MORNING OF A
CRESCENT MOON

Morning of a Crescent Moon

a novel

N.J. SCHROCK

Morning of a Crescent Moon

© 2026 by N.J. Schrock

Editors: Terra King, Stephanie Thompson
Cover and Interior Design: Emma Elzinga

Indigo River Publishing
3 West Garden Street, Ste. 718
Pensacola, FL 32502
www.indigoriverpublishing.com

Ordering Information:

Quantity Sales: Special discounts are available on quantity purchases by corporations, associations, and others. For details, contact the publisher at the address above.

Orders by US trade bookstores and wholesalers: Please contact the publisher at the address above.

Printed in the United States of America

Library of Congress Control Number: 2025928185
ISBN: 978-1-969935-03-9 (paperback)   978-1-969935-04-6 (ebook)

First Edition

With Indigo River Publishing, you can always expect great books, strong voices, and meaningful messages. Most importantly, you'll always find . . . *words worth reading.*

*This book is dedicated to the miners who gave their lives
at the Battle of Virden:*

Frank Bilyeu, Springfield, Illinois
Abraham H. Brenneman, Girard, Illinois
Joseph Gitterle, Mt. Olive, Illinois
William Harmon, Girard, Illinois
Ernest Kaemmerer, Mt. Olive, Illinois
Ernest Long, Mt. Olive, Illinois
Ellis Smith, Mt. Olive, Illinois
Ed Welch, Springfield, Illinois
*and to my grandfather, James (Dutch) Peacock, and my father,
James D. Peacock, who worked at the Virden North Mine and
were beneficiaries of the right to collective bargaining.*

Contents

On July 4, 1897, the United Mine Workers of America (UMWA) called a nationwide strike to gain higher wages and safer working conditions. In January 1898, the UMWA reached a landmark agreement with mine owners for a pay scale increase and an eight-hour workday. But Illinois operators located in Pana, Carterville, and Virden refused to honor the agreement. In April, the Chicago-Virden Coal Company, the largest coal producer in Illinois, locked the miners out of the mine. By late summer, the miners had been out of work for months. With both sides unwilling to compromise, tensions rose until a deadly conflict seemed certain.

Virden, Illinois, approximate location about twenty-five miles south of Springfield.

The laboring man's only property is the right to labor, which is as dear to him as the capitalist's millions, and he has the same right to carry arms in defense of his property as the capitalist has to protect his millions.

Illinois Governor John R. Tanner, from an interview with the *St. Louis Post-Dispatch*, October 10, 1898, p. 2.

Chapter 1

Arrival

August 1, 1898, Monday

Hovering above the earth, an aeronaut enjoyed the isolation afforded by a modern, lighter-than-air craft, a basket suspended under a bubble of silk spun by worms and filled with hydrogen gas. The balloon allowed its occupant to become a creature of the sky, leaving behind its humble beginnings to commune with the clouds.

It rose higher and higher in a peaceful blue silence while the wind stroked its lines. The air thinned; the balloon drifted south toward a distant thunderhead. A release of hydrogen checked its rise. The aeronaut controlled the rise and fall, but not the balloon's direction. "The wind blows wherever it pleases."

Slowly, it descended through low clouds that parted like a curtain to reveal railroad tracks coming from the north and running south, cutting through a town, surrounded by flat land and green fields that spread to the horizon. The balloon's path followed the tracks south.

On the northern edge of the town, west of the tracks, a blackened city block with a gray pile of rock and a three-story tower came into view. A coal mine. A peculiar activity surrounded the property. Men were building a wooden fence around it. Across the tracks to the east of the mine lay an open field.

As the balloon continued south, leaving the mine behind, the scenery changed. Wooden and brick buildings surrounded a large, shady town square animated by pedestrians and wagons. Houses with green lawns lined the streets in every direction until they ran into farm fields. Directly below the balloon, a man and three children pulled a small wagon of red and green objects across the train tracks.

At the south edge of town sat a smaller coal mine, still and quiet. Beyond it were corn fields and the distant thunderhead, lit briefly by lightning. A large dog walked along a dirt road, away from a farmhouse with no animals and a crop of weeds.

A couple of miles farther south, the balloon slipped lower. The aeronaut would have to land or drop weight. A train approached from the opposite direction, its passengers visible through open windows.

A woman's face. The flash of a white handkerchief.

The aeronaut released a sandbag, and the balloon rose.

꘎

Cate dabbed sweat from her upper lip and forehead with a handkerchief as the train approached Virden. Movement outside the open window caught her attention. A sandbag dropped from a bright red balloon, drifting over a field not far away. Slowly, the craft ascended. For a brief moment, Cate envied its suspended, silent detachment from life on the ground, its ability to unload a weight.

For most of the trip, the warmth and rhythmic swaying of the train had made her drowsy, partly because she hadn't slept well the previous night. She'd been anxious about the trip, about starting again in a new place, and about her new job. Would she be up to the task? Or would she have to abandon it as she did the last position? The previous night's worries lingered in the back of her mind as drowsiness fled.

Two rows forward, a young man looked back, flashing bright green eyes like Lieutenant May's. For a few seconds, she couldn't breathe; the odor of May's rotting flesh came back to her. May should have been a young man like this one with two good legs. Instead, he was wounded near Cuba at the beginning of the war with Spain four months ago. Gangrene set into the wound, and he ended up in the Maryland hospital where Cate worked as a nurse.

Lieutenant May was beyond help, and he knew it. The day before he died, he asked Cate to open a window. A cool breeze visited the stagnant room. He managed a smile and said his dying wish was to be kissed by a pretty girl. She said, "Should I go find one?" He held out his hand. With no one around, he pulled her to him for a kiss, sweetly done. But in that instant, she learned the taste of death. It waited in his breath and on his feverish lips.

Not long afterward, she quit. She had to for self-preservation. She left behind the wounded and dying young men, but not the guilt of leaving the hospital short-staffed. Memories of their faces and mutilated bodies brought fresh tears, even today.

She blinked them away.

"Are the Virden miners still striking?" asked the passenger with the green eyes to the man across the aisle.

"Yes, and there's trouble brewing. The operator wants to bring in scab workers like they did in Pana."

"Strike breakers? That's trouble."

"If he does, there'll be a bloodbath."

At the word bloodbath, Cate's chest tightened. Unable to get enough air, she turned her attention to the passing scenery.

"Arriving Virden," the conductor announced.

Several seats behind Cate sat a Black family of four, two parents and their children, a boy and a girl. They were on the train when Cate boarded in St. Louis. The kids grew increasingly restless and needy. Could they get a soda? Or ice cream? Their mother hushed them in short, whispered replies. Turning toward the window, the boy leaned out as the train slowed and pulled into Virden. Just as quickly, he backed away, saying, "Papa, those men are all White."

"It'll be fine, son. Better get used to it."

"They don't look happy."

The mother told them to gather their things.

Cate rose with her handbag and stepped into the aisle. The slowing motion of the train carried her forward as the brakes squealed.

With her first step from the train, she paused. Ten men stood near the platform, their mouths in straight lines, hats shading their eyes, fists clenched. One of them held a shotgun. Her second foot worked up the courage to step down as a middle-aged man approached her right. His breath came urgently. "Any Negroes on the train?" He smelled pungent and smoky, like creosote.

Cate blinked, trying to fathom why on earth he would ask such a question. "Just one family toward the back. A couple with two children. Why?"

"Is that all?"

"That's all I remember, but I didn't survey the passengers."

The man pushed behind her and aimed his next words at the Black family getting off the train. "There'll be no scabs in this town. Get right back on board."

The father stepped down first with his family behind him, wide-eyed but following. "We're anything but scabs. I'm the new part-time preacher for the Black church." He extended his hand. "Reverend Elijah Bellwether. And you are?"

The offer of a handshake wasn't returned. "Any more of you getting off?"

Reverend Bellwether withdrew his extended hand and offered instead a broad smile. "As far as I know, I was the only preacher on board. Why? You need preachers?"

The only answer given was the thud of luggage being unloaded.

A short, stout woman elbowed her way toward the train, parting the gathering of men like a bear through corn stalks. "By God. Don't you men have something to do besides hassling people getting off trains? Back up, and let that young woman through! She's my niece."

"Aunt Alice!"

"Glad you made it, Cate. Ignore these loafers." She paused to look at Cate. "You've gotten so tall and thin. Grown another few inches, I see. Come over this way. I got Clyde to bring his wagon."

Cate pointed to two trunks on the platform. "Those two are mine."

Alice flung her next words to the men, still frozen in place. "Some of you here help get these trunks into that wagon. Just because the mine's idle don't mean you should be."

One of the men said, "Now Alice, you know William would of been down here too if he'd a lived to see our trouble."

"Yeah, well the only place you'll find sympathy right now is in the dictionary, not from me."

When the trunks were loaded into the wagon, Alice turned to Clyde. "Just put them on the back porch. We'll be down there in a while. And thank you."

"Sure thing, Alice. Anything else you need me to do?"

"Not now. Thanks again." She lowered her voice and said to Cate, "I have Clyde for dinner sometimes, so he owes me. When you're a widow, it's useful to have a man owe you favors." She pointed toward the north, and they began walking that way. "I'm sorry I wasn't here right away. Kept getting stopped by people wanting to talk my leg off."

The men with grim mouths continued to watch until no more passengers disembarked, at which point they dispersed.

Nearby, a middle-aged Black couple greeted Reverend Bellwether's family with hugs and handshakes. They loaded their luggage onto a cart and pulled it away from the station as the train continued its route north. Cate waved to the kids, and they waved back.

When the squealing of the train faded, Alice motioned across the tracks to the west. "Let's head over to the drug store uptown and get you a cold drink or ice cream. We have time before the storm comes if we get it."

The sound of distant hammering came from the north. Several blocks away stood a building with a three-story tower.

The lot was partially surrounded by a wooden fence.

"What's going on over there?" Cate asked.

Alice shook her head as if disgusted. "Fred Lukins is building a stockade around his mine and houses on the inside. Brought in carpenters from out of town. Virden men wouldn't touch the job."

"Does that have something to do with the strike?"

"It has everything to do with the strike, or as the miners call it, the lockout. They'd work if they got the pay that was agreed to in January, but he won't pay it."

Several people passed the two ladies on their way uptown. Cate expected the same quiet village she remembered from when she was twelve but instead found the street full of activity. They passed several shops, including a drug store, a barber shop, a saloon, and a meat market. Nearly every passerby greeted them with a "Hello, Alice."

"You've been away a long time." Alice hugged Cate's arm.

"Ten years."

"Do you remember Virden?"

"Not a lot, just that it was a nice place to visit."

"It's a nice place to live, too, when we don't have miners show-ing up from all over expecting trouble. This part of Jackson Street is the levee. We'll go to the drug store on the north side of the square. The levee gets drifters from the train station."

At the next corner was the Farmers and Merchants Bank, and the town square spread to the south. Two customers entered the bank, one dressed in bib overalls, the other in a light gray summer suit. Both nodded to the two ladies.

"And this is our uptown. You can get about anything you want here and some things you don't want."

Cate pointed to the shaded park in the middle. A few adults sat on benches while children chased each other, jumping on and off an elevated platform with railings and a roof.

"What goes on there?"

"This time of year, band concerts every Saturday night. St. Louis and Chicago ain't got nothing on Virden."

Paved streets, Cate thought, *is something St. Louis has over Virden.* A wooden walkway lined the square in front of the stores, but a wide dirt road with wagons and carriages circled the central park area. Low areas held puddles. Dry areas produced dust. At the edges, conveyances waited for their drivers to return. A Black man shoveled manure into a cart.

As though reading Cate's thoughts, Alice said, "The city's going to make this all brick in a couple of years."

In half a block, they stopped in front of a drug store. The window declared the shop had a druggist, medicines for all ills, ice cream, and soda.

Nearby, two young men, one Black and one White, stood with five kids, two Black and three White, along with two wagons. One held vegetables, and the other contained boxes labeled "Eggs." Both men looked in Cate and Alice's direction. The Black man's eyes turned away, but he still briefly nodded and tipped his hat. The White man did not look away. He looked directly at Cate, smiled, and tipped his hat. "Afternoon, Alice."

Alice nodded. "Noah, Luke, same to you."

Cate paused, momentarily struck by the man's deep blue eyes. She turned to go in and caught sight of him through the reflection of the drugstore window. He watched her still.

The door was propped open. Patrons, drinking sodas or eating ice cream, sat at the bar and at tables farther back. Fans whirled lazily under a high, decorative-metal ceiling. Alice motioned to one of the first tables, and they sat down. "Those two men outside are an interesting pair. You'll meet all these people in time."

For the first time in several days, Cate felt a cool calmness come over her. The lingering anxieties hadn't gone away, but they occupied a smaller space. The town and its people were taking form and substance. They were becoming real and easier for her to imagine fitting in with, like the firm, contoured back of the solid wooden chair in which she sat.

The soda-fountain bartender, a tall, gray-haired man in an apron, white shirt, and bow tie, came over to the table. "You have a visitor, I see, Alice."

"This is Cate, my niece. She's going to be teaching school this fall and keeping me company. Cate, this is Phineus, a good man to know. He sells ice cream."

Cate nodded, smiled. "A pleasure to meet you, Phineus."

"Welcome to Virden, Cate. What'll you ladies have?"

"The usual for me. Vanilla ice cream, one scoop, and water with ice."

"Do you have Pepsi?" asked Cate.

"You mean Brad's Drink? I don't have the new bottles in yet. Where you been getting it as Pepsi already?"

"St. Louis." She pictured her dad's store and his new refrigerator case with Pepsi bottles lined up like soldiers on display, and she felt the briefest flicker of homesickness.

"That explains it. I'm still working on the bottles I bought three months ago. I'm glad they're changing the name. When people ask for a cola, and I give them a Brad's Drink, they say, 'Who's Brad?'" He tapped the table. "One Brad's Drink with ice, an ice cream, and an ice water coming right up, ladies."

"You sure you don't want ice cream?" Alice asked her. "You could stand to put some meat on your bones. Still got a good bustline though."

Cate responded by watching the other customers. She remembered her mother saying how one never knew what would come out of Aunt Alice's mouth. She knew her aunt meant well, though.

"I was thin when I was your age," Alice added, as if aware she had hit a tender point. "That seems like forever ago."

"I've picked up a few pounds. I look healthier than I did when I came back from Maryland."

"Your ma wrote me that you had a hard job and got sick. She was worried she'd lose her only child left."

"My heart broke every time a young man died until I had no heart left for it. I think teaching young kids will be good for me, and I can still apply my nursing skills as the school nurse."

"Too bad you got that scar. You have a nice complexion otherwise."

Cate put a hand to the scar on her left cheek and pushed the dark memory from her mind. "I'll tell you about it sometime." Phineus delivered the drinks and ice cream. She took a sip of her cola and realized the other customers were giving them more than a passing glance. "Even in a town of over two thousand, people still recognize a stranger?"

"That or it's your looks. Your mother was a beauty. Still is. You have her light complexion, dark hair, and brown eyes. William said your father fell for her as soon as he seen her."

Cate's father had admitted that many times. "You and Uncle William seemed to have done well here."

14

"We did. He could of been a grocer like your dad, but he hated dealing with the public. Moving around to follow the mine work got old, but it was steady and paid well until the recession of '93."

"Dad's grocery business suffered then too. He risked a lot giving so much food on credit, and I learned charity and generosity. That's what led me to go into nursing and now teaching."

Alice nodded. "Your dad is a good man. He helped William and me out once too when times were hard. You probably didn't know that. When William got hired at Lukins's new mine here, we thought we had it made. We'd saved. Having no kids helped, and we were able to buy that house, which didn't leave us with much. He thought he'd work many more years. Finish his time out here, but his lungs just gave out when he got the flu. Miner's asthma does that."

"Dad took his passing hard."

"I'm glad William had the years he did, and I have a roof over my head. There's a lot of good men who are miners as long as they're not also drinkers. But there's also plenty of wealthy farmers and bankers in town. You'll meet 'em."

Cate took a long sip of her cola and sighed, thinking how coming to Virden to look for a husband wasn't on her list of priorities. To change the subject away from the town's eligible bachelors, she said, "This tastes good after all morning on a train."

"I was sure surprised when you wanted to go into school teaching, and not in St. Louis. Your ma wrote me she was glad you were getting away from a beau."

Cate fiddled with her napkin. "Victor. They didn't like him, and when I broke up with him, they celebrated. But he keeps trying to see me again. I was glad to get this job, put some distance between us, and come to a nice, quiet farming town."

"I'm not sure how nice and quiet Virden will be with this strike. The talk gets hotter all the time, and no end in sight. We're all just hoping it'll somehow blow over."

Alice turned her attention to finishing the ice cream. A cooler breeze blew in from the back. Wagons and carriages rolled by outside, and Cate realized that Virden's unpaved roads muffled the sound of their wheels, unlike the clatter from St. Louis's brick pavers. Silverware met glass and ceramic. Patrons conversed. Cate picked up fragments of their conversations and grew confident she could put her health and her life together here in this community of farmers and merchants and miners.

Chapter 2

Visitors

August 2, Tuesday

The doorbell startled Cate from reading *Dracula*. Its continued ringing filled every corner of the house and propelled her off the sofa.

At the door stood a boy of about five or six. Cate's heart skipped a beat. He looked so much like her little brother, Joey, who died at the age of seven. His hair was so blond that it was nearly white, and he cranked away on the doorbell until his blue eyes met hers when the ringing fled the house, but not her ears. Her brother might have acted the same way.

"My goodness. Are you trying to wake the dead?" Cate asked him.

He pointed behind him. "No. I'm selling tomatoes." He wore a gray T-shirt and denim overalls. The rolled-up pant legs covered most of his shoes and touched the ground. The right shoe had a hole large enough to see his big toe.

Cate joined him on the porch and knelt to look him in the

eyes. Her pink, flowered dress covered the hole in his shoe. She felt like giving him a hug, but held back. Maybe someday, if she got to know him.

The tomatoes waited just beyond the front steps in a wooden wagon, its sides worn shiny. The metal handle rested on the footpath.

"Will you show me what you have?"

He led the way to the wagon.

"What's your name?" she asked him as she inspected his tomatoes. They were shades of pink to red and nested in a single layer on gunny sacks.

"Harry McCall."

"Well, Harry, how much are your tomatoes?"

"A penny apiece or four for a nickel."

Hesitating a second, she said, "Shouldn't that be five for a nickel? Or even six for a nickel?"

"No. If you want more than three, then you can pay more."

"Usually, merchants give customers more for less money."

His brow wrinkled. "I ain't usual, and if you want more tomatoes, then you pay more."

"I see. Did your mom or dad set these prices?"

"I ain't got a mom or dad, just Noah. But he's only half a brother. And he's old like you."

"Well, I'll take these three tomatoes." She pointed to the ripest ones.

His hands were too small to hold a tomato securely, so he handed them to her one at a time using both his hands.

She opened her apron, using it as a carrier. "Let me get my pennies. I'll be right back."

After she paid him, he turned the wagon around and headed

back to the wooden walkway that ran east toward the town square, wheels squeaking in protest. Not two minutes later, just as she was finding where she had left off in *Dracula*, the doorbell rang again, this time softly and tentatively.

A girl who looked to be a couple of years older than Harry stood on the porch with a basket of sweet corn. The color of her hair matched the corn tassels. Her faded blue dress had a torn pocket hanging open. "I have the best sweet corn in Virden. A penny an ear. Want some?"

Harry stood waiting out on the walkway. Cate pointed to him and asked, "Are you, by any chance, related to Harry?"

"He's my brother."

"Why didn't you come at the same time?"

"Noah says not to. We have to sell the tomatoes first 'cause they won't keep. If we all came at the same time, you might only buy the corn."

Cate wished she could ask her in and repair her torn pocket, but as with Harry, she thought *maybe someday*. Instead, she said, "I see. Let me get more pennies."

When Cate went to get her change, the kitchen window framed another boy to the west with a wire mesh bucket of red and green peppers.

Back on the porch, she said, "I'll take four. And is that four pennies or a nickel?"

"Four pennies. Harry thinks he can make deals with people."

Cate handed her the pennies. "And what's your name?"

"Beatrice. Or Bea for short." She smiled, showing two new front teeth.

"Is that another brother over there?"

"That's Ellis. He's selling peppers."

"And the corn is more important to sell than the peppers?" Cate motioned for him to come on into the yard. "How much are your peppers?"

Ellis had dark hair, and Cate guessed him to be around twelve. His pants didn't reach his ankles. He wore shoes and no socks. "A penny apiece," he said in a direct, business-like manner. Cate could picture him grown up, well-groomed and handsome.

"I'll take a red one and a green one." She gave both of them their money and collected the corn and peppers in her apron. "You know, you can bring everything all at once next time."

Ellis hesitated before leaving. "Thank you. Are you the new teacher?"

"Yes. I'm Miss Merry. I'll be teaching the primary grade."

"Then you're in for it. You'll have Harry. He's starting the primary grade." He smiled, and two dimples appeared. "And, Miss Merry, I hope you will be one of our best customers. Come on, Bea. Noah will want to hear about Miss Merry."

They headed toward Harry, who waited on the walkway in front of the next house. Across the street, the young man her aunt had greeted as Noah tipped his hat to her and followed well behind the kids as they headed uptown. She waved and smiled.

꙳

That evening, Cate fixed baked chicken, sliced tomatoes, sweet corn, and sautéed peppers.

Alice said, "Those McCall kids come to see you?"

"How did you know?"

"I seen them going around on my way back from work. Theirs is a sad story."

"Oh dear. My heart went out to them without knowing

anything about them. They were so polite and earnest in selling the vegetables. I felt like buying all they had and giving them hugs."

"The older brother is Noah. He's about your age. His dad died in the Diamond Mine disaster up by Chicago when he was young. His ma then married George McCall and had the three kids. George adopted Noah so they'd all have the same name. They came to Virden so George could work the mine. She died not too long after the youngest was born. Then, about the time Noah was to graduate from Virden High School and go off to Blackburn College, George died of pneumonia. With no other kin in the States, Noah took care of them and went to the mine to do it."

"I saw him watching from across the street."

"He's about the best non-father father I've seen. And a right good gardener too. I says to him one time, 'How's a young, good-looking guy like you not found a wife?'"

"He says, 'I'm not looking. I have a hard enough time feeding what I got.'" She shook her head. "A lot of miners had to leave town when they couldn't feed their families. They've been out of work for over a year now."

"Too long to be without a job."

"George had at least bought that house Noah and them live in. It's just west a few blocks. That colored man he was with yesterday is his mining partner, Luke. Him and his wife, Claudette, raise chickens and trade Noah eggs for vegetables. So, they get by—just."

Cate reached over to squeeze Alice's hand. "Thank you, Aunt Alice, for taking me in and letting me stay. I hope I'm not in any way a burden."

Alice met Cate's eyes and blinked. "A burden?" She squeezed

Cate's hand. "When I came home this evening and smelled supper already cooking, I realized how lonely I've been, and I felt so glad you're here now to keep me company. And I ain't been eating right. I come home and don't feel like cooking for myself. You're no burden. You'll liven things up around here."

Cate went over to Alice and gave her the hugs she didn't feel free to give the McCall kids.

August 3, Wednesday

After breakfast, Alice folded the wet cloth over the washtub and dried her hands on a towel. Cate still had a few dishes to dry.

Alice leaned toward the window and then backed away. "You're going to get an earful. I got other things to do this afternoon, so I'll leave you to it." She picked up her bag of cleaning supplies and headed out the back door.

Before Cate could finish drying the last plate, the doorbell rang. She set the dishcloth down, wondering who her aunt was trying to avoid.

Beyond the front door screen stood a hefty woman in a peach-colored, flowered dress. Her face was expressionless as though posing for a photo, but her hat gave an impression of being ready to fly off because of all the feathers adorning it. When the woman caught sight of Cate through the screen, she smiled and waved. "Are you tired yet of all the rain we've had since you arrived?"

Cate let her in and offered her a seat on the couch in the front sitting room. "Would you like some water or tea, or maybe some Lincoln cake?"

"Just cake, please. I do love a good Lincoln cake. I don't need the tea. It's hot enough without drinking tea. I came to introduce myself, seeing as how we're neighbors. I live just a couple of blocks further down the street. I'm Dora, and you must be Alice's niece, Cate. I heard you're one of our new teachers. You're a pretty thing, but how'd you get that scar on your cheek?"

"It's a long story. I was attacked one night while walking home from work. Let me get the cake." Cate didn't continue the conversation until she returned with the piece of cake. "I'm going to teach at the primary school. I chose it over nursing, for now anyway. I haven't regretted the switch, but then I haven't taught my first class yet."

"I thought you might be at the teachers' institute in Carlinville this week."

"No, I didn't find out about it in time, and the principal said there will be others."

"That's the truth. Those teachers seem to have an institute every few weeks—keeps them out of the classroom, is what I think."

Dora took a bite of cake, which failed to interrupt her talking. Cate felt relieved that the conversation veered away from herself. She was beginning to suspect that anything she told Dora would make its way all over town.

"I'm sure you'll like Virden. We usually have such a gay, active town, but I'm afraid we're not giving you the best impression with all these miners upset about the strike. But Mr. Lukins, whom I've always found to be a nice man, is taking his case, I hear, to the UMWA board in Springfield on Monday, and I hope they decide that the miners should go back to work and end all this strike nonsense. It's hurting the merchants in town with the men out of work and all." She took another large bite of cake.

"What is the UMW…A?"

"The United Mine Workers of America. Mostly a bunch of troublemakers."

"Well, but…"

"I just hope it don't get as bad as it's been in Pana. You've probably heard all about Pana by now."

"Well, no…" Cate hesitated, knowing that she was about to hear all about Pana.

"Everybody knows about it. The mine owners brought in Negroes to work the mines. They work cheap. My cousin in Pana says they claim it's a lot better than being in Alabama, even if they make lower wages than what our miners want. Our miners here are just causing too much trouble. Why, poor Mr. Dalby says he may have to go out of business. And it's just a matter of time before the rabble rousers from other towns like Mt. Olive and that crew of General Bradley's show up."

"General Bradley?"

"Oh, he's one for the books. A cock-of-the-walk he is. He must think he's something. During last year's strike, he marched his boys—I call them boys because they're acting like it, marching around instead of working—all over Central and Southern Illinois instead of staying home and taking care of their families. But what does he care? He's single and a *rounder* from what I hear. Got caught 'getting a little sport' as he called it in one of those houses last year. He dresses like a dandy with a silk top hat, coat, and cane. But he's a good-looker, that's for sure, with those black eyes and combed-back hair. Well, I'm sure we'll all get to see him because he'll come looking for trouble, and he'll find it unless they settle this strike."

"I do hope so. The students must worry about…"

"I wanted to make sure that you know about the band concert Saturday night, starting at eight. We have one nearly every Saturday night. E. P. Kimball is the Virden High School band director, and he also publishes *The Virden Record*. Anyway, they give such wonderful performances, even if he is a Democrat. It's the highlight of the week. One advantage we have living only a few blocks from the square is that we'll hear it whether we show up or not. And it'll drown out the noisy boys."

"Noisy boys?" Cate asked, although she would have preferred to hear more about the concerts.

"Haven't you heard them? Young boys with nothing else to do have been congregating under the new streetlamps in the early evenings and making all kinds of racket with their games. I knew those streetlamps would cause problems when they put them in, but no, the town had to have streetlamps to be, as they said, civilized and ready for the twentieth century. I don't know if I'm ready for the twentieth century if it means more streetlamps, telephones, union strikes, and noisy evenings. And then there's that Standard Oil depot going in. One of these days, it'll get struck by lightning and take the whole block and then some out. Mark my word. It's not good."

"Goodness." Cate began feeling a bit sorry for Dora and her negative attitude. She wondered what had made her that way, but Dora continued steering the conversation.

"Well, you're a pretty young thing and will be wanting to meet other young people in town. We do have an elegant young set. I can introduce you to some young working people, and maybe you'll meet a nice young man. They'll all be looking at you, but we do have some other pretty teachers who have come to town, so you'll have competition."

"Well, I'm really just trying to get settled in, and…" But Cate stopped herself from sharing further, realizing she might as well be talking to a passing train.

"Just stay away from the coal miners. What a rough crowd they are, and if you marry one, you'll never know if he's coming home on a stretcher. And coal dust everywhere, I hear. I advise marrying a man with a clean, steady job like my husband. He works for George Sewall at *The Virden Reporter*, the Republican newspaper. That's how I know all the important news that goes on in town. Well, I have to be off. It was so nice getting to know you, and I do hope you'll stop by for a visit someday, especially before school starts. And you'd be welcome at the Presbyterian church, but we're remodeling right now. We always have cake and cookies. And your cake was delicious. Did you make it?"

"No, Aunt Alice did—" Cate was about to add that the recipe was hers, but she didn't get the chance.

"Well, she's a good cook. You'd do well to take lessons from her. The best way to a man's heart is through his stomach, I always say."

Dora whisked herself out the door.

Cate exhaled, releasing the breath for all the words left unsaid for the last half hour.

Lincoln Cake

From *'76 a Cookbook*, p. 171. edited by the Ladies of Plymouth Church, Des Moines, Iowa, Mills and Company, Printers and Publishers, 1876.

Two cups of sugar, 2 eggs, a half cup butter, one cup sweet milk, four cups of flour, two teaspoons baking powder and flavor to the taste.—Mrs. M. R. Kellogg

Later that afternoon, Cate felt like getting out. Yesterday's rain had kept her in all day. Plus, she needed to open a bank account. The rain had stopped, but the sky remained overcast. She put on a yellow cotton dress that matched her cheery mood and a straw hat. She picked up her handbag and took Jackson Street east toward the public square. At the intersection of Church Street, she recognized the primary school where she would soon teach. She wondered how differently she would view it once she knew her students and their lives.

Along Church Street to her right were two churches and maybe a third farther down. A sign proclaimed the nearer one to be the Christian church in existence since 1882. A man with clippers trimmed its bushes.

He waved and walked toward her. "Can I help you? You look lost."

"No, only lost in thought, trying to decide which way to walk."

He offered his hand but realized it was dirty and withdrew it. "I'm Reverend Goos. That's G-O-O-S, not like the bird." He smiled and wiped sweat from his forehead with the back of his hand.

"I'm Cate Merry, Alice Merry's niece."

"Oh, our new primary grade teacher. Welcome to Virden! We're very fond of your aunt, and we'd be pleased to have you in our services."

"Thank you, Reverend. I'll attend, probably this Sunday."

"Let me know if I can do anything for you. Anything at all."

"Thank you. I will." She pointed past the Christian church to the next block. "Is that the Presbyterian church?"

"Since 1856. It's undergoing extensive remodeling. The next block down has the Methodist church. And there's the Baptist church next to the school where you'll teach."

"I can see why this is Church Street."

"Would you like to come in and visit?"

"Thank you for the offer, but I'm going uptown and want to get back home before lunch."

"Well, I'll see you on Sunday, and we can visit then. Good day, Miss Merry."

As she turned again toward the town square, fragments of a verse from the book of Hebrews came to mind: "…we are compassed about with so great a cloud of witnesses…let us run with patience the race that is set before us…" She considered again the school and the new job and longed to do right by the children she would soon receive. *Grant me the skills and patience, whatever they may be.*

By eleven a.m. on the town square, the doors of many stores were open, welcoming shoppers who came and went. Men leaned against lampposts and raised unsettled politics through blue tobacco smoke, while wagon wheels raised dust that settled on the nearest objects. Music from the park's bandstand faltered, stopped, and started again in practice for Saturday night's concert. A carriage deposited two women with a whispering of silk and lace and gardenia not far from the corner where Cate stood. A wagon delivered flour to a grocer.

After walking three sides of the square, Cate was pleased to have found more than she might have expected for a small town relative to St. Louis. She found two banks, hotels, grocers, five-and-ten-cent stores, dress shops, and your run-of-the-mill doctor and lawyer offices. On the west side was even an opera house billing a play put on by the ladies of the Christian church called the "Old Maids' Convention."

She went into a few shops and picked up the needed items she hadn't brought with her. In the Bank of Virden, a tall, smiling, mustachioed young man in a three-piece suit introduced himself as Henry and welcomed her to the area. Cate introduced herself and explained that she was a new primary school teacher and that when she was hired, she was told she could have an employment-based savings plan since she was single. He happily opened an account for her and then walked her toward the door when she was ready to leave.

"I would happily show you around town, Miss Merry, if you would like an outing."

"Perhaps, once I'm settled in," Cate said with a smile. She didn't mean to be rude by declining, but she was not yet ready to be seen riding around town with a man she knew nothing of.

"Will you be attending the Christian church with your aunt? That is where I attend."

"Yes, I will."

"Perhaps I can escort you there on some days."

"Thank you again, Henry. But for now, I'll see you there." She left doubting that he was this friendly to all his customers.

Her last stop was Dalby's Five and Ten for candy. She loved lemon drops, and Aunt Alice didn't have any. The store, like many of the others, had a wooden floor, a decorated metal ceiling with fans, and wooden shelves and bins holding merchandise. But, relative to the other stores, its goods seemed scant. She found a bag of lemon drops and headed to the front.

The female clerk wore a white, crocheted cardigan despite the heat. To a young woman holding both a baby and a cloth doll, she explained, "Mr. Dalby isn't buying homemade dolls." She stopped and blinked with downcast eyes, pausing to regain composure. "I'm afraid he might not be able to restock the bins. He said the miners' strike may put him out of business." She pulled out a handkerchief and blew her nose.

Cate, interested, listened and waited for her turn.

The customer stood still, unblinking, like the embroidered eyes of the cloth doll she held. The woman had pulled her red hair back in a tight bun, but a strand fell loose. Her blue flowered dress was patched in several places. The baby on her hip kept reaching for the doll. She spoke in an Irish brogue, "Aye, you think the strike hit you hard? My husband's a miner. We have no cash income other than from the miners' fund. We barter for everything, but some things you can't trade for. I'm just trying to make a few coins."

"I'm sorry, but we are not in the market for homemade dolls."

"Can you check with Mr. Dalby?"

"I don't need to. So far today, he's turned down canned goods, clothing, toys, trinkets, and toppers. He hopes to restock, but he said he can't unless the strike ends soon."

The woman's shoulders slumped. A tear ran down her cheek, and she gave the baby the doll.

Cate felt sorry for the woman and her situation and had a solution for them both, so she stepped toward them. "I might be able to use a doll like that. May I see it?"

The woman wiped the tear away and shifted the baby. "Really? I'm Maeve. You need a doll?" She handed Cate the doll. It was carefully made with embroidered features, including blue eyes and black eyelashes. It wore a finely stitched blue dress with gathers around the waist.

Cate stroked its yarn hair. "This is nicely made. I would like four dolls. A man, a woman, a boy, and a girl."

The store clerk snickered and squinted at Cate, making her sharp features and crow's feet even more pronounced. "What do you need dolls for? Ain't you that new teacher?"

"I am," she said to the clerk. Turning to Maeve, she added, "I learned in nursing school that young children often struggle to talk about something that makes them sad or scared, but they can act out their fears with dolls because the dolls aren't really them. Dolls were quite useful to me as a nurse, and the idea just occurred to me that I can use them as a teacher."

Maeve said, "I'd like to make the dolls, but I don't have a lot of material. My neighbor loaned me the scraps to make this one, and I promised to pay her back when I sold it."

"I can supply the material. I live with my Aunt Alice about three blocks from here. I'm going there now. Would you like to come with me or stop by later?"

"I'll come now." A smile showed stained teeth with one missing.

Cate laid her money for the candy on the counter. She and Maeve said goodbye to the clerk, and they headed around the corner and down Jackson Street.

Maeve shifted the baby.

"Would you like me to take her for a while?" asked Cate.

"Oh, no ma'am. She's not but a featherweight."

Cate found the woman interesting and wanted to know more about her situation and background. "Do you have more children?"

"I have one at home. Brian—he's my husband—he's looking after Oscar. Oscar's going to start school. Will you be his teacher?"

"I will if he's in the primary grade. I want to visit my students before school starts after I get a list of the ones who signed up. Maybe I could visit Oscar when I collect the dolls?"

Maeve hesitated. "Our humble abode won't be to your liking. I could bring him by your house or the school when I have the dolls."

"Well, we can decide later."

"Brian won't believe I got a customer. He said there weren't anyone going to buy homemade dolls in these times. People who have money, he said, buy store-bought dolls. And the miners won't be buying toys anytime soon."

"We're here." Cate motioned to the house.

Maeve stopped at the front walk. "What a nice house. What does your uncle do?"

"He was a coal miner, back when the pay was better. And he and Aunt Alice never had any children."

Maeve's eyes widened. "A coal miner?" She shifted the baby again to the other side. "I'd love to have a house like this someday. I've heard others complaining that all of us new immigrants have ruined the salaries. I'm sorry about that, but we were even worse off before coming over here. We're going to help get those wages back up with this strike. I'm behind it all the way."

Cate patted Maeve's back and then led the way to Alice's material scraps. She had shown them to Cate when they compared hobbies and discovered they both liked sewing. Alice told her she was welcome to whatever she wanted.

Maeve searched carefully through the material pieces as though they were gems not to be scattered. "How do I know what I can take?"

"Take whatever you think you could use for the four dolls."

Maeve picked through the scraps until she had what she thought she needed. She looked at Cate and opened her mouth as though she had a question but then didn't say anything.

Cate prompted her. "Yes?"

"How much do you think you'll want to pay me to make these?"

"How about fifty cents a doll? Two dollars for the four."

Maeve's eyes didn't blink. She inhaled sharply. "Two dollars?" She reached over and gave Cate a hug. "Brian ain't never going to believe this. Two dollars! I might be able to get some school clothes after all."

Cate walked with her to the front. The sky to the west had turned dark blue. "I hope you don't get wet. I could lend you an umbrella."

"Wouldn't hurt me to get a good bath on the way home. That sky looks like we could get a real frog strangler."

Cate laughed and waved her on her way.

Chapter 3

Band Concert

The Virden Reporter

Friday, August 5, 1898

The Virden H. S. C. Band will give a concert in the square Saturday night, commencing promptly at 8 o'clock. The following programme will be given:

March—"Popular Swing" ... Brooke

Waltzes—"Cupid" ... Vandercook

Selection—"Mountain Echoes" ... Dalby

Tuba Solo—Selected ... H. G. Kirkpatrick

Overature—"Oriental" ... Bleger

Selection—"Star of the Sea" ... Kennedy

Comique—"My Angeline" ... Johnson

Overture—"Cubaneon" ... Beebe

Serenade—"Waves of Memory" ... Blanchard

March—"DeMolay" ... Hall

E. P. Kimball, Director

August 6, Saturday

Cate was eager to attend the band concert in the public square after hearing about it from Dora and Alice. She enjoyed frequenting concerts in St. Louis, especially ones down along the river, and she wondered what kind of musical entertainment a small town like Virden would offer. The rain stopped during the night, and a less humid wind from the north blew in, drying out the puddles, although the street was still muddy.

She put on a lightweight, ivory cotton dress with just enough lace at the neckline and sleeves to distinguish it from an everyday dress. Ivory was one of her favorite colors because of the way it contrasted with her dark hair and eyes. Her only jewelry was an Illinois Watch Company pendant. She checked the time on it and said goodbye to her aunt, who had cleaned wallpaper all day. "The old gray mare ain't what she used to be. Besides, I'll hear it from the front porch," Alice explained.

The sun set, leaving the sky a cloudless shade of lavender. With all the recent rain, everyone's grass was spring green. The air near the front porch carried the scents of the butterfly bush at the corner of the porch and the pink Duchesse de Brabant rose off the sitting room window. Cate filled a small handbag with a handkerchief, some change, a pencil, and a small pad of paper. She checked the time. Seven-thirty. Half an hour until the concert started.

She spotted Noah McCall pulling the two youngest kids in a wagon—one of their vegetable wagons, Cate guessed—while Ellis walked beside him.

By the time Cate approached the front walkway, Noah and the kids were only a few yards away. She waved and waited for them to catch up to her. "Good evening. I'm Cate Merry. That's Cate with a C. Alice Merry is my aunt. And you must be Noah."

Noah removed his hat. His dark hair shone in the waning light, and so did his smile with the same dimples she'd seen on Ellis. "Nice to meet you, Cate with a C. I'm Noah, and this is Ellis, Bea, and Harry, my siblings, but I think you've already met them. I heard you're the new primary grade teacher." Noah's blue eyes shone violet in the evening light. She felt a sudden warmth for this young man who could be doing other things with his time but chose to spend it with his half-siblings. Knowing that made him somehow even more attractive than he already was.

"You heard right," she replied.

"Well, then, you will have Harry in class. He's starting school this fall, aren't you, Harry?"

Harry didn't make eye contact with her. He mumbled, "I guess so."

Noah shook his head and shrugged.

Cate smiled and nodded. She knelt and looked into Harry's face. "We're going to have a lot of fun this year, Harry. Just wait and see. I think you'll like school."

Noah said, "Would you care to walk the rest of the way with us? And we have a wagon for those who get tired around nine o'clock or so."

"I'd like that. I don't know anyone or know what to expect. I do hope I won't need your wagon."

"I hope not either. The teasing that I'd get from my buddies would be unbearable if I hauled you home in a wagon."

He smiled, and she laughed, and the awkwardness of having just met dissipated.

The walk to uptown took less than fifteen minutes. At first, small talk filled the space between them. They remarked about how glad they were that the rain held off for this evening. Noah said he thought that the Virden High School band gave a good concert.

"I heard that from Dora, and I saw yesterday's *Virden Reporter*."

"Well then, you're up on all of Virden's high-society news."

"She mentioned that the band director, Mr. Kimball, publishes *The Virden Record*. Doesn't it cover the society news also?"

"It does some, but it does a better job of covering Democratic party politics, the miners' strike, and issues that are of less interest for *The Virden Reporter's* subscribers."

About half a block from the town square, they crossed an alley and passed a large shop window that said "Laundry." A young Asian man leaned against the doorway with his hands in his pockets. His white linen shirt looked freshly pressed, as did his tan trousers. Noah greeted him. "Good evening, Hop. Going to the concert?"

He answered with an accent, "No, I hear the music from here, and sometimes I get customers."

"Have you met Miss Cate Merry, our new primary school teacher? Cate, this is Mr. Hop Long, a good man to know."

Hop answered, "We've not met. Good evening, Miss Merry."

"A pleasure to meet you, Mr. Long. I'm sure that I'll be stopping by when I need special laundry services." From the view she had into the shop, it appeared immaculate and emitted an odor of soap and lavender.

They found the public square filled with people of all ages. Families mingled together as women greeted each other, laughed, and called to their kids, who raced around the park. Some of the men talked among themselves in small groups. The streetlamps came on, and many glanced upward as though the sun had come out. Cigarette and cigar smoke participated in the conversations until rising above it all. The band tuned instruments and arranged music on stands.

Noah and the kids led the way across the street to the park. A man leaning against a light pole and talking to other men called to Noah. "Quick work, Noah." He looked at Cate. "Noah likes to be one of the first on the job." The group laughed. Cate felt herself blush, which always made the scar on her cheek more pronounced.

Noah shook his head. "Ignore him." He pointed toward an ice cream stand. "Harry convinced Phineas to exchange tomatoes for ice cream, so they're anxious to collect."

Cate said, "My dad's store sells ice cream. It's one of his best-selling items this time of year."

"What kind of store does he have?"

"A grocery store in St. Louis."

"I like to make ice cream in the winter when I can get ice from setting a pail outside, but isn't it best in the summer?" He smiled, showing his dimples.

"Certainly." Cate hoped her blush had gone away.

"Phineus will have ice cream for about an hour until his ice melts or he runs out. I'm glad he's willing to barter with the kids."

"I like ice cream too. I'll follow you over there."

Noah parked the wagon and told Harry and Bea to wait while he stood in line. Cate ordered her ice cream first and joined the wagon off to the side. While Noah waited, he glanced toward a woman standing a few yards away, who then shimmered toward him. Her light blonde hair and pale green eyes shone against her pink silk dress. "Hello, Noah. Nice to see you this fine evening." She inspected Cate before directing her attention back to him.

He tipped his hat. "Good evening, Jenny. I hope you enjoy the concert." He took the ice cream to the kids, and the woman turned away after taking one more look at Cate, who couldn't resist smiling and waving. Cate wondered what possessed her to do something that might aggravate this woman whom she didn't even know.

After a few licks of ice cream, she had to ask Noah, "The woman who spoke to you—you seemed to brush her off."

"Her family is one of the wealthy ones whose every move makes *The Reporter*."

"So why not talk to her?"

He leaned toward her and lowered his voice. "We liked each other in grade school into high school. When I couldn't go to college and went to the mine, her dad caught me on the street one day and told me in no uncertain terms to stay away from his daughter or I'd be sorry."

Cate's eyes widened. "You're serious?"

"And so was he. Dead serious. And he has the money to do it. So, I say 'hi' when she speaks to me and move on."

"I'm sorry."

"No need. I know now she's not my type."

The band struck up the first song, "Popular Swing," before she had the chance to ask him just what *was* his type.

Instead, Cate said, "Thank you for seeing me uptown. I'll walk around. I wouldn't want to cause you more teasing or hinder your love life."

He shook his head and smiled. "That's not a problem."

"Maybe I could walk toward home with you when you're ready to leave?"

"Certainly. I'll find you later."

The breath of a dozen high school teens went into wind instruments, and bows drawn across strings all merged into music, filling the park and spreading out in four directions across town. Cate imagined Aunt Alice sitting on the porch and receiving this gift. Talkers leaned in toward the ears of listeners so that the music wouldn't steal their words.

Cate had nearly finished her ice cream cone when two boys ran toward her in pursuit of a skinny gray dog. She held out the cone's last bits, and the dog stopped to take it, allowing one of the boys to grab the leash. She laughed and asked them if he was a good dog. The older boy said, "He ain't a bad dog, but he likes to get loose, and we don't want the dog killer to get him."

"The dog killer?"

"Yeah. One of the men who shoots strays. Don't you know anything?"

"I'm new in town. I see your dog likes ice cream."

"Everybody likes ice cream. I'd of eaten the ice cream too."

She handed him money to get two ice creams. "Here, I don't need more. You can get some if you give your dog the end of the cone."

The boys' eyes grew round at the coins she handed them. They mumbled their thanks, already running toward Phineus.

Buoyed by the music, she began a circuit inside the park. When the song ended, Cate caught snippets of conversations before the next one started up. Some Pana miners, recently released from jail, would be suing. The situation in Pana was tense between imported Black scabs and striking miners. Elderly women complained of noise late into the evenings ever since the streetlamps were installed. Others muttered of boys with slingshots and air rifles causing problems, though Mayor Noll was slated to go after them. Because of a rainy month, root maggots damaged the corn. Someone wished the new Standard Oil facility would get struck by lightning. Italian immigrants replaced Canadian rail workers. The next song started up and drowned out the chatter.

"Miss Merry, isn't it?"

She turned to find Reverend Bellwether. She spoke up to be heard over the band. "Hello! How are you settling in after that welcome we received at the depot?"

"Just fine, thanks. We haven't formally met. I heard your aunt call your name. I'm Reverend Elijah Bellwether, and this is my wife, Minnie, my daughter, Tami, and my son, Isaac."

Minnie said, "We're doing just fine, Miss Merry. Most people have been very welcoming."

"Please call me Cate. What grade will your daughter be in?"

Minnie patted her daughter's head. "Tami will be in kindergarten."

"They call it primary grade here, and I'm the teacher this year."

"How nice!"

"I plan to visit my students before school starts."

"Come any time, Miss Merry—Cate. We live down near the Black church."

The music reached a crescendo, making conversation more difficult. The Reverend managed to say above the music, "Nice to see you again." They shared a wave, and Cate continued her walk, filled with the satisfaction of having met another of her students.

N.J. SCHROCK

A few yards farther, Maeve sat on a blanket with the baby. She waved and stood as Cate came closer. Leaning toward Cate, she said, "I started on them dolls."

"I'm so glad."

Maeve invited her to join them on the quilt. But Cate declined, choosing to continue her stroll. Maybe she would meet more people ahead—she wanted to become familiar with the town and its people as quickly as she could.

As the band finished a song, Cate caught movement on Springfield Street. Some teenage boys and young men watched a weaving rider on a bicycle. One of them began singing, "Daisy, Daisy, give me your answer, do!" and laughed at him.

The sound of a gunshot rang through the square, and screams brought conversations to an end. Across the park, a man stood with a pistol aimed skyward. A group of men surrounded him. They exchanged shouts. Cate heard only fragments of what they were saying, partly because their words overlapped.

Noah touched her elbow, and she jumped. He said, "I'm sorry. I didn't mean to startle you, but I think it's time for me to take the kids home."

She nodded, and they headed toward Jackson Street. He told Ellis to pull the wagon, which again held Harry and Bea, while he walked behind them with Cate. The corners of Harry's mouth were down, and his face was red. He rubbed his eyes and looked like he was close to crying when he said, "He didn't shoot a dog, did he?"

Noah answered, "No, Harry. They don't shoot dogs in a crowded square."

When they were in front of the school, Cate asked Noah, "Harry likes dogs?"

He answered her in low tones that would be hard for Harry and Bea to hear over the squeaking wagon wheels. "He loves all animals. A couple of months ago, he was playing in the yard when he witnessed the dog killer shoot a dog running across Heaton field near our house. The shot caused the dog to tumble like a rabbit, and Harry ran screaming over to it. It was a bad thing for him to see. It's given him nightmares. I learned last winter that if I go hunting, I can't clean the rabbit or squirrel in front of him. I take them to my friend Luke's to clean."

"Goodness. I can understand how he feels. Harry reminds me so much of my younger brother who died several years ago. He was only seven."

"I'm so sorry. I don't know what I'd do if I lost one of these kids."

"It's about the worst thing that can happen." The wagon was well out of hearing range. "What was tonight's gunshot about?"

"I don't know exactly, but the guy with the pistol is a guard at the mine. The mine manager, Fred Lukins, hired guards so he could continue building a stockade around the mine. The men standing around the guy with the gun were miners. He probably felt threatened."

"Is a stockade really necessary?" She felt a tightening in her stomach. What was a conflict that didn't seem to involve her when she arrived had become far more real now that she knew something of this miner and his family.

"To do what Lukins has threatened to do, it will be. He needs a barrier to keep miners out if he's going to operate the mine with scabs. Word has it that's what he plans to do if men don't go back to work soon at the pay scale he wants, which for us is not enough. But there's some good news. The mine operators have agreed to meet on Monday and present their case to national and state union leaders. They claim that they'll abide by the decision made by union leaders. I hope so, and maybe we can end the strike before we have problems like in Pana."

Somber music found its way down Jackson Street as Noah and the kids said their goodbyes to Cate. They also waved and said goodbye to Alice, who sat on the porch swing, moving it to the slow pace of the music. Cate joined her on the swing.

"Hey, why'd the music stop all of a sudden?"

"Trouble on the square between a mine guard and some miners."

"I guess it's starting."

Chapter 4

Painting by the Tank

August 8, Monday

Cate was setting up an easel on the front porch when Clyde stopped with his horse and wagon. "Hello there, Cate. Is your aunt Alice around?"

From the kitchen window, Alice called, "Be right out."

Clyde secured the horse's reins and hopped down from the wagon. When he stepped onto the porch, he asked Cate what she was doing.

"In St. Louis, I loved to paint the riverfront, but the closest to that I've seen here is a drainage ditch. So, I thought I'd paint that flower garden." She pointed across the street.

Clyde rubbed his chin. "You know, I'm going west of town and right by a peaceful, good-sized pond we call the tank. It was built by the railroad for water. There might be a few swimmers, but you could set up somewhere away from the beach. It's a nice spot, and you'd find something to paint."

Alice appeared with a half-bushel basket. "How much do you think they'll want for them apples?"

"I'm not sure how many they have or the price. I'll pay, and then you can pay me."

"All right, but don't go above fifty cents. I like apples, but not if they're going to cost me an arm and a leg."

"I won't let them overcharge, Alice." Turning back to Cate, he said, "I could drop you at the tank on my way to the apple farm and pick you up on the way back. I'll be a couple of hours."

Cate consulted her watch: nine thirty. A couple of hours would make it eleven thirty. She could get back to Aunt Alice's in time for lunch. "Why not? Let me get a parasol and supplies."

On the way to the tank, the wagon jostled and jerked because of ruts in the road, and Cate wondered how the pioneers went all the way to places like Oregon riding on the seat of a wagon—or walking. And what if a woman were pregnant?

About a mile west of town, Clyde pulled off the main road and onto a narrow path with bushes on each side. A turn to the right opened the view to a small lake with a sandy beach. On the opposite shore ran railroad tracks and beside them rose an elevated water tank. Four adults and several kids played on the beach and in the water. Clyde stopped the wagon in the middle of a circular drive. "Here you are. Will this suit your need for a water picture?"

"Yes, thank you. It's lovely out here. I'll see you when you return."

He pulled out his watch. "About eleven thirty. See you then."

She jumped from the wagon, motioning to him that she didn't need help, picked up her parasol, a shoebox of art supplies, and a leather-bound sketchbook from the back of the wagon, and waved goodbye.

Cate chose a pathway between a few bushes that led to a spot under a large elm tree, north of the pond's beach but still along the shore. Near the tree's trunk, a wooden bench offered her a seat, and she took it, finding it cleaner and more comfortable than sitting on the grass. Beyond a road running west and atop a hillside, gravestones waited among scattered trees. Small American flags, noting veterans, waved beside many grave markers. The faces of the men, young and old, who died in the Maryland Veterans' Hospital came alive again in her memory as did their cries of pain, their fears, and the stench of iodine and death. Clyde's wagon headed west down that road, interrupting her train of thought. She turned back to the lake.

She opened her notebook and began a pencil sketch of the view across the lake, including the water tank and the trees beyond the track. The swimmers disturbed the surface of the lake, so she imagined the trees' reflections on calm water above a cloudless sky.

The laughter from the beach, the chirping of a cardinal in the elm, and the scent of water and grass receded as she became absorbed in capturing the scene. After laying out the sketch, she wet her brush and began applying watercolor paint, starting with horizontal strokes of deeper blue at the top, fading to a lighter blue at the horizon. Next, she defined the trees on the opposite shore, and then the water, mirroring the trees and sky. She would wait until the sky and water dried to add the water tank and its reflection. Wiping her brush on a cloth, she held the painting-in-progress at arm's length and compared it to the actual scene. It wasn't detailed, but it could be used to paint a version in oil on canvas at home.

"Hello, Cate. I thought it was you up here."

Because of her concentration, the sudden voice behind her caused her to jump. But she recognized the voice and turned toward him, smiling. "Hello, Noah. You startled me."

He wore a sleeveless shirt and cut-off cotton shorts, both of which were wet over the tanned skin and muscles of a laborer. "Sorry. I thought I'd let the kids play for a while with Luke before I give Harry another swimming lesson." He examined her sketch. "Very nice. I can go and leave you to it."

"No, please, visit for a while. I have plenty of time to finish this before Clyde gets back." She motioned to the bench, inviting him to sit. "So, you're giving swimming lessons to Harry?"

Down at the beach, Harry practiced kicks in the shallow water. Luke stood in water to his hips with his young daughter on his shoulders, and he tossed Bea and Ellis out into deeper water. They were the source of the laughter. When they swam back to him, he launched them again.

"I'm wet. I'll sit here," and he found a spot in the grass where he could see both her and the kids playing at the beach. He rested his right arm on a raised knee. "I want them to learn to swim. It's one of life's essential skills."

Cate pinned up a loose lock of hair and laid her painting on the grass to dry. "Hold that pose. I'd like to sketch you if you don't mind." She chose a blank page from her sketchbook.

"OK, but I'm not sure why you'd want to."

"Practice on the human figure." Her pencil traced a line from the top of his head down the back of his neck and along his spine to his shorts.

He glanced at the back of her notebook and then at the movement of her eyes. "Teaching swimming, because you never know when you might accidentally be in water over your head?" she asked. When he turned toward her, she traced the contour of the right side of his face, along his cheekbone, and down along his clean-shaven jawline.

"Right. My father couldn't swim and drowned in the Diamond Mine accident up in Braidwood. Maybe he would have drowned anyway because so many miners were trapped, but being able to swim would have given him a better chance of getting out."

"Oh dear. What caused the accident?" For a moment, her pencil paused at his collarbone, her attention arrested by his story.

"In February of '83, we were living in Braidwood. My dad was a miner there. We'd had a lot of snow and then an early thaw. Most mines were closed because the superintendents were worried about flooding from all the standing water in the fields. But Dad's mine didn't close. The operator was more worried about making money than about the miners' safety."

He blinked and looked away. "I was eight. Mom and I heard the whistle for trouble, so we ran to the mine. I remember people rushing around, yelling and crying. We heard how water from the fields suddenly broke through a pathway into the mine. Hundreds of miners were working at the time. The main escape flooded, and seventy-four miners never made it out. One of them was Dad. As a kid, I kept imagining water rushing down the mine tunnels and drowning men and mules."

"I'm so sorry, Noah." Her pencil moved again, defining the rise of his biceps and the slope down to the elbow resting on his knee and a similar line in reverse under the arm.

"Incidents like that one—and it's only one of many—have made it clear that too many times operators put money before people. That's one reason miners are taking a stand here in Virden."

"So, is Fred Lukins that type of operator?"

He was silent for a few seconds. "I honestly think Mr. Lukins is a decent chap. He's personable to talk to. He has a nice wife and a mother-in-law who lived with them until just recently, and three sons. He helped to build Virden's economy. T.C. Loucks is the president of the company, and I think he may be the one taking a harder line against the miners. But I suspect neither of them wants to set a precedent of having the miners tell them how to run the business, so they've dug in their heels on the issue of wages. And we've dug in our heels, and I'm worried about how all this is going to end."

"What happened after you lost your father? How did you end up in Virden?" A few long strokes of her pencil captured his long legs and bare feet. She then focused her attention on his face.

"Mom and I went through some difficult months. She cleaned houses. We raised a garden. That's why I like gardening. It gives us food security, well, at least for vegetables. In the fall, she married George McCall. He knew my dad. George was one of the lucky ones to get out of the mine. He moved us to Virden in '85 because he'd lined up a job at the Virden South Mine, which was the only one here at the time."

"And your mother and George had Ellis, Bea, and Harry?" When his face turned toward her to answer, she quickly marked the positions of his eyes, nose, and mouth. She started with his mouth and carefully defined the line of his lips.

"Yeah, and then Mom died not long after Harry was born. She had a tumor and internal bleeding. I helped George with the kids as best I could. The neighbor lady, Martha, looked after them during the day. George paid her. That helped me stay in high school. But in the winter of my senior year, George got pneumonia. His lungs weren't good. Black lung, the miners' disease, they call it. And then George died."

"Oh Lord, Noah. That sounds like something out of a Dickens novel."

"Things are better now. As Father Clancy says, 'The Lord doesn't give you more than you can handle.'"

"So I've heard, but I'm not so sure." With a few more marks, she captured his eyes and nose, but a pencil sketch did not do justice to their color.

Noah's attention may have been on the past or the kids at the beach. Their laughter and voices mingled with the engine of an approaching train. It hissed and squealed to a stop next to the water tank. Two men from the train crew jumped off and prepared to take in water for the engine.

Noah continued. "The whole story starts earlier if you want to know more."

"I do want to know. I think I have you now." She turned the sketch around so he could see it.

"Yes, you do." He smiled. "You're a good artist."

"Please continue."

"In '65, toward the end of the war, George was wounded in battle. He woke up on the battlefield, thirsty and disoriented. He sat up and heard gunfire. A voice called to him from a stand of trees, where a Black man knelt behind bushes. He said, 'They's shootin' Yankees,' and motioned for George to join him. George crawled over to the bushes and realized the man was probably an escaped slave, yet the man shared his water with him. They hid out as straggling Rebs walked by. George learned his name was Lucius. The plantation he'd worked on had been overrun and sacked by Union troops, so he high-tailed it with no destination in mind except to go north."

"So, what happened to Lucius?"

"George knew the war was about to end and that Lucius had very likely saved his life. They wandered the area for miles until they found the Union troops. George gave Lucius some money, supplies, and a letter to George's family explaining who Lucius was in case George didn't make it back. He told Lucius that if he could get home without getting killed, he'd help him get a job. Well, they met up in Illinois and worked a few mines until getting jobs in Braidwood. Lucius made it out that day also. My mining partner, Luke, down there on the beach, is Lucius's son."

"Oh my! That's quite a story."

A breeze ruffled the pages of her notebook and the surface of the water. Cate pinned up another strand of hair that had come loose, conscious of Noah watching her and not the beach.

"It's not over," he said. "Lucius moved his family to Virden when he'd heard from George about the better mining conditions. When I graduated from high school, I suddenly had three kids to support. I don't have any other relatives in the States, and I couldn't put them in an orphanage. Luke was already working at the Chicago-Virden Mine—we call it the north mine. Lukins bought it in '93 when it was still under construction. Luke and Lucius helped me get hired. You have to have an experienced miner take you to the mine and show you the ropes."

"So, your stepfather, George, and Luke's father, Lucius, met during the war, then both got jobs in mines up north, and eventually both ended up in Virden. And then you and Luke became mining partners when you needed a job."

"That's it. I've learned from the best. Luke can really mine the coal. His dad was a good miner too, but I don't think his health is good enough for him to go back to work when the strike is over. He's been living in Springfield with Luke's sister."

Cate could imagine how Luke, this muscular Black man, tossing the kids in the water, could probably chisel out tons of coal. But she still pondered another point. "Why did you go to the mines? Surely there were other jobs you could get with a high school diploma."

"At that time, the mine was still paying a living wage. And, if you work your way up and become a mine examiner or engineer, you can make even more money. I could see a way to provide for the family by going to the mine. With my father and stepfather being miners, I saw the pride and brotherhood they had in the trade."

"I see," Cate said, but she wasn't sure she did.

"On September fifth, District Twelve of the union is erecting a monument in Braidwood and having a commemorative parade for the fifteenth anniversary of the accident."

"Are you going?"

"Ha! I can't afford a ticket. I'm saving from our sales to buy the kids school clothes, and I need more canning jars."

"I think Aunt Alice has more jars than she needs."

"I'd sure be willing to borrow them this fall and return them when they're empty."

"Doesn't the miners' union give relief money?"

"It amounts to eighty-six cents a week. I'm not complaining. It's better than nothing, but it doesn't take care of family needs." He started to get up but stopped. "So, that's the story of how I got here in Virden with three siblings to take care of. Again, I'm not complaining. I love these kids, but my life now isn't what I'd imagined when I was in high school." He turned to look at her. "What about you? What made a city girl like you decide to teach school in Virden?"

"That's a long story. In short, I studied nursing and worked at a veterans' hospital in Maryland where I took care of mostly dying veterans, some wounded down near Cuba. I realized I just didn't want to continue with nursing for a while, and then another nurse and I had a bad experience on the way home one night. I'm still not over the fears I have from that. I grew tired of Maryland, tired of dying young men, and I didn't feel safe. I went home to St. Louis and reconsidered what I wanted to do. I already had the schooling to teach the lower primary grades, so I started applying. Virden was one of the places I applied to because Aunt Alice is here and just lost Uncle William not long ago. My nursing background helped get me the teaching job, so here I am getting ready to start a school year for the first time as a teacher."

"I'd like to hear more about the details sometime."

"I've held you up long enough. I believe that you have swimming to teach, and I have a painting to work on."

He stood to go, and his eyes fell on the pencil sketch she had made of him. "Are you keeping that?"

"Of course, if you don't mind."

He smiled and shrugged. She closed the sketchbook and returned his smile. "Clyde is picking me up in about an hour if you want a ride back."

"Thank you. I think we will."

Chapter 5

Fears from the Past

The Virden Record, Aug. 10, 1898

Numerous complaints reach me of the indiscriminate use of slingshots and air rifles by the boys in the city. I desire to call attention to the fact that city ordinances prohibit the use of both these, and if further complaints reach me, prosecutions will follow.

Henry Noll, Mayor

The cool morning air brought with it a break from the heat and humidity. Cate put on a lightweight green cotton dress and located her walking shoes and straw hat. She felt like she needed to get some exercise and to see more of the town, but she wasn't sure which way would be most interesting. While she was tying her shoes, she heard the squeak, squeak, squeak of Harry's vegetable wagon and got the idea to see which way the McCalls were going. She hurried out.

He stopped at the corner. She met him there and spoke first. "I'm on my way out for a walk, Harry."

"Where are you going?"

"Just out to see the town. Which way are *you* going?"

"Noah said we ain't been to Vinegar Hill for a few days and to go there."

"You *haven't* been. 'Ain't' isn't proper English. We'll talk about that after school starts."

"I guess." He looked down and then back up. "He also said don't stop at your house because you'll think I'm a bug."

Cate took a second to think about what Noah could have meant and then laughed. "Oh, Harry, he meant a *pest*. No, you're not bugging me."

As usual, Bea was coming next and Noah behind her, so Cate waited for them and asked, "Where's Ellis?"

Noah said, "Good morning, Cate. He stayed home, and he's going to do some weeding. We didn't need three of us today." Then, addressing Harry, he said, "Harry, I told you not to bug Cate today."

Cate replied, "I've already told him he's not a bother, and today, his visit was particularly welcome because I was getting ready for a walk to somewhere I hadn't been, but I didn't know which way would be the most interesting. So, may I walk with you? Harry says he was going to Vinegar Hill, wherever that is."

"Join us. I can give you a brief tour of the south side of Virden." He smiled. "Do you have walking shoes on?"

"Of course." She showed him her shoes with a low heel, which most of her shoes had. The top of her head still came to about his nose.

Noah told Harry and Bea to go on farther ahead. "We like to go to the south end, known as Vinegar Hill, because that's where the richer people live."

"I see. Why is it called Vinegar Hill? It's not a pleasant name."

"I have no idea. I've heard there's a Vinegar Hill in New York or somewhere out east."

"I appreciate being able to walk with you. I feel…" she hesitated for the right word, "vulnerable walking alone even though I know that Virden hasn't had problems with women getting bothered." She met his gaze and knew the concern in his eyes mirrored her own.

"No, we haven't, but we're getting more men from out of town because of the strike. And things may not get better anytime soon after this week's meetings."

"Oh? What's happening?" She stopped walking to face him, and he turned to face her.

"The top union officials nationally are meeting with the Chicago-Virden Coal Company operators, Fred Lukins and T. C. Loucks, to hear the company's side of the wage dispute. The operators have agreed to abide by the union's decision. Some union leaders say the forty cents a ton wage is fair, which was in the contract agreed to last January. Other mines are paying it. But the Chicago-Virden Coal Mine is the largest in the state, so Lukins and Loucks carry a lot of weight. I suspect Lukins is getting pressure from other mine operators to not pay the higher wage and break the union demands."

They began walking again. Noah called to Harry, telling him to go to the Lincoln tree. Now on Greene Street, Noah pointed to the south. "That's Vinegar Hill. We'll go over that way, but I want to show you something."

Harry stopped at a white, two-story house and went to the front door. When Noah and Cate caught up, Noah pointed to an oak tree in the backyard. "You see that oak tree? It was grown from an acorn picked up at President Lincoln's funeral in Oak Ridge Cemetery."

"Really?"

"That's Judge Balfour Cowen's house, although he hasn't been home lately. His health hasn't been good, but I hear he's moving back. His son is getting married in a couple of weeks. Judge Cowen's mother-in-law, Mary Bartlett, was at Lincoln's funeral and picked up the acorn and planted it here in 1865."

"Thirty-three years of growth. It's a fine specimen of an oak tree. Thank you for telling me that story. I loved history in school, and St. Louis has a long history. I'm glad to get to know some of Virden's."

"I like history too and wanted to teach it if I'd been able to go to college."

"Maybe someday you'll get a chance to go."

"It's not likely."

Harry hadn't found anyone at home and squeaked his wagon back to Noah. His shoulders slumped. "It's just an old tree." Noah knelt and tied Harry's shoe. "Which way now, Noah?"

"Go south and try to pick up the usual customers." Harry and Bea crossed Greene.

"So what might happen with the operators?" Cate asked.

"If Lukins refuses to go along with the union's decision, even though he had agreed to abide by it, he may bring in Black miners from Alabama as the operators did in Pana. That's why he's building a stockade. If he tries to do that, things will get violent."

"Oh dear, I hope not." She shook her head. "And here I thought I was coming to a nice, quiet village."

"I don't see how we'll avoid a serious conflict. There is no way the Virden miners, and other miners in the area, want to repeat the situation in Pana, where the Alabama miners were allowed to get off the train. They now work the mines, and there's constant conflict with the Pana people."

They walked slowly, partly because Harry and Bea were stopping at nearly every house. Most of the houses were two-story and well-kept. Cate noted, "The other oak trees are about the same size as the Lincoln oak. Is the neighborhood about thirty years old?"

"I suppose so. The 1860s would be about right for this neighborhood."

"Looks like Harry and Bea are getting some sales."

"That's why we come down here. Earlier, you said you preferred not to walk alone. Why?" He stopped and turned to face her.

She sighed and paused, considering how much to say. "Some of the nurses and I in Maryland had bad experiences being stopped and propositioned, or much worse, by strange men. We worked long hours and sometimes had to be out at night. Even in St. Louis, I didn't want to be in unfamiliar neighborhoods. I had a big dog that I walked with. He was a good boy, and I miss him. He died a couple of years ago." She sighed again, as though tired.

"I'm sorry to hear that," he said, just above a whisper.

"I know Virden isn't Maryland or St. Louis, but I can't shake the fears I have when I'm out alone. Maybe I should carry a walking stick."

"Cate, anytime you want to take a walk, we'll be happy to walk with you."

"When I get a list of my students, I'd like to visit them before class starts to help the students who might be shy. Primary grade can be scary for some kids. It was for me. Maybe you could tell me where they live. Aunt Alice is out most days with the family that she cleans and babysits for, so I'm on my own."

"I'd be happy to help with that too."

August 13, Saturday

The day had been cloudy, and the clouds overstayed their visit, showing no signs of leaving as evening approached. Cate studied her image in a mirror near the front door and pinned on a narrow-brimmed straw hat.

Alice sat darning socks near a lamp in the sitting room. "Are you going out? It might rain."

Cate picked up an umbrella from the stand near the door. "I thought I'd see if there's a concert tonight. I've been busy preparing for school and haven't been out all day."

"Oh, they'll have one unless it starts raining hard or gets windy. Going alone?"

"Looks like it. No one else is on the street." She glanced at the clock. Seven-thirty. "I'd better get going. Want me to bring you anything like popcorn?"

"No, I can make that at home and not pay two prices for it."

Cate started to say that popcorn wasn't expensive, but she reminded herself that Aunt Alice must have lived through many years where she and Uncle William had to be frugal. Pinching pennies wasn't a habit easily thrown off—nor were her own insecurities.

Out on the walkway, she considered going back for a light jacket. The thermometer outside the kitchen window had said seventy-five, but if the rain did come, the temperature could drop. Not wanting to go back inside and risk being late, she thought, *It's not too far.*

At the square, the crowd was lighter than usual. Cate wondered if the farmers and farm workers, who must make up more than half the population, knew it was going to rain and stayed away.

"Miss Merry, how nice to see you this evening."

Cate turned to find Maeve with her little one in a faded, blue baby carriage. It looked like something from decades ago, but it still served its purpose. "Maeve! I'm glad to see you. I came by myself and was wondering who I'd find to talk to."

"You're smart to bring an umbrella. I did too. You know it's going to rain when the farmers aren't here." She gently pushed the carriage back and forth to keep the baby sleeping.

"I wondered about that and was thinking the same thing."

"Only three weeks until your school starts. Oscar isn't looking forward to it, but I told him he'll like it. He'll be doing some fun things. And he said, 'Like what? I hope we're not playing with your dolls.'" She laughed and added, "Five-year-olds can say the funniest things. You're in for an interesting year."

Cate laughed too and nodded in agreement. "In primary grade, we don't expect a lot. We'll learn the alphabet, taking it one letter a day. They'll learn their numbers and how to count. Draw shapes. And maybe, most importantly, how to behave around others and to sit still when they're supposed to. I'll teach a lot of these through games. You're welcome to visit any day if you like. I've heard that parents are encouraged to come for a visit."

"Oh, I might. Maybe on a day when you could use some help. I hear it'll be a large class."

"I'm sure on some days, help would be appreciated. I can send a note home with Oscar if I think there's a day when you could help me."

Heated voices came from a group of men to their right.

Maeve said, "Oh, not another argument this week."

The group was only a few yards from the bandstand. The band director had been waiting while the band members tuned their instruments and were in position to start the concert. While he had noted the argument, he continued with the program, tapping his director's wand on the music stand and telling the band they were ready to start. With another tap, tap, tap, they launched into a particularly robust march. The group of men who had been arguing broke up, but not before exchanging glares and finger-pointing.

Maeve nodded to someone across the square and excused herself to talk to them. Cate waved her goodbye, then stood alone in the sparse crowd and found a half-vacant bench. The other half was occupied by a teenage girl and a boy around three or four. Cate smiled at them and then focused her attention on the band. The music seemed particularly loud this evening, as though the clouds were keeping the sound in and not letting it escape to the stars. The march finally ended, and in the quiet, the child turned to Cate and said, "Did you get your face hurt?"

The teenage girl with him said, "Shh. That's not nice."

Cate touched her left cheek. "Yes, I did. Some men pushed me against some bricks. It just happened about three months ago."

The girl said, "That must have been scary."

Cate nodded and turned away to listen to the next piece, another march. She wondered if all the kids in her class would ask about her scar. She should just tell them the first day, not any details, but enough so they wouldn't ask more questions. She thought about the class preparation she had been working on and what the students would be like. The back of her head began to ache. She tried to relax her shoulders, but it wasn't going to get rid of the unease, the loud music, the tobacco smoke, the strangers milling around, so she stood up to leave.

The girl apologized again, and Cate said, "Oh no, it's not that. I guess I'm just not feeling well tonight."

She headed for Jackson Street and let the music recede. She passed under one of the new streetlamps, a five-globe affair. Some boys played a boisterous game of tag around it. Two blocks away from the square, the music had followed her, but not the light. She looked back and saw two men behind her. They were silhouetted against the light from uptown, and she couldn't see who they were, but they were maybe around six feet tall. The farther into the darkness she went, the more her unease grew, and an unwanted memory walked with her.

Early May. Around midnight. Lilies were blooming, and their scent was in the air as Cate and Sylvia, one of the other nurses, walked together toward their apartments, which were only a couple of blocks apart. They had just gotten off an eight-hour shift that had turned into twelve hours because of the arrival of new casualties from Cuba. Working nonstop, the two women felt exhausted.

They cut across a small park diagonally, which took them into an area that was not well-lit. Cate, feeling uneasy, reached for Sylvia's arm to turn back when she noticed four men following. They were well-dressed and, she suspected, from their staggering, drunk. She tried to ignore them, but their laughter caused her to look back again. A couple of them met her gaze. She said to Sylvia, "Those men back there worry me. They're drunk. Let's walk faster."

Sylvia turned to look. "They're not looking for two exhausted nurses. They can afford to buy girls for the night."

The men, still laughing, lurched for Cate and Sylvia and were on them before the girls had a chance to get away. Both girls screamed, but within seconds, Cate found her right arm twisted behind her and her face against a brick retaining wall for a drainage ditch. A handkerchief was stuffed in her mouth. One man held her arms while another fumbled with her skirts. She could hear Sylvia's muffled screams and assumed the other two men were on her. The man who was on Cate had pulled back far enough, trying to get under her clothes, that she could aim a kick hard between his legs. He yelled in pain, and she was able to kick him again before jerking free of the other man, who was so drunk, he could barely stand up.

Cate threw herself at the man who was on Sylvia. A few seconds later, two police officers joined the fight and soon had the four in handcuffs.

One of the officers said, "What are you two ladies doing out after midnight? Should we arrest you also for soliciting?"

Cate had never wanted to slap a man so much in her life. And the men in handcuffs on the ground, she wanted to kick senseless. "We're nurses who just got off a long shift because of new casualties coming in, and you want to blame *us* for being attacked?"

The officer was young, probably early twenties like Cate. "I'm sorry, but women just can't be out after dark in some parts of this city."

"This is where we work and live!" Sylvia screamed at him through her sobbing.

Cate told the officers, "We'll be pressing charges against these men." And then to Sylvia, she asked, "Did he...?"

Sylvia was crying so hard that her answer was barely audible. "No, but it was close."

The second police officer, who was equally young, said to Cate, "Ma'am, you're bleeding." And he pulled out his handkerchief and pointed to her cheek. "You better get that treated."

She felt her cheek and realized she'd been injured. "I'm a nurse. I know what to do. You're a police officer. Do you know what to do with men like these?"

He answered, "We don't tell you your business. You don't tell us ours."

The next morning, Cate and Sylvia went to the office of a nearby attorney and arranged to file a suit against the men who had molested them, but when the attorney looked into their case, he found they had never been charged with anything.

Cate, with a bandaged cheek, and Sylvia, with eyes still puffy, sat across from him in his office. The desk was clean, and so was the trash can, his suit, and the windows behind him, through which they could see the park where they had been accosted. Cate said, "How could they not be charged?"

"One of their fathers came to the station and probably paid a pretty penny. I doubt it was the first time."

Sylvia's shoulders slumped, and her eyes filled with tears. "What about us? And they might do this again to some other poor women."

The attorney put his hands up, palms toward them, as though he were innocent. "There's little any of us can do about it if the law doesn't charge them with something. They didn't succeed in raping either of you, so no real harm done other than a scraped cheek."

Cate could feel her face getting hot and knew it must be quite red. "This is outrageous. Four wealthy young men can act like hoodlums, molest two nurses returning from a long shift, and suffer zero consequences. Where is justice?"

He shrugged. "They have the clemency of wealth." He leaned back in his chair. "And without actually raping you, you won't have to worry about a longer-term consequence. The scrape will heal."

Cate pointed to her cheek. "I'll be scarred. This was more than a light scrape."

"I'm sorry, but there's nothing we can do. The police won't give out the names of people they don't book."

꘏

Cate glanced back at her followers again and took a deep breath. This was August in Illinois. In a nice, friendly, small town called Virden. Things like that wouldn't happen here. But the two men following Cate were getting closer. Alice's house was now only a block away, and she made a run for it. She felt her hat come loose and fly off, but she wasn't about to stop for it. She could get it tomorrow. She took the steps up to the porch two at a time and rushed through the front door, out of breath and disheveled.

Alice looked up from her mending. "Goodness, Cate. You look like you seen a ghost."

Cate leaned against the wall and worked to catch her breath. "Two men were following me."

"Who? Did you get a good look at them?"

Cate sank into one side of the couch and put her face in her hands. "I couldn't see who they were. I was just reminded of the men who gave me this scar."

A knock at the front door made both women jump. Alice said, "I'll get it."

Cate used a handkerchief to dab sweat from her face and neck.

Alice opened the door. "Noah. Won't you come in?"

He had Cate's hat in his hand, and he took his own off. "Cate, Henry and I saw you drop your hat when you ran. Was there something wrong?"

Cate let out a sigh. "So, it was you and Henry." Her hand shook as she held it out to take her hat. "I didn't know who you were."

He stood holding his own hat. "But what scared you?"

She touched her cheek. Tears in her eyes reflected the lamplight. "Memories of how I got this scar." She sniffled and used her handkerchief. "I'm sorry. It has nothing to do with you. Another nurse and I were attacked while walking home from a late shift. I'm sorry I alarmed you."

Alice went over to the couch and put her arm around Cate.

Noah turned his hat over in his hands. "I'm sorry we scared you. You were across the square from us when we saw you leaving, and we thought we'd follow you home, but just didn't catch up before you ran." He put his hat on. "Well, I'll leave you two for tonight." He turned to go, but then added, "You know, Cate, you and Alice should let me know if you need anything or feel threatened."

Cate had her face in her hands.

Alice nodded, "Thanks, Noah. Where are the kids?"

"I left them playing board games with the neighbor. I decided to take a break and walk uptown and back."

"Well, have a good evening. And thank you for returning Cate's hat. If it does rain tonight, it wouldn't be worth much in the morning."

Chapter 6

Spiders and Keys

August 16, Tuesday

In *The Virden Reporter*, Cate had noted ads for Lorton's claiming they had everything a good grocery store should have. Cate hoped so, because she wanted to make veal pot pie and had a list of ingredients she needed.

At Lorton's butcher counter, she ordered the veal and began chatting with the butcher. His name was Adam, and he already knew that she was the new primary grade teacher. Cate guessed that he was thirty, so he might have a child around five or six. But he confirmed that he did not; he was a resolute bachelor.

The customer behind Cate spoke up, "I have a primary grader this fall, and he's right here with me."

Cate turned to find a boy who was tall for five. He had curly, brown hair and hazel eyes. "Hello, young man. What is your name?"

"Nolan. And you'll be my teacher?"

"Yes, I will. I'll try to visit my students before school starts if I haven't met them around town."

The mother was quick to add, "No need to come by our house now you've met Nolan. I can't keep the house in order good enough for a teacher."

"Oh, there's no need..." Cate's reply was interrupted by a woman's scream from near the produce.

The woman screamed again, and the butcher hurried to the produce counter.

Cate and the other customers converged on the scene of the scream. The woman stood with one hand over her mouth, and her face was turning as red as the tomatoes. She pointed with her other hand. "It's there!" The finger shook. "It's in the bananas!"

Out from among the bananas crept the biggest and hairiest spider Cate had ever seen. The circle of customers backed away a couple of steps.

A man in a three-piece suit next to Cate stepped forward. "I'll get it. Stand back! It's probably a tarantula. Adam, can I get a jar with a lid?"

Adam produced a jar while the customers stared at the spider. The spider stared at the customers. Adam handed the jar over, saying, "Here you go, Dr. Boyer."

In one swift motion, Dr. Boyer used a cucumber to knock the spider into the jar. He put the lid over it, then said, "I know just the thing." He went to the other side of the aisle, and when he came back, the jar was filled with liquid, suspending the spider. "A little alcohol, and this spider isn't going to bite anyone."

Cate was disappointed that he had felt the need to kill the spider, but she understood why. Its legs still twitched slightly, and she wondered if it was suffering. She felt sorry for it, even if it was a spider. It was another living thing, just trying to get by. "The high school biology class might want it," she said. "It really is a magnificent specimen of a spider."

All eyes turned to Cate.

The frightened woman had backed up, shaking visibly. "Take it away, then! It's horrid."

Minutes later, Cate emerged from Lorton's with the ingredients for a veal pot pie and one possible tarantula in a jar filled with alcohol. The new principal was a high school teacher, and she wondered if she might find him at the school even though classes hadn't started yet. If he wasn't there, maybe someone else would be.

She took the groceries home and walked to the high school. People referred to it as the East School, since it was on the east side of town. It was a two-story brick schoolhouse, the first story of which, she had been told, was built in the 1860s. She found the door to the high school ajar. When she entered, her footsteps echoed on the wooden floor. Through another door, a man sat working at a desk. He wore a white shirt with the sleeves rolled up. The window behind him provided a breeze that came across the hallway to the open door.

He looked up from his papers and stood up. "May I help you?"

"Hello. I'm Cate Merry, the new primary grade teacher."

"And I'm Milo Loveless. Come in, come in." She held up the jar, and his eyes grew wider. "What? A tarantula?"

Cate explained what happened at Lorton's, including Dr. Boyer telling everyone to back up when no one had any intention of rushing in. Milo first laughed, and then he said, "I wish I'd been there! I imagine that stirred up the shoppers."

"I suggested that perhaps the high school biology lab may want it. So, here it is if you're interested."

"Certainly, we're interested! We don't get tarantulas in Illinois, if it even is a tarantula. The size of it indicates some kind of warm-weather spider." He spread his arms wide. "We have a large boa constrictor, which is very popular with the students."

"Well, I'll just leave Mr. Banana Spider here with you." She lightly set the jar on his desk and waited to ask another question.

He immediately picked it up to have a closer look. He held it level with his face, and from where Cate stood, the glass and alcohol magnified his glasses and eyes. He set the jar down. "I was going to stop by to meet you, Miss Merry. I believe you are living with your aunt, Alice Merry?"

"Yes, I am. And I did have one request, if it's possible. Would you have a list of my students? I was thinking about trying to meet them so that they're not so intimidated by the first day of school."

"Yes, I do. I can bring that list by tomorrow if you like—and the key to the building."

"Thank you so much. I have one other question. Why is the grade before first called the primary grade and not kindergarten?"

"It's just our history. You know, Virden became recognized as a town in 1852. I think when they decided to add a grade to precede first, they gave it the primary name. And I suspect they never changed it because, well, kindergarten sounds German, doesn't it? The town is historically English, Scottish, Irish, and Welsh, although we're getting more of an ethnic mix every year as more men come to work the mines."

"I see. I have a teaching degree, but as you may know from your predecessor, who hired me, I haven't yet taught school."

"I understand, but I also understand that the school board wanted someone with nursing skills because, well, accidents happen, and kids get sick, and so on. And they're aware some of our practices might be improved." He shrugged. "You'll do fine. Not a lot is expected of students in the primary grade. If the students can learn their letters and numbers and how to sit in class and play with other kids, then you've done your job."

"I appreciate the vote of confidence. Have a nice day, Mr. Loveless."

He moved the jar with the spider onto a stack of papers. "What a paper weight I have now!"

August 18, Thursday

The front porch caught a pleasant breeze from the north. Aunt Alice had just moved a scented geranium from the sitting room to the porch, and Cate caught its perfume when the breeze was just right. She rocked the swing with her dangling feet, heel to toe to heel, as she thought of the coming school year. Then, as though she had conjured him, Milo Loveless came from the direction of the high school and turned up the walkway to the house.

"Good morning, Miss Merry." He smiled.

Cate stood. "Hello, good morning."

"May I?" he said, indicating the front steps.

"Certainly."

"I have the list of students and your keys for the school."

"Thank you so much, Mr. Loveless. Please have a seat. I was just enjoying this morning's breeze before it fades." She gestured to the two chairs against the porch railing.

"Oh no. I can't stay. Today, I'm making the rounds of the teachers to give them our new keys—and to give you your first key. We had our locks changed so they're harder to pick. Desperate times require more desperate measures, as they say." From his pocket, he pulled a piece of paper and a hefty key about three inches long and offered them to her.

When she took the key, she felt more excited than she had for a long time—her new beginning had finally begun. "May I go to the classrooms anytime now?"

"Certainly, you may. Yours will be the first one on the right. The windows have a commanding view to the east toward the public square and Church Street to the south. It might be the best of the three classrooms."

"Lovely, I might go see it today." The key in her hand felt heavy, substantial, like her job as a teacher. She was beginning to feel the weight, and excitement, of getting young minds off to a good start.

"When you do, consider whether you need anything. The previous teacher, Miss Carmel, was very thorough and tried to supply everything in May for your start in September, but there might be something else you need. I'll be back for another visit well before school begins." He tipped his hat and went back down the steps. He then turned back toward her. "Oh, I almost forgot to tell you. The spider from Lorton's appears to be a Brazilian wandering spider. They can grow to be about six inches."

Cate's eyebrows shot up, and she took a deep breath. "Goodness. I'm glad he wasn't full-grown when we found him."

He nodded. "Good day, Miss Merry."

Yet again he hesitated before retracing his steps to join her on the porch. In a low, soft tone, he said, "Did you notice a man loitering over there, kitty-cornered to the west? I saw him earlier. Probably he's watching for someone, but you might want to keep an eye on him."

"No, I hadn't. Thank you for telling me."

Milo wished her a good day again and at last was off.

Cate sat back in the swing and tried to see if she could spot someone loitering. No one yet that she could see. She relaxed into the motion of the swing and considered what she knew she would need for the coming school year and felt the building anticipation of what she might find already there.

A couple of minutes passed. Two sparrows fought. A crow flew into the maple tree near the porch. The geranium's perfume came and went. Then, from around the corner of a storage building across the street, a man's face half appeared and then disappeared.

She waited and watched. A couple of minutes later, first the brim of a hat appeared and then half of a face. Yes, somebody was looking out from behind that building. But, she thought, he must be watching for someone to come down the street. It was broad daylight, and why should she worry about some man lurking around the corner? She had things to do today, starting with a visit to the school as soon as she gathered her hat and bag.

꘎

The key, again feeling heavy in her hand, turned easily in the lock as she opened the school's front door—a large, double wooden door. The superintendent who had hired her said they were planning to build a two-story brick building with a basement, but that was ten to fifteen years away.

Inside, she found an open space with closed doors leading to each classroom. The sound of her footsteps told her the floor was hollow below the wooden planks. Light came from overhead at the far end of the hall. A heavy rope dangled to ring the school bell on the roof. The first door to the right, the corner room, was now behind her. She turned toward it and put her key in its lock, unlocking her first year of teaching.

Milo was accurate in saying that the classroom had a commanding view. Large windows covered two sides of the wall in this corner room, making it a light-filled space that she could see spending many hours in.

In the window facing south, she watched as a man in a brown shirt and denim pants crossed Church Street and stopped behind an oak tree, concealing all but the brim of his hat. She saw the brim move forward, and part of his face appeared and then disappeared. He was no one she recognized, and she suddenly felt as wooden as the floor and walls. *So, a man is watching me,* she thought. *But why?*

Her mind started down the path of remembering again the night in the park… she shook her head and looked away.

A gravelly voice made her jump. "I stopped to say hello."

A tall, thin Black man with a heavily wrinkled face and slightly stooped posture framed the doorway. He smiled with the few teeth he had left.

Cate put her hand to her heart. "Oh! You startled me. I'm Cate Merry, the new primary grade teacher."

"I be William Williams, the janitor, but everybody calls me Uncle Billy. I have a small room in the back and keep an eye on things in the summer. Heard you come in."

"Nice to meet you, William."

"Uncle Billy. Been at this job over thirty years, since just after the war. If you have any questions, just let me know."

"Thank you so much, Uncle Billy."

He smiled and shuffled almost silently toward the back of the school.

No wonder I didn't hear him, she thought. She could picture him roaming the building like a security guard, although he wouldn't be much of a threat.

She went back to the front door and locked it from the inside. Composing herself, she began taking an inventory of her classroom. At the front of the room was the teacher's desk, on which sat a box of primary textbooks. Behind the desk, a long chalkboard extended from the door to the window facing Church Street. Across the street, the brim of the man's hat was still visible behind the tree. To the left of the door were hangers for coats and shelves for supplies. A box of pencils, a carton of crayons, stacks of paper in various colors, a box of chalk, and a yardstick waited patiently for summer's end. Along the top of the wall was the alphabet chart, printed in perfectly formed capital and small letters.

Cate walked to the opposite corner of the room. The windows to her left looked up Jackson Street, while those to her right opened her view along Church Street. Cate watched as ladies carrying dishes and bowls entered the Baptist church. She was sure that if she opened the window, she would be able to smell the food. Across the street from the church and toward the square, she recognized Long's Laundry. All of its doors and windows were open. Steam rose from a window in the back. A half block farther down Jackson Street was the town square, of which she could see part of the north side. Half a block away on her right, down Church Street, stood the Christian church just past where the man was still hiding. It also had a small gathering in front of it. Cate wondered if Thursday was typically a day for church gatherings.

Minutes passed as she stood there in the corner, taking in the view and deciding what to do. With these others around, she gained the courage to make a bold move.

She locked up her room, unlocked and locked the front door again on her way out, and headed straight for the tree the man had been behind. The brim of his hat was no longer visible, and when she got to the tree, no one was there. She wondered if he saw her preparing to leave the classroom. Again, she felt as wooden and immobile as the tree. Looking around, she saw no one suspicious. She headed for the square to pick up some eggs, thinking perhaps she would run into Noah's friend, Luke.

Men talked on street corners, on walkways, in the public square—more men than just a couple of weeks ago. As she passed one group, she overheard a man say, "Lukinsville is coming along." Another replied, "Oh, it looks imposing, but for real good fighting purposes, he should of used split logs and not one-inch pine."

She crossed the street and found a shady bench in the public square. The day was heating up. She dabbed at perspiration on her forehead. The light breeze from the north now came from the west and no longer felt so cool. Other women talked in small groups while their children played.

Across the public square, she saw Luke pulling his oldest child and cartons of eggs along a walkway that ran up to and around the bandstand. He paused to talk and sell eggs to any interested ladies.

Cate tried to look nonchalant as she approached him. "Luke, hello. I'm Cate. You don't know me, but I know you're a friend of the McCalls."

"Why hello, Cate. Noah's told me that you're going to be Harry's teacher." He reached into a carton in his wagon. "A fine day to buy eggs." He held a couple of large brown ones up to her. "Need any?"

"Yes, I do. I'd like half a dozen, please."

He counted them into a small brown bag.

"Luke, I know this sounds crazy, but I think there was a stranger following me. I saw him at the house, then outside the school."

Luke's eyebrows furrowed. "Where's he at?"

"I don't see him now. He may be somewhere close, and I'm not sure what to do. Even though the house is just a few blocks away, I'm uneasy about going alone."

"I see. I'm not the best person to walk a White woman home, so let me find somebody. There's plenty of guys here I know who could see you home." He scanned the square. "I see a couple right over there." He dropped the wagon handle to talk to the men a few feet away.

"You're Mabel, aren't you?" Cate asked his daughter.

The girl, who looked to be about three, nodded.

"Do you like selling eggs with your dad?"

She nodded again.

"Cat got your tongue?"

Mabel smiled and shook her head. Her braids and bows swung back and forth.

Luke returned with Henry, the banker. He was dressed in a suit and tie as he was when she met him. Luke said, "Henry is on his lunch hour and has the time to see you home. He works at the Bank of Virden. Henry, this is Cate, one of our new teachers."

Henry tipped his hat, revealing strawberry blond hair. He smiled, the corners of his amber eyes turning upwards. "We met a couple of weeks ago when Miss Merry came into the bank."

Cate nodded back and turned to pay for the eggs. "Thanks, Luke. I owe you one."

He smiled and shook his head. "Just don't tell Noah I had Henry walk you home." He turned and pulled the wagon away.

Henry said, "What was that comment about Noah?"

"I have no idea." She paused before looking back up at him. "Do you and Noah have some history?"

"Not really. Well, maybe a girl. Nothing now."

"Jenny?"

He drew back slightly in surprise. "How did you know?"

"A lucky guess. Thank you for the escort." She smiled and congratulated herself for putting two and two together.

"So, you have a stranger following you?" He motioned for her to lead the way.

"Yes. I've seen him twice, trying to be covert but keeping an eye on me. I can't imagine why someone would be spying on me."

"Maybe an ex-beau?"

"No. He's in St. Louis, and it's not him."

"Well, no worries. He won't bother us, or he'll wish he hadn't." He motioned toward his vest pocket, pinching it open to reveal a pistol nestled inside.

Her expression of surprise made him laugh. "We have a lot of strangers in Virden lately, many of them armed like I am. Some are here for the miners. Some for the coal company. I don't go around unarmed these days."

The comment made Cate wonder how many of the men around her were concealing a gun, but she put the thought away and tried to make small talk with Henry until he deposited her in front of the house. Cate could see Aunt Alice through the screen door and thanked Henry for his kindness.

"My pleasure. Any time you need an escort, let me know. Maybe I can ask you for a dance sometime when we have one?"

"I think that would be fine, Henry." She left him with the thought that he had a bit of Victor's pompous demeanor, which she didn't like, and she didn't see him as her type—whatever that was. But he was kind enough and someone who could be a friend if he didn't try to insist on being more than a friend.

That afternoon, when the kids came by with their vegetable wagons, Noah stopped to say hello. He wore a pressed cotton shirt and clean denim jeans. After their initial greetings, he paused and then rubbed his chin when he said, "I heard Henry walked you home from town this morning."

"Word travels fast." She held up her hand. "It's not what you think. I had a strange man who seemed to be following me, and I told Luke I was uneasy. He found me an escort home."

"What strange man?"

"I don't know."

"If you see him again, let me know."

Chapter 7

Visitors

"Hellooooo!" The knock on the door and the voice could be only one person. "I thought I'd stop by and see if you're settling in okay."

Cate rose from Aunt Alice's sewing machine, which she was checking to see if it was in proper working order. Aunt Alice hadn't used it for a couple of years, since before Uncle William died.

"Dora. Hello. Would you like to come in?"

"Just a friendly visit. I see that scar on your face has lightened a little. When did you get it?"

Cate took a deep breath, drew back her shoulders, and gathered the patience to explain the scar yet again. "Just in May. An accident on the way home from work. Please have a seat. Would you like ginger cookies?"

"Well, yes, if you have some."

"And tea?"

"No, no. I guess you heard about Mrs. Harrington dying."

"No, who was Mrs. Harrington?"

"She was Fred Lukins's mother-in-law. She lived with Fred and Nina for the last three or four years, but the poor woman's health has been in decline. It's a pity. She was only in her mid-fifties. That poor Lukins family. With all the striking miners that Fred has to deal with, now they have this."

"Loss of a parent must be hard."

"Do you have both your parents still?"

"Yes. And, so far, they're reasonably healthy, but they're only in their late forties."

"And are they in St. Louis? What does your father do—is he a teacher too?"

"They do live in St. Louis, but he owns a grocery ch… store." Cate checked herself, remembering that anything she told Dora would be all over town.

"How nice. A businessman."

Dora took a large bite of a ginger cookie and asked if Cate had any brothers or sisters.

"No. I had a brother. He died in the 1890 flu epidemic. He was only seven. So, now I'm an only child."

"Well, I wonder how they let you come up here to a town where violence could break out at any minute."

"I don't think they appreciate the situation. And, anyway, I'm not a miner or involved in the mine in any way, so I shouldn't be in any danger."

"Have you not noticed the number of strangers loitering around town?"

"I wouldn't know a stranger from the regular town folks."

"Well, there's plenty of strange men coming in, and a girl like you, as pretty as you are even with that scar, had better be careful to only go out in the day and with a companion."

"I appreciate your concern. I'll try to be careful." She wondered if Dora's comment was inferring that she needed a young man, maybe one of the town's eligible bachelors. "The mine operators did not agree to abide by the wage scale the miners want—and rightly so—so we're in for trouble."

Cate's spirits immediately sank, knowing what it meant for Noah and Luke and Maeve's husband and all the miners she didn't even know.

"I've heard it noised around town that Fred Lukins is going to completely enclose the mine with that fence he's building. It'll be a stockade so that he can bring in scabs. He's had trouble finding carpenters in town to help him with that. The poor man. And with the loss of Mrs. Harrington and all, I feel so sorry for them."

Dora took a breath and another bite. "Oh, and unfortunately, there's no band concert tomorrow. The bass player is sick. And here I promised you that Virden had a concert every Saturday night. Oh well, we'll have plenty more, probably through October or until the weather gets bad."

"I'm glad you let me know. I won't plan on going."

"There'll still be young people visiting around the square. We do get other fine concerts like Miss Maud Botkins, the violinist at Chautauqua, no less, who played at the Methodist church last Sunday."

With Dora taking another bite of a ginger cookie, Cate offered her news. "I was at Lorton's when the tarantula was found. That was my excitement this week."

"I read that in the paper. What a fright. I don't even want to look at bananas after reading that. I wish the apple crop was better this year. The price is too high to even think about canning them. We did get a lot of peaches and grapes, so I guess I shouldn't complain. I love this cookie. Are you willing to share the recipe?"

Ginger Cookies

From '76 a *Cookbook*, p. 197, by the Ladies of Plymouth Church, Des Moines, Iowa, Mills and Company, Printers and Publishers, 1876.

One teacup of molasses, one teacup of butter, a half tea-cup of sugar, a half teacup of water, one tablespoon of ginger, one tablespoon of soda, flour sufficient to roll.

—Mr. E. S. Speed, Rushville, Illinois

August 20, Saturday

Noah had in front of him a peck of peppers. He had rinsed them, and now they lay drying on the kitchen table, waiting to be cut up and canned. Their colors—red, orange, yellow, and green—made him smile.

Ellis sat at the table reading and looked up. "What are you smiling about?"

"I like the colors, and I think of them bringing back the summer sunshine this winter every time we open a jar. I wonder if I have enough jars, though." He sat down and considered the situation. "I'll need more for the tomatoes and other vegetables. Maybe I'll borrow some from Cate's Aunt Alice. We have a bumper crop of nearly everything with all the rain this year."

Harry interrupted his thoughts by running in saying, "Noah. Luke's here. He wants to talk to you."

On the front porch, Luke leaned against the left pillar and faced the street, but turned around when he heard Noah's footsteps. "Hi, Noah." His little Mabel was already playing with Bea in the front yard.

"Hey, Luke. What's going on?"

"I was downtown selling eggs, as usual, near the train station, and some guy gets off the train and immediately begins asking for Jackson Street and the way to the house of Miss Cate Merry."

"That's interesting. How old do you think he is?"

"Oh, late twenties, maybe thirty, and a real dresser. White linen suit and shiny shoes. Slicked back blond hair and a mustache."

"Hmm. What are you thinking?"

"If he were someone she wanted to see, wouldn't she have met him at the station?"

Noah put his hands on his hips and looked down the street in the direction of Cate's, even though her house wasn't visible from his. "I wonder if this guy could have something to do with that guy who was following her or the blighter ex-boyfriend."

"Blighter? That White-people talk?"

"Yeah, British. My dad would say it. A scoundrel. There's some guy in St. Louis she said she dated for a while. He asked her to marry him. She said no, but he wouldn't take no for an answer. I think his name's Victor." He thought for a few seconds more. "Maybe we should drum up a reason to see Cate. I want to ask her about borrowing jars, and you still have eggs to sell."

"Sounds like we could stroll through her neighborhood."

Noah spoke to Ellis. "Watch the kids for a few minutes, okay?"

Luke picked up Mabel and put her in his wagon. A few minutes later, they neared Cate's house and slowed. They stopped when they heard voices coming from open windows in the sitting room, while the pink rose under the window nodded in the light breeze.

Cate's voice said, "Victor, the answer is no and will always be no."

A man's voice replied, "But how can you continue to live in this god-forsaken backwater town among a bunch of farmers and coal miners?"

Noah and Luke exchanged glances. The muscles in Noah's jaw worked.

"I like it here, and that's my choice."

"Don't you miss me, darling?"

"Victor, I'm not your darling."

"You were at one time."

"No, that was you saying it."

"Don't you miss me? Didn't you love me?"

"No, I don't miss you. I do miss Ernie. I still miss him a lot." Her voice broke.

"Ernie, Ernie, Ernie. I wish he'd died sooner."

Cate's words came louder and between sobs. "Victor… that's… callous. Please leave. Now!"

"I came all the way from St. Louis, and I'm not going until you come with me."

"I don't care if you came from Timbuctoo, I'm not going with you."

"Your parents asked me to bring you back."

"That's a lie. My parents never liked you."

"I intend to rescue you from this backwoods hamlet and its country bumpkins. Good god, Cate, they don't even have paved roads."

Both Cate and Victor jumped when Noah's voice cut through the screen door. "The lady asked you to leave."

Cate opened the door for Noah and Luke. She dabbed at her eyes with a handkerchief. "Hi, Noah, Luke, this is Victor. Victor, these are friends of mine."

Victor clutched his hat and turned it around as he spoke. He pointed to Noah's pants. "Patches on the pants. Shoes need a good polishing. And gray socks in the summer? Let me guess, farmers."

Noah rubbed and flexed his fingers, hands extending in front of him. Luke stood behind him with his arms crossed. Mabel and the wagon waited in the shade on the front lawn. Noah repeated, "The lady asked you to leave."

Victor gave a nervous laugh. His face was the shade of a ripe peach. A strand of blond hair hung over his forehead. "And what are you going to do if I don't? Have your colored boy beat me up?"

Noah took a step forward, and Luke grabbed his arm to keep him from going closer.

Noah's cheeks turned pink, and he spoke with force. "He's not my colored boy. He's a good friend, and we're proud coal miners."

"Coal miners! Cate, honey, is this really what you want?"

Noah took another step forward when Luke let go of his arm. He put his hands on his hips. "You will leave *now,* or I'll get the sheriff. We're not here to beat anyone up. But we might drag you back to the train depot."

Cate thought the men couldn't be more different. One was a tanned, muscular laborer. The other a pale, pompous lightweight. She cleared her throat to regain her composure. "Victor, please go."

Victor stood uncertain for a few seconds, continuing to rotate his hat in shaking hands. With a face now drained of color, he pointed a finger at Cate as though pointing at a misbehaving child. "This isn't over between us, Cate. No man will ever love you as I do. You'll come to your senses sooner or later." He went around Noah and Luke and out the front door. His footsteps on the wooden stairs were his only goodbye.

Cate's shoulders relaxed. She sighed. "Thank you both. I think he had a spy follow me that day I had the strange man around. And then he probably reported back to Victor. I was hoping not to see him again."

Noah nodded. "Glad to be of service. We'll follow him and make sure he's on the next train to St. Louis..." He pulled his watch from his pocket, "which will be in about an hour."

Cate collapsed into a chair, sighing deeply before looking back up at the men. Her voice broke as she said, "Noah, don't think his derogatory comments mean anything to me. You know what I see when I look at you two?"

"Two poor coal miners?"

"No. I see two young men who are pouring their hearts and lives into caring for their families, and I love that about you. Victor is a vain popinjay who wouldn't be interested in me if my dad didn't own a successful business. I'm sorry you had to hear all that, but thank you for getting rid of him." She dabbed her eyes with her handkerchief and blew her nose.

Noah sighed. "Is there anything else we can do before we leave?"

"No. I'm okay now that he's gone."

Luke said, "Can I ask who Ernie was?"

"Oh, you heard that too?" She looked away. Her eyes were red and puffy. "He was my constant companion. Such a good boy. I loved him so much. He was a large dog I'd had since I was about ten. He never liked Victor and would growl every time he came to visit. His name was really Ernest, and he was nothing if not earnest."

Chapter 8

Jerry

August 23, Tuesday

Through the open windows of the kitchen, voices found their way to Noah. Voices that made him stop chopping tomatoes. A man's voice said, "Where's he at?"

A woman's voice, which Noah recognized as Gladys, a neighbor a few doors over, answered, "He's been lying in the shade over by the drainage ditch for two days. He's probably sick or rabid. You better be careful."

"You don't need to tell me how to do my job, Gladys."

Noah put down his knife, wiped his hands on a dish towel, and went outside. He followed behind the two and recognized the man as the dog killer for that part of Virden. He called to them, "What dog are you after?" Noah felt his stomach churn at the thought of Frank killing a lost dog, but sometimes they did have to be put down, especially if they had rabies.

Gladys yelled, "That mongrel that's been hanging around the ditch."

"Show me and let me see. He might belong to someone and just got loose."

"He's loose all right. He ate the mincemeat pie I set on the counter to cool so I could take it to the church luncheon. Put his paws up on the windowsill and his long snout through to the counter. Damn dog. Look at him over there sleeping it off."

Noah chuckled and said, "I'd eat one of your mincemeat pies too, Gladys, if I had a chance. That doesn't sound like something a dog with rabies would do."

"I spiced it up pretty good. I hope it gives him the shits." She put her hands on her hips. "Now what am I going to take to the potluck tonight?"

The dog killer stopped and pulled out a pair of binoculars. "Let's not get too close before we find out if he's rabid, wild, or what."

"Well, even if he ain't rabid, he's still a menace."

Noah said, "He's not acting like a mad dog. He's a good size, though. I can see where he could reach through your window if he stood on his hind legs."

Harry had come around the house from the front yard and saw Noah, Gladys, the dog killer, and the dog. He ran toward the dog, his blond hair flying, and he screamed, "Don't kill him! Don't kill him!"

Noah ran after him. "Harry, stop! We don't know if he's sick or hurt. He could bite you."

Harry reached the dog before Noah could, and he stopped a few feet away.

The dog sat up with all the commotion, and his ears perked up. Noah motioned to Frank to hold up and said, "Harry, *do not* touch him and get back to the house."

The dog's tail rose and fell a couple of times. He wagged it more when Noah said, "Good boy." Harry got behind Noah but didn't go back to the house. Noah edged closer. He put his hands on Harry's shoulders and blocked Harry's view of the dog. "Harry, listen to me. Please back up farther."

"But Frank's going to kill him!" Tears ran down his face. He wiped them away with a dirty hand, leaving a streak of brown.

"No, he won't. I won't let him. The dog isn't rabid." As Harry backed toward the house, Noah slowly reached out and stroked the dog's head. "Good boy. Good boy."

The dog gave him a lick. He had long brown and black fur and a collar. The fur was matted with mud, seeds, and burs in several places, and he had a notch out of his right ear. He did not have wild eyes, nor was he foaming at the mouth. He had friendly, almost pleading brown eyes.

Noah squatted in front of him. "Hi, boy. Can I see your collar?" A canvas belt with a brass buckle circled his neck. Noah had to brush the fur out of the way to read the lettering. Painted on the canvas was *G. Wagner*. "G. Wagner. Gertrude Wagner? I think I'm beginning to see how you got here." He stepped a few feet away. "Come on, boy," he said, slapping his thigh. "Will you come with me?"

The dog, panting, looked at him and then got up to follow. With one hand near the top of the dog's head and his other hand on Harry's shoulder, Noah walked toward Gladys and Frank, who lowered his gun. Gladys edged back behind Frank, saying, "Look at him. He's a mess. Noah, he could bite you any second. Frank, kill the bugger!"

Frank cradled the shotgun in his right arm. "It's okay, Gladys.

I've seen enough dogs to know this one ain't mad, and he ain't going to attack."

Noah pointed to his collar. "He has a collar that says G. Wagner."

Gladys's jaw dropped. "Gertrude Wagner? She dropped dead about a month ago!"

Frank gestured toward the dog. "I'd say he got out of wherever she had him and has been scavenging for the last month."

Gladys moved from behind Frank, but no closer. She was no longer yelling. "I seen her son and daughter-in-law in town not long after she died. Heard they come and cleaned out the house. They live in Chicago and probably had no use for a dog. Should of found somebody to take him, though."

Frank pulled out his pocket watch. "I got a meeting to get to. You want me to just put him down now?"

Harry cried, "No, no, don't kill him!"

Noah pulled the dog against his leg. "No, let me take him."

Frank motioned toward the north where the mine was. "You're out of work. You can't afford to feed no dog. He ain't gonna to eat them garden vegetables."

"I'll find him a home. He looks like a German Shepherd. Gertrude probably used him as a guard dog and herding dog for those sheep and goats she had."

Gladys waved him off as if to say "Good riddance" and headed home into the midday sunlight. Frank shouldered his gun and headed toward town.

Noah said to the dog, "I wonder what your name is. Come on, boy. I'll take you home and get you cleaned up."

The dog sat down and scratched his neck with a hind leg.

"Looks like I'd better send Ellis to get some flea soap."

Cate heard a knock at the door and set aside the broom. Aunt Alice had just left to visit a neighbor. The house was quiet. The evening sun cast a warm glow over the kitchen. It was her favorite time of day, and she planned to settle in with a good book, so she was disappointed at receiving a visitor. Beyond the screen door, she found Noah and his two youngest.

"Hello, Noah, Bea, Harry. You're out selling late, aren't you?"

Noah answered with a smile. "We're not selling anything tonight. I have something for you—if you want it, but I'm not sure you'll go along with it."

Cate couldn't imagine what he might have. Cantaloupe? Brussels sprouts? "All right. What is it?"

"I think you might like protection."

Dear God. Where is he going with this? I certainly don't want a gun.

Noah turned toward the front of the house. "Ok, Ellis. Bring him around."

Cate's mouth formed an O. Whatever she expected, it wasn't a dog. And a dog who looked a lot like Ernie, except he had patches of fur cut away and a notch in his right ear. "What? How? Who?"

Harry said, "His name is Jerry."

"Jerry?"

Noah explained that the dog killer was ready to shoot Jerry, mostly for stealing one of Gladys's mincemeat pies, and that he had a canvas collar on him with the name of a woman who had owned a farmhouse and died about a month ago. "The dog is now ownerless and homeless and, I guess, has been scavenging for the last month. We gave him a bath with flea soap twice and brushed him out. Ellis cut out the burs and tangles and maybe got a little overzealous with the scissors. We tried hard to get out all the dirt and fleas." Noah patted Jerry's head. "He seems like a good dog and needs a home. Gertrude probably trained him as a working dog. I thought I'd start with you to see if you'd want him. We can't keep him."

Cate, still stunned, went over and knelt before Jerry. In the places where the fur wasn't chopped up, it was the beautiful, varied-colored brown and black fur just like Ernie's. When she looked up at Noah, tears ran down her cheeks. "I'd be happy to take him. I'll have to convince Aunt Alice, though." Then she rubbed Jerry's ears. "Are you a good boy?" She gave him a big hug and stroked him. A wag of his tail assured her he was indeed a good boy.

"How do you know his name is Jerry?"

"We don't. It's the name that Harry gave him. You could call him whatever you want."

Harry added, "He looks like a Jerry."

"Well, I didn't know what a Jerry looks like until now. So, Jerry it is." She reached over to Harry, hugged him, then ruffled Jerry's fur. "Thank you so much for thinking of me, Noah. I hope Aunt Alice doesn't have a fit when she gets back. She's a particular housekeeper."

"Tell her you could use a bodyguard. You not only had the stranger Victor hired following you, but we're getting more men in town every week. And we'll continue to get more men coming in until this lockout is over. They haven't caused trouble, but..." his voice trailed off. "Jerry can escort you around town, and no one will give you any trouble. You won't feel so vulnerable, as you put it."

"That'll be a good reason for Aunt Alice." She gave Jerry another hug and promised him a treat if he followed her into the house.

Noah said, "Well, there is one thing you should know, Cate."

"What?" She wiped more tears from her cheeks.

"Uhm, he's, uhm, been modified."

Cate laughed so hard that more tears came. "You mean he's missing some of his equipment?"

"Uh, yeah. Gertrude must have had the vet do that so he'd be less likely to roam."

"That's fine with Aunt Alice and me, Jerry." She hugged him again. "Good night to you, McCalls, and thank you." She turned to go into the house and then hesitated. "You know, I think Jerry had to be providence, him showing up only three days after me telling you about Ernie."

"I think you might be right."

"Jerry, you and I were just meant to be together. Come on, boy."

The smell of baked chicken still lingered in the air. Jerry didn't hesitate to follow Cate into the house, wagging his tail.

On the way home, Noah said to the kids, "I think Cate and Jerry will get along just fine."

"I liked it when Cate hugged me," said Harry.

⚓

August 24, Wednesday

The sitting room clock struck one low-frequency chime for nine thirty. Cate set down *The Adventures of Sherlock Holmes* and listened to the crickets. She picked up her journal and did a quick pencil sketch of Jerry. She had made him a dog bed and put it in the corner by the window because he loved to look out. Somewhere, a dog barked, and he raised his ears.

Alice sat darning socks for the family she worked for. "I wish Clyde had brought back the cake pan." She sighed. "I need to make that marble cake for the bake sale bright and early in the morning."

"Is that the cake where you swirl together batters for a silver cake and a gold cake?"

"That's the one."

"Sounds delicious. Don't you have other cake pans?"

"This one has a sliding lid to keep the flies out."

"Maybe he'll leave it on the back steps tonight."

"I hope so, or it's the last time he'll get cake in my favorite pan."

Cate pointed to Jerry and then to the back door. "Come on, Jerry. Let's go out one more time before we go to bed." She found that he behaved like a working dog because of how easily he responded to pointing and simple commands.

Jerry padded behind her as they went into the backyard— she down the path to the outhouse and he to the back bushes. When Cate returned to the back door, she called him, and he came without delay. She'd had him one day, and he already knew his new name, or at least understood what she wanted him to do. She wondered what his real name had been. Maybe something similar, or maybe he was just that smart.

All the windows of the house were open, including in her bedroom. The heat of the day hadn't entirely escaped her room. Instead of closing her door all the way, she left it cracked open to give more airflow. Alice was also going to bed, so she turned down the sitting room lamp.

Alice's house was typical. The front door opened into the dining room. A sitting room was at the front of the house, to the left of the front door. The kitchen stood beyond the dining room toward the back of the house, with two bedrooms on the left. Cate picked up Jerry's bed and brought it into her room.

Cate changed into a short-sleeved nightgown while Jerry settled onto his bed.

Sleep didn't come right away. She thought of her upcoming visits to students, what they might be like, and how her parents were doing at home. The Virden Telephone Exchange was completing telephone connections, and the central switch would be located above the Farmers and Merchants Bank. Soon, every city would be connected to every other city, and she wondered how long before every home would be connected to every other home and if that was even possible. Wouldn't it be nice to be able to talk to her parents whenever she wanted?

The clock chimed ten thirty. She had lain awake nearly an hour and tried again to clear her mind. Jerry rose from his bed and went over to the bedroom door. Cate sat up. There was enough moonlight to see Jerry nudging the door farther open with his nose, and she wondered if he heard or smelled something.

Suddenly, he bolted through the door and let out a loud bark, followed by growling.

"Ouch! Ouch! Jesus, Alice!" yelled a man's voice. "Ouch! There's a wolf in your house!"

Cate ran from her room at the same time Alice emerged from hers with a lamp. In the kitchen, Jerry growled through his teeth that had Clyde by the pant leg, and he wasn't letting go.

"This damn dog bit me in the ass! Since when did you get a dog, Alice?"

Cate yelled, "Jerry. Stop! Release!"

Jerry let go of Clyde's pants and began barking again. Cate hurried over to him. When she managed to get him calmed down, she told him everything was okay, murmuring that he was a good boy.

"Good boy? That dog bit me."

Alice couldn't keep from laughing. "Clyde, you're lucky it was your backside and not something else. Did he draw blood?"

Clyde was rubbing his buttocks. "I don't think so." He looked at his ankle by the light of Alice's lamp. No blood there either.

Alice added, "Clyde, it serves you right, creeping around my house at ten thirty at night."

"Ah, Alice. The back door was unlocked, and I was just trying to return the cake pan."

"Well, why didn't you leave it on the back steps?"

"I was afraid you wouldn't find it until you blamed me for not bringing it back tonight."

Alice nodded with understanding. "Clyde, meet Jerry, our new guard dog, a German Shedder. I was wondering what he'd be good for besides eating and shedding."

Cate held Jerry around the neck. "My fault. I didn't lock the door on my way in."

Alice let Clyde out the back door. "All's well that ends well."

A knock came from the front door, and the neighbor lady's voice said, "Is everything all right, Alice? I heard such a ruckus."

Chapter 9

Visits to Students

August 25, Thursday

Cate had an umbrella, her handbag, and a list of student names. She'd left Jerry at home with Alice. He loved a walk, but some people found him a bit scary, and she was trying to avoid frightening her students. And she couldn't yet be sure how he would react in some situations like a crowded street. She consulted her list of students again. Some had house numbers, some just street names, and some only the section of town. One said, "Bartholomew White, Jr., Prairie Street."

Near the intersection of Prairie and Matteson, a group of boys was shooting rocks at cans with slingshots.

Cate called to them, "Hello, boys. Can you tell me where Bartholomew White lives?"

They looked at each other, and one pointed to a house. "Over yonder in that two-story house."

"Thank you."

As Cate walked away, they were snickering among themselves, and she wondered what was so funny about Bartholomew White's house."

The yard looked well-kept with flowers and bushes, although Cate found the beaded curtains in the parlor window gaudy. She knocked at the front door, and the woman who answered wore a dress with a low-cut neckline and a hem length around her calves.

Cate said, "Good morning. I'm looking for Bartholomew White. Is he at home?"

"Probably. He ain't here, though." She laughed, and two other ladies dressed similarly came up behind her.

Cate began to get a queasy feeling. "He doesn't live here?"

All three ladies chuckled. "No, he mostly lives down at the church, being the preacher and all. What you want with him?"

"Oh, I'm sorry. I want Bartholomew White, *Jr.* I'll be his primary grade teacher this year, and I wanted to introduce myself."

"Oh, honey, the Whites live a couple of blocks to the west. And you won't find any of them here. They've tried to shut us down. This being a Thursday, they're probably at the church getting ready for the Thursday night Bible study."

Cate felt the blood drain from her face. Three women, not dressed fit to be seen in public, were laughing at her questions, and she realized what she had stumbled into. "I'm sorry to bother you, ladies. Thank you and good day." Down the street, the slingshot boys laughed and ran away.

The next house on her list was a few blocks to the north near the Chicago-Virden Coal Mine. The sound of hammering from the stockade grew louder as she approached the address. The house needed a coat of paint. What was still on the wooden siding was a dirty-white color. A couple of goats ate grass in the front yard. Children's voices came from the backyard.

Cate knocked at the door and noticed a foul smell, which took her memory back to the injured ward at the veterans' hospital. *Please, dear God, don't let it be that*, she thought.

A second knock brought a small, thin woman to the door. She dried her hands on a gray dish rag and said, "We don't have any money to buy whatever you're selling, including religion."

The odor became stronger, but Cate pushed it from her mind. "I'm Miss Cate Merry, and I will be Arthur's primary grade teacher this year. I am trying to meet some of the students, so they'll be less worried about the first day of school."

"Worried or not, he'll be there, or he'll get a tanning." She tried to tame a couple of loose strands of hair. "He ain't here right now. He's out playing with some boys."

"I'm sorry, but what is that smell? It's the smell of…"

"That's Papa. He got a splinter in his leg that ain't healing. It's just getting worse, and we've no money for doctor bills."

"He needs to be seen immediately. I suspect that's gangrene. I know the smell from my work as a nurse."

"You was a nurse too?"

"Yes. Please get him to a doctor right away. Or I could look at it quickly, if you like."

"No, no, thank you. I'll talk to him. He won't want a leg amputated, though."

"No one does, but sometimes it's necessary to save the person's life. Think of all the men who wouldn't be here today if surgeons during the war hadn't amputated their legs."

"He's in no condition for a woman to see, and we don't need help deciding when to see a doctor."

The next residence was close to what was called the "colored church" at the corner of Prairie Street and Dye Street. The Reverend Elijah Bellwether sat on a chair in his backyard with a large piece of canvas stretched over his lap.

Cate cut across the lot behind the church and greeted him.

He stood up and smiled. "Miss Merry. What brings you by?"

"I'm trying to have a quick visit with students before school starts to help lessen any fears they might have about their first day."

"That's a fine idea. I think Minnie and Tami are baking cookies. Just knock at the front door. They'll be excited for your visit."

"May I ask what you're making?"

The Reverend motioned toward the canvas. "I'm a tent maker, just like St. Paul, although most of my tents end up in carnivals and circuses."

"I see. A noble profession in addition to being a preacher."

"I enjoy it, even if it doesn't make use of my education."

"Which is what?"

"Theology and history. I use the theology part, but no one is going to hire a Black man to teach history to White kids anytime soon."

She marveled at all the canvases laid out. "I wonder if adults would attend history lectures from a Black perspective. I'm sure I could learn a lot."

He shook his head. "I doubt it, but let me give it some thought."

Cate said, "I'll leave you to your work, St. Paul," and gave him a wry smile.

She knocked at the front door, and the pleasant odors from this house helped her forget those from the house where "Papa" had gangrene. It was gingerbread, if she wasn't mistaken.

Minnie came to the door, smoothing her apron. "Why, Miss Merry! Hello. Do come in."

"Hello, Mrs. Bellwether. Please call me Cate. I'm visiting my students before school starts. I've already met Tami, but I was in the neighborhood and thought I'd stop by to see if you have any questions."

Tami came from what Cate guessed was the kitchen, licking her fingers. "Hello, Miss Merry."

Minnie said, "Tami, go back in there and wash your hands." Then to Cate, "Please call me Minnie."

Minnie invited Cate to sit for a while and then went into the kitchen and came out with Tami, a plate of fresh gingerbread, and a pot of tea. They chatted about the upcoming school year and some of the activities they would be doing. The sitting room was plain and tidy with no clutter. A framed picture of Jesus hung over the couch. In this version, Jesus looks Middle Eastern and not blue-eyed.

"Minnie, this gingerbread may be the best I've ever had. And thank you for the tea."

They asked her to stop by anytime.

When she was back on the street, she thought, *What a range of households*. She knew this meant she would need to prepare for a wide range of students.

The next student on Cate's list was Oscar.

Cate knocked at the door that a woman a few houses down said belonged to Maeve, the dollmaker. Even though Maeve said Cate didn't need to visit her, Cate was curious about Maeve's household and wanted to meet Oscar. From the backyard came a clanking sound and male laughter.

Maeve came to the door, again holding the infant on her hip. "Why, Miss Merry! You didn't have to come to me. I can bring the dolls to you. They're almost done. Would you like to come in?"

"Thank you. This is my visit to meet Oscar and welcome him to my class."

"I'm sorry you missed him. He's down the street trying to sell firewood from his wagon. Him and a friend collected some yesterday, and he's just trying to make a few pennies."

Maeve's sitting room was clean but cluttered. A faded and fraying rag rug softened a wood floor and drew together the faded and worn furniture pieces. A hurricane lamp sat on a square table next to a sofa. From the wear on the sofa, Cate guessed the end near the table was a favorite reading or sewing spot.

Maeve pointed to where Cate's attention had been drawn and said, "That's where I do my sewing in the evening. Right near the lamp. I'll show you my progress on the dolls."

"I would like to see the dolls, but I don't need to interrupt your day if Oscar isn't here. What is that clanging coming from the backyard?"

"Oh, that's my husband and a couple of his friends playing horseshoes. I'll be so glad when the mine gets back to work. He helps me with the kids and other things, but I'd much rather have the money than his help."

"Do I hear some kids out back with the men?

"That's the other man's kids. I've told them to stay clear of flying horseshoes, or they'll wake up next week."

She pulled from a drawer in the sofa's side table four dolls without clothing. Two were clearly girls with long yarn hair. "I'm afraid they're not ready for decent company yet. Here's the clothes I'm working on." She had odds and ends of dresses, shirts, and pants.

"Maeve, these are going to be so nice. The kids will love them."

"They'll be ready well before the first day of school. I'll bring them by next week, if that suits you."

"That will be perfect." Cate turned to leave but hesitated. "One other thing that I was thinking about. Didn't I see you at church on Sunday, sitting in the back?"

"That was me. I like to come when I can and leave the kids with Brian. He's not much of a churchgoer. He's the opposite of a fair-weather Christian. He'll only go when the weather is bad, if then. And I sit in the back because I don't own clothes good enough to be seen in the same room as a lot of them other ladies."

Cate replied, "I'm sure they know that your situation is a lot different from theirs. From the conversations I've overheard, the people with money in church, like the Hendersons and the Bronaughs, are putting pressure on Fred Lukins to end this strike before things turn violent. And they know that better salaries for the miners will mean more money for Virden's businesses."

"I'm glad to hear it. Mr. Lukins might listen to them. But were you going to ask me something else?"

"Yes, I was thinking that we might be able to get fabric donations from the ladies at church and then start a quilting bee among the sewers in the congregation. I think a few of you who sew and can probably quilt. We could make quilts and raffle or auction them for the miners' fund that gets distributed to the families. Would you be interested in a quilting bee?"

"Would I! With Brian not working—and the other miners out—they can watch the kids while we ladies get together for a couple of hours and talk and sew. But where would we meet?"

"My house, well, Aunt Alice's house, will be glad to host. And I'll provide some light refreshments. How many ladies do you think we could get?"

"Let me think on it. Maybe four others. Can I talk with them?"

"Please. Let me know what they say next week when you bring the dolls."

As Cate left, she felt, if she wasn't mistaken, that she had just made Maeve's day.

Soft Gingerbread

From *Everyday Cookbook and Encyclopedia of Practical Recipes*, p. 196, Miss E. Neil, Mercantile Pub., 1892.

Six cupfuls of flour, three of molasses, one of cream, one of lard or butter, two eggs, one teaspoonful of saleratus [baking soda], and two of ginger. This is excellent.

August 26, Friday

Cate gathered her bag and an umbrella. The morning had started out clear, but clouds had begun to build. Jerry stood up and wagged his tail. Cate reached down and patted his head. "You know the signs already, don't you, boy? We're going out, and today you can come. We're going to the west, and maybe you'll get to see the McCall's. They're the ones who rescued you."

He wagged his tail harder.

Three blocks to the west of Alice's house was the address for a student named John. Several kids played in the yard. They ranged in age from around twelve to a toddler. All wore faded, patched, and dirty clothes. One of the older girls ran up to Cate and asked,

"Can I pet your dog?"

"If you're gentle."

"What's his name?" The girl stroked Jerry's head.

"Jerry."

The eldest boy came up and pointed to Jerry. "Hey, that looks like the stray dog that was hanging around a couple of weeks ago. What happened to his fur?"

"The McCalls rescued him from the dog killer and cut out all the burs, and I adopted him."

"Ain't no one around here got enough food to feed a dog. I'm glad he got a home. He looks like a nice dog."

"He is. Is John at home?"

The boy turned and yelled, "Hey, Stubs. Come 'er."

A woman with a baby on her hip came onto the front porch. "What he'd do now?"

Cate said, "I'm Cate Merry, and I'll be his schoolteacher. I'm trying to meet my students before class starts on September 5th."

The woman yelled back into the house, "Hey, Stubs, get out here and meet your teacher, and be nice." She went inside, and a short boy—even for five years old—came out.

Cate said to him, "You must be John."

The boy nodded. He kept his hands behind his back.

Cate said, "I'm Miss Merry. I'm going to be your teacher. Are you excited to start primary school?"

He nodded again.

"Do you have any questions for me?"

He shook his head.

She patted him on the shoulder and said, "I'll see you in about ten days then?"

He nodded and smiled.

The next house was the McCall's. The three and a half weeks since she met them seemed like a long time ago, but she had not yet been to their house. She had had no reason to go west, whereas every day they went east toward uptown and passed Aunt Alice's. Her curiosity had her wondering what she would find. A young man and three kids with no woman in the house: Would it be a mess? She hated to think of them living in squalor. So, she approached their address with a little apprehension.

Cate stopped in front of the house that must be theirs. It was a house like many others in town, small and square. Its wood siding needed a coat of paint. A white-washed picket fence surrounded the front yard, while a solid wooden fence blocked her view of the backyard. No one was in the front, so she let herself in the gate, climbed the steps to the porch, and knocked on the door.

A pair of feet came running. Harry shouted, "Cate!"

Cate waved. "Hi, Harry. I'm meeting all my students, and today I'm coming to your house."

He said, "I'll get Noah." And he ran off before she could stop him, leaving the front door open. With her curiosity not satisfied, she let herself in.

The front room was a small sitting room. To the left, she could see through a door into a bedroom. The bed was made. Directly ahead was the kitchen. The sitting room had a couch and two cushioned chairs, well-worn. Overall, sparse and clean. No flowers or frills. Next to the couch was a side table with a lamp and a book. She picked it up to see what it was. *Examination Questions for Certificates of Competency in Mining.* She leafed through it and realized she didn't understand the language or the pictures. She set it down when she heard the back door open, and Noah entered, followed by Harry.

Cate said, "I hope I didn't interrupt anything. I'm visiting my students before school starts."

"Not at all. Would you like to have a seat?"

"No, I'd like to get back before it rains. But I would like to take a peek at your garden where all those good vegetables come from."

"Right this way, then." Noah smiled and gestured to the back of the house.

A cutting board and red and green bell peppers waited on the kitchen table. The counters were free of dirty dishes. Noah pointed to the peppers. "I was just getting ready to can some more peppers."

"They're lovely, like Christmas colors."

The backyard was large, maybe a hundred and fifty feet deep. About two-thirds of it was a garden. Rows of peppers, tomatoes, and corn waited for maturity and harvest. Cate saw very few weeds. "I can't imagine how many hours you've spent spading the soil and hoeing, and I don't know what all."

"Fortunately, I like gardening, and when I'm out of work, I have the time. And I need to garden so that we can eat and trade vegetables for other things. If I didn't have a rent-free house and this garden, I would have had to find work somewhere else, like a lot of the miners did."

"So, you're saying that many have left town?"

"Right. When the strike's over, they'll come back."

Cate patted Harry on the back and asked him, "Do you have any questions for me about school? It's only ten days away."

"Cate, Will Jerry get to come?" He was stroking Jerry's back.

"Jerry will have to stay home."

Noah said, "Harry, you have to call her Miss Merry, especially at school because she's the teacher." Then, turning to Cate, he asked, "Do they need to bring supplies?"

"We appear to be stocked, at least for now. Just bring yourself ready to learn, okay, Harry?"

Chapter 10

Trip to the Vet

August 29, Monday

Sunlight reached the jar of marmalade on the breakfast table, and it glowed orange. Cate and Alice were eating poached eggs and toast when Alice said, "Well, a week from today, you start teaching."

Cate replied, "I've enjoyed some time off, but I'm looking forward to teaching."

"I'm cleaning a house in Vinegar Hill. What're you getting into today?"

"Jerry's going to the vet. I saw in the paper that the vet from Girard, Dr. Travis, would be at Clayton's Livery on Mondays. I thought I'd get Jerry a checkup."

"He's mostly a large animal vet, which is why he's at the livery. My friend Frances takes her dog up to Auburn. Seems like Virden ought to have our own dog vet if Auburn's got one."

After breakfast, Cate got Jerry's strip of leather with a slip knot that Noah had used to bring him to her. It reminded her too much of a hangman's noose, so she decided that Jerry would also get a new collar and leash, maybe at the same place where she planned to buy a garden spade. An investigation of Uncle William's tool shed the previous day revealed a well-used one with a rotting handle.

As Cate and Jerry passed now-familiar shops uptown, some passersby gave Jerry the eye. One man even had the nerve to say, "Must have been some fight, boy. Wouldn't want to see the other dog." He and the man he was with chuckled. Not wanting to engage in conversation with strange men, Cate smiled but kept walking.

Clayton's Livery Stable sat a half block from the train station. Cate and Jerry paused at its open door, which was large enough to drive a carriage through. The interior was the size of a large barn and extended the length of one block with an alley running along the side. Skylights let in daylight. Straw and hay bales everywhere made Cate think, *Tinderbox*. Beside her, Jerry sat down and panted.

Near the center of the barn stood two men and a gray horse. One man held the horse's reins and wore overalls. The other man, whom Cate assumed was Dr. Travis, wore a short-sleeved blue shirt and canvas pants. He ran his hand up and down the horse's right leg. Then he picked up the leg to look at the hoof, pulled a tool from his back pocket, and scraped around in the hoof before dropping the foot. He said, "I think it's just a sprain, Bert."

"I hope so. I don't know what we'd do without old Grayson. Can't afford another horse anytime soon."

"I'll give you a wrap for it, but Grayson needs to not pull any heavy loads for at least a week."

Bert slapped the horse on the side and then stroked it. "Well, old boy, looks like you get a bit of a rest."

Dr. Travis waved to Cate. "I'll be with you in a minute."

Bert paid the vet and led the horse out, nodding to Cate.

Dr. Travis called over to her, "Come on in." Then he went over to a bucket and washed his hands.

As Cate moved forward, Jerry stayed sitting. She had to tug the leather strap and encourage him to follow her. As she led Jerry in, the horses kept an eye on the dog, and he hung back, not walking alongside her as he usually did. When they stopped in front of the vet, Jerry sat behind Cate's skirt and faced the exit.

Dr. Travis dried his hands on a burlap bag. "What can I do for you?" He studied Jerry for a couple of seconds, and before Cate could answer, he said, "This dog looks familiar, but you don't. Have I seen him before?"

"I don't know. A friend of mine found him as a stray and kept the dog killer from shooting him. We've cleaned him up, and I've adopted him. He had a collar that said 'G. Wagner,' who, if it means Gertrude Wagner, died over a month ago."

"Of course. Gertie's dog, Jack. I recognize the notch in his ear. I treated some wounds after a tangle with coyotes."

"He fought coyotes?"

"Yeah. Gertrude said he protected her sheep. A real hero dog. And I also neutered him when he was about a year old."

"Oh dear. I guess I'm safe from coyotes, and maybe he won't wander off."

"I would say not if you keep the food coming."

"How old do you think he is?"

"He's not a young dog. Must be around six."

Cate pulled on the leash to get Jerry to stand up so that the vet could see him better, but Jerry didn't budge or look at the vet. "Can you examine him and see if he needs anything?"

"Sure." Dr. Travis pulled Jerry up by the waist, then prodded and probed, which Jerry tolerated by stopping his panting and looking up at Cate as if to say, *Is this necessary?*

The vet stood up. "I'm giving him a clean bill of health except for a sore on his left flank, which could use some cream."

"That's where a burr had buried itself deep. I've been trying to keep it clean, thinking it would heal without a bandage."

"Right, dogs aren't fond of bandages. You could get some Good Samaritan ointment at one of the drug stores or Climax Trading."

"I will. I've used that ointment before, but we don't have any at the house. Thank you, Dr. Travis. What do I owe you?"

"Oh, nothing. I didn't do anything. I'm glad that Jack has found a good home. It'd be a shame to kill a hero like Jack."

"I call him Jerry now, and he responds to the name."

"Well, like I said before, if you keep the food coming, you could call him whatever you want. Isn't that right, Jack?"

Jerry was still ignoring Dr. Travis and looking toward the exit. Cate thanked the vet again, relieved that he didn't find anything wrong. Jerry trotted along beside her on the way out.

The Climax Trading Company was on the north side of the public square, and she had walked by it many times, going to the drug store and the Bank of Virden. On the window, it advertised being the miners' place for supplies with J. F. Eyster as manager.

She and Jerry entered. The store had a high ceiling but no fans to circulate the August air, so it lay stagnant, and was distinctively different from other stores. It smelled like kerosene or wax. Cans of "Miners Sunshine" lined a section of one wall along with what looked like small metal teapots, a few larger metal teapots, picks, shovels, canvas caps, and lanterns that filled waist-high bins. Overalls, coveralls, shirts, and pants hung on racks.

A couple of men in dirty canvas work clothes talked to a man behind the counter, who, Cate guessed, was J. F. Eyster. One of the customers smoked a cigar. The smoke hung in the air around his head. He turned toward Cate, and she recognized him as the man who had commented on Jerry having been in a fight. He coughed a smoker's cough and said, "Well, look who just came in. Beauty and the beast."

Cate again just smiled—the comment was humorous—and she said nothing to avoid encouraging him or having to start a conversation.

The other customer laughed, but J. F. Eyster didn't. Instead, he said, "Ok, you two. Stop hassling my customers. You have what you needed?"

The men continued chuckling as they headed toward the door. The wisecracker patted Jerry's head on the way out.

J. F. Eyster, Cate estimated, was in his mid-twenties. He wore a white shirt with the sleeves rolled up and denim pants. She was now the only one in the store and had his full attention. "Good morning. What can I help you with?"

"I need a new garden spade and some Good Samaritan ointment."

"I have those. Let me get the garden spade. Are you the intended user?"

She nodded. "Yes."

"The ointment is right here in this cabinet." He put the ointment on the counter and went back to the middle of the store where a forest of shovels leaned against the wall. He hefted one of them, glanced back at Cate, set it down, and selected a smaller version. "I think this one will suit you just fine."

"Are you Mr. Eyster, the manager?"

"At your service. Jacob Franklin Eyster. And I recognize you as the new teacher, Miss Merry. Is there anything else I can get for you?"

"A dog collar and leash?"

"Sorry. Not much call for those in the mines. Dalby's or Furry's might have one. Anything else?"

"No, I don't think so." She hesitated, then pointed to one of the buckets labeled Miners Sunshine, Standard Oil Company. "What is Miners Sunshine?"

"That's the fuel for the miners' lamps on their caps and the parting lamps." He showed her a canvas cap with a bill and how one of the small metal teapots fit onto a front bracket. "The oil, well it's more like a wax, goes into the pot, and a wick sticks out of the spout."

"What's the larger pot for? Surely, they don't put that on a cap."

"No. No. That's the parting lamp. They go down the shaft with just the parting lamp lit, and then they light their cap lamps from the parting lamp and head down the entries to their rooms."

"Oh, I see. I think."

He rang up the sale, and she paid.

After a pause, she again spoke. "It's quiet in here."

"The lockout. Few of the miners will buy something from here until the strike gets settled. And I don't think they can break Mr. Lukins. So, I'm not making any money, but then neither are they." He had been studying Jerry. "Did he get in a fight?"

"Not recently." She offered him a handshake, which he accepted. "Good day, Mr. Eyster, and I do hope that you and the miners can get back to making money soon."

"Jacob, or J.F., please. And thank you, Miss Merry."

"Please call me Cate. Good day, Jacob."

Back on the walkway, Cate received what she felt were glares from a couple of men loitering in front of the store. Miners, she suspected.

At Dalby's, she learned the store was definitely going out of business. The clerk blamed it on the miners' strike and pointed Cate in the direction of the dog supplies. For a sale price, she found a bright red collar of sturdy canvas and a leather leash. There would be no mistaking him now for a stray. She pictured how nice it would look after she stitched "Jerry Merry" on it.

⁛🐖

August 30, Tuesday

"Noah! Come out here!" Ellis called from the front porch.

They had all been in the garden weeding, hoeing, and tying up tomatoes. Ellis had gone into the house to get a drink, and Noah was washing up on the back porch. The thought occurred to him that the boy had found a snake, or worse, a rat.

Noah opened the screen door and stepped onto the front porch. Sitting to the right, waiting patiently, was a wooden box labeled "Jars. HANDLE WITH CARE." He rubbed two days of stubble on his chin and wondered how the jars got there. The box looked new.

As they stood pondering it, Ellis said, "Maybe it was delivered to the wrong house."

"Well, let's see." He turned the box around until he found a place where a shipping label had been torn off. In place of it was a note: "Thank you for the dog. I needed him. Here is something you may need. —Cate"

Harry and Bea joined them on the porch asking, "What is it? What's it say?"

"It's from Miss Merry as a thank you for Jerry."

Bea twisted her face in concentration and looked up at Noah. "She gave you *jars* because we took her a stray dog?"

Harry said, "I'd ruther have a dog."

Noah tousled Harry's hair. "Maybe someday, but right now the jars don't eat anything, and they'll help us put away more food. I think I need to talk to Miss Merry. Kids, load some squash and corn in the wagon while I take these into the kitchen."

⁑

Cate shifted her weight onto her foot on the spade, and it sank a couple of inches into the soil. She stomped onto it harder, and it went in another inch. Then she lifted the spade with the small amount of sod and dirt she had excavated and turned it over. She surveyed how much needed to be done and how little progress she had made, even though she'd been trying to dig for several minutes. The wash hung limp on the clothesline. Cate wished for a breeze and felt a trickle of sweat run down her spine and another down the side of her neck. She tucked behind her ear the strands of hair that had come loose from her bun.

She again put one foot on the spade and tried to push it into the soil, almost hopping up and down on it. She didn't notice Jerry get up from under the shade tree and go over to the gate. Unaware she had observers, she stopped to wipe sweat from her forehead and neck with a handkerchief, and then she reached around to feel that her shirtwaist was already damp in the back.

"What are you doing?" Noah reached one hand over the picket fence, patted Jerry's head, and tried not to laugh.

She looked around, first with just her head, but then turned and leaned on the handle of the shovel. She wondered if the smile on his face mocked her efforts. "You must have oiled the wagon wheels. I didn't hear you coming."

"I did. I wondered if the squeak gave customers a warning we were coming, which might be good or not. So, what are you digging up?"

"Uncle William grew his garden here. As you can see, it's overgrown and a mess. Aunt Alice said she tried to do something with it last year, but she doesn't have time to give the garden the attention it needs. I thought I might put in fall lettuce or whatever grows in the fall."

Noah opened the picket-fence gate and motioned for the kids to bring the wagon in. "I got the canning jars. Thank you, but you didn't have to buy me jars. We've brought you some corn and squash, but they're a poor payment."

She wiped her neck again, wondering what she must look like. "I didn't buy them. My father, the grocer, sent them. I told him I wanted some canning jars. He probably assumed that I was going to do some canning, but I knew he'd send whatever I asked for. I'll write and tell him how they'll be used."

He opened his hand toward the shovel, and she handed it to him. He looked at it and said, "Where did you get this?"

"The Climax Trading Company. Uncle William's shovel had a rotten handle."

"Ah, yes. J.F. Eyster. You must have told him it was for you because he sold you a lightweight one, a young or small man's shovel, but it'll work. The kids and I are going to help—and no argument." He motioned for them to come over to the garden, which left Jerry free to wander back to his spot under the tree. "Bea and Harry, start pulling the weeds and piling them near the incinerator." Then, turning back to Cate, Noah asked her if she had a hoe. She retrieved one from a small shed next to the garden, and he had her hand it to Ellis. "Ellis, you can follow me with the hoe."

The plot was about ten feet on each side. Noah took his outer shirt off, leaving his T-shirt on. He pushed the spade into the soil and then leveraged the handle against his leg, pulling the dirt up and turning it over with ease. He commented on the soil being nice and black, adding that recent rains meant it had moisture, and her uncle may have used compost for fertilizer. He stabbed the piece he'd turned over a couple of times for a rough break-up. As he turned over more dirt, Ellis hoed it into finer soil, and Harry and Bea removed weeds. Soon, Noah had done one row and turned to come back toward her with a second row.

Cate stood there watching him work and feeling useless. She watched longer than she intended to. He stopped and smiled at her watching him, so she turned toward the house and said, "I'll get us something to drink."

From the kitchen, she continued to watch the progress in the backyard. The four of them made quick work of preparing the garden. Alice had told her how coal was mined. Cate pictured Noah using a larger, heavier shovel in the mine's dark tunnels with the flame of a miner's hat inches from his face, which would be black with coal dust—some of it finding its way into his lungs.

His partner, Luke, would be pulling coal away from the tunnel face where it would have been blasted loose with black powder. And she felt so sorry that men had to earn a living—a dangerous living—so that modern society could heat homes, run trains all over the country, and stoke factory furnaces.

She took a lemon from a fruit bowl where it had kept company with two of this year's expensive apples and a banana. She cut the lemon open and pressed one half into the juicer. Outside, the kids laughed, maybe at Jerry. He had come into the garden to investigate something they were looking at. And as she stood there smelling the lemon with its juice stinging a cut on her hand, she pictured Harry as a grown man delivering the eulogy for Noah and saying, *He was the only father I ever knew.*

A few minutes later, she came from the back door with a pitcher of lemonade and glasses. "Time for a break. I have lemonade. It's weak. I had only one lemon, and I'm not Phineus, so there's no ice. But maybe it'll taste good."

The kids came running, but Noah stayed tilling. "I'll just finish this up and then drink water. The kids can have the lemonade. They love it, and I can't grow lemons."

By the time the kids had downed the lemonade, he had finished spading and gone on to hoeing. "You don't have to do that, Noah. I can probably handle hoeing."

"Yes, I do. Honestly, it feels good to work. I was afraid I was getting soft, not shoveling coal every day."

She stopped herself before saying what she was thinking. *You don't look like you've gone soft.* "I haven't gardened before. What should I plant this time of year?"

"If you plant them right away, you could grow beets and carrots. Radish seeds could go in now. Then plant lettuce and spinach every week for a few weeks. We'll start getting cooler weather soon, but until then, you might have to water every day or two."

"No corn or tomatoes?"

Noah laughed and came over to a chair in the shade and sat down. "You really don't know anything about gardening, do you, city girl?"

"No, I guess I don't. But you wouldn't fib to me, would you, so that I keep buying your corn and tomatoes?"

"Certainly not." She handed him a cup of lemonade that she had set aside, as he asked her, "Are you up for a walk later this afternoon? I heard there's a wedding in Vinegar Hill. We might be able to see the festivities from a distance."

"Sure. Who's getting married?"

"Nell Furry—daughter of J.M. Furry, who has the Furry's store uptown—is marrying our judge, Herbert Cowen. It's at the Furry house at three o'clock. Sometimes, we just happen to be walking in the vicinity of something going on. You might get to see them come out."

"Jerry would like a walk, but they picked the hot part of the day for a wedding."

"Vinegar Hill has plenty of shade trees. The reception is from four to six, so they might not come out until after six. We could wander over that way, probably any time after four and see who's coming and going."

"What about closer to six when we might see them come out?"

"I'll come by at five thirty, and just you and I and Jerry can take a walk. I won't bring the wagon, and Ellis can watch the kids for a while."

At five thirty, Cate, Noah, and Jerry headed south toward Vinegar Hill and arrived a block from the Furry house close to six o'clock, at which point they slowed down. They were only half a block away when guests began streaming from the house. The newly married couple was easy to identify because they were the center of attention. The bride wore an ivory and light green dress. The groom wore an ivory linen suit. They got into their carriage and were whisked away.

"What lovely clothes everyone has on," said Cate. "I'm sure I'll hear about it from Dora. She'll have all the details."

"It'll be in the paper too. I think she may do some of the write-ups."

"I wonder why they didn't have it at a church."

"The bride is Presbyterian, and the church is under renovation."

"Oh, of course."

"Judge Cowen isn't one to like a fuss, so having a small service at the Furry home probably suited him. That's the Reverend Pomeroy at the top of the steps. I'm guessing he did the service."

"I imagine they're headed to the train station now for a honeymoon trip."

"Most likely. That's what people with money do."

"You'll have money again someday." She turned to him smiling, hoping to be encouraging.

"Probably not that much. They're likely going up to the Great Lakes or somewhere cooler. That's a popular place to go in the summer if you can afford it."

"My dad took us there one summer. To the east side of Lake Michigan. It was lovely."

As they turned to go, he said, "I've started studying to get my mining papers."

"What does that mean?"

"I could get a job that pays more, like a mine inspector or foreman or manager. Then maybe I could see what Lake Michigan looks like." He smiled.

Both were silent for a minute as the walk took them toward Alice's.

Cate asked, "Have you heard what one of the guys who roams the public square has started calling Jerry and me?"

He furrowed his eyebrows in concern. "No, what?"

"Beauty and the Beast."

Noah laughed for a block.

⸙

August 31, 1898

Virden, Illinois

Dear Mom and Dad,

I know this is my first letter for a while, but I've been busy getting ready for the school year. Only five days to go. I've been visiting students and preparing a schedule for classes. I've decided we're going to work on learning the alphabet by taking one letter a day and having the students bring an item that begins with that letter, or name something. I will also have lessons on hygiene and manners. I'm wondering, Dad, if you would be able to send me about thirty toothbrushes, drinking cups, and boxes of baking soda. The school isn't going to pay for those supplies.

I want to let you know that the canning jars were greatly appreciated. You probably thought that Aunt Alice or I was going to do a bunch of canning, but they were for the McCall family, whom I told you about—the ones who sell vegetables and gave me Jerry. Noah, the older brother, has been canning his vegetables, and the gardens are producing well this year, which has been wet. Noah came by to thank me for giving him the jars, and he found me trying to spade Uncle William's overgrown garden. He and the kids took over and had the spading, hoeing, and weed-pulling done in no time. So, now, I plan to put in a fall garden.

Jerry has been doing well. I found out from the vet that his name was really Jack, and he's been known to fight coyotes. Jerry stopped what he thought was an intruder one night around 10:30. He created a ruckus and bit Aunt Alice's friend Clyde, but he didn't draw blood. Clyde was trying to return a cake pan. How was Jerry to know? Oh, and he stole a steak. Aunt Alice unwrapped two steaks for us for supper one evening and had them sitting on butcher paper on the counter when she had to answer the door. When she came back, there was only one steak on the counter. Jerry sat on his bed in the corner, looking innocent. He got a chewing out from her. He hates for me to go anywhere and not take him. He's a people dog as long as you're the right people and not burglars or, apparently, coyotes. So, you see, I'm safe here in Virden. No need to worry about me.

Thank you again for the canning jars, and let me know if you can send the other things. Maybe in a month or so you can come for a visit?

Love,

Cate

Chapter 11

An Unexpected Trip

September 3, Saturday

G reen Street was quiet on this Saturday morning as the McCall crew went door-to-door with their vegetables. Ellis had stayed home, whitewashing the picket fence. Bea and Harry pulled the wagon filled with squash, tomatoes, and corn. Noah followed behind about half a block, thinking about how the garden produce would soon begin dwindling. Close to Vinegar Hill, he heard a woman's voice say, "Wait just a minute, Noah. I have something for you." He recognized her as Dee from St. Catherine's Catholic Church. She went into her house and returned with an envelope.

Noah called to Harry, "Wait up."

She was out of breath but smiling as she met him on the street. "We at St. Catherine's heard that there is a commemoration of the Diamond Mine Disaster in Braidwood on Monday. We also know that your father died in that mine, and we got up a collection for you to go to the ceremony."

Noah stood for a couple of seconds with his mouth open. "I much appreciate this, but I can't leave the kids, and I can't take them."

"I would be happy to have them for a night. My husband and I haven't had young ones around for a while. You take the train up on Sunday. We'll keep them after mass and until the late train arrives back in town on Monday. No more excuses."

Noah opened the envelope. It held enough money for train fare, some meals, and a cheap place to stay Sunday night. "Dee, I don't know what to say."

"Say you'll go and represent Virden."

He blinked back tears. "I will. Thank you so much, Dee."

September 4, Sunday

After the service at the Christian church, Cate chatted with Henry for a while on the front lawn. Alice was still inside visiting with friends. Henry usually made an effort to ask how Cate was doing, if she needed anything, and whether she wanted an escort anywhere.

"Thank you for asking, Henry. But I now have Jerry as an escort around town."

"I know he's some protection, but does he have this?" Henry opened his jacket to remind her of the revolver tucked into an inside pocket.

"Henry, I can't believe you brought that to church. What do you need it for this morning?"

"You never know. Walking to or from Church Street, I could get robbed."

Cate shook her head. "I haven't heard that we're having a problem."

"Maybe not yet, but we will have. You'll see." He nodded as if he had some kind of insider information that others didn't have. "Can I walk you home?"

As he was asking, Alice came out and said, "All right. I had to catch up on the gossip. Let's go home and get some lunch. I wish they'd start the service sooner, like the Catholics, then we could get out sooner."

Noah and his kids were lingering at the corner of Jackson and Church. Cate smiled at Henry. "Thanks. I appreciate the offer, but I think our escort is here. They're going our way."

Henry shrugged and turned away while putting on his hat. "Have a nice day, Cate."

They met Noah and the kids at the intersection. "Good morning. You all look nice," Cate said. "You must be coming from church."

Noah said, "We are, but we call it mass."

"I see. You're Catholic?"

Alice said, "I should a told you that."

Noah nodded. "Guilty."

Cate then noted, "Well, isn't it convenient that St. Catherine's mass is earlier, which means by the time you're heading home, we can walk home with you?"

Noah said, "I'm surprised Henry didn't try to escort you two home."

Alice waved her hand as if shooing away a fly, "Oh, he's harmless enough. A decent man, but one of those big-time operator types."

"He offered, but I told him that I had some escorts," Cate added.

They began walking. "How does Jerry like having to stay at home on Sundays?" asked Noah.

"He doesn't like it at all, but I left him in the sitting room where he can look out the window, and I gave him a pile of food for breakfast and a soup bone to work over."

Alice said, "He's a lucky dog. A lot of people in town would like to have that soup bone."

Noah unbuttoned his shirt sleeves and rolled them up.

Cate said, "I think you have something on your mind. And the kids aren't as lively as usual." Ellis, Bea, and Harry lagged behind, talking among themselves—mostly about the after-mass sweets from what Cate could gather.

"Yesterday, Dee from St. Catherine's gave me money to go to the commemoration at Braidwood. I leave on the three o'clock train this afternoon. I'll pack a few things, and then I'll take the kids to Dee's."

"Oh Noah, I'm so happy for you! That will be something you'll always remember. How nice of Dee to do that."

"She took up a collection at the church, so I'm committed to going. I'm not an experienced traveler. I'll have to find a place to stay tonight. I hate to leave the kids. All this should be exciting, but..."

They had arrived in front of Cate and Alice's house.

Alice told him, "You go, and for once, forget about your worries here." And with that, she headed up the walkway to the house.

Cate patted Harry's head. "Tomorrow is the first day of school, Harry. Are you ready for it?"

Harry nodded but wasn't convincing.

"I think that's another thing they're worried about," said Noah. "Not only am I going to be gone, but they're all starting a new school year."

Ellis kicked at a pebble on the walkway. "I'm not worried. It's just another school year."

Cate patted him on the back. "I know you're not, but…" She didn't get to finish her sentence before Jerry bounded out the front door.

They all greeted Jerry, who wagged his tail at being the center of attention.

She turned to Noah. "Well, safe travels."

"Are you worried about the first day of school?" he asked.

"Not much. What is there to be worried about?" She shrugged and smiled, making light of her actual concerns.

Harry pointed to the sky. "A balloon!"

For several seconds, everyone watched the balloon and its two passengers drift silently to the north.

Harry pulled on Noah's sleeve. "Can we ride in one of those?"

Noah ruffled Harry's hair. "Maybe someday, if the price for a ride comes down, and I get some money."

"I'll sell more tomatoes."

"You can't sell enough tomatoes to pay for a ride in one of those, Harry. But when we can afford it, I'll go up with you."

Cate shook her head. "I don't think I want a ride in the sky. I'll keep to the ground. I saw a balloon like that one from the train when I was coming into town, and I envied its detachment. I had a lot on my mind back then. But now, I want to be here." Everyone continued watching the slowly moving balloon. "I had on my hospital ward a captain who flew balloons for the Army. They gave a demonstration near Washington, and something went wrong. The man was burned by an acid they added to iron filings to make the hydrogen gas."

"I didn't know how they made the gas," Noah said. Then, in a softer voice as though musing to himself, he added, "You must have met a lot of interesting men working as a nurse."

"I did, but unfortunately, too many of them were dying by the time they made it to our hospital. Just victims of circumstance… which reminds me of something I find disturbing about the balloons."

"Which is?"

"You can't steer them. You go wherever the wind takes you."

Noah smiled, showing his dimples. "That may be a metaphor for my life."

The balloon had gradually lost altitude. Above Heaton's field, it dropped a sandbag.

The kids erupted, saying they wanted to get the sandbag before anyone else did.

"Okay, go get it," said Noah. "I'll be along pretty soon."

Jerry watched the kids run off and whined as though he wanted to follow them.

Cate smoothed the fur on Jerry's head. "Can we walk over there with you? I'd like to see it too."

"Certainly." Noah motioned to Jerry. "Let's go, boy."

As they set off at a brisk pace, Cate said, "I'll be interested to learn about Braidwood."

"I'll stop by on the way back and see how your school day went, if that's okay."

"Please do. I'll want to hear all about your trip, which will be more exciting than one day of primary grade."

"I wouldn't be so sure about that."

At Heaton's field, the kids stood around a burlap sandbag, trying to figure out how to get the heavy object into the wagon.

Harry ran toward Cate and Noah. "Cate, Noah, look! It's a *sandbag* from a *real balloon!*"

Chapter 12

School Begins

September 5, Monday

As Cate left the house, she told Jerry, "Stay." The fur between his eyes wrinkled, and Cate knew he didn't like her going out and not taking him. She checked his water bowl one more time, then closed the door firmly behind her. Aunt Alice was cleaning a house and would be back for lunch, so he would have company then.

Cate made an effort to relax her neck and shoulders, which had already tensed up. She tried to take her mind off what she would find on her first day of teaching, besides a room full of five-year-olds.

She thought about Noah in Braidwood and wondered how the commemoration ceremony would go. She looked forward to finding out after he returned on the evening train, though getting the kids would be his first priority. She hoped he didn't get in too late to stop by.

At the school entrance, Uncle Billy was tying the shoe of a boy who, Cate guessed, was probably a second grader. The boy said to him, "Thanks, Uncle Billy."

"You're very welcome, young man. Now go in and get smart!" He chuckled and stood up. When he saw Cate, he said, "I love the first day of school. Gets my old blood pumping to see these young ones and think about the futures they'll see that I won't be around for."

"Good morning, Uncle Billy." She patted his shoulder. "You saw quite a past, though—one they can never see."

"And I thank the good Lord for that, Miss Merry. When I was freed after the war, I felt like I had a future. I sure hope they never feel they don't have one." He rubbed his neck, his face solemn. "I also hope the miners can see their way to a future without a war. One thing I know to be true is if you're not free to work at what you want and spend the wages how you want, you're not free. You're a slave."

"You're a smart man, Uncle Billy."

"Well... I came from 'the school of hard knocks,' as they say. You have a nice day with your young ones, Miss Merry."

Just inside the school, one of the other teachers was directing kids to their correct rooms, either primary, first grade, or second grade. She had to ask some of them their grade, and others she greeted by name and knew where they should go.

To her surprise, Cate found her room already about half full. Kids were looking at the books and crayons and pencils, some excitedly while others more warily. A group of four girls admired the dolls. True to her word, Maeve had delivered them a few days ago, and they were nicely made and lovely. A group of boys clustered around a jar of marbles that Cate planned to use for learning to count. A few marbles had escaped, and they chased them across the room.

Two girls pulled a picture book from the shelf and studied it. One boy, whom Cate recognized as John, also known as Stubs by his family, stood in the corner, looking toward the public square. Cate went over to the boy and asked if he was all right.

He held up his right hand. The thumb was a stub and not the normal length. He said, "Do we have to play marbles? I ain't no good at marbles."

"No, you won't be playing marbles in class. Those are for learning to count."

"Good. I lost my thumb in a grinder when I was three."

"Oh dear." Cate pulled a book from one of the shelves. "If you like looking out windows, maybe you would like to see this picture book."

He clutched it to his chest and sat on the floor under the window. Cate wondered if he had ever seen such a nice book. Likely not, from his reaction.

The next few minutes saw more children enter the classroom. Cate greeted them with a smile and called them by name to help make them feel at ease and accepted. As they arrived, she realized that older siblings were dropping them off, which explained why so many were early. The older sibling needed time to get to either the west side school or the high school on the east side before their classes started.

Ellis McCall looked around the corner and into the room. He waved, and Harry came from behind him, saying, "Hi, Miss Merry."

She waved back. "Come on in, Harry. Ellis, have fun on your first day at the East School."

He nodded and slipped out, saying, "I have to hurry."

About ten minutes before class was scheduled to start, the school bell began ringing. In the hallway, Mr. Loveless pulled on the rope. Cate had expected him to be at the high school because he taught classes there. After the ringing stopped, he came over to her class.

"Hello, Miss Merry. Are you all set to begin the year?"

"I am. I'm surprised to see you here, though."

"I want to make the rounds on the first day of school, so I'm starting with the lower grades and will work my way up." And with that, he was gone.

Cate let the students wander the classroom, looking at the books and other items, until Uncle Billy rang the bell for school to begin.

"Good morning, students. I'm Miss Merry, and most of you have met me. I'm going to start by taking attendance, and I would like us all to be able to see each other. So, find a desk and bring the chair over here so that we're in a big circle, and I'll sit in this chair."

With the front windows behind her, she settled in to take the attendance. Around thirty young faces looked up at her, and Cate felt again the gravity of laying the groundwork for the rest of their lives. It was quite the opposite of what she had done at the veterans' hospital, where she was frequently dealing with the end of their lives. She had wanted a change, and with a sigh, she realized she had gotten it.

She began by calling out their first names and asking each student what they wanted to be called in class. Some of the names, like Beauregard, probably weren't what family and friends called the student. But she didn't expect to be confronted with their nicknames.

Arthur said he went by Squirt. Cate told him that he would need to be Arthur in class because she didn't want to call him Squirt. Then she offered Art or Arty as different names for Arthur.

He decided to use Arthur.

When she read "Harold McCall," Harry informed her that Harold was a bad boy. "Could you call me Harry like you do around Noah?"

"What do you mean that Harold is a bad boy?"

"That's what Noah calls me when I'm in trouble." And then he imitated Noah's older and lower voice, "Harold! Get in here and clean up your mess!" The other kids laughed.

"Yes, we can call you Harry."

The boy with the partial thumb said everyone called him Stubs.

"But your given name is John, and that's what I'll call you in this class unless you want Johnny." He chose Johnny. John was what his dad called the outhouse.

Beauregard didn't go by Bo because that's what people called his sister's boyfriend. She asked what they called him at home. He said, "Boo."

"I don't want to scare other students every time I say your name." The students laughed. "So, what if I call you Reggie?"

He smiled. "I like Reggie."

When she called the name Spencer Smith, a boy raised his hand but didn't say anything. She had two Smiths, and the other was a girl who volunteered, "He's called Spud, and we're twins."

The boy scowled. "I ain't a twin with no girl."

She yelled back at him, "Yes you are! Our birthday is the same day."

Cate said to her, "And I see that you must be Carol."

"Yeah, but I'm Crocus."

"Crocus?"

"I'm the first one up in the morning. An early riser, my mom says, and crocuses come up early in the spring."

Cate continued going through the roll and learning their preferred names when something outside the window distracted them.

Amanda suddenly screamed, "Mad dog!" and ran behind Cate's desk. "He's going to bite us. We'll get sick and die!" Becky followed her, saying Mandy was scared of dogs.

Cate turned in her chair to look toward the windows. "Oh, Christ!" burst from her mouth before she could stop it.

Jerry had his paws on the windowsill and was pulling himself through.

Harry said, "That's just Jerry. He ain't mad at nobody!"

One of the calmer boys raised his hand and asked, "Is his real name Gerald?"

Cate still had her mouth open and was just rising out of her chair when another asked, "What's wrong with his fur?"

≈

Cate and Alice sat on the front porch, hoping to catch Noah walking home after his trip to Braidwood. About twenty minutes after hearing the train come into town and then leave, Noah and the three kids came walking down Jackson Street. Alice and Cate went to meet him in front of their house. Jerry beat them there.

"We thought we'd waylay you, Noah," said Alice, "and find out how Braidwood was. You got here quick."

"Dee brought them to the station to meet me." He hugged Bea, who was hugging his leg. "Braidwood had a really meaningful tribute to the miners who died. I can tell you about it sometime soon. We're all tired tonight." Looking at Cate, he said, "Harry's been telling me all about his first day of school and how it was Jerry's first day too."

"Right. Like Braidwood, that's a long story that can wait."

Alice pointed to Jerry. "That dog was like one of them circus magicians. The doors were locked, and he busted out a window screen and headed to the school. I don't know how he knew that's where she was."

"Jerry's smart, that's how," Harry said.

Cate explained how she had taken him to the school several times before, so he knew his way and somehow knew that's where she was. "Once I calmed down one of the girls who's afraid of dogs, he sat over by the window and looked out or slept all day. He wasn't any trouble, but I'll try to keep him at home tomorrow."

Noah said, "Maybe he's feeling insecure, considering what happened to his previous mistress."

Alice turned to go in and then paused. "Noah, why don't you all stop by tomorrow after supper? I'll have some pie, and we can hear all about Braidwood."

Noah agreed. They could come back tomorrow, and they bid Cate and Alice good evening.

"Come on, Jerry," said Cate. "You've had a busy day. It's time you turned in."

꘏

September 6, Tuesday

On the second day of school, Cate told the class that they would begin learning the alphabet. She had a bowl of apples, a paring knife, and a chopping board on her desk.

"I brought some apples today. Does anyone know what letter 'apple' begins with?"

About one-third of the class raised their hands. She called on Becky.

"It starts with an *A*, like Amanda's name."

Amanda turned to look at her. "My name don't have 'apple' in it."

Cate said, "Very good, Becky. Amanda does begin with an *A*. The word 'apple' has five letters, and the first one is an *A*." She wrote APPLE on the chalkboard in capital letters, then wrote AMANDA next to it.

"Do you see how both 'Apple' and 'Amanda' begin with the letter *A*?" She demonstrated by circling both of the first letter *A*s. "We're going to learn all the letters of the alphabet and the sounds they make, and then we'll learn how to put them into words like APPLE. The letter *A* sounds like 'aaa' as in 'aaaapple' or 'ahy' as in Aaaamy." She chose an apple and began slicing off pieces. "You can come up and get a slice if you'd like."

Amanda and Becky declared they didn't like apples and didn't come to get a piece. A few of the kids ate their slices like they were hungry. She sliced, and they ate until the apples were gone.

Harry raised his hand. "If we do *B* tomorrow, will you bring in bananas?"

Cate replied, "Tomorrow, I want *you* to bring in something that starts with an *A* to show the class. We'll do *B* on Thursday, and I'll see if I can get some bananas."

Nolan raised his hand. "Don't bring in any tarantulas, Miss Merry."

Cate laughed. "No, Nolan, I'll make sure the bananas have no tarantulas in them. Class, Nolan was at Lorton's with his mother at the same time I was when a woman found a tarantula in the bananas."

"The tarantula was the biggest, hairiest spider as big as your hand." Noah made a spider shape with his hand. "And Miss Merry took it in a jar to the high school."

Tami asked what the high school needed a tarantula for.

"The high school biology class will study it. Now let's get back to the letter *A*. What else starts with the letter *A*?"

Arthur, who sat over by the window, pointed to it and said, "What about *A* dog?"

Cate was startled but stifled an expletive when she saw Jerry outside again with his paws on the windowsill, looking in. She had shut him in the sitting room with the windows cracked open, but not far enough that he could squeeze through them. He must have pushed one open wider.

After the class settled down again and Jerry was at the back of the room looking out the window, she pulled out three stacks of small tin cups. "I have something else with the alphabet that we're going to do today."

During the break yesterday, Cate noticed how all the kids shared one drinking cup. A teacher pulled water from the well, put it into a pitcher, and poured it into one large cup, which was then passed around. When Cate mentioned to the teacher how unsanitary the practice was, she was told that they'd always done it that way.

Cate tried to explain in simple terms that scientists had recently discovered how germs cause and spread sickness. She told her students how they should wash their hands and drink from separate cups so that anyone who might be sick wouldn't spread germs to the others.

"We can't see germs without something called a microscope, but they're all around us. And if we get too many of the wrong kind, they can make us sick. That's why I'm going to give each of you your own cup after I scratch your initials onto it. Soon, each of you will know at least the first letter of your first and last names."

Cate noticed Tami wiping tears from her eyes, so she asked her, "Tami, what's wrong?"

"My initials are TB. I don't want TB."

"You're right—your initials are TB. What is your middle name, Tami?"

"Marie."

"Fine. Then you're TMB, okay?"

Tami nodded and sniffled.

Arthur said, "I'd like my middle initial also, so I have three letters."

Cate said, "What is your middle name?"

"Sean."

Mentally, Cate pictured the three initials for Arthur Sean Stevens. "No, I think two letters are simpler to learn unless you don't like the two letters like Tami's TB, okay?"

Becky raised her hand, "Germs come from Germany. My grandpa was from Germany, and he died of TB."

ı✿

Alice came home at lunch and baked the pie that she promised the McCalls. It was an apple pie.

That night, Cate was quiet all during supper and seemed preoccupied. As they cleaned up, Alice asked, "Is school going okay? Or are those little devils getting to you?"

"Oh, they're fine. I just haven't been very good at anticipating their questions and what might come up. It's certainly different from dealing with adults."

"Some of those kids come from rough backgrounds. At least a couple of them have fathers who are drunk any time they have two nickels to rub together. And the mother of one of the girls works at that house near the corner of Matteson and Prairie."

"You mean the house…"

"That one, yes," Alice said, cutting her niece's description short.

"She doesn't live there, does she?"

"No, her grandma keeps her when her mother's working."

"Oh dear."

A knock at the front door proved to be Noah and the kids.

Alice opened the screen door. "You can go around to the back. We set up the folding chairs for the adults, a blanket for the kids, and a card table. I'll bring the pie out."

When they were all in the back, Alice brought out the apple pie with plates and forks. Cate followed, bearing cups and a pitcher of water. Alice cut generous pieces of pie for each of the McCalls. The kids took their pie to the blanket under the shade tree.

Noah asked Cate about class.

"Oh, it's fine. I guess Harry has told you all about it."

"Bits. I heard Jerry showed up again. They all now have their own cups with their initials on them, and Harry needs to bring in something that begins with the letter A tomorrow."

"That about sums it up." She sighed.

"Are they wearing you out?"

"I'm tired by the end of the day, but I'll get used to it. I am enjoying the class. The students are so fresh and funny and open to learning."

Alice said she wanted to hear about Braidwood.

Noah shared what was said by several speakers who remembered the miners who died. Their stories were heartbreaking and reminded him of how hard that time had been for his mother. "I think I mentioned this to you before, Cate, but incidents like Braidwood clarify for me what this current strike is about. Miners risk their lives every day, and we need to make a living wage. John Mitchell, the UMWA Vice President, put it best when he said that the miners just want enough money to live and to educate their children, and to be able to retire when they can no longer work. That should be the minimum we deserve."

He was quiet for a while and finished his pie.

Over on the blanket where the kids were, Jerry licked their empty plates. Cate put a hand to her open mouth. "Oh dear. Looks like those plates will need boiling water."

Noah laughed and then became serious again. "Before the strike, when I was working, I made a little less than two hundred dollars a year. I think you teachers make more than twice that, and you should because you've gone to school and have responsibilities as educators. But men who work in dark tunnels three hundred feet below the surface of the earth and risk dismemberment and death daily should at least be compensated enough to live above poverty."

"Seems like any reasonable person should agree with that. Why have salaries gone down when prices continue to go up?"

"Mostly because the operators can hire new immigrants at a lower wage. They come from bad conditions in Europe—sometimes famine or political oppression—and they think any job is better than what they had. And for a while, it is… until they realize we're recreating what they tried to escape in Europe. That's what it'll be like here if we don't demand as workers that we're paid a decent wage."

Alice asked him if he wanted to finish off the pie, adding, "Maybe you should try to get one of the top union positions."

Noah offered the last piece to the kids, and they took it to split, eating it from the pan. "I feel like I need to focus on the family. When this situation heats up, I'm going to have to decide on how much risk to take." He lowered his voice so the kids couldn't hear him. "I can't afford to get shot, or worse, killed. These kids would end up in an orphanage. We don't have any other kin to take them in. On the other hand, I can't do nothing and maintain my self-respect and the respect of my peers." He shook his head and looked away, absorbed in a picture neither Cate nor Alice could see.

Alice picked up the empty dishes. "You two sit here and talk. I'll take these in. Thank you, Noah, for stopping by. If it means anything to you, William would be right there with you. He's here in spirit."

꘎

September 7, Wednesday

The Virden Record, September 7, 1898:

The miners of the C. & A. sub-mining district held a meeting in Girard last week to elect officers. The following were elected: President, Dan Fogarty, Carlinville; Vice President, Ed Cahill, Virden; …

The miners at the south shaft walked out this morning.

The cause of the trouble is said to be the miners want to dictate to the operators whom they shall employ.

Fred Lukins returned from Chicago this morning.

꘎

September 8, Thursday

Cate stood at the corner of the building and watched her class during recess. Jerry sat next to her as though waiting for her to assign him a job. Some of the girls in her class played hopscotch. The boys were trying to play marbles, but their little fingers weren't coordinated, and the ones who brought their own marbles were more dexterous and winning more of the games.

Harry concentrated, pursing his lips and raising his shoulders. He missed a shot, and Reggie laughed at him. Harry jumped up and balled his fists, acting as though he was going to throw a punch but then thought better of it. Instead, he yelled, "That's not fair. You have your own marbles and play every day."

Reggie shrugged, "Get your own marbles, Harry."

Cate could guess what Harry was thinking. He didn't have any money of his own, and Noah had other things to buy besides marbles. She got an idea and called him over to her.

He came with his fists still clenched and his eyes down as though he expected to get into trouble. "I'm sorry, Miss Merry, but they're aggregating me."

"You mean aggravating?"

He nodded.

"Jerry is going to have a birthday party in a week or so, and he might have marbles at his party. You'll get an invitation."

"I'll be there if Noah says I can." And he ran over to the game again to witness Reggie beating Arthur.

Watching the girls at hopscotch and jump rope, Cate suddenly realized that Tami Bellwether was missing. She checked the other side of the building toward the Baptist church, but no Tami there. Recess was nearly over, so she let Uncle Billy know that he could ring the bell, and she went in to check for Tami in the classroom.

When she entered the room, Tami was sitting in front of the bookshelf that held the dolls. She had the girl doll in her lap and a brown crayon in her hand. She was trying to color the face of the doll brown.

"Hello, Tami. What are you doing?"

"I want her to be brown like me."

Cate sat down on the floor with her. The doll had a few marks on her cheeks, but the crayon was not doing a good job of coloring the cotton cloth brown. "Rather than coloring the doll brown, why don't I just get a brown doll?"

The school bell rang for the kids to come in and another class to go out. Within seconds, students were filing in.

Tami stopped trying to color the doll and looked up at Cate. "They don't make brown dolls."

Not used to seeing their teacher sitting on the floor, some students began to gather around Cate and Tami.

"I know the maker of these, and I can buy a brown doll. Would you like that?"

Tami nodded.

Harry stood near her left shoulder. "That makes you like Jesus."

Cate blinked at him. Their eyes weren't far apart. "What? How am I like Jesus?"

"Father Clancy said last Sunday that when they hung Jesus on a tree, he bought all of us, all colors."

"Well…" Cate wasn't sure what to say. "I'm sure Father Clancy is right, but these are just dolls, so I'm not like Jesus."

On the way home, Cate went by Dalby's and purchased a bag of marbles. Then she went by Sprague's for some plain brown cotton cloth, which she dropped off at Maeve's before heading home. She hoped that Aunt Alice had something in mind to cook for supper. It was only Thursday, and she felt worn out.

Chapter 13

The Camp Meeting

September 9, 1898

Services at the Christian church, Sunday, Sept. 11, morning and evening. Subject of the morning discourse, "The Noble Bereans." Subject of the evening discourse, "Pilate's Great Question." The public is cordially invited to attend the services.

The Virden Reporter

September 11, Sunday

Reverend Goos took the lectern, and murmurs subsided. He opened his Bible and said, "The word according to the book of Acts, Chapter 17: 'And the brethren immediately sent away Paul and Silas by night unto Berea: who coming thither went into the synagogue of the Jews. These were more noble than those in Thessalonica, in that they received the word with all readiness of mind, and searched the scriptures daily, whether those things were so. Therefore, many of them believed; also of honorable women which were Greeks, and of men, not a few.'"

He closed the Bible and bowed his head. A cough came from somewhere behind Cate. Another from the left. Reverend Goos cleared his throat and said, "Let the words of my mouth, and the meditation of my heart, be acceptable in thy sight, O Lord, my strength, and my redeemer."

Reverend Goos placed a hand on each side of the lectern and focused above the heads of the audience, as though seeing something above them all. "'They received the word with all readiness of mind, and searched the scriptures daily.' Those noble Bereans. I wonder—do we do that?"

After the service, Cate waved to Maeve and caught up with her as she was leaving. "Maeve, the noble Bereans gave me an idea for the quilting bee."

"I'm all ears."

"I have a book of Biblical quilt blocks. What if the quilting bee made a quilt of a Biblical block pattern? I can go through the patterns and pick one out."

"I think that's a fine idea. I hope we get material in cheery colors—something people will want to brighten a room. We'll get more money for it."

"I'm going to try to get the material within the next couple of weeks so we can start the bee soon. The first week of classes wore me out."

"I can't imagine a day with a room full of five-year-olds."

Alice joined them, and Cate explained her idea again. Alice said, "I don't have much time for hand piecing, but you're welcome to use my sewing machine, or I can use it to sew the blocks together."

They said goodbye to Maeve and began heading home, discussing who would cook and what would be cooked.

Noah and the kids stopped them at the corner where Cate and Alice would turn toward home. Noah said, "Good morning, ladies."

"Good morning, McCalls," said Alice.

"The kids and I are going to hear some lively music tonight. Would you care to join us?"

Cate said, "The band concert was last night. What's on tonight?"

"You'll see." He added, "I'll stop by at six thirty if you're interested."

⁊๑

At six twenty-five, a light breeze from the north promised a pleasant evening. The lack of recent rain meant lower humidity, and Cate and Alice were sitting on the front porch swing while Jerry lounged in the corner of the porch, looking around the neighborhood. His tail wagged, and the squeaking of small wagon wheels could be heard before the McCall crew came into view. Ellis pulled one wagon with Harry and Bea riding. Noah followed behind, pulling another wagon containing a two-by-six board, some wooden crates, and an assortment of other items. They stopped at the front walkway to the house.

Cate held a leather leash in her hands. "Can I bring Jerry?"

Noah nodded, "Certainly. We'll see how he is with crowds."

"Crowds?" She couldn't imagine what was going to cause a crowd on a Sunday night in Virden.

"You'll see." He smiled then asked, "Alice, do you want to come?"

"No. You don't need an old lady like me tagging along."

Cate was not surprised when Noah led them uptown. But her curiosity grew as he led them past the public square, along "the levee," and over the railroad tracks before turning north. The farther they got from the square where the usual events took place, the more her interest grew. Eventually, they came to a field with shade trees that Noah explained was Henderson's field. It was directly across the railroad tracks from the Chicago-Virden Coal Mine. What surprised Cate even more than the fact that they had arrived at an open field was that the other arrivals were mostly the town's Black residents. Noah pointed toward a spot out in the open and away from the crowd, which concentrated around a couple of shade trees. Using the board and the two wooden crates, he made a makeshift bench. Others were setting up seats and offering them to women and the elderly. Some spread blankets.

Cate said to him, "I'm glad you picked a spot in the open. With this cloudless sky, we'll be under the stars."

He took from the wagon a blanket, spread it nearby, and said to the kids, "Make yourselves comfortable. I'll get the snacks." Cate sat on the bench. Jerry didn't wait for an invitation to lie on the blanket, and he looked like he had settled in for whatever was going to happen. She started to shoo him off, but Noah said Jerry was welcome to share the blanket. Harry and Bea gave him hugs and pets while Jerry panted and smiled his dog smile.

Noah pulled a covered bowl from the wagon. "I'll be right back."

Several women spread a tablecloth over a long table. One added a vase of flowers, two hurricane lamps, and plates, while the other received dishes from the growing crowd. Cate watched Noah greet a few people and set the bowl on the table that was rapidly becoming the center of attention. He removed the bowl's cover, and a woman near him looked inside and clapped her hands. Other women looked in Cate's direction and smiled. Noah returned with cookies for each of them.

Reverend Bellwether and his family walked by and waved. Tami called, "Hi, Miss Merry." They pulled a much larger wagon than Noah's, and Cate could see wooden folding chairs.

Cate waved. "Hi, Tami."

People gathered, and excitement rose as the sun retired. A band began assembling under one of the trees, and its members tuned their instruments. Three of the band members wore miners' canvas hats without the pots for the flames. The fingers that swung picks, hacked coal from a rock face, and shoveled it into coal cars were now strumming banjos and guitars. A couple of men had wind instruments. One man had drums, and a woman tuned a fiddle.

Noah settled in next to Cate on the bench, and she felt the wood sink slightly from his weight. "You are now at one of the Black church's camp meetings. They're not to be missed if you like good music, but a lot of Whites in town only attend covertly." He made an invisible circle around them with his finger. "Look around, beyond the field, especially on the other side of the railroad tracks, and you'll see quite a few people loitering as it gets dark. They're close enough to hear but not close enough to be seen." He waved toward the rest of the field. "The field is owned by the same Hendersons who attend your church."

Cate twisted around on the seat. Behind them and across the railroad tracks were more than the usual number of people mingling along Matteson Street. The western sky turned orange. The Virden North Mine tipple stood silhouetted against it, as though watching the gathering above the partially completed "Lukinsville" stockade. The orange light coming through the missing boards reminded Cate of a jack-o-lantern missing teeth. The silhouettes of mine guards in the tipple were evident, and they had an excellent view of Henderson's field and the concert.

Stars began to fill the sky overhead. Fireflies answered their twinkles from the grass before launching themselves into the air as though to join the gathering of stars. Kids ran around trying to catch the fireflies. Over by the food table, Luke and his wife, Claudette, whom Cate hadn't met yet, and their kids laughed with another couple.

Reverend Bellwether took a spot in front of the stage and clanged a supper triangle.

"I'd like to say a few words before we get started. This might be our last time to get together for a couple of months. We all know that some kind of trouble is brewing with this strike, and I'm afraid this brew will be strong. You've all heard the rumors. The mine management wants to bring in Black miners from the South. You've all made lives here in Virden, and my family is making a life here too. We like this town. We send our kids to the schools. We shop in the same stores. If Black scabs are brought in, we're going to need to call on the Lord above for his help, and we'll have to keep our heads down. If any one of you needs help, ask any one of us. We'll be there to help."

A voice from the crowd said, "We're goin' to need more than prayers, preacher."

"You all know the scripture. 'And we know that all things work together for good to them that love God, to them who are called according to his purpose.' And, 'We are troubled on every side, yet not distressed; we are perplexed, but not in despair; persecuted, but not forsaken; cast down, but not destroyed.' Let's see what tomorrow brings. Today has its troubles enough. Now let's get the music going and have fun while we can."

The band began with spirituals even White churches had adopted. "I Know the Lord's Laid His Hands on Me" was followed by "Were You There (When They Crucified My Lord)?" Then came "Down by the Riverside." Currents of low and high frequency voices and rhythmic clapping blended to vibrate hearers to the core. Each song was livelier than the last. Soon, no one was sitting. Cate rose when Noah did and swayed and clapped to the music. The strains reached into the heart and grabbed the soul. After several gospel songs, the music picked up pace again, and the band played what their director introduced as a new kind of music called Ragtime. Then they did something called Jazz, which was catching on in St. Louis. The later the hour became, the more heated the singing and dancing. The climax came crashing down to "Swing Low (Sweet Chariot)." *But still my soul feels heavenly bound, coming for to carry me home.*

When the notes from the song faded, only the crickets sang. Noah pointed to Harry and Bea asleep on the blanket, one on each side of Jerry, who lay still with his ears up and eyes open. Noah said, "Time to head home. I need to pick up my bowl first."

Cate turned to him and was glad that the night hid her tears. "Thank you so much, Noah, for inviting me. That was the most incredible concert I've ever been to."

Chapter 14

An Invitation

September 13, Tuesday

The postman came whistling up the front walk. "Hello, Harry and Bea. What are you two up to?"

Bea spoke without looking up. "We're making jewelry."

Harry scowled. "Yeah, and it's not that much fun."

"Harry's trying to make a dog." Bea lifted a chain of white clover flowers. "Want a necklace, Mr. Greer?"

"Why no, Bea. Thank you, but you can keep it. I could use one flower for my lapel, though."

Bea picked the largest clover she could find and handed it to him.

On the front porch, Ellis lounged in the swing, reading a book.

"And what are you reading, Ellis?"

"*Red Badge of Courage.* I finally got it from the library. It had a waiting list."

"That's a good one. I was in the war, you know, and I like that one."

In the kitchen, Noah halved ears of corn and put a pot of water on to boil. A ripe tomato sat on a platter, ready to slice, while navy beans simmered. He heard voices outside and moved toward the front door.

Mr. Greer brought a blue envelope up to his nose and sniffed, implying it was scented. "Somebody has mail—an interesting piece this is. I'm running late today."

Noah took the blue envelope and a flyer with advertisements.

Mr. Greer's words brought all three kids in to see what was in the envelope.

Noah turned it over. The only thing on the envelope was "The McCalls" and their address. If he wasn't mistaken, it smelled of roses.

Ellis said, "I'll open it if you won't."

Mr. Greer chuckled. "Mind if I wait to see what it is?"

"Not at all." Noah dug in his pants pocket, pulled out a pocketknife, and used it as a letter opener. Inside the blue envelope he found a white notecard with an ink drawing of a dog on the front. He opened the card.

"What's it say?" came from all three kids.

"Noah, Ellis, Bea, and Harry, you are all invited to Jerry's birthday party on September 17 at eleven a.m. Bring no gifts, just an appetite. Jerry has requested hamburgers and ice cream. Please RSVP. Your friend, Miss Cate Merry."

The message was initially met with a stunned silence, followed by cheering. "A birthday party with ice cream!" Harry said. "What's a hamburger?"

"I had one in St. Louis." Mr. Greer said. "It's a sandwich with a ground beef patty inside, and it's *good.*"

Ellis said, "What's an RSVP?"

"As a postman, I know the answer to that too. 'Répondez S'il Vous Plaît,' which is French for 'respond if you please.'"

Noah smiled. "Well, aren't you this evening's expert. I just knew it meant that we needed to reply."

"Can I go respond right now? We can go, right?" begged Ellis.

"Of course, we can go. Wouldn't want to miss Jerry's birthday party."

Bea tilted her head in thought. "We ought to take Jerry *something.* What would a dog want?"

Noah said, "You could make him a flower necklace."

Harry scowled. "He's a boy. He don't want no flowers around his neck."

Bea punched him on the shoulder. "He might."

Noah reminded them, "The card says to bring only an appetite, but, Ellis, you can go reply to Cate. Ask her if we can bring something from the garden for the hamburgers."

Harry and Bea said they wanted to go too, so all three headed toward Cate's house at a half-run.

Noah yelled after them. "Don't stay long. Supper is almost ready."

The Virden Record, September 14, 1898

Judge H. H. Cowen and bride returned from their wedding tour Saturday evening, having had a delightful trip on the northern lakes.

Owing to the absence of some of the members of the band, there will be no concert Saturday night.

Mr. and Mrs. John P. Henderson issued cards Saturday announcing the approaching marriage of their daughter, Miss Almira Louise, to Mr. Howard T. Willson of Chicago. The wedding will take place at the Christian church at 6 o'clock Wednesday evening, Sept. 28.

[Reprint from *The Canton Ledger*:] The aeronaut business is evidently feeling the effects of competition the same as all others. A few years ago, from $125 to $200 was demanded for a balloon ascension and parachute drop. A week before the K. of P. picnic in Canton, an aeronaut submitted a written proposition to the committee that he would make an ascension and parachute drop for $75. No attention was paid the communication, and the day before the picnic a telegram was received saying he would give his exhibition for $12.50. This was certainly a big drop in price.

[Comment by Virden townsperson:] If the ascension was as tame as the one recently given in Virden, the last price would be too much.

⋆

September 15, Thursday

On the shelf in Cate's classroom, the cloth people lined up, waiting for the students to arrive. There were dolls from a light-colored muslin material representing a White family: a man, woman, boy, and girl, plus a little baby that Cate hadn't thought to ask Maeve to make. Besides this family, Cate had just laid out a family with the same members where the material was cinnamon brown. Both families had similar clothing. Males wore denim overalls, and the girls wore pink and yellow dresses. The babies were in white gowns as though ready for a christening.

In this second week of class, Cate introduced role-playing and considered the dolls a success. She had the students take turns acting out situations in their lives and gained insight into what they were thinking and where she could direct her instruction. She had a bedtime role-play in mind for today around learning to brush their teeth.

As students filed in, she began putting a crayon and a blank piece of paper on each desk, starting with the ones nearest the windows. From the other side of the room came a squeal when Tami found the family of brown dolls. She held the woman in an embrace and showed it to Amanda. "Look, Amanda. Dolls like my family."

Amanda picked up the male doll. "I never seen a doll that color. They're like gingerbread people."

Tami picked up the boy doll also. "Are not. Maybe you're sugar cookie people."

Cate called over to them, "Now, ladies. Sugar cookies or gingerbread—both are sweet."

Amanda showed the doll to Cate. "I'm using this doll for my letter G. Gingerbread. Wouldn't that start with G?"

Cate was nearly done distributing crayons and paper, so she had made her way over to the girls at the shelf. "You are right, Amanda."

Arthur's desk was nearby. "But she ain't gingerbread. She's colored. That starts with a 'C' like cat and crayon."

Cate turned to him, "Arthur, do you remember what we said about saying 'ain't'? Say 'is not' instead. And we can call the doll gingerbread-colored, just like you are almost gingerbread-colored after being out in the sun all summer."

"I ain't colored."

"No, not when we use it to mean a Black person. But aren't we all different shades from white to brown?" She didn't wait for a reply but took her place at her desk.

"Just like Jerry," replied Arthur. "He has all the colors in one."

Jerry sat on his mat in the corner by the windows. When he heard his name, his ears perked up, but he stayed in place, looking like he was trying to figure out if someone was telling him to do something.

Tami brought the female brown doll to Cate. "If I want to buy this doll, how much would she cost?"

"She's not for sale."

"But I want a doll like this one. There aren't any in the stores."

"I'll write down the name of the woman who makes them for me, and maybe your mother can buy you one."

She skipped back to her desk with her pigtails bouncing.

Chapter 15

The Birthday Party

September 17, Saturday

When Cate heard the familiar wagon wheels, she turned to greet her guests and motioned them to come inside the gate. Jerry was already on his way to greet them. Under the shade tree in the middle of the yard, a blue and white checked tablecloth covered a rectangular table. On it sat a glass cake stand with a yellow cake visible through the glass lid. Blue metal cups and a glass pitcher of a light-yellow liquid waited beside it. A metal-domed platter held something not yet visible.

Both women wore ivory cotton dresses with the sleeves rolled up. A light breeze swayed blue and yellow paper lanterns hanging from the tree. Toward the back of the property in the opposite corner from the outhouse was a smoldering fire pit. Equipped with a grating, it looked ready to cook something.

Noah took from the wagon two large, ripe tomatoes and a bunch of lettuce. "We brought a contribution, but I don't feel like it's enough."

Cate pointed for him to set them on the table. "You're contributing yourselves. Jerry wouldn't be here to have a birthday if you hadn't rescued him, so he wanted to celebrate his birthday with the McCalls."

Jerry had gone back to lying in the shade with Harry petting him. Harry called over to Cate, "How did you know when his birthday is? Dogs can't talk."

Cate put the tomatoes and lettuce on a plate. "That's true, but I thought it would be fun to pretend it's Jerry's birthday." She began slicing the tomatoes. "What do you all like on your hamburgers?"

None of them said anything. Noah grimaced. "Well, I have to admit that they've never actually had a hamburger. Mr. Greer's description is all we know about them."

Cate stopped slicing and turned to him. "Oh, I see. Well, they're popular in St. Louis. You cook a ground beef patty—I have those still in the house—and you put it inside a bun like these." She lifted the lid of the metal dome and revealed bread rolls about the size of Noah's fist. They had been sliced in half horizontally. "Then you put on the hamburger whatever you like, like mustard—I mixed up some today—ketchup—I bought that—tomato, onion, lettuce, maybe pickles. Some people like mayonnaise, but I didn't make any."

Alice had been checking the fire and came toward the table. "The coals are ready if you want to start cooking. I'll go get the hamburger."

"Thanks, Aunt Alice." Cate continued slicing and said to Noah. "I have some special drinks. Lemonade for the kids, and something for you down there with the ice cream." She covered the sliced tomatoes with an inverted plate and then reached down and pulled aside a wool blanket, revealing a barrel with a metal canister surrounded by icy water. Two bottle necks stuck out from the water. She pulled one out, removed the cap with an opener, and handed it to Noah. "I have two of these, but they're both for you. I shouldn't be seen drinking. The Women's Christian Temperance Union might try to get me fired."

Noah took a drink. "Oh, that's so nice, Cate, and unexpected. What if the WTCU sees me here drinking? I can't remember the last time I had a cold beer."

"You're Catholic. It's okay." She smiled, and so did he. "I do like a glass of wine on occasion, but I wouldn't drink it out here."

Noah took another draw from the bottle. "Oh wow. That's so cold and so good."

"I asked the grocer for the best-tasting one. I don't know much about beer."

Harry cried out, "I found a marble over here under the tree."

Cate called back. "You can keep it. There are more if you look."

His eyes grew large. "Really. For keeps?"

"Certainly. I guess I lost my marbles." She laughed.

Bea called to Harry. "Here's another one under the table."

Soon, all three kids were looking for marbles. Jerry followed the kids to see what the excitement was about and sniffed the marbles.

Alice brought a covered platter from the house and carried it to the fire pit. She and Cate laid round, flat, ground beef patties on the grating. Cate turned to Noah, "We have some wooden folding chairs in the shed. Could you bring three?"

Alice added, "Just two will be fine. I have a meeting to go to, and I'll be leaving."

Seconds later, he was back with two chairs, and Cate motioned for him to bring them over by the fire pit where she was standing under a small shade tree.

"These will take a few minutes for each side, and then we'll eat. I expect the kids will have found the marbles by then."

Noah motioned toward the table and the lanterns and the kids hunting marbles. "Cate, thank you for all of this. The kids will talk about it for weeks."

"Noah, I really appreciate you knowing that I could use a dog. And even before that, you and Luke ran off Victor—I hope for good this time. You've helped me feel like Virden could be home."

"I'm glad to hear that." He hesitated. His eyes focused on the burgers, and he noticed there were about twice the number they needed. "There is so much riding on this strike. I couldn't begin to put on a party like this one. I can't afford to even buy meat, except when I get my eighty-six cents a week from the miners' union or we have a good sale of produce."

"I didn't want the kids to come to the party and just eat banana cake and ice cream, so I got the idea to make hamburgers. I'm earning a good salary now, and I saved money when I was working as a nurse, so I'm not straining my budget to do these things."

"I hate feeling like I can't return the favor."

She flipped the hamburgers with a spatula. "You've done a lot for me, so let me do this party for you and the kids."

Harry and Bea came running over to the fire pit. Bea opened her hands first. "Look what we found."

Harry was out of breath. "Yeah. We might have them all now."

Noah motioned with his hand, "Harry, come here a second." When Harry was in front of him, he pointed to his untied shoe, then turned him around and put him on his lap. With his arms around Harry, he tied the boy's shoe and turned him loose.

Cate was struck by how gentle those arms were with Harry. The same arms that could spade hardened topsoil almost effortlessly.

She pointed to a bucket near the back steps. "Harry, there's water in the bucket at the corner of the house. You can wash the marbles off. And there's a bag to put them in."

Noah said, "Kids, you need to share. Each of you should have the same number."

Harry said that Ellis had given them the ones he found. Ellis was now petting Jerry under the shade tree and looking bored with his chin on one hand.

Cate called to them, "The hamburgers will be done soon. Wash your hands in the bucket after you rinse the marbles."

Noah took another long pull on his beer, and Cate noticed for the thousandth time how blue his eyes were. He looked down at his hands and said, "If we don't win this strike, I'm not sure what I'll do or Luke or the other miners who will be out of a job. The wage the company wants is barely enough to feed a family, and it's not enough to properly clothe them. Higher education is at best a dream. But if we can get a wage increase and an eight-hour day and a six-day week out of the strike, then I'd like to have a party after I get a few paychecks."

"I'll hold you to that. Now, we are ready to eat hamburgers. We can eat near the table, and the kids can sit on the blanket."

Hamburgers and buns were distributed. Everyone picked their choice of toppings, and the kids went to the blanket with their plates while Jerry tagged along.

Cate told them, "Kids, you need to watch your burgers and not get them too close to Jerry's nose. He's a known thief. He stole a steak from the kitchen counter a couple of weeks ago."

Noah grimaced. "A *steak*?"

"Yeah. Aunt Alice had some choice words for him, but he's learning."

Ellis hung back from joining Bea and Harry, and Cate wondered if, at twelve, he was probably wanting distance from the younger kids. She said to him as he finished outfitting the hamburger, "Ellis, if you want to get another chair from the shed, you can sit over here. Also, I have a book that you might like if you haven't read it. I found it the other day when I was unpacking the latest box my mother sent."

"Really?"

"*Treasure Island*. Have you read it?"

"*Treasure Island*? No, but it sounds like something I'd read." He retrieved a chair and set it near the kids' blanket.

Noah brought the two chairs under the large shade tree. After he was satisfied that the kids were set to eat, he bit into his hamburger. With a mouth half full, he put a hand to his lips and mumbled, "Oh, this is so good!"

"I'm glad you like it. I'll have leftovers. You can take some patties home to break up and put into vegetable soup or reheat them or whatever."

For several minutes, the talking ceased as hamburgers disappeared. When everyone finished, Cate called Jerry over to her and gave him the rest of her hamburger. "I can't eat a whole one." Jerry looked up at her as if to say, *I can. Got more?*

Noah pointed to him, "That dog is going to get fat."

"I'll try not to let that happen. We'll have to walk a lot, won't we, Jerry?" He wagged his tail.

"That's one happy dog."

"I hope so. I really love him, and I've had him for less than a month."

Cate stood up and revealed the cake under the glass cover. She asked if they liked gold cake with bananas added. Noah said they did. Bananas, like lemons, weren't something he could grow in the garden, and unless one of the ladies at church brought one to a potluck, they didn't get banana cake.

"I was careful at Lorton's picking out the bananas after what happened last month."

"I heard the tarantula specimen is popular with the high school students."

"So I've heard."

All three kids gathered around with their plates to get a piece of cake. Cate uncovered the lid to the vanilla ice cream and scooped some out for each of them.

"Oh wait," she said. "We haven't sung Jerry 'Happy Birthday.'"

After a round of "Happy Birthday, Jerry," Cate said, "That singing ought to have the WCTU wondering what we're drinking."

She then put a scoop of ice cream on the grass for Jerry.

"He'll get a brain freeze," said Noah.

After everyone had seconds of cake and ice cream, there wasn't any left. Cate and Noah carried the picnic items into the house, and Cate came back out with the book for Ellis and a box for Bea.

Ellis studied the pirate picture on the front and said, "Thank you, Miss Merry."

"You can keep that one. I have another copy in St. Louis. If you want a quiet place to read, you could go to the front porch. I don't mind."

He looked to Noah, who nodded.

Bea asked what was in the box, and Cate opened the lid. Inside were assorted buttons and string. "Aunt Merry has a huge collection of buttons, and I picked out some interesting ones. Harry told me that you make jewelry from clover. Have you ever made it from buttons?"

She shook her head. "Can I play with them?"

"They're yours."

"For keeps?"

"Yes, for keeps."

Turning to Noah, Cate said, "I'm going to brew some coffee. Would you like some? Or there's the other beer left."

"I'd love some coffee. Can I take the beer home if you don't need it?"

"Of course. I'll get the coffee started."

"I can bring you some pumpkins in about a week."

"I'd love pumpkins for bread and pies."

Bea was busy with the buttons, and Ellis was already absorbed in *Treasure Island* on the front porch swing when Harry asked if he could use the outhouse.

Cate replied, "Of course." She carried some more of the party items into the house while Noah went to check on Harry. She rinsed out the ice cream tub at the well pump and was drying it when Harry and Noah came from the outhouse. Harry said to Bea, "Bea, go see. Cate has *toilet paper!*"

Cate laughed and asked Noah, "Don't you have toilet paper?"

He rubbed his chin in embarrassment. "That would be a luxury right now."

She gave him a puzzled look. "Well, what do you...?"

"It varies. Paper from advertisements or corn cobs."

Cate's eyes widened. "Corn cobs?"

"And a washcloth and a pitcher of water. What? Have you always had toilet paper?"

"Certainly."

As they carried the final picnic items into the house, she said, "You are so good with these kids."

"They're like my own, especially Harry. I changed his diapers."

"You're a saint."

"No, I'm not, but I hear you're like Jesus."

"Oh, let's not go into that."

Gold Cake

From *'76 a Cookbook*, p. 174, 1876.

Yolks of twelve eggs, five cups of flour, three cups of white sugar, one cup of butter, one and a half cups of cream or milk, a half teaspoon of soda and one teaspoon of cream tartar.

Beat the eggs with the sugar, then stir in the butter, softened by the fire; dissolve the soda, and sift the cream tartar with one cup of the flour; mix all together, then sift and stir in the rest of the flour. Bake in a deep loaf pan.

Chapter 16

Father Clancy's Reception

September 19, Monday

Cate and Alice finished cleaning up supper. While they were enjoying the evening on the front porch where they could catch a cool breeze, Noah appeared from the west, heading toward uptown. He stopped at the front walkway. "Good evening, ladies."

Alice invited him to join them, but Cate could tell from his hesitation that he had something on his mind. She rose and went out to greet him with Jerry padding after her.

"Where's the kids, Noah?"

"They're with Ellis and the neighbor, Martha." His hands were in his pockets, and he seemed reluctant to ask her a question. He had on pants and a shirt similar to what he wore on Sundays. She broke the awkwardness by asking him, "So, what are you doing with your free evening?"

"I heard at mass yesterday that the ladies are throwing a reception tonight for Father Clancy. He returned from Ireland on Saturday. No one mentioned a party to him, so it's supposed to be a surprise. And it's a nice evening to be out, so I thought I'd go down to St. Catherine's and welcome him back." He hesitated a couple of seconds and added, "You're welcome to join me if you'd like an evening walk."

"I would love an evening stroll, and so would Jerry. Can he come?"

"I don't see why not. And if you don't want to stay, I'll understand."

"Why wouldn't I want to stay?"

"Well, we're a bunch of Catholics, you know."

"I'll try not to act too Protestant. I won't be expected to cross myself, will I?"

He laughed. "No."

"Good, because I'm not sure how. Let me get Jerry's leash."

On the way, they talked about the birthday party. Noah told her again how much fun the kids had and thanked her. He said they were still talking about it two days later.

Cate reached down and scratched Jerry's head. "Jerry says he enjoyed it too, didn't you?"

"What dog wouldn't enjoy a hamburger and ice cream?"

Many more people mingled around the town square than usual for a Monday evening. Most of them were men, and they were congregating on the east side, toward the train depots.

Noah groaned. "Oh, I forgot about the welcoming committees for the evening train."

"Who are they expecting?"

"They're expecting a trainload of Black miners from Alabama. They're sure Lukins is going to try to land some within the next few days if what they've heard from St. Louis is correct."

"What do they plan to do?"

"Keep the Blacks from getting off the train. We don't want to repeat what happened in Pana, and the best way to stop it is to prevent any scabs from getting off a train."

Cate saw that some of the men carried guns. "Are you going to have to help keep watch?"

"Not yet. Enough miners are coming in from out of town with nothing else to do."

"Can you avoid it? Seeing all the guns is giving me a bad feeling."

"I have a stake in the strike also. I need to make a living, feed and clothe the kids, give them whatever education they want." He hesitated, "But, like I said before, I know what would happen to them if something happened to me. They'd end up in an orphanage. So I try not to take too many risks."

"I don't want anything to happen to you." She linked her arm through his. "May I?"

He smiled. "Of course."

They reached the train station. Twenty to thirty men milled around talking, smoking, and coughing the miners' cough. Cate and Noah crossed the tracks and left the group behind.

A streetlight at the intersection near St. Catherine's revealed a crowd opposite what Cate and Noah had left at the train depot. Children played tag under the streetlamp as adults gathered at the residence next to the church, which Cate assumed was the priest's. Chinese lanterns, goldenrod in vases, and red, white, and blue streamers decorated the yard. A small band was assembling near the church steps.

"I should explain," Noah said, "that Father Clancy visited his elderly father in Ireland. The congregation gave him about three months off."

Parishioners surrounded two men in dark suits and clerical collars. "Is he the younger priest or the older one?"

"The younger one. I think he's about thirty. He's well-liked, and we're all glad to get him back. The other priest is Father Davis from Auburn."

Cate said, "I can stand back here with Jerry. But you should go closer."

"No need. I can hear from here." A few of the parishioners looked their way and waved. Noah nodded and waved back. "I'll go over and say hello to him in a bit."

Father Davis tapped a spoon on his wine glass to get everyone's attention. He said a few words about welcoming Father Clancy back, then Father Clancy shared how glad he was to be back and how thankful he was to the congregation for allowing him so much time off to see his father. His voice broke as he explained that his father's health was deteriorating. He probably wouldn't live much more than a year. The visit was bittersweet because, as happy as they were to spend time together, they knew their parting would be for the last time in this life. Yet, he was thankful they had the opportunity to say goodbye because how often do we lose someone and wish we could have said a few last words, like, "I love you"?

Several parishioners dabbed their eyes and nodded. Cate wondered how many of those here had left behind family in the old country that they had no hope of ever seeing again.

Father Clancy gave other details of the trip and had everyone's attention, except for the kids', whose voices carried over with the light of the streetlamp. He said he set sail on the Lucania on July 2 and arrived six days later in Ireland.

Noah leaned toward Cate. "Only six days to cross the Atlantic. I would love to do that."

Cate nodded. "It's an experience to be in the middle of a vast ocean and arrive in a foreign land."

His eyebrows went up. "You've been to Europe?"

"I went with my parents to Spain a couple of years ago. I'd love to go again."

"Spain? Why Spain?"

"My mother is Spanish. My full name is Catalina, which is why I'm Cate with C."

"You'll have to tell me about it sometime."

Father Clancy finished his story and thanked everyone for coming. A woman took charge by telling congregants to help themselves to refreshments and that they were honored to have a few members from the Virden High School band, which promptly struck up an Irish tune.

Noah lightly touched Cate's back. "Let me greet Father Clancy, and I'll get us something. There's probably wine. Would you want any?"

"I'd love some, but no. I would take some punch, but I don't need cake. I just had some of Aunt Alice's apple pie at home."

"Even better than cake."

"There's some left when we get back."

As Noah returned with two glasses of punch, a middle-aged woman approached them. Before Noah could introduce her, she introduced herself to Cate as Dee and said she understood that Cate was the new primary grade teacher. Then she asked Cate, "Are you sure the WCTU won't get after you for drinking with us Catholics?"

"I'm drinking punch, but I don't think a glass of wine is a sin. Jesus drank wine."

"Exactly! That's what we think too. The WCTU has that 'holier-than-thou' attitude that can be hard to take in their weekly newspaper column."

Noah intervened. "If some men didn't get drunk and drink away their salaries, then maybe the WCTU wouldn't be so opposed to alcohol. They have a concern that I can understand."

Dee shook her head. "Some men aren't everybody. They want to outlaw alcohol, period. Then where would we be?"

"Teetotaling, I suppose," he said with a smile.

Dee shook her head again, but smiled and wished them a good evening.

After Noah gave his regards to Father Clancy and returned their cups, they left the glow of the Chinese lanterns, the occasional laughter, and the children's voices on the night air to retrace their steps back home.

September 20, Tuesday

Cate opened the classroom windows before the students arrived. The temperature was expected to be in the 70s and pleasant. Jerry took his seat on his mat in the far corner as usual.

Tami was the first student to arrive. She smiled her white baby teeth and skipped over to Cate. "Guess what, Miss Merry."

"What Tami?"

"Guess."

"You are feeling good today?"

"Yes, because I'm going somewhere on Thursday. Here's a note from my mom." She still showed her broad smile.

"Oh, I'll miss you. What's going on?"

"It's the Emancipation Day celebration in Springfield, and we're all taking the train up there to celebrate."

Cate made a wide-eyed, open-mouth expression as she read the note from Minnie Bellwether. "Well, that *is* exciting. What happens at the Emancipation Day celebration?"

"It's as much fun as the Fourth of July. Maybe funner. There'll be free food and rides and fireworks. We won't get home till late. If it's too late, I might not be here on Friday either."

"That sounds like a good time. I'm sorry you'll miss class, but I'll think about how you're having so much fun."

Tami skipped over to her desk.

As the class filled, Cate wrote a big letter "J" on the blackboard. The bell rang, and she quickly took attendance as the kids talked among themselves.

"Good morning, students. Attention on me, please. How is everyone this morning?"

In unison, they all said, "Ready to learn." Cate was pleased that two weeks into the school year, she had them saying they were starting the day "ready to learn."

"Today, the letter we're learning is the letter *J*." She pointed to the letter on the board. "We mentioned yesterday what sound it makes. I brought something today that starts with a *J*. What do you think it might be?"

The students were silent for a few seconds, then Harry, in the back of the room and only a few feet from Jerry, raised his hand. "Jerry?"

"That's right! I brought Jerry."

Arthur said, "But you bring Jerry every day."

"I do, but today, he's my letter *J* object. I'd like to see what you uncovered at home that starts with the letter *J*."

The kids had the usual interesting assortment of objects. Amanda brought a jelly jar with no jelly or jam because she said her mother didn't trust her not to drop the jar and waste the jelly. Oscar brought a small jug. Arthur said he brought his jaw and pointed to it. Tami said she brought joy and then did a happy dance that made everyone laugh.

When Nolan's turn came, he got up from his seat, went to the door, and motioned to someone outside the classroom. In stepped Uncle Billy, and Nolan said, "I brought a janitor." Uncle Billy smiled, took a bow, and went back into the hall.

Bart said that his dad told him if anyone brings a job—which starts with a J—he'd like them to bring it to him. And so the class continued presenting objects like a glass "jewel." The final object was a joke, which Spencer brought up on a piece of paper for Cate to read.

"This joke, the note says, was told by President Lincoln. It says: Lincoln was walking along a road one day when he met a woman, who, in passing, said, 'You're the ugliest man I ever saw.' Lincoln replied, 'Well I can't help it.' She said, 'No, but you could stay at home.'"

Cate wasn't sure how a class of five-year-olds would take such a joke, but they laughed. Every day, she tried to find a food item that began with the day's letter, because during the first week, she had realized that some of the students came to class without having had breakfast. She found their obvious hunger heartbreaking. Some of them couldn't bring lunch either, so she always had fruit or something extra on hand. "Today, our food item is jerky. This one is made from dried beef. Come up and get a piece, and bring your cup. You might want some water from my jug—which, as Oscar told us, also starts with a *J.*"

Chapter 17

The Quilting Bee

September 24, Saturday

By one o'clock on Saturday afternoon, Cate and Alice had the living room ready for the quilting bee ladies. A fresh pot of coffee, linen napkins, china cups, several dessert plates, and forks waited on a side table. They pulled out the dining table, which usually sat against one wall, and opened its leaves to accommodate seven women. Alice spread a white linen tablecloth to cover the mahogany wood, and Cate added several sheets of cardboard, stacked in the middle, along with pencils and pieces of writing paper.

Agnes arrived a few minutes early. "My word, Cate, the smells coming from this house may draw in the neighborhood." The elderly woman leaned on her cane and looked through the front door screen. Cate smiled and let her in. The top of Agnes's head didn't come to Cate's chin. She wore a lavender-gray flowered dress and a crocheted shawl.

"Agnes, did you walk all the way from Vinegar Hill?"

"That's what keeps me healthy. You young people think you have to take a train or wagon everywhere, and now some cities have *auto*mobiles. What? Do they move themselves?" She smiled, revealing only a few teeth left. "I walked from Indiana to Illinois and was five months along with my third child, so what's a few blocks down the street?"

"I don't know how you did it. I admire the spirit and strength of you pioneers. Here, Agnes, have this cushioned chair."

"We weren't wearing these corsets you women squeeze yourselves into nowadays. And, we didn't have much choice about a lot of things back then. If the men wanted their own land or a new start, we got up and went. We lost a lot of us over the years. I still sometimes think of my sister, Dorothy."

She paused, and her eyes seemed to focus on an empty spot a few feet away. "She died trying to give birth to her first. It just wouldn't come out, and no midwife around. She was one of the first ones buried in the Virden Cemetery. We're not sure where her grave is anymore. The marker was just a wooden cross and blew away in a windstorm. It was weeks before we realized it was gone."

A knock at the door brought Helen, Caroline, and Betsy.

Helen, a hefty woman around sixty, came in saying, "Cate, this is what heaven is going to smell like."

Alice came from the kitchen carrying a cake. "What? Coffee cake?"

"Coffee cake. I'm an authority on baked goods, and I haven't smelled anything that good coming from the Palace Hotel with their fancy baker."

Caroline greeted Cate with a kiss on her cheek. "Now, Helen," she said, "heaven will smell like lilacs. I have that on good authority—my mother." Caroline was a forty-something, thin woman with blonde hair.

Helen sat heavily on one of the chairs at the table. "What? Did she come back from the grave and tell you that?"

"No." Caroline took another chair. "One of the last things she said was, 'I smell lilacs.' It was in January—the dead of winter. She died later that afternoon."

"I didn't know that. I always liked your mother. A good woman if there ever was one. She could make the best silver cake, and she gave me her recipe. May she rest in peace."

Caroline patted Helen's hand. "You look tired today."

Helen sighed, "The last few days. Been doing some cleaning before winter sets in and going at it too hard. No rest for the wicked." She fiddled with her spoon. "I went to the doctor and complained about being tired. He said, 'Well, Helen, you're no spring chicken anymore. You can't work like you did when you were thirty.' I told him it didn't take a medical degree for that diagnosis."

Cate stepped back so she could see Helen's ankles under the table. "Helen, you look like your ankles may be swollen. You might want to elevate them on a hassock in the evening."

Betsy hadn't taken a chair yet. "Cate, is there something I can help you with?"

Betsy was in her early twenties and petite, not much taller than Agnes, and recently married. She wore her light-brown hair braided and pulled back into a bun. From the loose drape of her dress, Cate suspected she might already be pregnant. "You could help hand out the cake and the coffee."

Alice cut the cake while Cate filled the coffee cups. Alice asked, "Who are we missing?"

Maeve's voice came through the screen. "Me! Hello every-body. Sorry. I hope I'm not late."

"Come on in," Cate called to her. "Find yourself a seat at the table. How are you today, Maeve?"

"Oh, fair to middlin', I guess."

"Why? Anything wrong?"

"The neighbor kid has some kind of croup, and the baby's starting to cough too. But I can tell from the smell of coffee and—is that coffee cake?—that I'll soon be doing a lot better."

Cate and Betsy handed out coffee cake and coffee.

After the first bite, Helen said, "Alice, this not only smells like heaven, it tastes like heaven. And, Caroline, as much as I liked your mother, she's not eating lilacs in heaven."

"No, I suppose not."

After a few seconds of just eating and not talking, Betsy said, "Isn't it a little scary around town with all the strange men showing up?"

Helen took a sip of coffee and said, "They're not looking at a hefty matron like me, but I can see where you young women might be uneasy."

"I have Jerry and take him with me just about everywhere." Cate nodded toward Jerry, who had been waiting near the door to the front sitting room. "I had a bad experience when I lived in Maryland, and Jerry helps me feel safer."

"What happened?"

Cate's eyes were on her coffee cup. "Oh, that's a story for another day."

Betsy said, "My husband, Colin, says Lukins plans to bring a load of Negroes from Alabama to work the mine, so Colin goes down to the station every day for a few hours to meet the trains."

Maeve finished the crumbs of her cake. "Well, we don't want the kind of working conditions here like we saw in West Virginia. They had nine-year-olds working in the mines. And they worked twelve-hour days, six days a week. I told Brian we're getting out even if we starve before he finds work in Illinois. It ain't no fit life what they have in them places. Our miners and the other Illinois miners are doing right by fighting it now."

Alice handed Helen a spoon for her coffee. "William would of had a hard time believing what's going on now. He always considered Fred Lukins to be a real decent man. And, he had his mother-in-law, Mrs. Harrington, living with him these past few years. How many of our husbands would want our mothers living with us?"

Betsy laughed and said, "Colin might like it because my mother's a real good cook, and I can't seem to get the hang of it."

Helen stirred sugar into her coffee. "I don't think Nina Lukins has gotten over her mother's passing last month. Nor has the Baptist church. The Lukins family has been dealing with a lot, but that doesn't mean I sympathize with strikebreaking. For everyone concerned, I hope we don't have bloodshed. If we do, Cate, you better get your nursing bag dusted off and stocked up."

"I hope it doesn't come to the point where I need my nursing skills. Let's talk about something more pleasant, like quilt making." While the ladies finished their coffee cake and took to sipping coffee, she went on. "You know we're all here to make a quilt to auction off and give proceeds to the miners' fund for feeding their families. Are we all agreed?"

The ladies all nodded. A couple of them asked her what she had in mind. Alice started clearing their dishes from the table.

"I'm thinking that maybe we could start with a simple block based on a Bible verse and see how that goes. I have a book on Bible-block patterns, and a Jacob's Ladder is a simple block. The blocks on that one come together into a nice design." She showed them an example from the book. "It's only two square sizes. The smaller squares are sewn into four patches, and the larger square is cut diagonally and the diagonals sewn to the opposite color."

Agnes said, "That is a nice pattern. I've made it a couple of times. We'll need light fabrics and dark fabrics to get the effect when it's put together as a nine patch."

Cate brought a bushel basket lined with a sheet over to the table and set it on the seat of her chair. "And I have the fabric! Many ladies at church donated freely to this stash, and we have Aunt Alice's also if we need it." She spread several samples on the table.

They began fingering them and commenting on their fine quality.

Helen picked up a fabric that looked new. "Did this beautiful pink come from Mrs. Henderson?"

"I believe it did. She mentioned having a lot of scraps from Almira's wedding dresses."

"That explains the lovely pink. It would work for some of the light patches. It's never been on anything that's been worn. I hear Almira's going to have one of the prettiest weddings anyone's ever seen next Wednesday."

"You know Maxie Henderson. She'll go all out for Almira's wedding," said Agnes.

Cate picked up one of the pink pieces and felt its fine weave. "I don't know Almira. How do you know she'll have a big wedding?"

Agnes replied, "Almira's their only child, and being in farming and banking, they can afford to go all out. I'm happy for them."

Turning to Cate, she said, "Did you know that Maxie started the Christian church from the Girard Christian church?"

"No, I didn't."

"And I hear she's going to be the matron of honor."

Cate pulled out a piece of light green cloth to show them. "She was generous with fabric for our quilt. I was told the Henderson's field across the tracks from the mine is theirs."

"Yes, for many years."

Cate said, "If we like the Jacob's ladder pattern, I can cut out two cardboard squares in the sizes we'll need, and I have some cardboard for you to trace and cut out your own squares. Maybe today we could all put together one block each and see how they go."

"How many will we need to do?"

"One block should end up twelve inches square, not counting the seam allowance. If we each make just five blocks, we'll end up with thirty blocks and a quilt five feet by six feet."

Alice said, "I've already told Cate that I don't plan to do the hand sewing. I do enough darning for the people I work for. If you each sew your five blocks and drop them by here a couple of days before the next meeting, I'll sew them together on my machine. Cate also got a donation of muslin backing and cotton batting. The next time we meet, we can do the quilting."

Helen stood up. "Thank you, Cate and Alice, for figuring this all out. I'm anxious to get something done. But first, I need to go out back and see a man about a horse."

Cate pointed toward the back door. "Toilet paper is on the porch. I meant to take it out earlier."

Before she left the room, Helen said, "I wonder how much money the quilt will raise."

Betsy stroked the pink fabric. "Maybe Mrs. Henderson will buy it since it'll have some of Almira's wedding material in it."

Eyebrows went up, and someone said, "Wouldn't that be nice."

Coffee Cake

Breakfast, Luncheon, and Tea, Marion Harland, 1892. p. 332.

- 5 cups flour, dried and sifted
- 1 cup butter
- 2 cups sugar
- 1 cup molasses
- 1 cup made black coffee—the very best quality
- ½ pound raisins, seeded and minced
- ½ pound currants, washed and dried

- ¼ pound citron, chopped fine

- 3 eggs, beaten very light

- ½ teaspoonful cinnamon

- ½ teaspoonful mace

- ¼ teaspoonful cloves

- 1 teaspoonful—a full one—of saleratus [baking soda]

Cream the butter and sugar, warm the molasses slightly, and beat these with the spices, hard, for five minutes, until the mixture is very light. Next, put in the yolks, the coffee, and when these are well mixed, the flour, in turn with the whipped whites. Next, the saleratus, dissolved in hot water, and the fruit, all mixed together and dredged well with flour. Beat up very thoroughly, and bake in two loaves, or in small round tins.

The flavor of this cake is peculiar, but to most palates, very pleasant. Wrap in a thick cloth as soon as it is cold enough to put away without danger of "sweating," and shut within your cake box, as it soon loses the aroma of the coffee if exposed to the air.

Chapter 18

Tensions Rising

September 24, Saturday Evening

Cate and Maeve stood in the public square a few yards from the city hall. The band had been playing but was on a break to change some members and bring in different instruments. The ladies could now carry on a conversation without raising their voices.

Maeve said, "Oscar is really enjoying your class. I'm glad that you got him off to a good start in liking school. I was so afraid that he'd hate sitting at a desk and having to concentrate on something."

Cate began a reply, which she cut off when they overheard a group of men arguing a few feet away. "You're either *for* us or *against* us. You can't have it both ways. Which side of the stockade are you going to be on when the train arrives?"

The group of about six men stood in two groups of three as they traded verbal volleys. Everyone in the vicinity of the group stopped their conversations and turned to watch.

"*I'll* be on the inside. That's what Lukins is paying me to do."

"As a pit boss, you're also supposed to have the *men's* best interests in mind. Why side with Lukins and his robber barons?"

"Because they'll win, just like what happened in Pana. They're going to pay workers what they want to, and you aren't going to dictate your own salaries."

"We just want the contract agreed to last January. Most other Illinois mines are honoring it. If we give up here, at the largest producing coal mine in Illinois, and take a lower wage, other mines will follow the leader. Thousands of miners across the state will be poorer."

"You're not going to have a choice."

A man on the side of the miners pointed his finger at the man across from him. "And what about you? Are you going to hoist convicts underground?"

"Hell, yes, if that's what Lukins pays me for."

The miner's face was within inches of the hoisting engineer. "When we win this fight, you're going to be out of a job. We'll get that in the contract. And we'll see that you," he stabbed his finger at the air again, inches from the man's chest, "lose your hoisting papers."

Several other men now surrounded the group of six. Maeve pulled on Cate's arm to move them back a few more feet to outside what was becoming a circle of angry men.

A man stepped from the outer circle toward the inner group. "Wait, men. Our fight isn't now on a Saturday night with our families here. Save it for the station when the train comes in."

A man on the pit boss's side pointed his finger at the last speaker. "And that'll be soon enough. If you keep that train from landing the Alabamans, Lukins said he'll hire even more armed guards for round two."

"Let him. We're armed too. And we're pretty good at shooting rabbits and squirrels, so we won't have any problem hitting security guards and ex-Chicago policemen."

The next remark was drowned out by the band and brass instruments belting out "Popular Swing." The miners turned and went their separate ways.

Cate had been so caught up in the exchange that she was startled when, inches from her ear, Noah said, "Cate, can we walk you and Jerry home? We're getting ready to leave if you're ready."

She sighed, releasing a breath she didn't realize she was holding. "Yes, thanks. Let's find Aunt Alice and see if she's ready to go."

Maeve waved goodnight to them and told Cate to stay safe.

Cate found Alice visiting with a woman she cleaned house for. When Alice saw her approaching, she said goodbye and joined Cate, Jerry, and the McCalls. "Are you heading home?"

Noah replied, "We are. Would you like to join us?" Harry and Bea were asleep in the wagon. Ellis took the handle and pulled them ahead of the adults.

Alice waited until they were outside the public square to comment. "Thank you, Noah, for seeing after us. William always said you was a good boy."

Noah laughed and kept his voice low so as not to wake Harry and Bea, although they had just slept through the band music. "Good old William. He helped me whenever he could in the mine. I wonder what he'd think of all this trouble."

Alice thought for a few seconds and said, "He wouldn't like it, but he wouldn't back down from it either. He'd be doing his shift at the train station like everyone else. I don't think he'd like all these outside miners sticking their noses in our business, though."

"Why?" Cate asked.

"Their being here is a help and a worry," Noah replied. "We need their numbers to show solidarity, especially with so many of Virden's miners gone to other jobs. But we're worried that some of them are hot-heads, and they have good reason to be. Many come from area mines where the conditions are much worse than here in Virden. Some of them were put in the mines as young as nine."

Alice nodded. "Like that General Bradley? We haven't seen him yet. You think he'll show up?"

"No doubt, but I haven't heard when. We're pretty sure a train from Alabama is coming soon, maybe tomorrow. We're going to be at the station in full force for the next couple of days."

Cate felt a spasm in her stomach. "Are *you* going to have to be at the station?"

"I'll be down there tomorrow."

"What about the kids? It's a Sunday, and they won't be in school."

"Ellis will watch them with backup from my neighbor."

"Are you…" her throat constricted so that she could hardly finish her sentence, "…going armed?"

"Only for self-defense and intimidation. I have no intention of shooting anyone."

The ladies kept silent. After a few seconds, Noah asked, "How did the quilting bee go? Wasn't it this afternoon?"

Cate's throat was still tight, and she felt like she couldn't talk.

Alice took over, describing the ins and outs of the ladies' productive afternoon.

"I can't wait to see the quilt." He touched Cate's arm and then bent down to pat Jerry's head. "Good night to you all."

Alice headed into the house. Ellis, half a block ahead, continued pulling the wagon.

Cate cleared her throat. "You'll be careful, won't you, Noah?"

"Of course. I have three kids who would be in a bad way if something happened to me, and that worries me a lot."

Cate nodded and led Jerry into the house, thinking, *What more should I have said?*

ᙁ

September 25, Sunday

The guest minister had given an energetic sermon on the temptation of Jesus in Luke, Chapter 4, and he focused on the devil offering Jesus power and kingdoms if Jesus would worship him.

As Cate was leaving and in line to shake the minister's hand, the woman in front of her said to him, "Now, Preacher, were you implying that those in power are there because they serve Satan?"

"Not at all, ma'am. But sometimes I hear people say that if God put a man in power, then we have to go along with whatever he wants. I was pointing out that Luke 4 says Satan can put men in powerful positions too. We have to have discernment in an election year, like this year, as to whom the powerful are serving."

She replied, "Well, you should preach that one to the congregation across the street." She waved goodbye, leaving a frozen smile on the minister's face.

When Cate had his attention, she greeted him and shook his hand. "I can't imagine having to come up with a sermon every week and then have it criticized."

The minister's smile softened and warmed. He shrugged. "It comes with the territory."

On the walkway in front of the church, three of the quilting bee ladies had gathered. Cate joined them while Alice stayed behind to talk with the women responsible for the Henderson–Willson wedding on Wednesday.

Cate joined Betsy, Helen, and Agnes. "Good morning, ladies."

Betsy's brow furrowed, and she spoke in a low, conspiratorial tone. "My husband, Colin, he was at the train station when the load of Negroes came in this morning."

A sudden shiver ran down Cate's spine. "This morning?"

"Yes, this morning about six o'clock."

The ladies each exclaimed a different version of "What happened?"

"Someone came for him late last night. It was raining, if you remember. He took his oiled canvas and a big club. I started crying, but he said he had to go."

Helen shook her head. "Naturally. These miners are itching for the confrontation."

Betsy continued. "He said they waited all night, knowing the train, a special, had to be getting close because of where it was reported last night. Then about six o'clock this morning, they could hear it coming, and he said there must have been about three hundred miners around the tracks as it came into town."

Everyone's eyes were on Betsy. She cleared her throat and continued. "He said the train had guards. Some of them and some miners stuck their heads out to see what was going on, and then one of the guards motioned for the conductor to keep going, and it headed out of town as fast as it could. You might have heard them cheering after that."

Cate thought back to the early morning. "I thought I heard something like shouting, but it wasn't gunshots, so I didn't worry. Jerry sat up and looked out the window."

Helen spoke in a lower-than-usual voice. "That letter T.C. Loucks put in *The Reporter* on Wednesday was like kicking a hornet's nest. The miners gave a blistering response, I heard, in the *Springfield Journal*, but we don't get that. I'll read it this week in Wednesday's *Record*."

Agnes raised her hand that held the cane. "Maybe things will settle down now, and we can put this ordeal behind us. I'm tired of all these strange men in town. It's not good for the town's image either, with them sleeping in the public square and on the street. It's not safe."

Betsy wiped her eyes with a handkerchief. "I'm afraid only blood will end this standoff, and I don't want it to be Colin's, especially not now."

Helen lowered her voice even more. "Betsy, are you...?"

Betsy nodded. "I told Colin I don't want him getting in trouble at the station, but he says they're trying to prevent trouble. He said Lukins and Loucks have promised to hire more guards and try again." For a few seconds, the voices and laughter of other congregants filled the space between them. Then, she went on. "Colin said this morning the miners had mostly clubs and some pistols, but if he brings in more guards, they'll have to arm up too."

In spite of the warm sunshine, Cate felt cold. The mood was broken by Alice coming from the church. Cate patted Betsy on the arm. "I'm glad that, at least for now, everyone is safe. I see Aunt Alice, so I'll say bye for now. But if you need me, let me know."

Alice's gait, a hurried stomping and elbows flying, suggested she had something to say. "Cate, I just talked with Maxie

Henderson, and they could use a couple more people to help clean up after the wedding. If we do that, we'll get some of the flowers and plants."

"But isn't that on Wednesday?"

"The wedding ain't until six, and it'll be the wingding of the season. It'll outdo the Furry-Cowen wedding. And we'll be able to see it from the back."

"I can help. I'd like to see the wedding, and I didn't expect to be invited."

"I'll tell her to put you on the list too. Let's head home and cook something for lunch, and I'll tell you about the train coming in this morning."

September 28, Wednesday

Even after a day of school, Cate still felt excited about going to Almira Henderson's wedding and was glad she had agreed to it on Sunday. Both she and Alice put on ivory cotton dresses, gloves, and felt hats. Cate's hat was pink, and Alice's was green. They had heard that Almira's colors were pink and green. Although they weren't going to be in the wedding, they didn't want to show up in a clashing color.

"How'd your class like the pumpkin tarts for the letter P?" Alice asked.

"None were left. Too many come to school hungry. Harry informed them that the pumpkins were from *his* garden."

At five thirty, just as they were ready, a knock came at the front door. Cate found Henry dressed in an elegant gray suit. He said, "I heard that you two would be at the church for the wedding, so I would like to offer an escort. We can't be too careful with all these strangers around. And I assume Jerry isn't invited."

Cate laughed. "No. I don't think the wedding needs Jerry. He's in my bedroom with a bone and getting better about being alone."

"Then, it would be my pleasure to escort you ladies."

"We're just now ready and would be happy to have an escort."

As the ladies left the house, he offered one arm to Cate and one to Alice.

A block away, Noah stopped the wagon, and the kids stopped. They intended to see if Cate and Alice wanted more pumpkins after depleting their supply with the tarts. He said, "Wait, kids. Cate's going out."

He knew where they were going. Tonight was the wedding of the season. Noah had made the mistake of reading what the wedding was going to be in *The Virden Record*. A friend showed him a copy. Carpenters erected a platform at the altar so that everyone would have a good view of the vows. It was going to be a double-ring Episcopal service with an impressive number of bridesmaids and groomsmen. Almira's colors were pink and green. Carnations and plants would abound around the sanctuary. One of the ushers would be the publisher of *The Virden Reporter*, George Sewall, just back from three weeks in Colorado for a journalist's convention. Noah read the article and thought—*ah yes—the advantages of generational wealth.*

Standing there, watching Henry escort Cate and Alice to this extravagant wedding, he felt jealousy more keenly than at any other time in his life. His mother and then stepfather had worked hard to keep the family fed and clothed. He'd had a good shot at a college education—until the untimely deaths of his father, mother, and then George. The burden of raising three kids was his and his alone. Even if the miners got the raise that they were fighting for, Noah going to college was out of the question until Harry was at least out of high school. And then he would be, what? Thirty-five and too old. The best he could hope for was to give them a better opportunity than he had. He felt a headache coming on at the back of his skull.

Harry said, "Noah. What's wrong?"

Ellis said, "I think Noah's jealous of Henry."

Noah didn't expect Ellis to be that perceptive at twelve, but he was almost a teenager. Noah reached out and rubbed both their heads.

"Let's go home, kids. We'll catch Cate some other time. The pumpkins will keep."

While they were walking home, he thought, *What if I were Black like Luke—then how disadvantaged would I feel?*

Chapter 19

The Fundraiser

September 30, Friday

Cate and Alice sat on the front porch swing, gently moving it backward and forward. They wore light woolen dresses and cardigan sweaters. The weather now felt like fall. Jerry lay near the front steps, looking around the neighborhood. His fur was filling in nicely, and the light breeze lifted the longer strands.

Alice sighed. "Sometimes I think my life is like this swing. I move forward and then go back. I clean a house one day, and it has to be done all over again a week later. We fix supper. We wash dishes, and then we do it all again for the next meal. You, though, teach these kids things that they'll take with them for the rest of their lives. Some of them will go somewhere."

"I like seeing them learn, but I wonder how many of them will remember me when they're thirty."

"Some will. Some won't. I imagine those soldiers you took care of in Maryland remember you."

"Sadly not unless they're doing that from the grave. The majority showed up in bad shape to the ward I worked in. We healed some, but so many died."

Jerry's ears perked, and he sat up and looked down the street.

"She's out later than usual," said Alice. "I'm sure I must have something to do." She left the swing and went indoors. Jerry gave a low whine as Dora neared the front walk and turned in.

Cate said to her, "Good evening, Dora."

Dora mounted the steps to the porch. "A good evening to you, Cate. Alice sure made herself scarce when she saw me coming."

"She remembered something she had to do before bedtime. How have you been?"

"Oh, can't complain, I guess, and better now that our weather has cooled down."

"Care to have a seat?"

She chose one of the wrought iron chairs. "Thanks, don't mind if I do. Those swings make me dizzy." She took about five seconds to catch her breath before starting in with what was on her mind. "No one can say that Virden's been boring lately with all these miners in town."

"No, it's not boring. Aren't you worried about being out alone in the evening?"

"No, I don't turn any heads. My husband said he could see five separate fights from the second-story window of *The Reporter* today. George Sewall's back in town. He went to Colorado to the National Press Convention. Said he didn't recognize the town. I don't know where it'll all end. And Sheriff Davenport went back to Carlinville on Tuesday after deputizing some men Lukins brought in. No one in town wants that job." She shook her head in amazement.

"Is that a swan feather in your hat, Dora?"

"It sure is. Isn't it ridiculous that the Audubon Society thinks we shouldn't kill birds to decorate our hats? What did the good Lord put the birds here for anyway?"

"Eat insects? Provide eggs?"

"Well, a lot of women at the fair this week had feathers in their caps."

"A good time, the state fair?"

"I heard it was. I didn't go. I heard about it from Gladys, who, by the way, asked me to ask you how Jerry was doing."

"He's a good boy, and I'm glad Noah rescued him for me."

"Have you ever seen the grass so green in September? Looks like you or Alice need to mow."

"I'm thinking I'll do it tomorrow since it's Saturday."

"Going tomorrow night to the miners' auction, aren't you, so you can bid on your man's pie?"

"My man's pie?"

"Your Noah."

"He's hardly *my* Noah. What is the auction?"

"It's to raise money to help feed the miners who are in town. I wish they'd go hungry and leave, but the bleeding hearts—of which there are quite a few in this town, like Mrs. McWhinnie, who's been making coffee for them—want the rest of us to help feed 'em. Fortunately, I have a husband and an excuse, but you, especially with your teacher's salary and a young man who's a miner, will be expected to bid on a pie."

"Dora, Noah and I are not... we don't have any agreement..."

"Well, anyone can see the way he looks at you. He'll want you to bid, but you won't be able to outbid Jenny. She gets his goods every year to make her dad mad."

"Jenny will bid on Noah's pie?"

"Guaranteed. You'll want to be there to watch it even if you're not going to bid."

Cate took a deep breath and let it out. "I'll see."

"Maybe you have your sights on Henry. I seen you walking to Almira's wedding with him."

"He stopped by on the way and offered to escort Alice and me. That's all."

"I wasn't invited, of course, being Presbyterian. And with George, *The Reporter's* editor, being an usher, he had a ringside seat to what went on. Maxie or Almira must have given E.P. Kimball a write-up beforehand because he had a description in *The Record* of what the wedding was going to be on the day of the wedding. I think that was counting their chickens before they hatched. Anything could of happened, and it might not have come off as planned, but then, Maxie wouldn't have allowed that."

"It was a beautiful wedding."

"The social event of the season it's been called. Things will slow down a bit now with Almira gone off to Chicago with her banker husband, and Nell Furry settled down with Judge Cowen, and the Gelders gone off to Pennsylvania for the winter so those kids can get some higher-society education than what we have here in Virden. What a time we live in now. People going east and west and all over."

Cate didn't say anything. She felt relieved that she was not dashing off to Pennsylvania or Colorado.

Dora stood to go. "Well, it is getting dark, and I should be going. Here's something you can listen for on Sunday, Cate. Us Presbyterians will ring our steeple bell from the furnace room in the basement of the church now that the remodeling is done.

We've gone all modern. We'll be cozy and warm with our furnace heating, while you at the Christian church will be jockeying for seats near one of the stoves."

"I guess so, as long as the south shaft can supply enough coal for our stoves."

"There's a rumor of a resolution to the strike, but it's just a rumor. Tell Alice I said hello and not to run off the next time she sees me coming."

And with that, she headed toward the front steps as Jerry watched her go. He came lumbering over to Cate as if to say, "Isn't it time for bed?"

She buried her face in his fur. "You're a good boy. Let's go inside."

October 1, Saturday

> Firedamp
>
> The term firedamp, in America, is usually understood to mean any explosive mixture of marsh gas [CH4, methane] and air.
>
> —*Examination Questions for Certificates of Competency in Mining*, p. 63, 1907.

Luke stood on Noah's front steps with his hands on his hips. "Why aren't you busy baking a pie?"

Noah leaned his chair back against the front wall of the porch, closed his eyes, and crossed his arms over his chest. Noah said to Harry and Bea, who were on the porch swing, "Why don't you kids go around back and play. Luke's here to visit." They jumped from the swing, and the screen door slammed after them as they ran through the house calling for Ellis.

Luke adjusted his canvas hat farther back on his head as he took a chair next to Noah's. "Ok, partner. What's eating you this morning?"

Luke opened his eyes and righted his chair. "Nothing."

"Now, I know better. So, why aren't you busy baking?"

"I don't plan to go to the auction."

"You have to go. You're an eligible bachelor, and you brought top dollar last year. And it's for a good cause." He studied Noah for a few seconds. "Maybe Cate will buy your pie instead of Jenny this year." He rubbed his chin. "Now wouldn't that be entertaining to see those two bidding for your goods. Ha!"

"I think Cate doesn't think of me that way."

"Why would you say that? That girl likes you."

"Dora came by this morning to ask if I was going to stand with a pie at the miners' auction. I said I might. I'd have to think about it. She then said Jenny would probably buy it again this year if her dad didn't stop her because Cate wouldn't. I asked how she knew that Cate wouldn't, and she said she'd teased Cate about being my girl, and Cate let her know that she wasn't my girl."

"Now we're digging out what's bothering you. Cate. You guys have a falling out?"

Noah shrugged. "No, not at all. But she was escorted to the Henderson–Willson wedding on Wednesday by Henry."

"They go to the same church. Have you asked her to be your girl?"

"Well, no, but…"

"So, what else could she have said? Sounds to me like Dora was fishing for gossip, and Cate wouldn't supply it."

"I don't know. I don't care to stand on the auction block with my pie and be bid on. It's demeaning."

Luke shook his head and fixed his eyes on Noah. "Christ Almighty. I've heard a lot of White-ass whining, but that one does beat all. You're telling me," he pointed to his chest, "a Black man, that you don't want to be auctioned off. My pa was auctioned away from his family when he was ten years old. How about *that*? I don't want to hear your White-ass whining."

Noah leaned forward, putting his elbows on his knees. He covered his face with his hands and then ran his fingers through his hair. "You're right. You're right. But I still don't want to do it."

"Oh, you're going to do it. The miners' fund needs you. Claudette and I laughed ourselves sore watching Jenny have to outbid that Girard girl last year and pay five dollars for a pie."

"That Girard girl got married recently to the guy whose pie she bought. I dodged that one. I don't need some random girl thinking because she bought my pie that she's got some claim."

"Not even Cate?"

"I told you she's not going to bid."

"I'm tired of hearing this bull crap. You're going to the auction if I have to have Claudette bake the pie, and then I drag your sorry carcass all the way uptown." He stood to go but didn't leave the porch. "Well? Am I going to have to come back down here?"

Noah took a deep breath and sat up. "Okay, okay, just remember, you might have to rescue me from some firedamp girl like that one from Girard last year."

"You could use a firedamp girl."

"Get out of here. I have a pie to bake."

On his route home, Luke just happened to go by the Merry house. No one was on the front porch, and he hesitated to go to the door. He took the street along the side of the house, and luck was his. Alice Merry was hanging laundry on the clothesline. Cate sat under a shade tree. The lawn mower next to her waited for the rest of the backyard to be cut.

Jerry trotted over, wagging his tail. Luke stopped outside the picket fence and tipped his hat. "I wonder if I might have a word with Miss Merry."

Cate waved to him. "Of course, Luke. Would you like to come sit with us?"

"Oh, no ma'am. I'm just here to make sure that you know about the miners' auction tonight."

At the fence, she said, "I heard something about it from Dora. It sounds like a good cause, so I thought I'd go, but how does it work? I don't want to just buy some miner's pie. And then doesn't he have to walk me home, or…?"

"Yeah. That's usually how it's supposed to go, but you can decide what, well, where, uh…"

"I get the idea."

"I just came from Noah's. I twisted his arm and threatened him until he agreed to participate."

"I can see why he wouldn't be keen on it."

"We need him there. He brings in top dollar for a pie. Jenny makes sure of that."

"Oh, I see. So, you're suggesting that I might be interested in outbidding Jenny for his baked goods?"

"If you are interested. But, well, he heard from Dora that you said you wasn't his girl."

"Wait, what?" Cate looked away while checking her memory and then looked back, her brow furrowed with agitation. "She told me I had to buy his pie because I'm his girl. I told her I wasn't his girl because I don't want it getting back to him that I'm going around saying I'm his girl. I don't know how he thinks of me. Dora needs to mind her own business."

"Aah. I thought it might be something like that. I'll leave you to decide what impression you want to give him." He started to step away and stopped. "I've known him and partnered with him for years. He's a man of strong feelings and loyalties. Whenever he falls for some woman, it'll be hard. So, if you're not interested, don't bid."

"I'll give it some thought."

"Just between you and me, he seemed down this morning. I suspect Dora's visit had a lot to do with it—or maybe you going to the big Henderson wedding with Henry." He tipped his hat again. "Good day, Miss Merry."

"Call me Cate, please." She added, "And I didn't really go with Henry. He stopped by and we walked there together."

He nodded and called to Alice. "And good day to you too, ma'am."

Cate sat in the shade for a few minutes with her Aunt Alice, then rose abruptly and said, "I need to get to the bank before it closes."

⁓

At six thirty, evening had settled in. The streetlamps were on, as were the bandstand lights and other lanterns hanging around the public square. On his way uptown, Noah avoided walking by Cate's house. He didn't want to have a conversation before the auction. She should come on her own volition and bid if she cared to with no pressure from him.

On his way to the table collecting the pies, he spotted her with Jerry. She wore a sky-blue cotton dress trimmed with lace. Her dark hair shone under the lights of the lanterns, and he flushed at the thought of what might be coming. She was talking with a group of ladies and didn't see him.

A man with a megaphone mounted the stairs to the bandstand and said, "Ladies and gentlemen! If I may have your attention, please, we will get started on our auction to raise money to help feed the striking miners and their brothers who have come to Virden to help end this strike."

He pointed to a tent that had been set up next to the bandstand. "We'll start with the baked goods just in case the rain makes a comeback. Behind the first table, we have five eligible bachelors and their goodies."

Giggles came from the ladies among the bystanders. Five men, dressed in suits, stood behind each of their baked goods. A couple of them waved and smiled. The other three looked uncomfortable. One wiped the sweat from his forehead. Another adjusted a tie. The third looked off over the heads of the onlookers and toward the corner streetlamp. People in the park migrated toward the auction tent. The auctioneer started the bidding on the first man's cake at a quarter.

Cate left the group of women and made her way toward the tent. She was looking for Noah when her attention was drawn away by Jenny, who had come from behind her. She spoke to Cate in a low voice. "So, are you here to bid on Noah's pie?"

"I might. Are you?"

"Of course. He'll have something pretty sweet. And I always outbid anyone who tries to beat me." She smiled and turned away.

Cate smiled and waved to Miss Agnes, who had witnessed the exchange between Cate and Jenny from a few feet away. Cate had paid her a visit earlier in the day, and they had, in Cate's opinion, such an interesting chat. Miss Agnes told her stories from her life as an early settler—a breed of woman that was dying out fast. Tonight she wore a dress that would have been in style during the war. She bent over her cane and smiled back.

Cate wandered through the crowd while the first group of five was auctioned off. Jeering comments on the quality of their baked goods entertained the crowd. Noah stood with the second group of five just outside the tent, waiting his turn. He pulled at his collar, loosening the tie a little. His hair was combed back smoothly. To Cate, he looked like one of those good-looking men in a catalog sketch.

When his group's turn came, his eyes searched the crowd. They found Jenny, who smiled at him, and he returned the smile. He finally found Cate and Jerry toward the back. She waved. He nodded, and then his attention was drawn away to the speaker. He tried to find her again, but she wasn't there.

When the bidding came to him, the announcer held the pie up and asked, "What kind of pie did you bring, Noah?"

"Grape. From my own grapes."

"Who baked it for you?"

"No one. I baked it myself."

"Well, this is as fine a looking pie as I've ever seen. It has a lattice top and is nicely browned. Well done, Noah. Now, ladies, surely a man who makes such fine baked goods deserves a fine bid. As I recall, his pie last year got the highest price at five dollars. Now, who will start the bid?"

Jenny raised her hand and placed a generous bid of five dollars.

Many in the crowd laughed. Someone suggested that was the end of the bidding.

And then Miss Agnes bid ten dollars.

Jenny's head swung toward the frail old lady leaning on her cane, and she said, "Fifteen dollars."

Miss Agnes calmly raised her hand and said, "Twenty dollars."

"What do you want with his pie?" asked Jenny.

"Maybe I like grape pie," said Miss Agnes.

"Twenty-five dollars," said Jenny.

"Thirty dollars," said Miss Agnes.

The bidding went back and forth with increasing gasps from the crowd and increasing hesitation on Jenny's part while Miss Agnes coolly outmatched all of Jenny's bids.

When at last, Miss Agnes said, "Oh, let's get this over with. Fifty dollars."

Jenny turned away, saying, "Well, I hope you enjoy your fifty-dollar grape pie! It'll be sweet enough."

Miss Agnes just smiled and waved at Noah, who was standing behind his pie with his mouth open and cheeks flushed.

Toward the back of the crowd, Luke was doubled over laughing, and Claudette had a handkerchief dabbing away at her watering eyes.

After the rest of the five miners had been auctioned off, Miss Agnes came over to Noah. He asked her, "Miss March, why?"

She replied, "I'm not so old that I wouldn't like a good-looking man to escort me home."

"I can do that. Shall we go now, or would you like to stay?"

"Let's go now. I can't stand around like I used to. These things wear me out." She pointed with her cane. "Let's take Dean Street." She noticed Noah searching the crowd. "Are you looking for someone?"

"No, I think she's gone."

After they walked a few slow blocks, they arrived in front of Agnes's house. She tapped her cane on the walkway. "We can part here. And don't worry, you don't have to kiss this old cheek. I was just a proxy for someone else, and you need to take her the pie." She handed him a blue envelope.

Noah, trying not to drop his pie, opened it, aware that a few fellows had trailed them to find out what would happen. He glanced at the note, smiled, and quickly put it into his jacket pocket. He gave her a peck on the left cheek. "Thank you, Miss Agnes."

Alice arrived home from the fundraising to find Cate and Jerry already home and Cate changing into a flannel-weight dress. Alice said, "I thought maybe you'd left when I couldn't find you."

"I decided Jerry and I weren't in the mood for crowds."

"You missed it. You'll never guess what happened. Agnes paid fifty dollars for Noah's grape pie. I think she must finally have hardening of the arteries and gone senile."

"Really. Fifty dollars?"

"Now what would old lady Agnes want with Noah's pie?"

"I'm sure we'll find out sooner or later. What did Noah say?"

"I don't know."

"Did you bid on anything?"

"There weren't any miners old enough for me to bid on one." And she laughed. "I threw a quarter in their kitty jar."

Footsteps on the front porch and a bark from Jerry led Alice to see who was at the front door. The moonlight revealed Noah, holding a pie. "Hello, Mrs. Merry. I have a delivery. Is Cate home?"

Alice opened the screen door but didn't invite him in. She took the pie and said, "Yes. Just a minute."

Jerry greeted Noah, and Noah greeted him, rubbing his ears. "How are you, boy? Have you been a good boy tonight?"

After putting the pie on the kitchen table, Alice found Cate. "Maybe I should a known you'd do something like pay fifty dollars for a pie. Noah's waiting on the porch. The pie is on the kitchen table, and it's a beauty."

Cate found Noah waiting with his hands behind his back, smiling. She motioned toward the porch swing. "Thank you for delivering the pie. Can you sit for a while?"

When they were both seated, he spoke first. "Cate, fifty dollars is a month's salary for you. Why?"

"Maybe I like grape pie." She hoped her smile was visible in the moonlight. "And I heard something about the buyer being entitled to a kiss."

"I already gave the kiss to Agnes."

"You kissed Agnes?"

"On the cheek."

"I'm jealous."

"I'll make it up to you, but I don't think I have enough experience to give a fifty-dollar kiss." The night was quiet except for unidentifiable sounds coming from uptown and an occasional dog bark. "Cate, do you remember when I first saw you?"

"Certainly. Uptown on August first."

"No, it was before that."

"How could it be? I'd just arrived on the train from St. Louis."

"I remember it clearly. We were both about twelve, and you were in Alice's backyard playing with a couple of the neighborhood girls when I walked by with some friends. One of them said the Merrys had guests from St. Louis. And that's when I saw you."

"I had no idea."

Cate could make out Dora about a block away, heading in their direction on her way home. "The identity of your buyer won't be a secret for long."

Alice came halfway out the front door. "There's a grape pie on the kitchen table calling my name. Are you two coming in for a piece, or what?" And then she retreated into the house.

Cate stood up and said, "I'm going to get a piece of pie, but I haven't forgotten about that fifty-dollar kiss."

Chapter 20

The Mishap

October 4, Tuesday

Cate helped a few of the students put on their jackets after the bell rang. The afternoon grew increasingly darker, and gray clouds threatened rain. Just outside her classroom door, Uncle Billy tied Tami's shoe and told her not to trip.

Back at her desk, she sat down and sighed. The day went by fast. She'd been busy, so these few minutes after the children left the classroom were one of her favorite parts of the day. She could sit and reflect on what went well and what didn't go so well. Jerry waited in his corner near the windows for her to finish up and watched the kids in the schoolyard as though looking for trouble.

"Trouble" was a word that had come up in the morning's lesson on the letter *T*. Arthur said that his dad said there was going to be "Trouble" with a capital *T* when Mr. Lukins brings in Negroes from Alabama. Sometimes, the level of understanding of these five- and six-year-olds surprised Cate, and she wondered what she thought when she was their age. Tami said the problem wasn't that they were Black like her, but that Mr. Lukins would need a smaller stack of money to pay them, and he liked to keep his money. Then Tami said that her name started with a *T*. The other *T* items were more predictable: a teddy bear, a turnip, a wooden turtle, and the apple "tarts" she had brought. Then, she drew a large picture on the chalkboard of the tarantula she took to the high school. With all eyes on the board, they talked about spiders—yesterday's letter *S*—and tarantulas.

Cate sighed again and put away papers and pencils from the top of her desk when a scream and cry came through the open window as Jerry barked. She hurried to the window. Out near the schoolyard gate stood the Clemmons boys' horse. The older boy, who attended the Westside School and was, Cate guessed, in about fourth grade, cried and held his arm. Lynne, who was in the second grade at the primary school, also cried and stood nearby.

Cate grabbed her nurse's bag on the way out of the classroom with Jerry right behind her.

The boy on the ground continued screaming and crying but not moving. As Cate got to his side, she could see he was badly hurt. His shoulder bulged at an odd angle and appeared to be dislocated. His elbow bled and was probably broken or cracked. He cried, "I can't move! It hurts! It hurts!"

One of the other teachers came to Cate's side and told her he was Gregory Clemmons, Lynne's brother, and that he came every day to pick Lynne up from school. She asked Cate what she could do to help.

"Can you get Dr. Shriver? I think he's in on Tuesday afternoons. If not him, then get Dr. Boyer or one of the other doctors."

The boy looked like he was in so much pain that he might pass out. His eyes were rolling around behind half-closed eyelids.

He needed sedation and his shoulder reset before anything else could be treated. But a sedative or anesthesia wasn't something she was prepared to give him from her nurse's bag, and it might not be what the doctor would want.

She tried talking to him. "Gregory, can you hear me? This is Miss Merry. I'm a nurse. I've sent for a doctor who is going to fix your arm." She brushed the hair from his sweating forehead.

"Ouuw! Don't touch me. I can't, I can't..." He gasped for air.

Cate addressed another of the teachers. "Can you get everyone back and tell the students to go home. There's nothing they can do to help." She looked around for Uncle Billy and found him near the schoolhouse door. "Uncle Billy, do we have something that could be used as a stretcher to get him inside when the doctor comes?"

Uncle Billy nodded and said, "I'll come up with something," and went inside.

Then, she spoke to another teacher. "Do you know the parents? Someone should take Lynne and the horse and get Gregory's parents."

The teacher nodded. "I can take care of that. I'm glad I'm not a nurse."

A few sprinkles began to fall. Cate tried to hover over the boy in a way that would protect him from getting wet. The crowd lingered, with most of the onlookers standing back except for one man who came running up. He said to Cate, "I'm Edgar Day. My house is just over there. If we can move him, we can get him out of the weather until the doctor comes."

Cate nodded. "Uncle Billy has gone for something to move him on."

She continued to talk to Gregory in soothing tones, but she wasn't sure he could hear her.

Uncle Billy returned. "I think this might work to carry him inside." He held in his hands two broomsticks with a blanket stretched across them and held in place with safety pins.

Cate said, "Uncle Billy, you're brilliant."

He replied, "No ma'am. I just went through the war, and my master was an officer. We had to improvise to get men off the battlefield."

Cate stood and patted his arm. A couple of the teachers came forward to help Cate and Uncle Billy get Gregory onto the make-shift stretcher. They carried him carefully so as not to jar him across the street to Edgar's house. Gregory moaned and cried with every jolt and movement. Edgar cleared a dining room table and added a folded quilt for padding. They laid the stretcher on it.

Each minute seemed like an hour, but in no more than ten minutes, the teacher who had gone for Dr. Shriver arrived with him. Both of them were out of breath.

Cate stroked Gregory's hair. "Dr. Shriver is here now, and he's going to take care of you."

Dr. Shriver still wore his white office coat. He leaned over the injured boy, then gave Cate a grave look. Cate nodded that she knew what he was thinking.

He took a bottle of chloroform and a cotton cloth from his bag and wet the cloth with the chloroform. He held it over Gregory's nose until the boy relaxed. Then Dr. Shriver asked Cate to hold the boy while he reset his shoulder. With a skillful jerk, the shoulder was back in its socket. Gregory was still asleep.

Dr. Shriver went to work on the boy's elbow. "This is fractured and maybe shattered. He's going to be laid up for a while.

What happened?"

Cate handed Dr. Shriver everything he requested as she told him what she knew. "I didn't see it, but another teacher said that Gregory came to pick up Lynne. Lynne spurred the horse forward, and Gregory lost his balance and put his arm out to catch himself."

Dr. Shriver nodded as he worked on the elbow. "Makes sense, given the injury."

"I've seen him come to pick Lynne up some days. I assume he goes to the Westside School and that they live out of town because of the horse. I don't see them every day."

"They do live a far distance for the boys to walk." He continued bandaging the elbow.

Gregory started to move and groan, so Dr. Shriver reached into his bag and pulled out a vial of morphine and a syringe. "This will keep him quiet the rest of the day. We need his parents to come and take him home. I can check in on him later." After the injection of morphine, Gregory relaxed and again fell asleep.

Dr. Shriver sighed and said, "Well, I've been meaning to come and talk to you anyway. While we wait, let me tell you what I'm thinking."

"Okay." Cate wondered what he would have to talk to her about. She wasn't about to leave a teaching job and become a private practice nurse until she was well over her experiences from the veterans' hospital.

The doctor leaned on the table. "You know that we'll have trouble if Lukins brings in the Alabamans. We have hundreds of miners in town just itching for a confrontation. Lukins now has an estimated fifty guards inside the stockade. A man in charge of Thiel detectives arrived today to supervise them. They're arming themselves with Winchesters, and many of them are sharpshooters. Virden could turn into the wild west."

Cate felt perplexed. "But, what do I need to do?"

"We may need all the doctors and nurses we can get. The miners are getting communications along the rail lines, and they believe that we'll get the scabs in about another week. Can I ask you to stay ready with your bag of supplies equipped to bandage wounds? If you hear shooting, wait until it stops, and then see who you can help. I'm not sure where I'll be, or the other doctors, for that matter. We'll need patients stabilized until a doctor can get to them."

"Of course. I can do that. I would have done that without your asking me."

He rubbed his eyes and looked tired.

A woman rushed through the front door in near hysteria. "My boy, my boy! How is he?"

A man followed her. "Doc, how's our son? Lynne told us what happened."

Dr. Shriver explained that Gregory's injuries were serious, and they needed to keep him quiet. His instructions, however, faded into Cate's background as she thought about what she might be called to do when the trainload of strikebreakers arrived in Virden. She began making a mental list of what else should be added to her nurse's bag.

·

The clock on the mantle struck seven. Cate and Alice settled down to their respective hobbies. Alice darned socks and other items for the family she cleaned house for in the morning. Cate had two more Jacob's Ladder squilt blocks to finish before Sunday's quilting bee. They had not lit a fire because the temperature outside was in the low sixties, but it was a cool, humid sixties. A fog settled over the neighborhood, and they couldn't see beyond the house across the street. Instead of lighting a fire, Alice put on a pot of coffee. After it had percolated for a few minutes, she removed it from the heat. Raindrops tapped on the window, and Cate reconsidered lighting a fire.

Unexpectedly, Jerry barked. Footsteps on the front porch, followed by laughter, drowned out the tapping rain. Cate said, "I'll get it. I can't imagine who's coming on a night like this one."

In a line outside the front door, she found the McCalls with two umbrellas that they were collapsing. She opened the door for them. "Come on in. What brings you out on such a night?"

Noah ran his fingers through his hair and said to the kids. "Leave the umbrellas on the porch." Then, turning to Cate, he said as he came through the door, "We were looking for a *U* word for Harry for tomorrow, and one of the kids suggested 'umbrella.'"

"That was me," said Bea with a smile.

"Thinking about an umbrella gave them the idea of taking a short walk in the fog because they like the fog and think it's spooky."

Ellis said, "Yeah, it's like in the scary books where there's a haunted house."

"I didn't think it was really going to rain, but we took two umbrellas on our stroll in the fog to uptown and back. We weren't far from your house when the rain started, and Harry got the idea of finding out how the Clemmons boy had fared."

By now, they were all standing around the living room, including Alice, who had just come in from the kitchen. She said, "The accident at the school will take Cate a while to tell. Why don't you sit and have some of the pumpkin pie I made this afternoon from your pumpkins? And we just made a pot of coffee."

Cate could tell from the way Noah's eyes lit up that the pie and coffee were something he'd like, yet he said, "We didn't come to eat your food. There won't be any left after this crew eats."

"You got more pumpkins?" Alice asked.

"Oh yeah. We had a bumper crop with all the rain this year."

"Well then, we can make more pie. Bring me another pumpkin to make another pie. Come on into the kitchen."

In no time, Cate and Alice had six plates and forks out. When a piece of pie was on each plate, Cate said, "Oh, I almost forgot what we put in the cooler." She went out to the back porch and came back with a bowl of whipped cream and a bottle of milk. "We whipped some cream since the weather was cool."

Noah shook his head. "I don't know what to say."

Alice stabbed her fork at him and said, "Say you'll bring me more pumpkins."

"I promise to get you more pumpkins."

Cate suggested Ellis bring two chairs from the dining room to add to the four around the kitchen table. When they were all settled in with their pie, coffee for the adults, and milk for the kids, she began to fill them in on what happened. "Harry probably told you that Gregory Clemmons fell off the horse that they ride to school, and he put his arm out to catch his fall. Fortunately, he didn't get a head injury, but his arm was dislocated at the shoulder, and his elbow was broken. He was in a lot of pain and will be out of school for some time."

Alice said, "He's lucky you were there and that they have a school nurse now."

Noah agreed and said that type of injury may bother the boy for the rest of his life.

As the kids finished up their pie, Cate said, "I have some picture books and story books on the shelf in the sitting room. Maybe you kids would like to look at them while I talk to Noah for a while?"

Full of pie, cream, and milk, the children nodded along with Cate's plan in contented silence.

She showed them where the bookshelf was and pointed to the books that each of them might find interesting. When she came back to the kitchen, Alice had started cleaning up.

Noah told her, "I can wash the dishes, Alice. You baked the pie."

"Well, I'll let you. I have some darning to do, and I'm not sure I want to hear again what Cate has to tell you."

His eyebrows wrinkled, and he looked at Cate.

Cate rolled up her sleeves, poured hot water from the stove into the dishpan, and began washing the small plates and forks. She pointed to a towel for him to dry them. "Dr. Shriver talked to me while Gregory was sedated and we were waiting for his parents to come."

"And what did he say?"

"He said there would be trouble for sure when the miners from Alabama arrive. He asked me if I could help treat the wounded once the shooting stops."

"Cate, I don't want to think of you anywhere near the train depot or the stockade. I don't think even the guards that Lukins has in the stockade would deliberately shoot a woman, but there may be stray bullets from both sides."

"He said to wait until the shooting stops."

"It could start up again for some reason." He waved his hands and the dish towel as he spoke.

"Here, give me that." She took the towel. "One more dish to dry. There." She replaced them in the cupboard and the forks in the drawer. "Let's have another cup of coffee, if you have time."

They sat at adjacent sides of the kitchen table. She straightened a doily in the center. On it were the salt and pepper shakers and a sugar bowl with a silver spoon sticking out. "What do *you* plan to do when the train arrives?"

He sighed. "I plan to be at the depot. I have to support my brother miners. We're all fighting for our livelihoods." He paused. "No, more than that. We're fighting for our lives and our kids' lives. We deserve a living wage. We go into that mine over three hundred feet underground. Some of the main tunnels now have electric lights, but we may have to walk a half mile into pitch darkness with the only light being the flame in our headlamps. We handle explosives, and we never know if one of us will be carried out on a stretcher or trapped and not make it out at the end of the day like my father."

Cate tried to picture the conditions in a coal mine three hundred feet below the sunshine, and she shivered.

He went on. "Virden has good conditions, a seam of coal thick enough we can stand up and not have to crawl on our knees as my father had to in England."

"He had to crawl into the tunnels?"

"Oh yeah. You have no idea how bad conditions can get in some mines. That's why some of these miners from outside Virden are so militant. General Bradley will show up in Virden any day now. He helped get the miners in South Central Illinois to go on strike a year ago. The strike of '97 helped us get the agreement in January for eight-hour days and forty cents a ton wages. Bradley says in his speeches that he began working at a mine when he was nine years old. Many mines have boys that young underground. And some mines in Pennsylvania and West Virginia and other places pay the miners in script, which is only good at the company store."

"I can't imagine sending a nine-year-old hundreds of feet underground to work in a coal mine."

"I think Fred Lukins is dead wrong about bringing in the Black miners from Alabama, but I give him credit for getting some things right. When he bought this mine in '93, it was still under construction. He wanted to make it a modern mine with modern equipment. He doesn't hire boys. He pays in US dollars, and he hired Black men at the same pay scale. But over the last couple of years, I'm sure he's been under pressure from investors and other operators not to let the miners dictate what their wages will be. It's as though Virden is the showdown between big money operators and labor. If we let big money win, we'll never have the quality of life that we—that everyone working eight-hour days at honest labor—deserve. If the strike fails, I'm not sure what I'll do."

"What do you mean? What can you do?"

"I stayed in Virden through the strike last year, and we won an agreement for higher wages and an eight-hour day. But since Lukins refused to honor the national agreement and locked the miners out, I haven't had a paycheck. It's been months. I'm scraping by because I have the house that Mom and George bought, so I haven't wanted to just pick up and find work elsewhere like a lot of miners did. Having a place to live with no rent and room for a garden has kept us going, but it's not long-term. I'm going to have to look for something else if we don't get this pay raise. I don't want these kids to grow up knowing nothing but poverty."

"And if you do get the raise, you'll go back to the mine?"

"Yes, but I have plans for getting a better job."

Cate thought about the book she'd seen lying open in his house. "I'd like to hear your plan, Noah, if you wouldn't mind sharing?"

"I mentioned to you before that I'm studying to get a mining certification that will help me get a job like a mine manager or a mine examiner. When I'm thirty, I could even try for an inspector job if I get qualified. They make almost ten times what I make when I'm working."

Cate took his hand that was closest to her. "I'm so glad that you have plans to get away from the jobs where you'd be at higher risk. I don't like to think of you going to work every day and not knowing if you will come home."

Noah didn't say anything for a few seconds. He blinked back tears. "Cate, I know that whatever is going to happen in the next few days could be dangerous. I could even get killed. But it's something I *have to do* because it's all about my future, the kids' future—our future."

She leaned over and put an arm around him, resting her head on his shoulder. "I know. But also, I'm a nurse, and I have a duty to help heal the injured. So, I'll be right behind you, bandaging wounds or whatever needs done."

Ellis came into the kitchen. "Miss Merry, can I borrow this book?"

She straightened up and recognized the book as one she had recently read. *Dracula*. "Well, if Noah says it's all right, but it's maybe…"

Noah asked, "Isn't that the book that came out last year? Some half-dead people suck the lifeblood from living people and turn them into beings who are half-dead like they are?"

Cate nodded. "Right. It's a bit rough for a twelve-year-old."

"I'm thinking, though, that it's a metaphor he might learn something from."

Chapter 21

A Passing

October 5, Wednesday

Cate closed the door to her classroom, and she and Jerry headed out of the school. She had her umbrella in one hand, partly because today's letter was *U*, and partly because it was still cloudy and foggy.

Caroline and Betsy stood just outside the schoolyard gate. Their eyes were puffy and red. Betsy dabbed at hers with a handkerchief. As Cate approached them, she dreaded to ask the question that had to be asked. The thought briefly crossed her mind that maybe the Clemmons boy had taken a turn for the worse, but then she would have heard that news through Mr. Loveless. Something else had happened. "Ladies, what's wrong?"

Caroline swallowed hard and choked out the words. "It's Helen. She died suddenly. At home. Harriet, the woman she shared a house with for years, sent her handyman by this afternoon to tell me. He said she's a wreck. She and Helen were really close, living together all those years."

Cate felt riveted in the spot just inside the gate. Helen had seemed tired but otherwise fine at the quilting bee, not even two weeks ago. Cate's shoulders slumped. "Oh dear. That's awful. How did it happen?"

Carolyn sniffled and blew her nose. "I went to see Harriet when I heard the news, to see if she needed anything. She looked terrible and was just staring at Helen's chair in the sitting room."

Cate led Jerry through the gate. "Would you two like to walk home with me and talk about it?"

Betsy said, "I need to get home and work on supper. I'll see you, Cate. And Caroline, thanks for coming by and letting me know." She hugged Caroline and then Cate.

Carolyn said she also needed to go soon. "Harriet said that Helen made a comment about coffee cake and collapsed in the middle of the sitting room floor." A tear rolled down both of Carolyn's watermelon-pink eyes.

Cate leaned over to Carolyn and hugged her. "When you find out about arrangements, will you let me know?"

Carolyn nodded. "Harriet said Helen had her quilt blocks done and was going to bring them by your house today. She gave them to me." She pulled a flat bag out of her shopping basket and handed it to Cate.

"Thank you so much. And please let me know if there is anything I can do. I don't know Harriet, so I'm sure she doesn't need a visit from me."

"I'm taking her supper tonight and told her she can stay at my house if she wants. You know how the first night after someone's passing can be."

When Cate got home, she unclipped Jerry's leash and sat down on the couch. She opened the bag of Helen's quilt blocks.

They were all lovely color combinations. The top one was Almira's wedding pink, ivory, and green. She turned it over and viewed the stitches. They were small and had been carefully done. Within the last couple of weeks, Helen had spent several of her last hours on Earth bringing together individual pieces of fabric and joining them in beautiful ways to form five unique Jacob's ladder quilt blocks. The other four ladies and Cate were putting together their own blocks, spending their precious time doing it. And then these thirty blocks would come together into a quilt that had a value and function far beyond that of the individual blocks. The work was, in a way, Cate thought, almost sacred.

A tear ran down Cate's cheek. And she wondered what she, herself, was contributing to with the hours of her life that would come together with others toward something bigger. She blinked. A tear ran down the other cheek and onto the pink fabric. She clutched it tightly in her hands and pressed it to her chest. *Thank you, Helen.*

๏

October 7, Friday

Alice sat down in her chair with a sigh. "Thank goodness it's Friday, and I'm not working this weekend. Right now, I'm not worth the powder to blow me to hell."

Cate finished sewing her last quilt block. She removed her thimble and put the needle in its case. The other ladies had already brought their blocks, and Alice planned to sew them together on Saturday after Helen's funeral. The next quilting bee was on Sunday afternoon.

"There, I'm finished." Cate held up a couple of blocks for Alice to see. The darker blues, greens, and purples surrounded the lighter colors—ivory, tan, pink, and white. The light from the lamp shone through the fabric, making it look like stained glass.

Alice handed Cate a newspaper that was thicker than the weekly Virden papers. "Here. I'm tired, including my eyes. Clyde gave this to me and said we might want to read it. It has a lot of the goings on that we're not privy to. You could read it to me if you would."

Cate unfolded the newspaper. The *Illinois State Register*, Friday Morning, October 7, 1898. She read the headline. "Governor Northcott Acts." She paused and then said, "Shouldn't it say Acting Governor Northcott since Governor Tanner is in Washington?"

"I wonder if he left the state on purpose so Northcott would have to deal with whatever happens here."

Cate read, "The subtitle is, 'Orders Sheriff Davenport to Disarm Strikers.'"

"That'll happen over their dead bodies."

"Another subtitle is 'Says Miners Must Be Made to Leave Virden and Farmers are to Be Deputized—Several of Lukens' Guards Captured.' They spelled his name wrong. It's Lukins with an *i*, not an *e*."

"These journalists get a lot wrong, but they get enough right, and you and I aren't going to be in on what's really happening."

"I wonder about this: 'Several of Lukens' Guards Captured.'"

"What'd they do with them?"

"It says, 'The twenty-five hundred visiting miners...' Do you really think there are that many?"

"There's too many is how many."

"'The visiting miners are on guard, and this morning captured four of Manager Lupkens'—misspelled again—'force who had sneaked out of the stockade to spy out information. The deputies were marched to Girard at the point of weapons and warned not to return.'"

"I'm glad they didn't shoot 'em, or people won't like the miners."

"It says that the sheriff's brother, 'Doc' Davenport, is in the stockade, and they don't lack, quote, 'material comforts.'"

"What? Do they have women in there?"

"No, I don't think that's what they mean."

"Well, those guards are supposed to be ex-police and security men from Chicago and St. Louis, and you know how they are."

"No, I can't say I do, but this says Lukins has a telephone and has been using it. He wants the sheriff to have the governor send in the state militia. He was afraid last night that the strikers would try to destroy the stockade. The sheriff wanted to swear in some of Virden's citizen miners to be deputies if they'd agree to protect the mine property, and they refused."

"No, they wouldn't do that. It'd put them against their own brother miners. That sheriff don't know nothing."

"Mayor Noll has ordered all the saloons closed."

"The WCTU will love that."

"The article says the miners have plenty of money, and their provisions are costing a hundred and fifty dollars a day."

"And just think. Your fifty dollars fed them for at least one meal." She chuckled, then added, "The McWhinnies have been down there night and day, feeding them and handing out coffee for the last two weeks. Mary McWhinnie says the miners are sleeping in barns and storerooms and boxcars and anywhere they can. Well, go on."

"The sheriff told Acting Governor Northcott that he could not protect the town but would do his best. Northcott told the sheriff to disarm the miners and send them out of town to wait."

"Not going to happen. Northcott is a moron, but what can you expect from a Republican?"

Cate continued, "Now here's something. The next title is 'Tried to Kidnap Lukens. Strikers Made an Attempt to Secure Manager of Chicago-Virden Shaft.'"

"Ha! I don't like what he's doing, but I'm glad they didn't get him."

"According to this, Loucks and Lukins were allowed to board the train at the depot and go to Springfield."

"Maybe they were glad to get him out of town."

"And General Bradley is coming along with four hundred followers, but they've been held up in Jacksonville."

"We knew he'd make an appearance."

"The reporter actually interviewed Lukins. He, Lukins, says, 'I just came to Springfield to get a square meal. I took dinner at the Leland today, and I tell you I enjoyed it.'"

"The Leland! I guess he did enjoy it! That's the high-end eating in Springfield."

"Here's an interesting comment from him. I'm not sure we should believe it. 'I understand,' said he, 'that a miner said to one of our guards who is on duty at the stockade, and who goes into town and circulates among the strikers, that in case it came to a fight, the Virden miners will not go against the stockade, but will send the ignorant Pollocks and other foreigners who are with the crowd of men from the other places to do the fighting. This comes to me from the guard, and I believe it is the truth.'"

Alice shook her head. "Oh, he's wily. He's trying to stir up bad feelings among the miners. The Virden men are down there in the middle of what's going on."

"I agree. I heard that the local union guy, Ed Cahill, has been telling all the miners *not* to go up against the stockade because it would be suicide." Cate's last words hung in the air with the ticking of the clock pendulum. "That's all the article really has. It doesn't make me feel better about the situation. I'm worried for all concerned."

Alice nodded toward Jerry. "Look at that dog. Sleeping like a baby with no worries."

"His ears are up. Jerry's always listening."

He raised his head.

"He's edgier when I take him to town with so many people, especially men walking past us."

"I'm glad you have him." Alice got up stiffly from her chair. "Well, we have Helen's funeral tomorrow. I hate funerals. And tomorrow night, there are supposed to be speeches before the band plays."

"Are you going?"

"I'll stay clear of uptown, but you might want to take Jerry and go. Noah will almost certainly be there." She turned down her lamp. "I'm going to bed. Goodnight."

"Goodnight." The clock struck nine. Cate listened to its chime fade into the walls. She wished she could stop the coming trouble. Men who now walk Virden's streets might not be alive a few days from now. Their bodies could be lying lifeless in a morgue by next weekend. And for what? A temporary victory? Labor battles would have to be fought again and again and again where the interests of profit diverged from the interests of employees.

When she looked at the bigger picture, the struggle seemed futile. But when she thought about Noah and his three siblings, she knew that a stand must be taken. He had to do it for himself and every brother miner, or nothing would change.

October 8, Saturday

Alice and Cate hired a covered carriage for the funeral rather than going in Clyde's open wagon. Clyde offered to drive them to the cemetery, and they accepted—Alice and Clyde in front, Cate and Noah in back. He took her hand as she looked at the passing fields of brown cornstalk stubs and black dirt. Gray clouds hung low, threatening rain, even though the barometer remained steady and no rain was forecast.

Cate adjusted her black shawl and took in the ominous horizon before speaking the first words since picking up Noah. "I'm glad it's not too cold." She turned to face him. "Thank you for coming."

"I didn't want to see Henry escorting you as he did to the Henderson wedding, although my best suit has seen better days." He leaned over and kissed her cheek with lips warm and moist. Alice and Clyde carried on, looking straight ahead in their own conversation.

She placed her free hand on his arm and squeezed it.

"If you're up to it," he said, "there are going to be some speeches this evening before the band concert. Would you like to go with me? The neighbor will watch Harry and Bea. They don't need to hear what'll be said. Ellis might want to come."

She dropped her hand from his arm to nestle it inside his palm. "Yes, I'll go. Thank you for asking."

At the Virden Cemetery, mourners gathered around an open-sided tent. The site was near the western edge and higher up a hill than the older graves toward the east. Clyde parked the carriage as close to the tent as he could. Many other carriages lined the narrow lanes within the cemetery. Men helped ladies out of the ones that had just arrived. Nearly everyone wore black except Hop Long, who wore a green-gold silk suit.

Cate checked the time on her locket. Ten minutes until the service. She said to Noah, "Let's walk around for a while. I'm not ready to go over there yet."

He nodded, and she took his arm. They walked down the hill toward the older graves. She could recognize some of the last names and wondered about their connections with the living people she knew.

Noah pointed to a grave on their left. "He was a brother miner. Died from a rockfall. One of our few fatalities."

"Do you know many others? Recognize their names?"

"Yes, so many friends and people I've known here. Over this way," he pointed to their right, "is my mother and George." The simple headstone told only their names and dates and nothing about their lives.

Cate took a deep breath and looked up at the sky. "How do we come down to just a name and two dates?"

"We don't. We live in the memories of those who knew us."

"But when they're gone, we're names and dates on a headstone."

He made no reply for a few seconds. "I'm sure you'll hear from the Reverend that this isn't the end."

"Oh, I know. But to those left on this Earth, it is for now." She nodded toward the gathering on the hill. "Shall we go back?"

The quilting bee ladies had come together in a group, so she and Noah joined them. Carolyn and Maeve were already wiping away tears. They each gave Cate a heartfelt hug. Betsy blinked back tears and hugged her next. Agnes leaned on her cane, solemn and silent. Cate wondered how many funerals Agnes had been to in her lifetime. Harriet stood near the preacher, her eyes fixed on the coffin as though she expected it to do something.

The Reverend began the service in the usual way by saying they were here to honor the life of Helen, a friend of many in the town. He read from the usual scriptures that promised a resurrection.

"Blessed are the dead which die in the Lord from henceforth. Yea, saith the Spirit, that they may rest from their labors, and their works do follow them."

He continued, "God shall wipe away all tears from their eyes; and there shall be no more death, neither sorrow, nor crying, neither shall there be any more pain: for the former things are passed away."

Every time Cate heard these words in church or at a funeral, she couldn't help wondering, if God was going to do that, why not do it now? Why wait?

As they joined in unison for Psalm 23, "The Lord is my shepherd; I shall not want…" Cate felt her composure erode. She couldn't stop the tears and a feeling of heavy weariness.

Harriet, still staring at the coffin, prefaced the closing prayer by saying that it was Helen's favorite and not in the Bible. Her voice was steady as she recited the prayer of St. Francis.

Lord, make me an instrument of your peace:
where there is hatred, let me sow love;
where there is injury, pardon;
where there is doubt, faith;
where there is despair, hope;
where there is darkness, light;
where there is sadness, joy.
O divine Master, grant that I may not so much seek
to be consoled as to console,
to be understood as to understand,
to be loved as to love.
For in giving, we receive,
in pardoning, we are pardoned,
and in dying, we are born to eternal life.
Amen.

No one moved. A bright red cardinal sang in the pine tree behind the minister. A breeze from the west ruffled skirts and hats. A few sprinkles of rain fell.

Harriet repeated the last line again: "And in dying, we are born to eternal life."

⁂

By six forty-five p.m., the band began setting up even though a chance of rain was predicted. The bandstand had a roof, and they had a guaranteed audience of hundreds of miners. Their performance would go on unless a stiff wind blew up.

At least thirty miners kept watch duty around the stockade. Many other miners slept wherever they could manage to get out of the weather until they had a shift patrolling the stockade. They worked in three six-hour shifts to ensure that no one entered or left the stockade without their knowledge.

On this night, many miners came to the public square for food, coffee, and companionship. Interspersed among the miners were interested parties, but not many children.

Noah and Cate, with umbrellas by their sides and Jerry between, arrived a few minutes before seven.

Across the street from the square, Cate paused and took in the scene. She wished she could capture it in a painting. The warm-white light from the streetlamps on each corner of the square and in the center cast shadows in a cool blue. Some faces were fully lit, but most were only half so. People engaged in lively conversations that held their full attention, while others listlessly milled about.

Noah stepped onto the street before realizing Cate was no longer next to him. "Cate, is something wrong?" he called back.

Her gaze did not waver from the scene. "Not really. I wish I could paint this picture here and now."

"We'll have more evenings like this until the train arrives. You could bring your sketchbook next time."

"No, the scene is too complicated and dynamic. It would be best done from memory to capture the feeling and not the details." With that, she broke her concentration and patted Jerry on the head. "Come on, Jerry."

As they neared the edge of the square, a man standing with a group of three miners called over to them. "So, Miss Merry, gotten your fifty dollars' worth yet?"

She waved. "He's working on it."

Noah made a gesture to the group of men that she couldn't see and then pointed to a large tree. "Over there, under that tree.

We can hear and also be protected if we do get rain. I haven't seen any lightning."

A few of the men they passed spoke to Noah, but most, Cate guessed, were strangers from out of town. Under the large oak, Cate found she could stand on a root near the base and have a better view of the bandstand.

At seven o'clock, a man, whom Cate guessed to be in his thirties, climbed the steps to the bandstand and faced the crowd. The band stopped setting up and waited.

Noah said, "That's Ed Cahill, the local union leader."

Ed signaled for a tuba to blow loudly.

Jerry whined. Cate stroked his head. "It's okay, boy. It's okay."

Ed's voice filled every corner of the public square. "Can I have everyone's attention?" He paused for a few seconds as the voices quieted. "I think most of you know me. I'm Ed Cahill, the local union representative. I have something to say about what came out in the paper yesterday. I've heard talk around town that I don't like."

A few men clapped. One shouted, "We don't like it either!"

Ed waved down the comments. "Yesterday's *Illinois State Register* printed a comment that it claims Fred Lukins made. I don't know if he did or not. If he did make this comment, it was to stir up disagreements among the miners." He paused again to let some rumbling die down. "According to the *Register*, a Virden miner said that we intend to let the quote 'ignorant foreigners' storm the stockade. No Virden miner I know of has said that. It's absolutely *not* true, and I'll tell you why."

Ed paused. Murmuring died down. Occasionally, someone coughed.

"For one, we here in Virden don't want *anyone* storming the stockade. *No one!* Is that clear? Storming the stockade is a fool's errand. It would be suicide with all the guards armed with Winchesters, and we don't want to get ourselves killed. You can't enjoy a pay increase if you're dead."

He paused again for a couple of seconds while his words hung in the air. "Secondly, if miners damage the mine property, public opinion will turn against us. Currently, we're peaceful miners simply trying to earn a living wage. If we destroy property, we'll be viewed as anarchists. You remember the Haymarket Riot in Chicago of '86? A bomb turned a peaceful protest into chaos, and several of the protesters were charged with anarchy. Four were hanged."

A few in the crowd shuffled their feet, but most eyes remained on Ed. "The most influence that we can have is in the court of public opinion. Although many people wish we'd stop stirring up trouble and go back to work, we are going to continue to demand that we get the living wage of forty cents a ton and the eight-hour day that was agreed to last January. And so far, we have enough public sympathy for our fight. If we destroy the mine property, we destroy not only the means of our livelihood, but also the public's opinion of miners."

He stabbed the air with his right hand.

"So, let me be clear. *We are not anarchists.* We're trying to build here the kind of country we want to live in. We do not want a loss of life. We do not want anyone storming the stockade. The train from Alabama is expected to arrive this coming week. You'll hear from the union leadership within the next couple of days about our plans for meeting the train. It's a special that Lukins hired. That's all I have to say. Good evening." And he left the bandstand.

Cate turned to Noah. "Well, that was clear enough."

"Yeah, but not all the out-of-town miners were here to listen to him, and I think some do want to tear down the stockade as a symbol of taking down robber barons."

Chapter 22

The Second Quilting Bee

October 9, Sunday

B y two o'clock on Sunday afternoon, the quilters began arriving. Betsy was first and asked what she could do to help.

Cate said, "You can help pour coffee after everyone gets here."

"Oh, what a beautiful cake! It's so white." The table wasn't set, but a cake sat in the center.

"It's a silver cake." Cate smiled. "I baked it this morning before church and iced it after."

Agnes tapped the front door with her cane.

Behind her stood Carolyn. "I don't know what happened to the sun this month. I've forgotten what it looks like." She put her wrap on a hall tree near the door.

Agnes left her sweater on.

Cate motioned toward the fireplace. "I didn't start a fire because this isn't a large room, and I thought with all of us, we might get warm. But let me know if anyone prefers a fire."

Agnes took the first seat she came to. "I've gotten cold-natured in my old age, but today I hope to work up a sweat pushing a needle through fabric." She pointed to the cake in the middle of the table. "Is that an angel cake?"

Cate nodded. "You're close. It's a silver cake. It has butter in it. I first got the idea of making an angel cake in memory of Helen, but if you remember, she mentioned liking a silver cake last time. So, that's what I made."

She retrieved the pot of coffee from the kitchen and asked Betsy if she could start pouring. When she returned with the dessert plates and forks, she set them on the table. "Alice sewed the quilt blocks together yesterday, and I ironed it. She can really get that pedal going, and she had it done in a couple of hours. You're all going to be pleased with just how lovely it turned out. I can't wait to show it to you, but let's eat some silver cake first." She cut the cake, and Betsy gave each lady a piece.

Carolyn looked toward the kitchen. "Isn't Alice going to join us? And what about Maeve?"

"No. Even though it's Sunday, they're both working with Mary McWhinnie to feed the miners uptown. Alice doesn't care for hand quilting anyway. She says it's too slow. She likes to throw everything, except darning, on the sewing machine. Maeve said she'll come by sometime and work on it with me."

Agnes swallowed her first bite and said, "Alice never was one to take life slow or waste time. Cate, this cake is delicious."

"Thank you." Turning to Betsy, she asked, "You live close to the stockade. Do you feel safe?"

"Colin told me that if I hear shooting, I should go into the closet and not come out until it's all over. I said, 'I might need to check on you to see if you're hurt. And they wouldn't shoot a woman, would they?' He said probably not deliberately, but there could be stray bullets."

Carolyn shook her head. "I can't believe it's coming to this. Why can't they settle it peacefully?"

"They're going to try to," said Becky. "Colin said the Virden miners want to be at the depot to meet the train and have Sheriff Davenport stop it from going to the stockade. Then they're going to talk to the men from Alabama and convince them to go home. They'll even pay them to leave with some of the union money."

Cate added, "I've heard the same from Noah. No one wants this to come to shooting, but with all the guns on both sides, I don't see how they'll prevent it." Her next statement waited for a few seconds while the ladies ate silver cake. "I'm glad Mayor Noll closed the saloons. We certainly don't need drunk men getting trigger-happy."

Carolyn set her coffee cup down a little firmer than usual. "When women get the vote, we'll put a stop to all the drunkenness. That's why I'm a member of the WCTU."

Agnes met Carolyn's eyes. "And that, I'm afraid, is why women are going to be kept from voting anytime soon. The men want to run things their way. They always have. And if they want to drink, by God, they're going to drink. I wish the WCTU would stop kicking a mad dog and wait until after women get the vote to bring up taking away the liquor." She looked at Betsy and then Cate. "What do you ladies think? You're a young woman with a future to look forward to."

Betsy shrugged. "I haven't thought about it too much and don't care to read about politics. I'd probably just vote the way Colin wants me to."

Carolyn's next comments came with more volume. "What men are afraid of is that their wives won't vote the way they want them to. How many women are bullied by their husbands day in and day out? But when she gets in a voting booth, he won't be in there. They're suffering, and women's suffrage means she can check the box she wants to. Some wives will vote the *opposite* way out of spite, and *that's* what men are afraid of."

Their attention turned to Cate, who hadn't given her opinion yet. "When I lived in Maryland, a group of women, including me, went to Washington and marched near the Capitol building for women's suffrage." She took a sip of her coffee. "We were arrested, roughly handled, and spent a night in jail, which was not pleasant. The jail was deliberately kept cold."

Betsy hadn't moved a muscle since Cate started speaking. "Is that how you got the scar on your cheek?"

"No, that happened one night when a friend and I were walking home. We were accosted by a group of drunken young men. I was thrown face down against some rocks, and that caused the scrape. Fortunately, a couple of police officers heard our screams and stopped the men from doing much damage."

Carolyn put a hand over her heart. "Lord, help us. What's our modern society coming to? If those men hadn't been drinking, it wouldn't have happened. We're nearly in the twentieth century, and women still aren't safe from drunks on the street."

Agnes waved the top of her cane. "Carolyn, men are going to molest women whether they're drunk or sober."

Cate added, "The really maddening thing was that they got off. One of their fathers showed up and paid some money, and the incident was forgiven. The police claimed that they didn't get their names, so we couldn't even try to have charges brought."

Cate stood up. "Let me get the table cleared so we can go to work."

Betsy jumped up to help her. Soon, the food was cleared away, and Cate went to Alice's room. She returned within seconds and held up the quilt top. The ladies oohed and aahed.

Agnes reached for a corner of it and examined a block on the edge more closely. "This square has to have been done by Helen. I recognize the fine needlework."

Cate's eyebrows went up. "Why yes, it is one of Helen's."

"I've worked on quilts with Helen before, and many other women, and each has her own unique handiwork. I'd recognize Helen's anywhere."

A pensive silence came over the group until Cate said, "Let's get to work. I also ironed the muslin backing and have the batting fill ready."

꘎

By four thirty, the ladies had quilted themselves out. They first basted together the quilt top, cotton batting, and muslin backing with large stitches. Then they spent the rest of the time sewing the three layers together with small stitches that were the "quilting." Cate asked if anyone wanted another cup of coffee.

Agnes said, "I think I'm about done for today, and I'd like to get home. I can't quilt for hours like I used to."

Others agreed that they should go home and fix supper.

Cate suggested they could meet either the next weekend or in two weeks to finish up the quilting and sew the binding around the edges.

Jerry, who had slept all afternoon on his dog bed, suddenly jumped up and barked.

About five seconds later, a knock came at the front door. Cate found Noah waiting on the porch. "Noah, what a surprise." On the front walkway stood Bea, Harry, and a wagon containing pumpkins. He said, "I know you're having some ladies over, and I thought they might like a pumpkin. I'm not charging."

The quilting ladies gathered their things to leave. Agnes was the first to the door. "That is very thoughtful of you, Noah. Please let me pay you, though."

"No, Agnes. They're free to you ladies for working on a quilt to raise money for us miners. If you show me which one you like, I'll deliver it so that you don't have to carry it home."

"That's mighty nice, Noah. I'll see you down at my place then." She pointed to one and smiled.

The others picked up a pumpkin and left with their goodbyes. On the way past Cate, Agnes patted Cate's arm and whispered, "I think he's a keeper."

When they were gone, Noah turned to Cate. "General Bradley and about sixty men from the Mt. Olive area came to town earlier this afternoon."

"Really? What does that mean?"

"I heard he spread the word that he'll have something to say tonight uptown around seven. I want to hear him. Want to go?"

"Yes. I wouldn't want to miss the famous General Bradley."

"Women claim he's a good-looker."

"Now I *am* curious. I'll bring an umbrella."

"I'll come by at six thirty."

Silver Cake

from '76 a Cookbook, p. 174 [1876]

Whites of twelve eggs, five cups of flour, two and a half cups of white sugar, one cup of butter, one cup of cream or sweet milk, one teaspoon of cream of tartar, a half teaspoon of soda. Beat and mix as follows.

Beat the eggs with the sugar, then stir in the butter, softened by the fire; dissolve the soda, and sift the cream of tartar with one cup of the flour; mix all together, then sift and stir in the rest of the flour. Bake in a deep loaf pan.

~

Bradley's Speech

Noah, Cate, and Jerry arrived at the town square just before seven o'clock. To Cate, the evening felt like a repeat of the previous night: overcast, threatening rain, and hundreds of miners milling around, most conversing in small groups. Alexander Bradley was not hard to spot. Only one man in the crowd wore a silk top hat, a Prince Albert jacket, and rings on his fingers. He was taller than average, slender, and clean-shaven. He carried an umbrella, swinging it forward and back as he walked. The General wandered through the crowd, shaking hands and speaking a few words to each group or to any miner who approached him. As he worked his way toward Noah and Cate, Noah said, "Here he comes."

His silk hat shone under the lights. Its brim cast his black eyes into blue shadows. A few feet from Cate and Noah, his eyes turned in their direction, and he greeted Noah, "Evening, brother." Then he smiled and moved on.

Noah said, "Well, what did you think?"

Cate smiled and felt the urge to tease Noah. "He certainly is a good-looker. He's too fine to have coal dust hiding his face."

"Hey." He made a motion as though pulling a knife from his heart, smiling.

"I didn't say he was my type. A bit too much of a show-off. If he's a poor miner, how does he afford those rings and clothes?"

"No family other than his mother to take care of, and from what I hear, she can take care of herself. She runs a small store."

"I wonder why he's not married."

"Marriage could hinder his flamboyant style, especially if he had little mouths to feed."

General Bradley made his way to the bandstand at seven o'clock and strode up the stairs with his shoulders back. He waved his right arm wide, holding the umbrella and his left hand in his pocket. "Gather round, not just you miners and your families, but anyone who wants to free the mine workers of America from the terrible thralldom in which they've been held by operators for so many years—anyone with a stake in the future of miners. The General has something to say."

Conversations broke up as each individual's attention shifted toward the bandstand. Cate caught a couple of comments from men nearby, which revealed to her their divided opinions.

"Give them what for, General!" someone yelled.

"Looks like the Mt. Olive dandy will impart his wisdom," said another in a low tone nearby.

"We're with you, General!" came another shout.

General Bradley waved his umbrella again, just missing the ceiling of the bandstand, and said, "The General would like to make a few comments."

Cate noticed that he referred to himself in the third person and wondered if doing so allowed him to emphasize his honorary title.

The crowd became nearly silent. A baby cried and was quieted. A dog barked somewhere to the west. Tobacco smoke hovered in the still air.

"Many of you know me, and some of you don't, but I thank you all for listening. I'm going tomorrow up to Springfield to see the acting governor, or governor, or whoever is keeping the seat of power warm in Illinois. I want to make sure he knows our plight and ask for tents and supplies. I was deeply dismayed to see the conditions you men are sleeping in, especially given this cool, damp weather."

From someone in the crowd, "Give Tanner our regards, General!"

Bradley nodded. "Oh, I will. For those who don't know me, my family came from England when I was four years old. By the age of nine, I picked slate in Devil's Hole near Collinsville. The mine wasn't called Devil's Hole because it was a pleasant place to work. So, I'm a slate picker, a shovel stiff, and a mule driver down in our good earth. I wasn't born with a silver spoon in my mouth. And I know you brothers weren't either. I consider all you miners my brothers."

Cate noticed that he spoke as though he was a little out of breath, and she wondered if he already had miners' lung. Perhaps, if he'd gone to work in the mines at nine, he did. She guessed he was now around thirty.

He paused to let some scattered clapping die down.

"I know some of you have heard this, but many of you haven't. When I was a boy, I came across an almanac with a drawing of two chicks pulling at a worm beside a pond. The caption read 'United We Stand.' A picture next to it showed the worm pulled in two, and the chicks falling into the water. The caption read, 'Divided We Fall.' The same goes for the United Mine Workers. United we stand. Divided we fall."

Many applauded as he paced back and forth, making eye contact with individuals in the crowd as though he spoke to them for that brief second. "Four years ago, I had a life-changing experience. I marched in Washington with Coxey's Army, and that taught me the power of banding together. Last year, we miners marched from town to town in South Central Illinois." He stomped a foot like he was marching with the naming of each town. "Mt. Olive, Belleville, Staunton, Worden, Edwardsville, Glen Carbon, Collinsville, O'Fallon, Du Quoin, Pinckneyville, Coffeen, and everywhere in between."

Cheers went up with each town mentioned. "We induced our brothers to join the national strike. And in January, the UMWA negotiated a favorable contract with operators that Mr. Lukins now refuses to honor. So, it's time again that we unite as brothers in a common cause."

More applause.

"Some of you may feel discouraged because we just went through the big strike of last year. But the fight is not over. The battle is here, again, in Virden."

He then projected his voice louder and pointed at the crowd with his left hand on each word he emphasized. "The *battle* for workers' rights, the right to exercise the only power we have, which is the right to *organize*, will be under threat—*again*—and *again*—and *again*. It'll be fought in a thousand places: in *coal fields*, in *factories*, in *railways*, in *dockyards*, and *anywhere* workers are not paid the *living wages* they deserve for pouring the hours of their lives into their labors. Laborers deserve a living wage for eight hours of work—*especially miners*—when we risk our lives every damn day we go down into the pit."

He shouted the next sentence. "We want the contract we agreed to last January. An eight-hour day, and forty cents a ton."

The audience gave him vigorous applause.

"Last year on our march, along with the American flag, we carried another flag. Who remembers the slogan on the Peach Banner that the young ladies of O'Fallon helped us make?"

Several voices from the audience called out, "Peace on Earth and Goodwill to All Men!"

He nodded and continued pacing. "That's right. 'Peace on Earth and Goodwill to All Men.' So, remember, no nonsense and no violence! Any destructive act on our part will be maligned and misconstrued. We need the public's favor. Let's approach the business at hand *soberly* and *peacefully.* I understand Mr. Cahill said the same last night. We can *win,* but *not* with violence."

He bowed to the crowd. "Thank you for letting the General have his say." And he jumped off the bandstand. But there was no disappearing into the crowd for General Bradley.

Chapter 23

Preparing for Trouble

October 10, Monday

Cate closed her umbrella just before stepping inside the schoolhouse. On the way to school, she tried to keep herself and Jerry dry by maneuvering the umbrella while she carried a basket of rolls and held onto Jerry's leash. The thermometer at the house said sixty-two degrees, but it felt colder to her. She took a couple of steps away from Jerry because she knew he would shake himself off. Then she pulled out an old towel she had brought to wipe the area of the floor. His long fur could really shed water. She bent down and gave him a kiss on the top of his head and told him he was a good boy. Then she unclipped his leash and said, "Okay, Jerry, go to class." He trotted over to her classroom door.

Uncle Billy laughed from across the hall. "I just love to see that dog do what you tell him to. I think he'd go through fire for you."

"Let's hope he doesn't have to."

"I meant fire from bullets. I had a master during the war who had a dog a lot like that one, and he would take messages down the line."

"Goodness. That was heroic. I hope we don't need Jerry to do that." She unlocked her classroom door, and Jerry trotted over to his bed in the corner.

As she was hanging her wrap on a hook, Milo Loveless's voice came through her classroom door. "Good morning, Miss Merry."

"Oh, Mr. Loveless. I wasn't expecting you."

"I stopped by early because I want to talk with you before the students arrive."

"Would you like to have a seat?" She pointed to the other adult-sized chair in the room besides the one at her desk.

"No, this won't take long. I'll talk to the other teachers next, but I wanted to talk to you first. You have a unique location in this classroom."

"Yes, I do."

"These windows that look toward the town square make this classroom vulnerable if bullets start flying."

Cate began to feel even colder than when she'd entered the classroom. She looked toward the windows and nodded.

"Superintendent MacMillan is asking parents to keep their children indoors until further notice. But many of the students live quite close to the stockade, so we're advising parents to send them to school. And we encourage them to escort their children to and from school. Mothers are quite in agreement with the plan."

"I can see why, especially if they live anywhere near the mine."

"The high school, being a few blocks south and east of the train depot, is far enough away from the stockade. To be on the safe side, we'll keep the students away from windows. And the Westside School is well away from the depot and the stockade, so it should be safe."

Cate knew what was coming next.

"However, the primary school is so close to the public square that it could be in the way of stray bullets. And, as you well know, your classroom is the one with windows facing the town square." He went over and stood by Jerry. "I can almost see the train depot from here."

Cate had one hand in the other and tried not to rub them together as though she were freezing, which she was. She wished he had given her time to light the stove. "How soon do you think trouble will arrive?"

"The miners have had their spies all along the railway from Alabama. They can't predict how long the train will stop at each place, but the best guesses are sometime between Tuesday afternoon and Wednesday evening."

"So, my students and I are okay in this classroom today?"

"Yes, but if you hear any shots from anywhere, you should move them to the interior hallway immediately. Have them get down low and move out of the room. We could have some kind of conflict between miners and guards even before the train arrives."

"I understand. What about tomorrow and Wednesday?"

"I may know more in the morning. I'll stop by again before class. And remember, any sign of gunfire, have the students duck down and go into the hallway."

"Thank you, Mr. Loveless. I understand." She hesitated and then added, "Did Dr. Shriver tell you that he asked me to check on the wounded once the shooting stops?"

"He did. As long as the other teachers can supervise your class, use your nursing skills. I'm afraid they'll be needed."

The footsteps of one or two other teachers sounded in the hallway, and he left to talk to them.

At the stove in the center of the classroom, she pulled a couple of pieces of wood from the bucket that Uncle Billy kept supplied and worked to light a fire. Jerry settled himself onto his bed, and she said to him, "Jerry, I don't know if I like you looking out the windows this week. Maybe you should stay at home now."

At the mention of "home," his ears perked up.

The first student arrived, and Cate cleared her desk, thinking about how she would prepare the students for what was to come. Today was the letter *X*, not the easiest to build a lesson around.

When the students had all arrived and were in their seats, she asked them if they remembered what letter they would learn today. Most of the hands went up.

Arthur said, "I want to know what you brought to eat today that starts with the letter X. Pa said no food starts with an *X*."

Cate laughed. "Your Pa is probably right, but I did bring something for our letter today." She removed the lid from her basket, pulled aside the cloth covering, and held up a hot cross bun. The buns brought a smile to every face, and some students wiggled in their seats in anticipation of a bread roll. She showed them the top of the bun. What letter do you see?"

Several replied, "An X."

"Very good. This is a hot cross bun. It's usually made around Easter, and before baking, the baker makes the sign of a cross, which, if we turn it this way, is an *X*. These have raisins and cinnamon in them. Come up and get one. Bring your cups also, if you'd like some water."

Arthur said, "My Pa'll wish he'd thought of this food with the letter *X*."

The students devoured the buns within a couple of minutes, so Cate asked if anyone else had brought in something.

Harry came to the front with a pirate's map. He and Ellis drew it based on the *Treasure Island* book that Cate gave to Ellis. The map showed water and hills and a black X where, he said, the treasure was buried. She said to him, "What a smart idea, Harry. I never thought about an *X* on a pirate's map. Tell Ellis I said thank you for helping with the letter *X*."

One student had cut out a picture of a xylophone from a catalog, and no one else had anything.

Cate said, "I have something else that starts with the letter *X*, but I couldn't bring it in."

The students sat silently, waiting for the revelation.

"Three years ago, a college professor in Germany discovered a type of light called X-rays. He figured out that if you shine X-rays on your hand, you can see the bones. He took a picture of his wife's hand. So now, scientists are working on making a machine that doctors can use to see if you have a broken bone."

Oscar raised his hand, and Cate called on him. "Dr. Shriver could have used that for Gregory Clemmons."

"Yes, he certainly could have used one to see how many of Gregory's bones were broken."

She came to the front of her desk to get even closer to the students. "I have something else that we need to do this morning. You all know about the miners who are in town." Heads nodded. "Principal Loveless came by to talk to me this morning, and he wants us to practice getting to a safer place if trouble starts."

Amanda asked, "What kind of trouble?"

"Maybe gunshots. No one will try to hurt us. But if someone fires a gun, a bullet could come through our window because we're not far from the public square."

Bart said without being called on, "My dad says there'll be trouble all right. The miners will blow holes in any coloreds getting off a train."

Tami's eyes teared up, and she didn't wait to be called on to say, "I'm colored, and my family got off the train. They can't shoot them because they're colored, can they?" Her eyes looked at Cate, pleading.

Cate handed her a clean handkerchief. She patted the girl's back. "They want to keep them from getting off the train, and they don't want to shoot anyone. I heard their speeches in the square the last couple of nights."

She moved toward the door. "For us to be safe, just in case we hear a gun fired, we're going to practice getting down low, like a tarantula spider, and going into the hallway. Arthur, would you like to show me how you can get down low and go into the hallway?"

Arthur did a commendable job of crawling to the hallway with the rest of the class laughing.

"Well done, Arthur. Now I want all of us to do what Arthur did."

"Even Jerry?" asked Harry.

"Yes, even Jerry. But he's already on all fours, so it will be easy for him. He's going to want to be wherever the rest of us are."

Chapter 24

On the Eve

October 11, Tuesday

At three thirty, a light rain fell. Cate, umbrella deployed, and Jerry hurried along the north side of the square. She thought about how the day had gone with the students. She had a hard time keeping their minds on the schoolwork. Several of the students said their fathers claimed the train from Alabama would be in Virden tomorrow. Cate felt like they were all on a runaway train heading for a break in the tracks and a derailment. She tried to focus for a while on the letter Y. A couple of girls wore yellow ribbons. Amanda brought in a yam, and Harry insisted it was a sweet potato. He said he knew because he grew them. Cate had a yardstick and some yarn. They practiced going into the hallway. She wondered where Noah was and what he was doing.

After school, Cate walked uptown. When she and Jerry arrived at Matteson Street, which ran parallel to the railroad tracks, many miners and reporters congregated around the smaller depot, the J&S. She recognized the reporters by their notepads and hurried writing. The C&A depot, where the train would arrive, sat across tracks on the east side and had even more miners and reporters. Cate and Jerry turned left and walked away from the depots and in the direction of the stockade.

Miners crowded the porch at the O'Neill Boarding House. An elderly woman with a small dog handed out steaming coffee. Its aroma managed to reach Cate in spite of the tobacco smoke. Farther north, she saw the house she had encountered over a month ago, the one where the ladies were not appropriately dressed to appear in public. A queue had formed out the front door.

A man walking in the opposite direction stopped her and suggested the area was not safe for a woman to walk in, even if she had a German Shepherd. Bullets, he said, didn't go around women or dogs. She explained that she had to see a friend and wouldn't be long.

The stockade became more impressive the closer she came. The Springfield paper said the miners compared it to the Morro Castle in Cuba. The walls rose well above her height, and sentry posts rose above the walls. Barbed wire ran along the top of the wall. Guards stood in the sentry huts looking down, their guns clearly visible from a block away. Miners, also carrying guns, walked around the outside of the stockade, ensuring no one came or left, according to what Cate had heard.

A man with a notepad and other equipment stood outside the stockade south gate and called up to a guard. "I'm with the Associated Press. Mr. Lukins said I can come in." Soon, the gate opened just enough to let the man through, and then it quickly closed.

Three miners who had been standing near the stockade approached Cate and Jerry, so she turned to the west. Maeve's house was only half a block away.

By the time she reached Maeve's house, the rain had let up, but dark clouds still hung low. As she stepped onto the front porch, Maeve came to the door to meet her. "Well, what brings you by, Cate? You really shouldn't be over here." Maeve opened the door so Cate could come in. She left her umbrella on the porch to drain.

"Maeve, you're not safe here either." Cate gave her a hug, and Maeve squeezed her hard enough to let Cate know she appreciated the concern.

"Nonsense. I have a husband, and you just have Jerry."

"And where *is* Brian?"

"Down at the train station."

She sighed. "I've been thinking about tomorrow. My students told me their dads claim the train from Alabama is coming tomorrow."

"Aye, that's what we've heard. I'm afraid for what'll happen."

"Parents have been asked to keep their children indoors and away from windows."

Maeve nodded. "I plan to. Oscar's staying home. The weather's not fit anyway."

"But, Maeve, you're so close to the stockade. It's only a block away. You could have bullets flying in your direction."

"We're planning to stay on the side of the house away from the stockade."

Cate hesitated, but then went through with her plan. "I have another suggestion. My classroom, as you know, has windows facing the town square. We're well away from the stockade, but if there is any shooting in the square, Principal Loveless is worried about a stray bullet coming toward the school. So, for the last two days, the kids have been practicing crouching down and going into the hallway if we hear any gunfire."

"Good idea. What does that have to do with me?"

"Because of how close you live to the stockade, you and the baby might be safer bringing Oscar to school and staying there. And I could use the help. Dr. Shriver has asked me to help care for the wounded as soon as the shooting stops—if there is any. That leaves the other teachers to watch my students, and they have their own to worry about. You could, if you want to, come to the school in the morning and help me with my class. Then, when something starts, I'll have help with the students and a backup for when I have to leave."

Maeve didn't say anything at first. "This is getting serious, isn't it? I don't like the idea of you going out to care for the wounded. The shooting might start up again." She blinked back tears. "But for me coming, I need to talk to Brian and see what he thinks. If he agrees, I'll be down by eight in the morning. They're guessing the train will come at midday."

"Midday? So, we will get the trouble in the middle of the school day." Cate sighed. "Here's another option. If Brian doesn't like the idea of you going to the school, you could go to Aunt Alice's house. She's going to stay home and would be happy to have you there."

"Let me think about it. I don't like the idea of not being at home to meet Brian in case he gets wounded."

Cate nodded. "I understand. I'm going to go to Betsy's next. Even though she's just a block farther, she might want to come to Aunt Alice's, especially in her condition."

Maeve said, "There's a rally tonight in the square. Are you going?"

"I hadn't thought about it. Maybe."

They gave each other another hug, and Cate and Jerry headed back out, but this time away from the stockade.

$\cdot\bullet$

Black Damp

A molecule of blackdamp is composed of one atom of carbon and two atoms of oxygen and is designated CO2; this gas is also called carbon dioxide, carbonic-acid gas, and chokedamp.

—*Examination Questions of Certificates of Competency in Mining*, p. 62, 1907.

A light rain fell all day but tapered off by six o'clock. Cate hoped for a knock at the door and was relieved when it came. She wanted to go to the square with more of an escort than just Jerry.

She let Noah in and kissed his cheek. "I'm glad you came by."

"I'm going uptown. The miners are preparing for the train from Alabama. It's coming tomorrow, probably midday."

"I heard that from Maeve this afternoon."

"I want to be with everyone tonight and hear what is said. Would you like to join me?"

"I would. Alice is already uptown helping with the food, but I had some things to do for class tomorrow and haven't left yet. Jerry and I are ready."

Noah held his miners' cap, and he showed it to her. "We've been asked to bring our miners' caps with the lamps. I'm not sure why. But, for anyone who is not a miner, the request is to bring a candle or small lamp."

Cate hesitated, but then said, "No problem. Let me get a candle." She tucked one in her bag, then picked up her umbrella and Jerry's leash. They headed to town.

They passed Hop Long, smoking in the doorway to his shop. He said hello and then asked Noah, "Any chance they're bringing in Chinese to work the mine? I heard they threatened to do that in Pana."

Noah said, "No, this train is definitely coming from Alabama."

Hop nodded and smiled. "I wouldn't mind if they brought Chinese girls."

Noah laughed. "Sorry, Hop. No sign of that. You're so close to the square that you might want to get away before midday. You're welcome to go to my house."

"No thanks. I may have cleaning business coming in."

The mood on the square seemed to Cate almost festive. Laughter and loud conversations filled the air. Given that the arrival of the train from Alabama would happen tomorrow, she was surprised that the mood wasn't more solemn, and she said so to Noah.

They stood at the outside corner of the square, taking in the view. He said, "Maybe knowing that the confrontation will come tomorrow is a relief. After weeks of anticipation, something is finally going to happen."

"For better or for worse."

"And the *St. Louis Post-Dispatch* published an interview with Governor Tanner. He said that he will *not* send in troops to prevent the miners from intercepting the Alabamans. He said that the working man's capital is their labor, and he wasn't going to help the operators bring in convicts from Alabama to work in an Illinois coal mine. I was up here when that news broke, and we were all encouraged that we can stand our ground without militia troops interfering."

Cate nodded. "That is big news."

"For once, a governor has sided with the working man and not big business."

"It's an election year. I wonder if that had something to do with it."

"Probably. But what it means is that at least one politician finally cares about what the voting public wants and not just what the wealthy want."

"I'm surprised that Tanner, as a Republican, would do that."

"So were we, but we'll take it."

When they entered the public square, Cate wondered if some of the men had been drinking. They seemed more jovial, and she wasn't oblivious to the looks she and Jerry were getting. She took Noah's arm, and he put his hand over hers.

Alice was helping to serve coffee, and a lot of it was being poured. Cate recognized Minnie Bellwether and Mary McWhinnie also there. A brick fireplace contained a wire grid upon which sat several large coffee pots. When one was drained from the servers, another was set up and put on to percolate. Bread rolls and cookies were spread out on a picnic table covered with a red, white, and blue cloth.

They worked their way to the center of the square, and they came upon Luke and his wife, Claudette. They greeted each other at about the same time that a man, whom Cate didn't recognize, stood on the bandstand and asked for everyone's attention. Noah whispered to her that he was one of the state union leaders.

"Good evening, brother miners! I hope you've gotten some coffee to warm you against this damp weather. And about that, the barometer is rising, and the prediction is for clear weather in the morning, but it will be much colder. So, find a place tonight out of the elements to sleep. We need you ready to defend your brothers tomorrow."

A shout came from the crowd. "We're ready!"

He raised his hand in a fist, then dropped it. "As many of you know, we had some good news from the papers this morning. Governor Tanner said he will not send in troops to stop the miners from preventing the Alabamans from taking our jobs." He waited until the vigorous applause and cheers died down. "Across the country, operators want to declare the right of the so-called free market, and to hire who they want. Yet, they ask for troops to be called in to stop laborers from striking. How free is that? Apparently, they want it to work just one way."

Cheers erupted from the crowd, but next to Cate, she heard Claudette say, "They're not all convicts who are coming. Somebody needs to set that man straight."

"Here's the plan for tomorrow. We know that the train carrying the Alabamans will likely arrive about midday. The Virden miners have agreed to take the lead and meet the train at the C&A station, where we want to talk to the Alabamans and convince them to go back home. Our fight is not with them. It's with Lukins and Loucks. We've pleaded with Sheriff Davenport to stop the train there. We don't know what he'll end up doing, but we expect the first fighting, if it comes, will be at the train depot. We want to be there to try as best we can to stop any bloodshed before it starts. But if it does start, we expect it there. We will conceal our weapons until fired upon. And we will only fire into the air until fired upon. We'll have miners south of town to alert us with shots in the air that the train is arriving. We will also have a Virden group at the north end of the spur where it joins the main line north of Henderson's field to try to stop the train there if all else fails."

He paced the bandstand much like General Bradley had done. "The rest of you, line the tracks, but be prepared to take cover if bullets start flying. We can't be standing out in the open, letting the bullets rain down on us from the stockade. I know some of you Black miners came down from Springfield to support us, and we appreciate it. We really do, but we're telling our Black miners to lay low. When the shooting starts, it might be hard to tell you from the scabs, even if it's not them we're fighting. We can't guarantee your safety."

Someone shouted, "What about us out in the field across from the stockade?"

"Be prepared to lie low and take some kind of cover, behind hay bales or whatever you can find. Some of us are meeting later tonight, and you'll get more instructions in the morning. But, when you hear the warning shots fired south of town that the train is coming, get ready."

Cate realized that Claudette was no longer standing with them.

"Oh hell," Luke said.

As soon as the union speaker was finished, Claudette mounted the steps to the bandstand. The crowd began to heckle her. "We don't need no *woman* telling us what to do, especially not a colored one."

Luke rubbed his face and looked at Cate and Noah, "Now they've gone and done it. They've made Claudette mad."

Cate said, "I want to hear what she has to say."

Luke nodded, "Oh, you'll hear it all right."

Claudette, rather calmly but forcefully, called to the crowd. "I have something to say, and I'm going to say it, or you're going to have to haul me off here kicking and screaming."

She paused.

The heckling continued with comments like, "Luke! Get your woman off the stand!"

Luke's reply was immediate, "Hell no. There's blackdamp here. Let it ventilate!"

The heckling continued until Claudette yelled above the noise of the crowd.

"I got something to say! Some of you single men might not be used to being lectured by a woman, but I got something to say."

She raised her voice even louder and raised her right hand, which held a piece of paper. "I have here a letter from one of the so-called scabs that is coming on that train."

The union leader who had just spoken yelled, "Listen up!"

The crowd noise simmered to a murmuring and the occasional cough.

She surveyed the crowd, making eye contact with many of them.

"It's from a miner's wife, my cousin, who's a good writer. It says, 'Dear Claudette, I have such happy news to tell you. Some men came down from the north and told us about the mining jobs in Virden. They said miners had left to fight in Cuba, and they are shorthanded in Virden. We heard the wage of thirty cents a ton and thought about the opportunity to get out of Alabama.

So, Isaac and I decided to pack up the kids and come. I'm sorry to spring this on you all of a sudden, but we are so excited to be heading your way and getting out of our current bondage. We were told there are miners' houses waiting for us, so you won't need to do anything but maybe make one of those cakes of yours to celebrate. We'll see you soon. Love, Bella." Claudette wiped tears from her cheeks.

Someone yelled, "They're still scabs and criminals."

Claudette waved the letter. "Let me tell you what you're shooting at if you shoot at the Blacks on that train. Being from Louisiana myself, I know something about how it is down there. Most of the so-called *criminals* from the South aren't *real* criminals. Ya'all know what they do down there to get miners to work under worse than bad conditions and low pay?"

The audience grumbled but listened.

"They find a Black man and drum up some bogus charge and throw him in jail. After he's sat there for a while without a trial and not earning for his family, they say, 'You want out? We'll let you out if you work at the mine. You can work out your sentence there.' The Black men go to work in the mine for a wage that is lower than yours. So, when they're told that they can come up here for a little better pay and not face that kind of slavery, they're just trying to do better for their families. They're men like you are, just trying to make a living."

Someone yelled, "They're Negro criminals."

She pointed at the crowd. "I've seen ya'all come out of the pit. And you know what? You're *all* Black when you come from that pit. I can hardly tell which of you is my husband. You're *all* Black with the dust from those long-dead plants that are being used to run our factories and heat our homes. You *all* risk your lives together. You *all* bleed the same color of red. You *all* deserve a living wage. These Alabamans deserve the chance for a living wage. Maybe not here in Virden. But that's all they're trying to get. If you shoot one of them, you're shooting innocents, and you'll have more than coal dust on your hands. You'll have blood on your hands. And I pray to God that we don't have to run our factories on blood." Her heels hitting the steps on her way off the stand resounded throughout the square.

Another man took the stage. This one was older than the first man.

"I'm going to be brief. You may be wondering why everyone was asked to bring their miners' caps or a candle, and I'll get to that. I'm so glad the rain has held off." He breathed as though out of breath.

He paced the bandstand, addressing the crowd as broadly as he could. "I met Mary Harris Jones last year. Some of us have started calling her Mother Jones, and I think she likes that title. The woman is a force to be reckoned with. I'd like to share a couple of things she said to me. One is that too many company owners, the Chicago-Virden Coal Company included, want to *divide* the working class because they know that our power lies in our unity."

He took a few seconds to consider what he would say next and to catch his breath. "Yesterday, I took a walk out east of town. Just needed to get away. And I witnessed a barn raising. About twenty of you citizens raised a barn in one day. One day! Think of the cooperation and labor that went into that so that this farmer's animals and feed will be sheltered from the wind and cold this winter."

He pointed to the crowd. "Well, there's another kind of wind blowing, and it's been blowing for years and getting stronger. It's the wind of the wealthy. A hot wind. A scorching wind. The rich get richer, while the poor get poorer. Look it up. What kind of greed denies the working class a living wage? The only way that we can stop this desiccating wind, this wind that will rob us of our lifeblood, is to band together and build structures that block that wind." He took off his hat, smoothed his hair, and put it back on.

"I'm not talking about wooden or brick structures. I'm talking about *human* structures. Human minds, human will, human organization. If we band together, if we *organize*, we will see a labor barn raising like no one has seen in the history of this great country. We're building a human structure to help shelter us from the wind of the wealthy." He paused again to catch his breath.

"You miners go into the mines every day and work hard, and you risk your lives in one of the highest-risk occupations there is. And like me, you can end up in poorer health, especially with weak lungs. You deserve a decent, middle-class living, not this barely scraping by, if that. Sometimes, we can't even scrape by. But you have to *demand* it. The capitalists aren't going to give it to you out of the goodness of their hearts. If there is one thing we've learned, it's certainly that. The wind does not care where it blows or what it damages."

"The United Mine Workers is the structure that will help us gain the safer, more secure, more prosperous living that we all deserve for risking our lives to fuel the industries and the industrialists who don't mind reaping their rewards off the sweat of our brows."

"Mother Jones said something that has stuck with me to this day, every word. She said," and the speaker used a higher pitched voice with an Irish brogue, "'Someday we will have the courage to rise up and strike back at these great "giants" of industry, and we will see that they weren't "giant" after all—they only seemed so because we were on our knees, and they towered above us.'"

The man held up in one hand his miners' cap, fitted with the small metal pot. In the other hand, which he raised, he held a large metal pot.

"You miners know very well what these are." He pointed to the large pot. "For those of you who are not miners, this is a parting lamp. When men are being lowered in the cages, they stand close together, and we can't all have our headlamp flames already lit. So, we have a parting lamp. When we get to the bottom, each man lights his lamp from the parting lamp. The passing of the flame sometimes feels almost sacred to me. Given the hazards of working underground, we can't be sure that when we go down those entries to work that we'll get everyone back again. Several times, I've lit my lamp with someone who wasn't with us by the end of the day."

Nods went throughout the crowd, and a chill went down Cate's spine.

"We don't know what tomorrow will bring. Some of us standing here tonight might not be alive by tomorrow night. I'm going to light this parting lamp, and I'd like everyone here in the square to pass the flame and light your headlamp or candle and hold them high so that Fred Lukins and the guards in the stockade witness the fire of our unity."

Starting from the parting lamp, flames lit other flames throughout the square. When everyone who had something to light held a burning flame, the speaker said, "Now hold your flame high, and let's make this country and our future the kind of place we want to live in. Join me in singing as loudly as you can *America the Beautiful.*"

Held high, the many lights shone down on the tops of their heads and pointed to the treetops and the clouds.

One of the Black singers who had been in Henderson's field during the camp meeting began humming the first bars of the song. A large man standing next to the singer encouraged everyone to join in, and he sang in a forceful baritone voice. Men outnumbered women in the crowd, and the low tenor of the men's voices and their unity of sound and words resonated in Cate's chest and filled her with a feeling of belonging. Jerry whined and then fell silent.

O beautiful for spacious skies,
For amber waves of grain,
For purple mountain majesties
Above the fruited plain!
America! America!
God shed His grace on thee,
And crown thy good with brotherhood
From sea to shining sea!

Inside the stockade, up in the tipple, the Associated Press reporter talked with one of the guards when the guard said, "What the hell? They're burning the town down."

The reporter looked through his binoculars and replied, "No, I've seen towns on fire. There's no black smoke. And… they're singing?"

All movement and voices in the stockade fell silent. The guard towers soon filled, but only the tipple was high enough to get a good view of the area around the town square filling with light and *America the Beautiful.*

Chapter 25

October 12

October 12, Wednesday

Cate woke up feeling tired. She hadn't slept well. The words from the speeches the previous evening still rang in her head. But she got up and went through her daily routine of washing up, dressing, feeding Jerry, fixing a light breakfast, and gathering her belongings for class. Today's letter was Z. She had a drawing of a zebra from a book, a big zero, and zigzag fabric. She had also baked zucchini bread two days prior.

Alice came from the kitchen, drying her hands on a dish towel. "Is today the letter Z?"

"Yes. I'm hoping to distract the students by making the letter Z special because we've arrived at the end of the alphabet. Every day, they've been more excited and distracted about the arrival of the train. What are your plans for today?"

"After the shooting's over, if there is any, and there will be, I plan to go up to the depot and see how I can help. Clyde said he'll come by and take me. He says he's ready with his wagon to haul away the wounded. I told him he'll be hauling away the dead."

Cate's eyes filled with tears, her mouth was dry, and she had a stomachache. Ever since her arrival in town, events had been leading up to today. She knew enough now about how the coal was mined to picture the fuse, or squib as they called it, being lit to ignite the blasting powder. This squib—the one between the miners, mine operators, and scabs—had been burning persistently for months. The train pulling into Virden would be the moment the lit fuse reached the powder. Instead of loading coal, they could be loading a whole lot of bodies. She shook her head to break the train of thought. "I'm glad you'll be with Clyde."

"I put together a bag of cloth strips, scissors, soap, boiled water, and carbolic acid."

"Good." She added, "Maybe add tweezers, a pocketknife, a sponge, and a small bowl. I have those in mine also."

Footsteps on the front porch brought Cate to the door while Alice disappeared back into the kitchen. Noah stood holding hands with Harry. He had dark circles under his eyes. "Good morning, Cate. Can Harry and I walk you to school?"

"Yes, thank you. I'm ready as soon as I get my coat. Come in." She took her coat from the hall tree and buttoned it. "The temperature dropped as predicted. At least it's clear today and not raining."

Noah nodded, swallowed hard, and blinked. "There is a crescent moon on the rise. My mother used to say that a crescent moon before a new moon foreshadows new beginnings. One way or another, today is a turning point."

"Yes," is all Cate could manage to reply without her voice breaking.

"Can I get a hug?" He asked. "I don't know what will happen today."

"You certainly can." She patted Harry on the head. "Harry, Jerry's leash is on the back porch. Can you get it?" He ran to the back. Cate wrapped her arms around Noah's neck. He smelled of shaving soap. She turned her face up, and they kissed, lingering in the moment. Reluctant to part, they held each other for several seconds. "Where will you be today?"

"At the depot with the Virden miners."

"Please try to stay out of the way of a bullet."

As they pulled away from each other, he said, "I'll do my best. I wonder if you should leave Jerry at home."

Alice came from the kitchen again just in time to hear his comment. "Good luck getting that dog to stay home when Cate goes to school. He's an escape artist. He'll either take out a window or a door after she leaves. And if he's running around loose, he'll get shot. We'll be loading his carcass onto the wagon. Let him go, I say."

Cate pulled a red handkerchief from her pocket and tied it around Jerry's neck. "This is in case he does get separated from me. It's more visible than his collar, and he'll look like someone's dog and not a stray."

Noah wiped away his tears. "If something should happen to me, can you and Luke make sure that the kids are taken care of? He knows I'm asking you this."

Cate's throat seemed to close up as it did when she was young and it was lightning outside.

Alice answered for her. "Of course we will. You just make sure that nothing *does* happen to you. I guess Bea is already at the Westside School?"

"Yes, and out of harm's way. Ellis went to the East School with a group of friends and one of their fathers." He turned to Cate and took her hand. "Cate, please wait until any shooting has stopped before you come out to help the wounded."

"Let's hope it doesn't come to that." She reached up and gave him a kiss.

"The only way there won't be shooting is if Sheriff Davenport stops the train at the station to let us talk to the Alabamans. If there's any attempt to unload them at the stockade, then there will be shooting. The miners are just not going to let them unload."

Harry returned with Jerry's leash. "I found it."

Cate attached it to Jerry's collar and said, "Let's go then. We don't want to be late."

Harry said, "Can I walk with Jerry?"

"Yes. He'd like that." Harry took Jerry's leash. Cate took Noah's right arm with her left hand and held her nurse's bag in her right.

Noah put his free hand over Cate's. "We're expecting the special train around noon, but we don't know for sure. You should have some time with your class to learn the letter Z."

She nodded, unable to talk again, and squeezed his arm. When she regained her voice, she asked him if he had any weapons on him.

Noah replied, "I brought my pistol for self-defense. I hope I don't have to use it."

Out on the walkway, they turned east toward the school and uptown. The rising crescent moon hung a couple of hand widths above the sun. Cate motioned to it. "I do hope whatever happens today marks a positive new beginning for the miners—and for us."

Noah leaned over and kissed her on the cheek. When they arrived at the school, Harry walked Jerry inside like it was going to be a normal day.

Noah said, "He doesn't quite know what's going on. He's heard there's a train coming in, and there could be a fight, but he doesn't really understand what that means. The kids haven't been around the miners talking lately, so all they know is what they've picked up or heard from their friends. Ellis understands a lot. I've asked him and Bea not to say anything to Harry that would get him upset. He's a sensitive little guy, even if he acts tough selling vegetables."

Cate looked into Noah's eyes and read his worry. "I'll try to act as normal as I can today, but if the class hears gunfire, I'm not sure what their reactions will be. There's nowhere in town that gunfire won't be heard. The town isn't that big." She turned toward the school door and then back to him. "I'd better go in. Let's meet up later—afterwards."

He nodded. Both of them blinked away tears.

As he walked away, she wished she had the power to stop events. Freeze time where they were. A tear ran down her cheek as she watched this young man, who had come into her life and was spending his youth taking care of three siblings, walk away into a dangerous situation. What if he didn't come back alive? The faces of some of the young men in the veterans' hospital came back to her, especially Lieutenant May's, and the open window and the taste of death. These men had given part of their youth, and some gave their lives to fight for Cuba's independence in a war she wasn't entirely convinced had begun for a good cause. Was it necessary? And today's conflict, was it necessary? She agreed with the cause of the miners. They had to take a stand. But did it have to come to violence? Was there no other way? She wiped away the tear. When Noah reached the corner of the square, he looked back and waved under a cloudless sky and crescent moon. She waved and turned to go in.

In her classroom, Cate found that some students were already there, particularly those who lived near the stockade. Most of the ones just arriving were being dropped off by an older sibling.

Maeve came in with her hair pulled back in neat braids. She brought her one-year-old and Oscar. For a few seconds, the two women looked at each other and knew what the other was thinking.

At the town square, Noah found the miners milling around in small groups, talking in excited tones, while others just stood and stared at the scene. About four stations of coffee distribution had a steady queue of men. Two UMWA tables were handing out ham and eggs. Noah wondered who had done all the cooking. He guessed that the union paid the hotels and boarding houses to supply the food.

He picked a line for coffee—he'd had breakfast at home with the kids.

The miners' conversations were somber. Men greeted each other and sometimes shook hands or patted each other on the back. Occasionally, someone laughed at an attempt to lighten the mood, but the laughter was tight and strained.

A light breeze moved the tops of the trees, and dozens of leaves floated down. Sunlight shone through them. Orange, gold, and red. Soon, they would join the others being trampled underfoot.

With the temperature in the mid-forties, some men stood in patches of sunshine to warm themselves after the last few days of rain. Noah had the horrifying thought that if they couldn't stop the gunfire, for some of the men standing in the sunlight of the public square, this day would be their last in the warmth of the sun. They knew it. Their families knew it, and the town held its breath.

After Noah got a coffee, he headed to the north side of the square, intending to take a walk, possibly to Henderson's field to see how the men camping there had spent the night. The ground under his feet was drier than it had been the night before. The cooler, drier weather was, in one way, a blessing.

Jacob Franklin Eyster pulled his wagon with two horses in front of the shops along the north side of the square. No one greeted him, but hundreds watched to see if he would go to the stockade. He steered the wagon down the alley next to the Chicago-Virden Coal Company store and tied the horses to a post in back. He went in through a side door. Within a few minutes, the shades came up in the front windows. One of his clerks, a young woman named Ada Beatty, came to the door, and he opened it to let her in. As he did, he stepped out to survey the gathering in the public square.

As Noah approached him on the walkway, he said, "Morning, Jacob."

Eyster nodded. "Any word on when the special is arriving?"

"I thought you'd be one to know that."

"Me? I went home to the boarding house last night to get some sleep. The miners aren't going to keep me informed."

"We're being told it'll come around noon or a little after."

Eyster nodded. "I like you, Noah. Stay out of the way of bullets."

Noah shrugged. "I'll try. You're not much older than I am, and I know you're just trying to run a business in a tough situation.

You and I have gotten along, so I suggest you keep your head down and don't come out of that store if you hear anything going on. You might want to lock up and go back to the boarding house. These guys from out of town could go after anyone associated with Lukins."

"It's not the friendliest environment at the boarding house either, even though we eat together every day. No, I'll stay inside and try to protect the store."

Noah extended his hand, and Eyster shook it. "The store is not worth your life, Jacob."

Some of the merchants worked to sweep the caked mud from the wooden walkway. A Bank of Virden employee worked on the walkway in front of the miners' hall, which had a thick coating of mud. He rinsed the planks with a pail of water and mumbled to himself, "I may be making this worse."

Noah smiled and spoke to the man, "Morning, George. Don't want dirty money?"

He laughed. "No, Mr. Henderson is very particular about keeping the bank clean."

Noah found the levee full of miners milling around, many warming their hands around coffee cups. Steam rose from the fresh pours. A tray of biscuits came from the saloon even though it was closed. A matronly woman held out the platter, and the men swarmed over to it. She told them, "Now, gents. Take just one. There'll be more." A young woman followed her with a bowl of hard-boiled eggs. "Eggs! Take just one until we get more."

Noah passed the group and did not attempt to get a biscuit or egg, even though the aroma of coffee, biscuits, and eggs was making his mouth water. Eggshells crunched below his feet, and he wondered how long these women had been serving up coffee and food. The front yard of the O'Neill Boarding House to his left was filled with miners, talk, and a diminutive elderly lady handing out coffee. An equally diminutive dog waited at her side.

Across Jackson Street at the J&S depot, a man with a wide broom tried to sweep around the gathering miners, but they were too distracted to move out of the way until he pushed the broom into their feet. Another coffee urn dispensed the steaming brew. Men sat or leaned against the leeward side of the building. No sign of a train, but none was expected, yet the tracks were littered with loitering men from the south edge of town all the way to the stockade. One of the railroad workers, whom he knew to be D. H. Kiley, waved to him as he crossed the tracks.

The larger C&A depot had scores of miners milling around. Noah recognized many Virden miners and decided to stop by the depot on his way back.

He then headed four blocks north to Henderson's field. It looked nothing like it had the night of the Black church's concert, when the air was filled with laughter, the smell of baked goods, and a warm breeze. Today, the field's grass had been trampled into a paste, and the cold air smelled of cigarettes, unwashed men, and coffee. Several small tents and lean-tos had been set up, forming a makeshift campground. Around forty men sat on hay bales. Hay clung to their clothing. When they conversed, their words were lost to the wide-open space, but each exhale brought evidence of their warm breath expelled into the cold air. Some smoked. Some walked around, trying to get warm.

Across the railroad tracks, the stockade stood ready and imposing, not only because of the wooden wall, but also because of the structures that rose above it. The mine's tipple, the equivalent of a three-story tower, had a clear view of the area. Several guards stood looking toward the field, as did guards in towers along each wall. An uneasiness spread from Noah's shoulders to the back of his head. They were under surveillance, and the surveyors were experienced and better equipped.

He spoke to a Girard man he recognized. "How's it going out here?"

"Cold and damp. I feel like I'll never be warm again. I did get some sleep last night."

Noah pulled a piece of straw from the man's sleeve. "In a barn, from the looks of your jacket."

"And we were glad to get it. It wasn't the Leland Hotel in Springfield, but it was a lot better than patrolling the stockade walls. And I'm glad that damn rain moved out."

"Do you know many of the guys out here?"

"Some. Most are from Mt. Olive and that area, and I got some family down there. A few are from Springfield and other towns around. They're getting all fired up by knowing the train's finally coming today. Do we know what time exactly?"

"Likely around noon or shortly after."

"Hey, you're Catholic, ain't you? St. Catherine's is putting out food and coffee. Some of the miners are getting warm and fed down there."

"I am, but I'm fine." He pointed to a couple of trees. "Not many trees around here or anything to hide behind. You're out in the open. What'll you do?"

"Duck behind the couple of trees and the few tents and hay bales, I guess. General Bradley got back from Springfield on the early train and said the governor wouldn't see him. He talked to the adjunct general, who promised to see what he could send, but it'll be too little, too late."

"Anything I can do for you guys?"

"Not unless you can stop that train from coming up to the stockade."

"I hope we can. I'll be there with the Virden men near the station, and we'll do our best. I heard that some of us will be north of the field also to cover where the mine's rail spur meets the main line at the north end." He held out his hand, and the man shook it. They clapped each other on the arm and said goodbye.

By the time Noah walked back to the train depot, he felt warm for the first time that morning. But the scene at the station brought back the chill. A crowd of men and women surrounded Sheriff Davenport. He could make out Ed Cahill's voice above the others. "Damn you then, Davenport. If you don't stop that train here, whatever happens down the rails is on you." Ed then left the center of the crowd and stood on the south side of the depot platform.

Noah went around the crowd to get to Ed and an older miner, Ben, standing with him. "Anything I can do?"

The older man turned toward Noah. "Hi, Noah. No, I'm afraid stopping a battle is out of our hands if we can't stop the train. The sheriff says only Lukins can tell him to stop it because Lukins hired it, and he refuses to have it stopped." He faced back to the south as though he might see the train coming. "I was in the war. Fought at Shiloh and other battles. This feels eerily familiar. The town is a black powder keg, and that train is the lit fuse. When it reaches the depot, we're going to have Shiloh all over again."

Noah blinked back tears, patted him on the back, and gave Ed Cahill a nod. Several women were still arguing with Sheriff Davenport. They were making a strong case for why they didn't want their husbands to get shot. Some cried, and some screamed and cried. Their voices faded as Noah headed back toward the public square.

At the school, Cate succeeded in getting the students to practice their spider crawl into the hallway. They laughed and raced each other. She didn't try to stop them from having fun with it. They also went through all the words that begin with the letter Z that they could come up with. There weren't many. Instead of going out at recess, they played games inside to the disappointment of the students. Teachers escorted students to the outhouses to relieve themselves around eleven o'clock, knowing they might soon be unable to go out for some time. Students in the classroom kept looking out the windows and not paying attention. At one point, Arthur stood at the window trying to see what was going on uptown. Cate had to pull his attention back into the classroom with a game of marbles.

Just after noon, a messenger came to each of the classrooms and asked to see the teachers in the hallway.

Cate turned to Maeve and said in a whisper, "Can you keep them occupied?"

Maeve nodded.

The man was out of breath, sweating and shaking. When all the teachers and Uncle Billy were together, he said, "The special has left Shipman and is headed to Virden."

Cate felt the blood drain from her face. A weakness came over her.

One of the other teachers, the most experienced of the three, asked, "When do you expect it to arrive?"

"Sometime after twelve thirty. We have sentries south of town. They'll fire warning shots when it comes into sight. When you hear those, you'll know that whatever is going to happen will happen soon." He put his hat back on and left.

The elder teacher said to the others, "Dear Lord, protect that man and all the others on both sides. Please spare us the carnage that could come."

The other teachers said, "Amen." Cate found praying nearly impossible. *Where was God in this?* she wondered.

Uncle Billy said, "My old ears don't hear like they used to. You ladies may have to tell me when you hear the shots."

All eyes turned to Cate. The elder teacher said, "Cate, you're likely to hear them best with the direction your classroom is."

The door to the schoolroom opened, and Mr. Loveless entered. "Ladies, I saw the messenger leave, so I assume you just got word that the train is about a half hour away. I'll be out here listening for the warning shots. When I hear them, I'll come in and go to Cate's class first and then the other two. We'll all meet in the hallway or the second grade classroom."

Maeve and two other women who were helping the teachers heard his remarks.

Cate thought that even Uncle Billy looked ashen. The time on her pendant read twelve fifteen. She and the other teachers returned to their classrooms. She had the students quietly play their favorite games. Jerry had been looking out the window most of the morning as though he knew something wasn't right. Cate wondered if dogs could sense fear, or, she thought, maybe he was hearing different sounds from the public square. But he wasn't his normal sleepy dog on his bed.

She was checking the time again when she heard the warning shots, distant but clear. Mr. Loveless came to her doorway and said, "It's time."

She turned to her students. "Class, it's time to do your tarantula walks into the hallway. Can you race like you did before?"

As they crawled toward the hallway, Cate had the impression Jerry was herding them. He wove in and out of the desks and was the last one into the hallway. Cate closed the door to her classroom and faced the kids, who were now sitting cross-legged on the floor. Some of the older ones stood in the back.

The pop, pop, pop of guns began within seconds. And then the pops came so quickly, they weren't distinguishable from each other, sounding like wagon wheels on gravel. Many children cried silently, while others were more vocal. The teachers tried to reassure them that they would be all right. They were safe in the school. The noise went on for several minutes—minutes that to Cate seemed like hours. *What was happening to Noah? How badly would these kids be traumatized by this?* Cate worked to suppress her thoughts and failed. One girl couldn't be consoled and cried out for her dad. She was near Cate, and so Cate tried comforting her. The other teachers were dealing with the anguish in their students.

Cate turned back toward her classroom door when she heard Jerry bark. The door was still closed. Arthur said, "Harry went back in the room."

Cate cried, "Oh Lord," and opened the door to see where he was. She found the classroom empty and the window toward the town square open. Jerry shot through the door, ran over to the window, and jumped through it.

Cate reached for her nurse's bag and returned to the hall. "I have to go. Harry just went out along with Jerry."

Maeve's eyes were red. "But the shooting hasn't stopped all the way."

Cate hurried out the door. She wondered how anyone would survive such a barrage of gunfire. How many men would she find wounded... or worse?

Harry was already entering the north side of the square when she laid eyes on him. He was screaming, "Noah! Noah!" Jerry was close behind him in quick pursuit.

⋅✿

At twelve forty, Noah was walking toward the depot when the signal shots from the south sounded. He stopped where he was in front of Clayton's Livery and felt frozen in place. The cold of the early morning suddenly rushed back, but he forced his feet to move forward toward the J&S depot, which was crowded with miners. Across the tracks, the C&A depot was also filled with miners. To the south, the train came into view. Noah stayed on the west side of the tracks, which were now lined on both sides with the hundreds of miners who had run over from the public square.

As the train approached the station, it did not begin slowing down. When Noah realized that it was not going to stop, but instead head toward the stockade, another cold shock went through him as though he'd been doused with water.

Railroad employee D. H. Kiley was in a position to pull the switch so that the train would take a side spur toward the south gate of the stockade instead of continuing along the mainline outside the stockade. Gunfire began, and he never pulled the switch. Kiley slumped to the ground just as the firing intensified. Guards on the train fired at the miners, and the miners fired at the train. Noah fingered the pistol in his jacket pocket and began to run toward the depot as the train rushed past. With brakes squealing, it pulled alongside the stockade a few blocks to the north.

A second later, the air was full of bullets, coming from every direction. The guards in the stockade were shooting not only toward the south in Noah's direction, but also toward the east and Henderson's field. Guards were also in a shallow trench between the stockade and the train, using the train as a shield to shoot at the miners in Henderson's field. Knowing that he could do little good from this range with his pistol, Noah turned back and headed toward D. H. Kiley to see how badly he was wounded.

Before he made it to the switch, a sharp pain struck his right leg. The next step forward with that leg filled him with such pain that he blacked out, collapsing amid the flying bullets.

Cate yelled as loud as she could, "Harry, stop! You have to stop!"

Harry kept running and yelling, "Noah! Noah!" His voice rang clear even above the gunshots, which were now tapering off.

Then, the firing stopped, and the yelling began—men's voices—but Cate was too far away to tell what they were saying.

Jerry caught up to Harry before he reached the Farmers and Merchants Bank and began nipping at Harry's clothes and barking. He got hold of Harry's jacket, which came off as Harry continued running. Dropping the jacket, Jerry pursued.

Several men in front of Clayton's Livery heard the barking and a child yelling. One of them said, "Look at that dog after the kid. I'll get him." And he leveled his rifle.

The man standing next to him hit the barrel of the rifle upward. "No, it's too dangerous. You might hit the kid. Besides, isn't that the teacher's dog?"

"Well, I'll be damned. What's he doing?"

"Looks like he's trying to stop the kid."

Harry stopped halfway down the levee with Jerry beside him.

From seemingly nowhere, women and wagons converged on the scene. Journalists poured from the train depots. Loved ones' names were called and shouted as the hunt for the wounded began.

Cate cursed her long skirts, boots, and lack of athleticism. Keeping her eye on Harry, she saw him cross the road, nearly getting run over by a wagon, and head toward the train depot. Jerry was now ahead of him and reached a man lying on the ground near the tracks. The man wore a hunting jacket like Noah's. He wasn't moving. Blood ran down the incline away from the tracks.

"Oh, dear God!" Cate wanted to stop Harry from seeing him, not knowing what condition he would be in.

Then the man's arm moved to force Harry down next to him. Jerry hovered above them.

Harry cried, "Noah, don't die! You can't die!"

Noah was fighting to stay awake, but his leg hurt with a pain he had never known. "Harry. I'm not going to die, but you have to get down. What are you doing here?" Noah held him close in an attempt to block any more bullets that might come from the direction of the stockade.

"I escaped like Jerry does—through the window."

Noah's breathing came hard as though he'd just stopped running. "Stay with me here until we get help. I can't walk. And it's not safe for you to run around."

"Are you going to be all right?"

"Of course, little buddy. I wouldn't leave you."

"Our mom and my dad left us."

"They got sick."

"Now you're sick."

Cate's voice came to them above the other yelling and moaning. "Noah, Harry!"

As soon as she reached him, she could tell he had a leg injury and did not appear to be bleeding anywhere else. "Noah, let me look at your leg."

He rolled on his back, keeping Harry close.

She pulled up his pant leg. "You've been hit close to the bone, and there's no exit wound."

"Cate, there have to be men in a lot worse shape than I am."

"Probably, but I'm going to get this wound disinfected and the bleeding stopped."

He thought he would pass out again when she poured the carbolic acid on his leg. He clenched his teeth and managed not to cry out for Harry's sake.

As she worked, wagon wheels stopped nearby. Clyde joined them, saying, "I brought the wagon."

Cate wrapped the leg, and the bleeding had mostly stopped. "Clyde, can you help get him into the wagon and take him to Aunt Alice's?"

A man nearby spoke. "I can help."

Clyde said, "Ben, you're hit too."

"Upper arm. Just a graze."

"Can you help me get him up?"

Cate asked, "Where is Aunt Alice?"

"She jumped out near the town square when she saw the first wounded man."

Cate said, "Harry, you need to go with Noah and take care of him. Can you do that?"

He nodded. "Can Jerry come too?"

"If he will."

Noah was loaded into the wagon, and Harry joined him. They called to Jerry, but he was not going to leave Cate's side. She waved them on, thanking God silently that Noah had only a leg injury, although it appeared to be a bad one. If the bone was shattered, the leg might have to be amputated.

Clyde called back to her, "I'll drop them off and be right back. Looks like there's plenty more wounded."

Ben added, "Cate, Henderson's field. It could be bad. We could see the stockade guards shooting toward the field."

She thanked him and surveyed both depots as they drove away. Several men lay wounded and were being attended by other men and a few brave women. She went over to one man who was down near the rail switch. He had been shot in the back of the head. The bleeding had stopped. He was barely alive, and she decided that she could likely do nothing for him, so she headed across the tracks with Jerry at her heels.

At the C&A depot, Betsy was crying and hugging a man. When she saw Cate, she called her over. "Cate, Colin was hit." Tears rolled down her face.

Blood came from a wound in his left side below the rib cage. She pulled up his shirt and examined the wound. "The bullet went all the way through and likely missed vital organs." She wet a bandage with disinfectant. "Colin, this is going to hurt, but I need to disinfect your wound and then stop the bleeding."

He nodded and clenched his teeth while she pressed the bandage around the wound and tied a wrap around his waist.

"Betsy, he's stable for now. There's not much bleeding. I haven't seen a doctor yet, but try to get him treated by one as soon as you can."

Betsy nodded and wiped at her tears. "Thank you so much."

Cate then headed north toward Henderson's field.

Every jostle of the wagon sent intense pain through Noah's leg. He wondered how badly it was broken. Noah reached up and pulled Harry's head down. "Harry, stay down. There might be more shooting."

"What's Cate going to do? She could get shot."

"No, Harry, I don't think anyone is aiming at Cate."

Tears still streamed down his face. "But you said stray bullets could hit me. They could hit Cate too. Or Jerry."

"I need you here to help me, okay, little buddy?"

Clyde turned back toward Noah. "There's a crowd now along the north side of the square. I'll go along the south side."

Noah tried to raise himself on his elbows. "Can you see what they're doing?"

Clyde stopped the wagon to study the situation. "Looks like Eyster just brought his wagon back up the alley."

Noah sat up as best he could. "Wait a second, Clyde."

From across the square, the men's voices weren't clear, but they caught snatches. "Get him. It's Lukins. Shoot him."

"Looks like Eyster from here, but they think he's Lukins," said Noah.

Eyster jumped from his wagon, leaving the horses in the alley, and ran into the back of the Climax Trading Company. The mob yelled at him to come out. A couple of men began shooting down the alley, and the horses dropped where they were.

Ada Beatty, with her hands up, came out of the store, and they let her go.

From the middle of the public square came a shout. "He's on the roof!"

Jacob Eyster ran from the roof of the Climax Trading Company across other stores to the east while taking cover behind chimneys. He fired a pistol down into the mob when he could, but they fired more shots at him. One bullet hit his stomach. Three or four buildings to the east, Jacob suddenly disappeared.

Clyde urged the horses forward. "We can't help him now. God save him."

Alice, on the east side of the square, tended a man bleeding from a head wound when the shooting started up again. About the time the man was loaded onto a wagon to be taken to the Clayton Livery, the mob hauled Jacob Eyster out of a building and into the public square, where they began beating him and calling him Lukins.

"By God, they're going to have to beat me too." She hurried into the public square and elbowed her way into the mob, yelling, "Stop it, you morons. This is Eyster, not Lukins."

Two police officers arrived and forced the beating to stop. Jacob Eyster lay still and unconscious or dead.

$\sim$

Cate heard the cries of wounded men in Henderson's field from a couple of blocks away. When she reached the edge of the field, she stopped and could no longer control the tears. Groans, cries for doctors, and wailing filled the air. The scene was far worse than what she experienced at the veterans' hospital. At least there, they weren't all crying out at once.

"I need a doctor over here," called one man, bending over another man.

"There are no doctors yet," replied a man nearby.

"Then I need a priest."

Wounded men lay all over the field, and the men who were able tried to help others. She recognized Father Clancy giving the last rites to two men. Their eyes stared at the sky. Jerry followed her into the field. She wished he'd stayed with Noah, but he was just a shadow and not causing problems.

Over near the stockade, a couple of women shook their fists at the guards in the tipple and guard towers. One said, "You sons-of-bitches, come down here so I can shoot you myself!"

Another woman threw a large rock with enough accuracy that a guard ducked.

The next person Cate recognized was General Bradley. His top hat was missing, and strands of hair fell across his forehead as he yelled for doctors. She was close enough to hear him tell Father Clancy that he would send a telegram for doctors, and he jogged off the field.

Cate started with the first man she came to. Many had wounds that were not fatal. She tried to conserve her disinfectant and bandages, but soon she was running low. One young man, proba-bly still a teenager, had wounds that she knew would be fatal. He had taken multiple bullets to the gut. Infection would inevitably set in and kill him within a couple of days. He was still awake, so she tried to comfort him and reassure him that doctors would be there soon. One of his friends said he'd stay with him. *Here I am again*, she thought, *caring for dying young men.*

She counted about six men who were dead, and two who would likely die. The six were carried off toward the depot. Several men needed a hospital. *Where are the doctors?* Cate thought. *Virden has three or four. Where are they?*

With all the wagons that appeared, the wounded and dead were carried to nearby houses within about an hour. Fatigue began to set in, but there was still too much to be done. She walked the few blocks back toward the depots and was told by a wounded miner to pay a visit to the O'Neill house to see if she could help.

Wounded miners filled the porch, but the cries from inside caused Cate to go past them and into the house. Men and women wept over the dead bodies lying in one of the rooms while a portrait of Father Clancy looked on. Blood soaked the carpet, and the stench of blood, feces, and gunpowder made her nauseous. With the dead beyond help, she returned to the wounded on the porch.

A man at the foot of the steps recognized her. He called in a weak voice. "Aren't you a nurse?"

She nodded.

"I need..." And he collapsed.

The wound in his arm wasn't fatal, but the bullet must have hit an artery, and his clothes were soaked with blood. Cate bandaged it the best she could with the supplies she had left. After treating several others, she began walking back toward the square to look for more antiseptic and bandages. Her clothes were splattered with blood. She had seen many wounded men, but under conditions found in a hospital. And even those made her want to quit the profession. She could not imagine following in the footsteps of Florence Nightingale.

In front of the Farmers and Merchants Bank, she encountered Dr. Shriver coming from his office in the back of the bank. He stuffed supplies into his bag.

They faced each other for a second and recognized the fatigue in the other's eyes. "You should go home now," he said. "Doctors are arriving from Springfield any minute."

"I hate to leave with so much work yet to do, but I've run out of clean bandages. And, doctor, Noah McCall has a bullet in his right leg. I think it hit his tibia, which is probably broken. He needs the bullet removed."

"Where is he?"

"At Alice Merry's."

He nodded. "I'll try to come down there this evening."

In the front sitting room, Noah lay on a fold-up bed that Alice pulled out of storage. The pain in his leg was throbbing and intense. Whenever he moved it, a jab came that made him feel faint. He lay as still as he could and watched the neighborhood through lace curtains. Wagons rolled by every few minutes. The ones heading toward the square were empty. The ones going west held one or more wounded men. Later in the afternoon, he saw at least one man who looked like a doctor, but not one from Virden. He couldn't sleep and wondered how the kids were doing at Martha's, where he had asked Clyde to take them. Alice occasionally came in to check on him and make remarks that she wished Cate would get home.

Around four o'clock, Cate passed by the front walk. Her clothes were filthy, and her shoulders drooped. Strands of hair had come loose. Jerry trotted alongside her. Noah waited for her to come through the front door, but she didn't. He called to her, but there was no answer. He wondered why she didn't come, and then he began to doze.

A kiss met his lips, and he opened his eyes. She had changed her clothes and put on an apron. He reached up to embrace her, even though every slightest movement hurt. "Cate. Cate."

"Noah, I need to look at your leg."

He nodded. "It's so painful. Something's really wrong. Will I lose it?"

"Not unless it's shattered or gets gangrene, and we're going to try to keep that from happening."

Alice stood in the doorway. "Cate, can I do something?"

"I need water that has been boiled for several minutes."

"I have that. I knew you'd need it."

Cate unwrapped the bandage and wiped away blood with a cloth she had wet with carbolic acid.

It stung, and Noah worked to not moan.

Cate noticed him clenching his teeth. She held a lamp over the wound. "I think I can see the bullet."

"Can you get it out?"

"Maybe. I saw Dr. Shriver uptown. He said he'd try to come by this evening."

"I don't want to wait to get it out. Can you please get it out?"

"Dr. Shriver can give you anesthesia. It'll be a lot less painful if he does it."

"It's killing me now. Just get it out, and maybe I'll get lucky and pass out."

"I'll prepare my long tweezers and get Clyde to help. Wait."

He laughed. "Where am I going to go?"

"Good point. Oh, and where is Harry?"

"I told him I was going to sleep and convinced him to go home and tell Ellis and Bea what happened. So Clyde took him home. Martha is watching them."

"Good. He doesn't need to witness a bullet removal."

While Cate disinfected the tweezers, a sharp knife, bandages, and her hands, Alice found Clyde.

Back in the sitting room, Cate propped Noah's leg up on a couple of cushions covered with clean linen napkins. Clyde held Noah's leg in place. She showed Noah the long tweezers that she planned to use. He nodded.

With as quick a motion as she could, she thrust the tweezers in and pulled them apart so they could grab a hard object, and she pulled it out. Noah had passed out.

She disinfected the wound again and pulled the hole together with a bandage, all the while hoping that Dr. Shriver, if he did come, would approve of her work. And she hoped his assessment of the leg was not as bad as she feared.

꜡

Noah woke up around nine o'clock in the evening. Cate was asleep on the sofa. He could hear Alice and Clyde talking in the kitchen but couldn't tell what they were saying. He tried to shift his weight, and the rustling, along with his moan, was enough to wake Cate.

She got up and placed a hand on his forehead. "You may be getting a fever."

"Is that bad?"

"It's a sign that your body is fighting infection."

"Gangrene?"

"No, not yet. That takes days to set in, and we're going to work to keep your wound clean."

"I'm really thirsty."

She came back with some lemonade and tea. "Do you need to relieve yourself?"

He hesitated. "Unfortunately, yes."

"I thought so. I'll have Clyde help you."

After Clyde came from the sitting room with a bottle of urine, he took it out back, and Cate went back in with a wash basin and sponge. "Let me cool you down a little."

A gunshot sounded, not as though it was close, but several blocks away.

They met each other's gaze, and Noah said, "I wonder what that was."

"Probably nothing good," Cate replied. "I thought the shooting was over."

"It was just one shot. We'll find out tomorrow."

She took the wet sponge and wiped his face.

"That helps me forget about the pain just a little."

"I'm glad. I think Dr. Shriver must have been held up. I have some willow bark for pain, and I'll give you that."

"I'm sure he had worse cases than mine, and he knows I had a personal nurse." He gave her a strained smile.

Clyde came in about an hour later. "I went to see what the shot was. The militia is all over town now, disarming everyone. One of the guards, Thomas Preston, didn't put his weapon down when they told him to, and they shot him dead."

"Oh dear," was all Cate could say.

Clyde added, "I also saw Dr. Shriver. I told him you took the bullet out, and he seemed relieved. He said he'd be by tomorrow.

He looked like death warmed over, poor man. He's been going at it all day."

Cate pointed to the couch. "I'll sleep here tonight."

Chapter 26

The Aftermath

October 13, Thursday

Cate lay on the sitting room sofa with a quilt over her. Noah had groaned frequently during the night while he slept. She wished that the doctor would come as soon as possible. He might have some morphine. Several times in the night, she had gone to Noah and offered him something to drink. Clyde had spent the night in the dining room with a blanket on the floor in case he was needed to help Noah.

At about six in the morning, Jerry scratched at the front door.

Cate woke up disoriented. She had finally been sound asleep after a restless night. "What's going on?"

Noah said, "Jerry is whining and scratching at the front door."

"The front door?" She went to see Jerry and found Harry curled up in a ball on the porch. He had his knees pulled up to his chin and a coat large enough to be Noah's pulled over his knees.

"Harry! What are you doing on my porch at this hour?"

"I came to see Noah." Tears ran down his cheeks, and his mouth formed an upside-down *U*.

"Well, come on in. He's awake now. He's still in the sitting room." She propped Noah up with pillows behind him. His injured leg remained on a cushion.

Harry ran to Noah's open arms. "Harry. What are you doing here, little buddy?"

"I dreamed you were bad sick. Are you sick?"

Noah sighed. "I am sick, but nurse Cate says I'll live. What are you doing wearing my coat? We could get three Harry's in there."

Harry rubbed his eyes and got up into bed with Noah.

"If you're going to lie here with me for a while, Harry, you have to not move. Every time I move, my leg hurts."

"Is the doctor going to cut it off?"

"I hope not. As long as it doesn't get badly infected, I'll be all right."

"If they cut it off, would you get a peg leg and be a pirate like the one in *Treasure Island*?"

"No, I wouldn't do that."

Cate asked Noah if he'd like some coffee; he said he'd love some. She came back a few minutes later with a cup of coffee for Noah and milk for Harry. She put a hand on Noah's cheek. "You definitely have a fever. I wish the doctor would get here."

Harry's eyes started to water again. "I don't want to leave."

"Does Martha know you're gone?"

He shook his head.

"Harry, Alice is fixing us some breakfast," said Cate. "After breakfast, why don't we go get Ellis and Bea, and you can all stay here and help take care of Noah?"

Noah said, "Oh, Cate. I hate having you and Alice looking after the kids also."

She touched his cheek. "You worry too much. We can handle it, and they'll be in school most of the day next week."

Alice announced that the pancakes were ready.

Just as they finished breakfast, someone knocked on the front door. Cate found Dr. Shriver on the porch. "Starting early, Doctor?"

"Yes, and fortunately, we have quite a few other doctors in town now."

Cate showed him into the sitting room. Alice said that she would take Harry home and collect Bea and Ellis. Noah asked her if she could tell Ellis he wanted his mine examiner book and clean clothes. Harry, in Noah's coat, waddled out, holding her hand.

Dr. Shriver's first words to Noah were, "You're running a fever."

"Yeah."

Cate opened the draperies, leaving the lace ones closed. Then she moved a lamp closer as the doctor removed Noah's bandage.

Noah's eyes watered.

"Noah, I can tell you're in a lot of pain."

"Yeah. A lot of pain," Noah echoed.

"If I do this, does it hurt?" He applied some pressure to Noah's lower leg and watched for his patient's reaction. Noah couldn't keep from crying out.

"Well, Noah, the wound looks like it should. You may run a fever for a while—your body is fighting the infection. I'm afraid, as Cate suspected, the tibia is probably cracked, or it wouldn't hurt so bad when I put pressure on it away from the wound."

"Oh God, Doc. What does that mean? Will it heal and be normal again? And how long will that take?"

"You're young and healthy. You'll have to stay off it for a few weeks. The good news is that it doesn't appear to be shattered, or it would feel different when I press on it."

"A few weeks? I have kids to feed and take care of."

"You can't do anything for at least several weeks. I can arrange to have a nurse sent around every couple of days at first if you can afford to pay her."

Cate said, "He doesn't need to hire a nurse, Doctor. I'm here."

Noah shook his head. "Cate, you have your class, and you don't need to take care of me."

"Well, we'll see about that. Classes are canceled for this week, anyway." Then she asked the doctor, "What happened to the guard that was shot last night?"

"He died. That's the reason I didn't get by here." The doctor began to rebandage Noah's leg after applying more disinfectant and a salve.

Noah covered his face with his arm, but it didn't hide his clenched teeth. He asked, "How many men died or were wounded?"

"Right now, the count is six miners dead and four guards and the railroad employee, D. H. Kiley. But we expect two more miners who were taken to Springfield to die. Their wounds aren't survivable. Jacob Eyster is still alive but might not survive his wounds. Maybe you heard that he was shot and badly beaten in the square. The coroner showed up last night and is starting an inquest into the whole skirmish."

Noah took a deep breath. "Who are the miners?"

"Surprisingly, none from Virden. The fatalities were over by the stockade, especially in Henderson's field."

Noah shook his head. "Damn, I'm so sorry to hear that. I was over there earlier in the morning."

"The Springfield and St. Louis papers have more details than I can give you. There was a Girard man killed, and one of the men in Springfield who isn't expected to live is from Girard. I don't recall names very well." He had finished with the bandage and stood to go.

Cate asked him, "Doctor, would you have a painkiller?"

"You mean something like morphine? That's in short supply right now."

Cate nodded. "I've been giving him willow bark."

"That's about as good as we'll have. I think the pain is going to get a lot better in a couple of days. I'll come back and put a splint on that, Noah. Do you have any crutches?"

Noah shook his head.

"I think I saw a pair in Aunt Alice's storage."

Dr. Shriver nodded. "Aah, yes, she sprained her ankle falling off a ladder a couple of years ago." He pointed his finger at Noah. "Put no pressure at all on the leg for at least a couple of weeks. As long as putting pressure on it is painful, the crack isn't healed."

Noah let out a moan, lay his head back, and closed his eyes. "What am I going to do?"

Cate patted his hand and said, "We'll work through this."

Dr. Shriver smiled and said, "I figured you two would."

After the doctor left, she put her arms around Noah and gave him a kiss.

"Now *there's* a pain killer you didn't mention to the doc," he said at last.

"My secret weapon."

"Cate, I... I love you." Tears flooded his eyes. "I wanted to propose sometime soon, and now look at me. Incapable of working even if I had a job."

She kissed him again. "I wouldn't let that stop you from proposing."

He pulled her down for another kiss. "I know we've known each other for only a couple of months, but would you marry me when I'm better?"

She smiled. "Yes, I will." Footsteps sounded on the porch. "I think your crew has arrived."

For the first time in days, Noah smiled. "I'm in a lot less pain now."

"If you don't mind, I'm going to take Jerry for a walk uptown and try to get a newspaper."

He held her hand. "I love you." Then he held out his arms to the three kids running into the room.

¡✎

The weather turned cloudy again. Cate buttoned her coat against the chill. She patted Jerry's head and then leaned down and gave him a hug, which always made his tail wag. He trotted along beside her as she walked uptown.

The public square, she found, had transformed into a military base. Tents, campfires, and equipment, including two Gatling guns, filled the space. Soldiers worked to set up more tents while some patrolled the streets in front of the shops. Whenever she passed a soldier, he pleasantly greeted her. The hundreds of miners who had been the square's occupants yesterday were conspicuously absent.

At Lorton's, Cate picked up an *Illinois State Register* and a *St. Louis Globe-Democrat*. Not many copies remained of either paper. Conversations recounted the personal experiences of the previous day and the men who were killed or wounded. Cate tried not to make eye contact with anyone so that she wouldn't have to describe how Noah was injured and how he was doing. But a brief conversation was unavoidable at the meat counter and the checkout.

In front of the Farmers and Merchants Bank, she paused to take in the scene. She had never seen anything like it. She took from her bag a sketchpad and quickly drew what she saw so she could show it to Noah and see his amazement.

From there, she went north on Dye Street to Reverend Bellwether's residence. Minnie greeted her at the door and invited her in. She wore a hat and jacket and was putting on gloves. "Cate, what a surprise."

Tami came running in from another room. "Miss Merry! Miss Merry!" She hugged Cate's legs.

Cate reached down and gave Tami a hug. "I came to see if you and the Black community are all right after yesterday's battle. But you look like you're going out. I won't keep you."

"Bless you. Yesterday, we stayed at home and kept low. We didn't trust all the miners not to mistake us for the Alabamans, even though we're Alabamans too. I don't know of any one of us who was hurt. Elijah went around to our houses, checking on everyone once the military came and took away guns."

"I'm relieved to hear this, Minnie. Do you need any food or anything?"

"No, we're fine for now. We feel like we can get out now that we're in a military base. So, today we're on a mission. We heard that the Alabamans are in Springfield at the miners' hall, and they're in a pitiful way. Elijah borrowed a wagon, and we're going to take some supplies up there. Claudette is especially worried about whether her cousin and family are there, so she's going with us."

"Goodness. How can I help? Can I make a donation?"

"I'm sure that would be much appreciated. We knew some miners when we lived in Alabama, and I tell you, those people don't have two nickels to rub together. They are the poorest of the poor, and now here they are stranded in Springfield with, I'm sure, no train fare back home."

Cate reached into her handbag. "Here is all the money I have with me. It's not much, but please take it. I can go to the bank on my way home."

"That is most generous. I'll let others know you contributed to the cause." She tucked the bills into her handbag.

Tami pulled on the side of Cate's skirt. "Do you think the doll family is all right?"

Minnie said, "She's been worried about those dolls. I don't know why."

Tami said, "They're in the classroom. Somebody could come in and rip them up."

Minnie and Cate exchanged worried eyes. Cate patted Tami's shoulder. "No, Tami. No one is going to do that. The school is locked, and the classroom is locked until Monday. You can check on them when you come to school."

Reverend Ball called from the back. "Are you about ready, Minnie? We should be going."

Minnie pressed Cate's hand and said, "Thank you again for stopping by."

Cate nodded and left them to get on with their mission.

Cate also wanted to see how Maeve and Betsy were doing.

Maeve answered her door and put her finger to her lips. She came out onto the porch to greet Cate and whispered, "Cate, good morning. Brian is finally sleeping. I took the kids next door for a while so he could rest."

"How is he doing? Was he injured?"

"A bullet grazed his head, and I thank God that was it."

"Has he had it bandaged properly?"

"Aye, a doctor from Springfield looked at it. How are you doing? You must have had quite a day yesterday."

"You could say that. I have Noah and his kids at Aunt Alice's. He took a bullet to the leg, and it's very painful."

"Well, he's in good hands, for certain."

"I'll let you get back to work. I want to thank you again for helping with the class."

"My pleasure, and it kept me and the kids away from the trouble."

When Cate left Maeve's, her path took her within sight of the stockade. Soldiers patrolled its perimeter. Men were visible in the tipple and the guard towers, but no one inside the stockade appeared to have a gun.

Cate did not find Betsy at home. No one answered the door, so she wondered if that was good news that Colin was doing well, and they were out and about, or if he had been taken to a hospital or a doctor. With meat and vegetables in her bag for supper, she decided not to tarry.

At home, Ellis, Bea, and Harry were all in the dining room. Ellis was reading. Bea and Harry had found—or Alice had given to them—a box of Tiddlywinks. They laughed as the disc Harry was trying to flip into the pot hit Bea in the chest. Cate hoped Noah wasn't trying to sleep.

Alice was in Cate's bedroom fixing the bed for Ellis and Harry. Alice said Bea could sleep with her if Cate was going to sleep on the sitting room couch again.

Cate said, "I have food for supper. I thought I'd bake a roast with vegetables."

Alice nodded toward the sitting room. "You go take care of your patient. I can put a roast on."

In the sitting room, Cate found Noah still propped up but asleep with a book over his lap. It was the book she'd seen when she visited their house: *Examination Questions for Certification of Competency in Mining.* Before she could turn around and let him sleep, he opened his eyes.

She asked him, "Do you need anything?"

He was pale, and the dark circles under his eyes were more pronounced. "I'm not sure."

She put her wrist to his cheek because her fingers were still cold from being outside. "You're still feverish. I can give you more willow bark."

He nodded. "Thanks. I think it's making my stomach upset, though."

"It can do that. That's a side effect. I imagine you're thirsty too."

He nodded again. "What do you have?"

"Lemonade, tea, coffee, milk, water, Pepsi—or rather Brad's Drink—or whatever you want that I could buy. I'm sorry that I didn't think to try to find beer, but I think there isn't any with the saloons still closed and the militia in town."

"Brad's Drink, please. And how was it uptown?"

"A military encampment. I drew a sketch. I'll get your drink and the newspapers I bought. And your medicine."

"I hear the kids laughing. What are they playing?"

"Tiddlywinks. I can tell them to be quiet if you want to sleep."

He closed his eyes and leaned his head back. "No, I like hearing them laugh." Then, he opened one eye to look at her. "I love you."

She blew him a kiss. "I'll be right back."

Over two sodas, they read the papers. She showed him her sketch. "I heard the soldiers spent last night in the opera house. This morning, they already had tents and campfires set up."

"I can't believe that's our town square."

Cate asked him, "Do you know any of the miners who died?"

"Some. I knew Abe Brenneman from Girard, but not well. I'd say he was mid-fifties. And I know who William Harmon is. This says he was taken to Springfield with wounds that are probably fatal. Good men, both of them. Frank Bilyeu from Springfield was also about fifty and a union organizer in last year's strike. I can't say I know the Mt. Olive men."

"Henderson's field was red with blood. I can't get it out of my mind, the groaning of the wounded, and worse, the silence and staring eyes of the dead. Father Clancy gave last rites to anyone who was dying, Catholic or not, since he didn't know the men from out of town."

Noah sighed and leaned his head back as though tired. "I hope something comes of this and the company agrees to the contract so these men didn't die for nothing." He straightened the paper onto his lap and sat up with a grimace. "This says that on board the train were over a hundred Alabamans, some women and children. Only a handful managed to get off, and only one was wounded. They're in Springfield now, trying to get back home or somewhere safe. I actually feel sorry for them too."

"I went by the Bellwether's house, and they were headed to Springfield to try to help them. I made a contribution. Minnie said those people are so poor, they wouldn't have money to get back home. She said Claudette was going too." Cate took his hand. It was warmer than it should have been. "You were reading the mine examiner's book."

"I could earn a much better salary and be underground only part-time. It would help us a lot."

"Salary aside, is it a job you would like?"

"Yes. It would help me send these kids to college and give us a better lifestyle."

"What would you do if you could do *anything*, and you didn't have to worry about the kids or money?"

"Oh, that's easy. I'd teach high school."

"Really? What subjects?"

"Math and history."

Cate laughed. "Math and history? Those don't usually go together."

"I know. But they're the subjects I like the most."

"I didn't know that."

He rubbed her hand and turned it over in his. "We haven't had the chance to talk about a future. And now this." He pointed to his leg and blinked away tears.

"Noah, we should consider how we might be able to get you what you want. Maybe we don't marry right away, and I work for a couple of years while you go to a teacher's college."

"I have no idea how that would work."

A knock at the door brought Dr. Shriver to the sitting room. "I have a leg brace that will help with getting up and not putting pressure on your leg."

He showed Noah how to put it on and asked how the patient was doing.

"He's progressing, but running a fever still. The willow bark helps with the pain, but any movement is painful."

Noah winced. "Just applying this brace is painful."

Dr. Schriver nodded. "It'll get better, but as I said this morning, it's going to take time." As he got up to leave, he said, "The smells from the kitchen are making my mouth water."

"Aunt Alice has a roast in the oven. You're welcome to stay."

"No, too much to do. I'll drop by tomorrow."

By eight o'clock in the evening, Noah's fever was higher, and he had chills. Cate lay down next to him and covered them both with a quilt.

He said through chattering teeth, "So, do you nurses do this for all your patients?"

"Not funny."

At two o'clock in the morning, Cate woke and felt Noah soaking wet next to her. She got up and retrieved a basin of water and a sponge. Her movements woke him up.

"I'm sweating."

"That's good. Your fever broke. I'm going to sponge you off, and we'll change your clothes, or you'll get cold again. Can you sit up?" She turned up the light of the lamp.

She unbuttoned his shirt and removed his T-shirt. His shoulders sagged. The lamplight accentuated the dark circles under his eyes. Cate wet the sponge and stroked it down his back, then over his neck and chest. He laid back and put his hand on hers to stop the bathing. "I'm exhausted, but you have to stop doing that."

"Why?"

He smiled. "Trust me. Just stop—I must be getting back to normal."

She kissed his cheek. "I'll get you a towel and a clean shirt."

Chapter 27

Improvement

October 14, Friday

Cate was in the dining room trying to keep the kids quiet while Noah slept. When she heard rustling from the sitting room, she went in to check on him. He was sitting up with his legs over the side of the bed.

She asked, "What are you doing?"

"With this leg brace and the crutches, I want to try to go out back."

"Are you sure?"

He took the crutches with one on each side and used his good leg to hoist himself up. "See?" He smiled.

"You seem better."

"I feel a lot better." He leaned his palms on the crossbar of the crutches, trying to put weight on them, then paused. "I feel like I could really use a good washing up."

"Aunt Alice has an enclosed shower in the corner of the porch. Uncle William set it up so he could rinse off after work."

"Really?"

"It's cool and drafty this time of year until you get the warm water spraying down."

"I would love that. I made one of those at home, but that's definitely too far for me to go." He cautiously took a couple of steps with the crutches. "Can you ask Ellis to help me?"

Cate called into the dining room. "Ellis, can you come and help Noah?" Turning back to him, she said, "Maybe you need a coat. It's chilly, in the forties."

"I don't plan on being out there long."

"You have one set of clean clothes from what Ellis brought you yesterday. I'll wash the sweaty ones today and start two buckets of water heating."

When Ellis came in, Noah told him, "If you can open doors and move chairs or whatever I need, I think I can make it outside."

Cate watched him slowly and carefully navigate through the dining room and kitchen. The back steps posed a problem. He was down one of them when he lost his balance, and the crutches flew in opposite directions. He landed face down but managed to soften the fall with his arms. "Ouch," was all he said. He pushed himself back up with his good leg while Ellis retrieved his crutches. "I'll definitely need a wash up now."

Cate felt an ache in her chest for this man who took care of others and could shovel tons of coal a day, and yet became so weak. She waited and watched them make progress toward the outhouse once Noah was on flat ground and used to the crutches. She took two buckets from the kitchen and filled them from the pump at the well, then carried them into the house. In the kitchen, she put one of Alice's largest pans on the stove to heat water for the shower. The one they usually used in the wash basin for warm water was already near the corner stove and warm. Alice had to work until at least lunch, but she had put an egg dish in the oven before leaving. Cate checked the dish and found it was cooking nicely, so she began to fry bacon and set the table.

Noah and Ellis took a while to make it back up the stairs and into the kitchen. Noah stood, leaning on his crutches and looking pale.

Cate said to him. "You look like the sooner you eat and get some rest, the sooner you'll feel better. Breakfast will be ready in about twenty minutes. If you don't need a lot of hot water, that bucket by the stove is already warm, and I have another one nearly warm."

"Perfect."

In the dining room, Harry and Bea were back to Tiddlywinks. Harry asked, "What are you gonna do, Noah?" He had seen Ellis with the bucket of water.

"I'm going to clean up."

"Can I help?"

"Sure."

Cate said, "Your clothes are there. Soap and a towel are here. Try not to get your bandage wet. I'll change it afterwards, but it shouldn't have water on it that hasn't been disinfected."

She handed Ellis Noah's clean clothes, the soap, and a towel, then asked Bea if she'd like to help her get ready for breakfast.

When the three males came from the porch, Noah leaned heavily on the crutches. "I feel so much better, but exhausted."

Cate pointed to the sitting room. "I changed your sheets, and you're having breakfast in bed."

"I won't argue with that."

After breakfast, Cate opened the drapes in the sitting room and again left the lace curtains to cover the window. The lace curtains allowed them to see out, but passersby could not see in very easily. Noah had enough natural light to read, so he picked up his mine examiner's book and sighed.

"Anything wrong?"

"I'm not sure my heart's in this subject today."

"Maybe you should just nap. I'll take Bea and Harry with me uptown. They'll get to see the encampment. It'll get them out and entertain them for a while. I need a few groceries."

"I wish I could get out. I hate sitting around."

"Want me to get you anything?"

He shook his head and leaned it back to rest. "I'm thinking the kids and I should go home tomorrow."

"Not a chance. You can't cook and take care of them. Stay at least a week."

"Maybe."

Uptown, Cate and Jerry walked Harry and Bea around the square three times so that they could see the soldiers, the tents, and the campfires. They found the Gatling guns especially fascinating. Then she took them into the dime store for two simple toys to entertain them. Harry picked out a top, and Bea selected a small stuffed dog. Cate bought a pirate book that Ellis would like. He had been reading almost constantly from Alice's selection of books, but many of them weren't exciting for a twelve-year-old.

Harry said to Bea, "What do you want a stuffed dog for? It don't do anything."

"I can hug it."

"You can hug Jerry, and a top does something."

She patted the stuffed dog. "I know, but I like him."

The hamburgers had been so popular at Jerry's birthday party that Cate bought the ingredients for those at Lorton's. Harry stood in front of the produce selection looking at the bananas. They matched his hair.

Cate asked him, "Would you like bananas too?"

"They cost too much."

"Not for me. We'll get some." She inspected them, making sure there were no tarantulas, and then selected two bunches so that she could also make banana cake.

At Alice's, Luke and his two kids were in the sitting room with Noah. Bea and Harry ran in to show Noah what they had gotten, and Luke laughed, but Noah gave Cate a look like, *You didn't need to buy them something.*

She smiled and shrugged. "I see you have visitors. Hello, Luke. Harry and Bea, can you take Mabel and her little brother and go play in the dining room? And please give Ellis his book."

After they left, Luke said in a soft voice, "I heard that I can congratulate you and Noah."

She smiled. "Yes, and now we have some things to figure out as he gets better. Can I get you two anything?" They declined, so she left to put away the groceries.

Noah told Luke, "I don't know what I'll do if I can't work for months."

Luke answered, "You worry too much. As Claudette says, 'We do the best we can and have faith that the Lord won't give us something we can't handle.'"

"But I could lose Cate."

"I don't think anyone who paid fifty dollars for a grape pie will be easily run off."

Noah leaned back and smiled but then became more serious. He asked Luke about the wounded and fatalities from the battle.

"Will Harmon from Girard died yesterday. Shot in the back, and from what I heard, had been in a lot of pain. He had to wait hours before seeing a doctor and going to Springfield, but they couldn't do anything. And Ernest Long from somewhere around Mt. Olive died last night. Shot seven times. He was only nineteen."

Noah groaned. "So, what's the casualty count?"

"Eight miners, four guards, and a railroad employee are now dead. Around forty were wounded. Eyster may survive, I hear. He wasn't given much of a chance right after they pulled him off the square, but he might make it. Hardly any of the men down at the depot were seriously hurt. The men up by the stockade and Henderson's field took the worst of it."

"I'm glad Jacob may make it. I never had anything against him."

"Ed Cahill kept the mob from storming the stockade, or the number of dead would be a lot higher."

"We'll have to thank him for his leadership and keeping his head during it all."

"Some of the men were so angry, they were ready to kill anyone who looked like a guard or a scab or Lukins. I'm not proud of it, but I stayed at home. Claudette would have shot me herself if I'd gone out to help."

"Any word about Lukins?"

"No one is allowed in or out of the stockade. A guard left yesterday to get a haircut, and the militia had to keep men from getting to him. So, for now, Lukins and his men are all holed up in the stockade. Some of the miners want to kill Lukins out of revenge, even if they hang for it."

"Well, he brought this on himself."

"Most miners from out of town have left, ordered out by the militia. Bradley and his Mt. Olive men are gone. They're having the funerals today for their miners, and Ed Cahill and some of the Virden men went down there. Same with the Springfield miners. The Virden miners who were on the scene during the battle are making a list of who was in the stockade shooting out, like some of the pit bosses who sided with Lukins, and they claim there won't be any agreement until these pit bosses are out of a job. They're not going to work alongside such men. I know I don't want to."

"No, that wouldn't work."

"Coroner Hart has started his inquest. Cahill testified yesterday and said he had begged Sheriff Davenport to stop the train at the depot."

"I was there near the depot and saw him pleading with Davenport, and the sheriff refused to do anything."

"So Ed told the coroner. He also claimed that the shooting started from the train and stockade. And, he thinks Kiley, the first one shot, was shot by one of these."

"I don't know why the guards would want to kill the man who was going to throw the switch to direct the train to the stockade."

"Maybe they mistook him for a miner."

"Maybe. Or maybe a miner didn't want that switch thrown."

"Lukins blames the governor for not bringing in the militia to protect his business interests, and the governor blames Lukins for trying to import criminals into Illinois. I hear there's a warrant out for Lukins's arrest."

Footsteps on the front walk made both men and Jerry turn to look just as Cate came in with lemonade. She stopped when she saw the view out the front. A well-dressed woman in a blue dress was accompanied by an equally well-dressed man in a three-piece gray suit.

Cate inhaled. "My parents." She set the tray down and went toward the front door, followed by a barking Jerry. "Jerry, hush."

Noah sat up. "What the?"

Luke chuckled and stood up. "Well, I best be going."

Noah pointed to him and the chair he had been sitting in. "No you don't! You're not going anywhere."

"Don't you have something to ask her father?"

"Not right away. I need him to warm up to me."

Neither said anything as they tried to hear what was going on with Cate and her parents.

They could hear Cate go out on the front porch. "Mama and Daddy, what are you doing here?"

A man's voice said, "We took the morning train up. Yesterday, we read about all the trouble in the paper, the riot and killings. Won't you come back to St. Louis with us?"

In the sitting room, Luke said to Noah, "Did he say, 'You need to come back to St. Louis with us?"

Noah groaned and whispered, "See! This is why I worry so much!"

The voices on the porch became inaudible from the sitting room.

Luke said, "Let's get you fixed up again." He took the comb from the bed's side table and flattened down some hair that was sticking up. "That's better. Can't do anything about the circles under your eyes or your sorry-White color."

"You have to get in that sorry-White description any time you can, don't you?"

Luke chuckled. "You'll do fine."

Within a few seconds, Cate came into the sitting room, followed by her parents and Jerry wagging his tail. "Noah, Luke, I'd like you to meet my parents, Joe and Lena Merry."

Mr. Merry had brown, thinning hair and hazel eyes. He was clean-shaven. Mrs. Merry had Cate's dark brown eyes and dark brown, but graying, hair. They both looked to be around fifty. Mr. Merry extended his hand and a smile to Noah and said, "You must be Noah. Don't get up." He chuckled. "I was kidding." Then he offered his hand to Luke, who had stood, and said, "And you must be Luke." They shook hands.

Mrs. Merry came over to Noah and said, "Forgive me. I'm European, can I give you a kiss?"

He nodded, and she kissed him on both cheeks. She approached Luke, and he offered his hand. "Nice to meet you, Mrs. Merry." She kissed him anyway.

Mr. Merry pulled up a chair. "Mind if I sit down? I've heard a lot about both of you."

Noah said, "I'm honored to meet you, Mr. Merry. How do you know me?"

"Cate's letters have been filled with you and your kids and her students."

Cate smiled and shrugged, and the ladies bowed out with the excuse of fixing lunch. Cate slid the door mostly closed after them, taking Jerry with her.

Mr. Merry said, "I'm sure they have girl talk to get to. Cate just told us that you were injured in the riot."

Noah stammered, "Well... it... uh... was more of a battle. The miners were there to protect our right to work and prevent the mine manager from bringing in scabs from out of state. The guards started it by firing on us. And, yeah, I got hit early on and was knocked down."

Mr. Merry nodded, "Maybe lucky for you. And what about you, Luke? Were you there?"

"Us coloreds were laying low. A few Blacks came from other towns, but those of us who live here didn't trust the out-of-town miners to not shoot us for scabs. I was telling Luke that my wife, Claudette, would have shot me if I'd gone out."

"She sounds like a smart woman."

"Yes, sir. I married up. She's pretty and a lot smarter than me." He exchanged a look with Noah. "A buddy of mine was there when Noah was hit, though."

Noah rubbed his eyes, shook his head, and said, "Mr. Merry. I can tell that you're about to get one of Luke's stories."

Luke continued. "One of my buddies seen it after the shooting stopped. He seen Noah holding his leg and calling for a nurse. One came up to him, and he said, 'No, you're not the one.' A couple of minutes later, another one came by, and he said, 'No I don't need you either. Go help someone else.'" Luke held up his right leg. "Then he started crying out, 'I need nurse Cate. I need nurse Cate.'"

⊷

The kids played in the dining room as quietly as Cate had ever heard them play. Cate and her mother were forming hamburger patties in the kitchen when they heard laughter from the sitting room. Mrs. Merry said, "What could they be laughing about?"

"Oh, Luke will have them entertained and break the ice if there is any."

"Do you think Noah will ask your father today?"

"I have no idea. He's worried about too many things. I'll let them know lunch will be in about twenty minutes. Clyde should be back with Aunt Alice any time now."

After Cate informed the men of lunch and went back to the kitchen, Mr. Merry got up and closed the door again.

Luke offered to leave, but Mr. Merry shook his head and turned to Noah. "I do have a question for you. I can tell from Cate's letters that she cares deeply for you and your kids. I'd like to know your intentions toward her if you don't mind my asking."

Luke sat motionless.

Noah swallowed with effort and said, "I love Cate, Mr. Merry. I want to marry her, but I currently don't have a job, and with this injury, I don't know when I'll be back to work, even if the mine opened today."

Mr. Merry nodded. "I see. If you could do any job, what would it be?"

"Cate asked me the same question earlier. I'd be a high school math teacher."

Luke said, "And a darn good one too."

Mr. Merry nodded again. "So, you like math?"

"Yes, I do. I'm studying this examiner's book to get certification to be an examiner or mine manager, and that would be a much better salary, but it'll take time."

Mr. Merry picked up the examiner's book and leafed through it. "There's a lot of math in here. Air flows. Pressures. Temperatures."

"I can do it."

Mr. Merry held up the book and read. "Here's a question. Goodness, there are a lot of questions, Noah, and it's only a little more than halfway through the book. It says, 'Find the horsepower of an engine having two cylinders thirty inches in diameter, and a five-foot stroke, when making sixty strokes per minute, with an average steam-cylinder pressure of thirty pounds per square inch, and an average back pressure of four pounds per square inch.'" He looked at Noah with an open mouth. "Good God, Noah. Can you work that?"

Luke said, "Was that in English?"

Mr. Merry laughed.

Noah assured him that he could work it.

Mr. Merry said, "I recently lost my bookkeeper. Died suddenly. A good man. He'd been with me since the start of my business. I met him on the loading docks down at the river. He'd been taught to take inventory and work with numbers, but his boss belittled him, called him names. I learned he was his boss's former slave. I watched him for a couple of weeks and finally asked him if he wanted to come work with me as I was starting a grocery business. I told him I couldn't pay much at the beginning, but if the business grew, I'd pay more. I guess his boss wasn't paying him much at all. What I offered to start was still more than he was making. He took the job and ended up being one of my best friends."

Noah cleared his throat and said, "I don't know anything about bookkeeping."

"If you can do the math in here, bookkeeping won't be a problem. When you can travel, you could come to St. Louis and see what the job would be and if you'd want it. And I wouldn't care when you did the bookkeeping, so you could take classes during

the day part-time to get a teaching certificate or your mining certification, whichever you want. Or, maybe take up a branch of
the grocery business. The bookkeeper job starts at ninety dollars
a month."

"Ninety dollars a month? I couldn't make that in the mines
without one of these certifications."

"St. Louis is a nice city to live in until you find the job you
want wherever you want to settle down—maybe back here in
Virden. We're getting the Olympics in 1904. The city is already
preparing for that. But it is a city, and not Virden. Think about it.
Talk it over with Cate."

The kids' voices came through the door as Cate opened it.
"Lunch is ready. I'll bring yours in, Noah. Can you stay, Luke?"

"No, Cate. I got some errands to run for Claudette, so I'll take
my kids and go. But thank you for the invite." He rose to leave.

"Tell Claudette I'll come for some eggs this weekend, and I
hope her cousin's family is doing okay."

"I'll bring some eggs by. You got enough to do." And he left
after shaking Mr. Merry's hand again and saying it was a pleasure
to meet him.

Mr. Merry followed him out of the room.

Cate came over to the bed and put her hand on Noah's shoulder. "You look paler than ever. Everything all right?"

"We're going to get our new beginning," he said, nearly chok-
ing on the words and blinking away tears.

Chapter 28

The Contract

The Virden Record, November 30, 1898

The following is the agreement entered into between the Chicago-Virden Coal Co. and its employees:

The price per ton pick mine run of mined coal shall be forty (40) cents; price per ton machine mined coal shall be thirty-three (33) cents; entry price for driving eight-foot entries per yard hand mining $1.35; entry price per ton machine mining thirty-eight (38) cents; room turning hand mining $2.50.

Engineer Wright to be removed on or before Dec. 10, 1898; engineer Appleton to be removed on or before Jan. 1, 1899, providing the Association of Hoisting Engineers refuse to reinstate him as a member of their association; the removal of pit boss Crouch on or before Dec. 10, 1898; the removal of pit boss Ralph on or before Dec. 10, 1898, if a majority of the miners of Auburn demand his removal on that date. Operators to be given ten days after Dec. 10, 1898, to secure a certified pit boss to take his place; the removal of Charles Evans on or before Dec. 1, 1898.

The stockade to be removed by the Chicago-Virden Coal Co.

An equal turn to be given all of the miners as far as practicable. Props to be sawed square on butt end after props now on hand have been all used. No blacksmithing to be charged in machine mines. No docking for loading of unclean coal. The method of dealing with those who refuse to load clean coal to be agreed upon between the superintendent and pit committee at the mines.

The miners and mine laborers expressly agree to observe the laws and constitutional requirements of the United Mine Workers of America regarding strikes, etc.

It is further agreed that the employees of the Chicago-Virden Coal Co. have agreed to observe such reasonable rules as the company may have for the proper government of their mines.

No employees to be discharged without good and sufficient cause. It is further agreed that all former employees shall be re-employed without discrimination.

The following scale of wages for day laborers agreed to: company men, $1.75; drivers, $1.75; track layers, $1.90; trappers, $1.75; timber men, $1.90; all other inside labor, $1.75; outside labor to be paid the scale agreed to between the Chicago-Virden Coal Co. and said top men during the resumption of work last June.

Signed by Chicago-Virden Coal Co.

T. C. Loucks, President

F. W. Lukins, General Manager

F. E. Halligan

Dan'l J. Keefe, Chairman

Signed by United Mine Workers of America.

John Mitchell

John Hunter

W. R. Russell

W. D. Ryan

Edward Cahill

Epilogue

On a hillside at the Virden Cemetery, about fifty people gathered on this August morning.

The preacher concluded with, "'For he is not a God of the dead, but of the living: for all live unto him.' And now, Congressman McCall has something to say."

Harry wiped his eyes and nose with a white handkerchief. Instead of a dark suit, he had on a white linen one. His blond-graying hair lifted on the breeze. He cleared his throat.

"Noah was the only father I ever knew. I could not have asked for a better father, and I want us to celebrate his life today."

He coughed and wiped his nose again. "I realized this morning that forty-five years ago today, Cate Merry came into our lives." His eyes turned to the gravestone next to the newly dug hole. The stone read, *Catalina Merry McCall, born 1876, died 1942.* "And Cate was the only mother I ever knew and my primary school teacher. Ellis, Bea, and I were with Noah and Luke that day, August 1, 1898. In later years, she would call it an anniversary." Harry nodded to an elderly Black couple, dressed in black except for the blue handkerchief the man used to wipe his eyes. "We were trying to sell our summer vegetables and Luke's eggs when she came fresh off the train from St. Louis, walking along the town square with her Aunt Alice. I'm pretty sure for Noah, it was love at first sight."

He sniffled. "I was only five that summer and fall, but I'll never forget it. We rescued a dog that I named Jerry, and we gave him to Cate. He was her constant companion for years. She had a birthday party for him that fall. She also paid fifty dollars for one of Noah's grape pies at a charity auction. Until we got Cate, Noah was my mother and father, cooking, cleaning, and caring for us. I tried once to call him Dad, but he wouldn't let me. He said George McCall was my dad, and he was just Noah. So, I always envied my nieces, Alice and Lena, who are really more like half-sisters, for being able to call Noah, Dad."

He shook his head at the memories. "But something I want for us to remember here today in 1943 is what else happened that fall of 1898. The Battle of Virden."

The elderly Black man and several other men in their sixties or older nodded.

Harry continued. "Here we are in 1943 in the Second World War, engaged in a fight for our way of life. Some of you are giving what you hold most dear to this war. Bea's daughter is a nurse in the South Pacific. Cate was so proud of her. My son is in England. And Alice has a son serving as a medic somewhere in North Africa. Many of you know that we lost Ellis in 1918 to the Spanish flu. Nursing was a hazardous profession in 1918, and he had become a good one. His death hit Noah and Cate hard. At the time, I was doing my part in France, and God, what an awful war that was. We thought it was the war to end all wars. I came back hoping I'd never send any sons to war. Well, we should have known better."

He paused and cleared his throat. "I want us to remember that in 1898, Noah and the Virden miners also fought a war. It was a different kind of war. It wasn't against some foreign enemy, some people who spoke a different language and had a different culture somewhere overseas. In fact, the enemy wasn't really even a people. The enemy wasn't Fred Lukins, who's buried not fifty yards from here."

He raised his voice and emphasized every word. "The *enemy* was the *perceived right* of a wealthy class to extract their wealth from the poorer classes, without giving them safe working conditions and a living wage."

He sighed and lit a cigarette. "Some people live to work. But most of us work so that we can enjoy living—a life of family, friends, and pastimes. But in the late 1800s and earlier this century, the rights of business operators were considered more important than the rights of workers. The Battle of Virden helped to change that. It showed that the power of workers lies in unity. Only by banding together were they able to get the operators to compromise. I'm glad that October 12th, Virden Day, is still observed here. My brother Noah was there and a part of that. And I am proud of him for it."

He looked at the ground for a few seconds to collect his thoughts and then shrugged. "Actually, I was there too. During the shooting, I escaped through the schoolhouse window to find Noah and was chased down by Jerry, who, we learned later, nearly got shot for his heroics to stop me."

A few of the mourners chuckled. Others sniffled.

"The fight for labor rights got even uglier in the thirty years after the Battle of Virden in places like Colorado and West Virginia. And the fight didn't end even then. In fact, it will *never* end. The important point is that when we see an injustice, we unite and stand up for what is right. And we're carrying on that fight here in 1943."

He turned and surveyed the many tombstones around him. "I look at Cate's marker, and other than giving her name and the dates of her birth and death, it says nothing about the life she lived, the teacher and nurse she was, and the mother she was. The same will be true of Noah's marker when it's engraved. We, the living, have to remember what they stood for and carry on the fight to make our lives and this country a place we're proud of and where we want to live."

He paused and ran his fingers through his hair. "Well, that's all I have to say. Thank you for coming."

"Thank you, Congressman McCall." The preacher then turned to the crowd. "Will you join me in saying the Lord's prayer?"

Harry's attention was drawn to motion in the sky: a balloon with one occupant, drifting east. Beyond the cemetery, it dropped a sandbag, and he recalled his five-year-old self saying, "Cate, Noah, look! It's a *sandbag* from a *real balloon!*"

As soon as the aeronaut released a sandbag, a light-haired man in the cemetery looked up and then quickly receded from view as the balloon rose and drifted eastward. Farm fields stretched in every direction, interrupted only by roads and rail lines.

The town of Virden appeared. Its streets spread out in regular blocks enclosing houses with green lawns. In the middle of town sat the town square with a shady central park. Cars and pedestrians animated the paved streets and sidewalks. The wind faltered and then pushed the balloon farther north.

A coal mine came into view. It had men on its grounds and smoke coming from a burner. An empty railcar rolled downhill toward the three-story tipple. Another railcar loaded with coal moved from the tipple and north toward the main line.

Across the tracks to the east of the mine lay a farmer's field. More farm fields reached toward the horizon. The balloon's ascent took it into low-lying clouds, and the town disappeared.

Author's Note

G ray clouds and a persistent wind from the west met me at the Virden Cemetery. Not many places seem so cold in March as an isolated Central Illinois cemetery with nothing to block the prairie wind. I had come to the cemetery on this morning to try to find Fred Lukins's gravesite. I had started research on this novel when I learned that he was buried in Virden, and I had been puzzled as to *why*. After all that happened in 1898 and his actions as the mine operator, why would he decide to be buried in Virden? He had lived in several places until finally retiring in Missouri.

John Alexander told me that Fred Lukins' grave was somewhere in the southeast section. I parked the car in the southeast section and began walking around. I wound my way toward the far end and then back toward the car. A bit frustrated at not having found it—this trip was before I realized that a search on the cemetery website would give a map with the exact location—I said to myself, and I think I may have even said it out loud, "Ok,

Fred, if you want me to find you, you have to help." I made my way back toward the car, feeling a little disappointed.

And then, there they were. Two modest headstones, much like many others in the cemetery, waited there, not far from my car. They were rectangular, about one foot by two feet, and only a few inches high. The one on the left said Nina Harrington Lukins, 1865–1942. The other said Fred W. Lukins, 1857–1926. The cemetery directory gave his date of death as January 14, 1926, which means he lived another twenty-eight years after the deadly battle. I asked the stone, "So why, Fred, did you choose to be buried in Virden?"

I turned back to the car and started it up. I pulled forward a few feet and looked out my driver's window, for no particular reason, and down at the stones that I passed. And that is when I saw another Lukins stone. I stopped the car and got out. On a stone that was a similar size to Fred's, it read Elmer H. Lukins, 1885–1918. To the left of it was Edith Lukins Crooks, 1881–1954. Surely, I thought, Elmer must be related to Fred with the stones so close together. But how?

Back at the Virden Library, I discovered the relationship. I found in a microfilm of the *Virden Recorder* the obituary of Fred W. Lukins. I learned that his body was brought to Virden the Saturday after he had died. It was accompanied by his widow and three surviving sons. Jessie and Elmer H. preceded him in death. Elmer Harrington Lukins was only thirty-three when he died. He married a Virden girl, Edith Gelder, and preceded her in death.

I felt I had an answer to my question, "Why Virden?" Fred and Nina had likely wanted to be buried in Virden to be near their eldest son, who had died in the prime of life. I also suspect that Fred had put the events of 1898 in the past and buried them also on that wind-swept prairie.

I couldn't leave the question in my mind of what had happened to Elmer that he died so young. And who was Jessie? I've discovered that historical research is never done. One question resolved always leads to other questions. The *Galveston Daily News* reported on March 5, 1893, that seven-year-old Jessie Lukins died in Galveston on March 3rd of rheumatism. A Streator, Illinois, newspaper reported her funeral a few days later. Fred and Nina lived in Streator in 1893. The timing of Jessie's death means that Fred and Nina lost their daughter only a couple of weeks before he purchased the property that became the Chicago-Virden Coal Company (March 18, 1893).

And Elmer? Further digging in the Virden newspapers revealed that by 1918, Elmer had become a prominent businessman in town and had been married for eleven years to Edith Gelder. And, like so many others in 1918, he came down with the Spanish flu and died of pneumonia in early November. The Gelder family's grief came through clearly in the obituary; they said he was like a son to them. Several years later, Edith went on to marry Nolan Crooks. A couple of years after her death in 1954, Nolan married Mabel Hart, the widow of Eugene Hart, Elmer Lukins's business partner. Mabel lived to be over one hundred. I remember Mrs. Crooks, and I wish I could talk to her now! My grandmother, Mary Peacock, was her house cleaner.

Historical Notes

The Virden Reporter is referred to below as *The Reporter*.

The Virden Record is referred to as *The Record*.

The Virden Record and *The Virden Reporter* merged into *The Virden Recorder* in 1921.

Weather conditions in the story are generally what they were reported to be in *The Record*, which recorded every week what the conditions were during the previous week.

Dedication: The names of those who lost their lives in the Battle of Virden are on the memorial in the town square.

Chapter 1. "The wind blows wherever it pleases." John 3:8 (NIV)

The Sanborn maps show the layout of Virden, Illinois, in 1894 and 1900. https://www.loc.gov/item/sanborn02206_003.

Chapter 2. Many of the items that Dora mentions are in *The Reporter* for August 5, including the teachers' institute and Lukins negotiating with the miners. The complaint of noisy boys at street corners under the electric lights was reported in the September 23 issue. George Sewall was the editor of *The Reporter*. E. P. Kimball was the editor of *The Record*.

Both the 1894 and the 1900 Sanborn maps show a public school (1900 labels it primary school) on the northeast corner of Jackson Street and Church Street, which is the location of the old Central School, built ~1915, and the current *Virden Recorder* building.

The Reporter had several notices on the Presbyterian church construction project during August and September 1898. On September 9, it said that the renovations to the church were nearing completion. One of the main improvements was the removal of stoves and the installation of a furnace.

The pastor of the Christian church was Rev. Lewis Goos. He came sometime in the spring of 1898 and left around the end of 1898. The weekly Virden newspapers list the churches, ministers, service times, and sometimes, the sermons that would be preached.

The names of the stores, merchants, and professional services, such as doctors, were taken from ads in *The Reporter* and *The Record*.

The "Old Maids' Convention" was a play advertised in the April 6, 1898, *The Reporter*. It was also known as "The Spinster's Convention" and billed as a comedy: *https://archive.org/stream/ spinstersconvent00chic/spinstersconvent00chic_djvu.txt*.

According to a Herndon's ad, fabric prices were from five cents to fifty cents a yard, depending on the fabric.

Chapter 3. According to the 1900 census, Hop Long was 21, born in China, and ran a laundry. The 1900 Sanborn map shows a Chinese laundry on the south side of Jackson Street in the first block west of Springfield Street.

Virden must have had "dog killers" to get rid of strays. A September 23 note in *The Reporter* said, "The dog killer has not been performing his duty in the southwest corner of town lately."

The Record reported on August 10 that Mayor Noll intended to prosecute any boys engaged in the "indiscriminate use of sling-shots and air rifles."

Other items of interest mentioned, such as the problems in Pana, the root maggots, the Standard Oil facility, and the Canadian rail workers, were all items in the Virden papers during August and September.

Chapter 5. Bakke, D. (2011 Jan 29). "Tree that dates from Lincoln Funeral Needs Attention in Virden." *The State Journal-Register.* *https://www.sj-r.com/story/news/2011/01/30/ tree-that-dates-from-lincoln/41748969007/.*

See also Wallace, Mary. (1975) *According to Gene.*

The Wednesday, November 16, 1898, issue of *The Record* reported Balfour Cowen's obituary. Previous issues had reported he was ailing.

Chapter 6. The August 19 issue of *The Reporter* said that a tarantula had been found a few days prior in a bunch of bananas at Lorton's. Dr. Boyer preserved it in alcohol.

Milo Loveless was reported to be the new Principal of the Virden schools. Periodically, each grade was listed and the names of the students with perfect attendance. A "primary grade" came before first grade. See the note on Chapter 12 for the location of the East School. One of the Virden papers mentioned that the high school had a boa constrictor.

Uncle Billy (William Williams) was a real person and a school janitor who was born into slavery. His obituary was in *The Reporter*, February 9, 1900.

The stockade around the mine was being referred to as Lukinsville. (*The Reporter*, Sept. 23, 1898)

Chapter 7. The August 17 issue of *The Record* reported the death of Mrs. Harrington, Fred Lukin's mother-in-law, on August 13.

Maude Botkins was a violinist at Chautauqua, and she did play at the Methodist church.

According to *The Reporter*, August 19, the band concert for August 20th was canceled because they didn't have a bass player.

The Reporter, Sept. 23, noted that the apples shipped in were too costly to can.

Chapter 8. *The Reporter*, August 19, noted that the Virden telephone system was underway.

Chapter 9. Newspaper notices said that churches had Bible studies on Thursday evenings.

The street currently known as Masterson was originally Matteson, as noted on the Sanborn maps. I recall my mother saying that her mother was upset when "Masterson Street" signs went up because it had always been Matteson Street. My mother's family lived on South Matteson Street for many years.

Chapter 10. According to an ad in *The Reporter*, "Dr. A. Travis, Veterinary Surgeon, Girard, Illinois, will be at Clayton's Livery Stable on Monday of each week. Patronage respectfully solicited."

As reported in many newspaper articles, Jacob Franklin Eyster ran the company store.

Both *The Reporter* and *The Record* reported on the marriage of Nellie Patton Furry and Herbert Cowen.

Sanborn maps show St. Catherine's Catholic Church on the southeast corner of Emmet and Jackson.

Chapter 12. In 1898, the first day of school was September 5. The August 31 issue of *The Record* said, "The brick building will be used for the high school, eighth, and seventh grades; the west building for the sixth, fifth, fourth, and third grades; the primary building for the second, first, and primary grades." Sanborn maps show the brick building was the old East School between Emmet/Greene/Holden. The West School was on the southwest corner of Finis and Jackson. The primary school was on the northeast corner of Church and Jackson Streets.

The UMWA commemorated a monument to the Braidwood miners killed. https://dn790009.ca.archive.org/0/items/braidwoodstory00donn/braidwoodstory00donn.pdf

I read that the practice of students using one drinking cup changed in the early 1900s.

Chapter 13. A book called *According to Gene* (1975, Mary Wallace) about long-time Virden resident Eugene Twitchell (1879–1977) says the following: "As Gene stood in front of the bank, he pointed to the north. 'There used to be a negro church down the street,' he recalled. 'I remember once when I was a small child, I ran away from home and went to one of their camp meetings in Henderson's Grove. I wanted to hear the singing.'" The "Colored Baptist Church" (1894 Sanborn map) or the "Colored Church" (1900 Sanborn map) was on the southeast corner of Prairie and Dye Streets.

Chapter 16. Both *The Record* (on Sept. 21) and *The Reporter* (on Sept. 23) reported on the reception given to Father Clancy, the priest of St. Catherine's Catholic Church, on his return from Ireland to see his father. Father John J. Clancy lived to be over one hundred, and Bill Heitzig tells his story in *My Days with Father Clancy and the Shining Village on the Hill*. 2012.

In *Sundown Town*, Kevin Corley depicts via historical fiction the events in Pana, Illinois, and to a much lesser extent, the Battle of Virden.

The Women's Christian Temperance Union (WCTU) had a weekly column in *The Reporter*.

The Reporter (Sept. 23) noted that Sept. 22 was Emancipation Day in Springfield, and a large group from Virden attended the celebration and returned on the evening train.

According to the Sanborn maps, the Palace Hotel was located on the north side of the square just to the west of the alley, and the Climax Trading Company was on the east side of the alley.

Chapter 18. *The Interocean* (Sept. 26) and many other newspapers reported "Negroes Didn't Stop. Armed Strikers Were Waiting for Them at Virden." Several hundred armed strikers deterred the train from stopping and unloading the Black miners.

On September 21, T. C. Loucks, President of the Chicago-Virden Coal Company, had an open letter in *The Reporter* explaining the company's position. The Virden miners made a reply two days later in the *Springfield Journal* and in the September 28 issue of *The Record*.

The Henderson–Willson wedding was reported in detail in both *The Record* (Sept. 28) and *The Reporter* (Sept. 30).

Chapter 20. The October 7 issue of *The Reporter* had described in detail the Clemmons boy's accident on Oct. 4 in the primary school yard.

Chapter 21. The *Illinois State Register*, Friday Morning, October 7, 1898, had the article entitled "Governor Northcott Acts."

During this period, Ed Cahill became President of the UMWA local district. He was reported in the papers as having prevented the miners from storming the stockade.

"General" Alexander Bradley's speech is a paraphrasing of the types of things he claims he said and other people claim he said. I took material from his memoir (*The Great Coal Miners' Strike of '97*), the Edward Wieck article, "General Alexander Bradley," in *The American Mercury* (1926), and at least one St. Louis newspaper. General Bradley did go to Springfield but wasn't invited to participate in the October 11 speeches at the State House. The governor was absent, so he met with Adjunct General Reese, who didn't commit to doing anything to help.

Chapter 23. The *St. Louis Post-Dispatch* (Oct. 10, p.2) published an interview with Governor Tanner where he says, "The laboring man's only property is the right to labor, which is as dear to him as the Capitalist's millions, and he has the same right to carry arms in the defense of his property as the capitalist has to protect his property."

Chapter 25. A photo of the O'Neill Boarding House shows miners congregating. On the left of the photo is an elderly lady with her dog. She reportedly helped to feed the miners.

https://macoupin.illinoisgenweb.org/images/oneillhouse1898.jpg

The Record (October 12 issue, which was published too soon to cover the battle) reported the weather on the 10th and 11th as rainy with temperatures in the 60s at six a.m. and six p.m. By the evening of October 11, the wind was from the northwest. *The Record* reports in the October 19 issue that October 12 was clear and cooler. At six a.m., the temperature was 44 degrees, the skies were clear, and the wind was from the northwest. By six p.m., the temperature was 59 degrees, the skies were still clear, and the wind was from the south.

The *Illinois State Register* (October 12 issue, p.1, published prior to the battle) reported that the superintendent of schools had asked parents to keep their children off the streets.

Bibliography

A partial list for the Battle of Virden (excluding the many newspaper sources).

Biggers, Jeff. Oct. 12, 1898: Battle of Virden. Zinn Education Project. https://www.zinnedproject.org/news/tdih/battle-of-virden/

Day, Marie. *Bloody Mine Riot of Virden, Illinois—1898. Lukins Ranch 1922–1928.* Dogwood Printing, 1989.

Feurer, Rosemary. "Remember Virden! The Coal Mine Wars of 1898–1900". *Illinois History Teacher*, 13, no. 2 (2006), 10–15. Also online: www.lib.niu.edu/2006/iht1320610.html.

Feurer, Rosemary. *Remember Virden, 1898, Illinois Humanities Council* (booklet). Copyright: St. Louis Bread and Roses, 1998.

Hicken, Victor. n.d. "The Virden and Pana Mine Wars of 189." Macoupin County ILGenWeb. https://macoupin.illinoisgenweb.org/mines/virdenpana1898minewars.html

John Alexander, host, *Labor History Today*, podcast, "The Battle of Virden," November 10, 2021, https://www.podbean.com/media/share/pb-men8a-10fe346

Markwell, David. "A Turning Point: The Lasting Impact of the 1898 Virden Mine Riot." *Journal of the Illinois State Historical Society*, 99, No. 3/1, (Fall 2006–Winter 2007), 211–227.

Mother Jones Heritage Project. (2007–2021) *Virden Mine War Tour*. Mother Jones Museum. https://www.motherjonesmuseum.org/virdenminewartour

O'Neill House photo: https://macoupin.illinoisgenweb.org/images/oneillhouse1898.jpg

Rosenow, Michael K. "Every New Grave Brought a Thousand Members: The Politics of Death in Illinois Coal Communities, 1883–1910". *Death and Dying in the Working Class 1865–1920*. University of Illinois Press, 2015.

Sanborn Fire Insurance Map of Virden, Macoupin County, Illinois. 1894, The Library of Congress. https://www.loc.gov/item/sanborn02206_001/

Sanborn Fire Insurance Map of Virden, Macoupin County, Illinois, 1900, The Library of Congress. https://www.loc.gov/item/sanborn02206_002/

Sangamon County Historical Society (2016). The Battle of Virden (1898). https://sangamoncountyhistory.org/wp/?p=9094

We Never Forget. The Labor Martyrs Project. https://weneverfor-get.org/we-never-forget-the-martyrs-of-the-battle-of-virden-oc-tober-12-1898/

Wieck, Edward, A. "General Alexander Bradley". *The American Mercury*, May 1926. Alfred A. Knopf.

Weinberg, Carl. "The Virden, Illinois, Coal Mine Massacre on October 12, 1898." Digital Research Library of Illinois History Journal, ed. Neil Gale. https://drloihjournal.blogspot.com/2019/01/the-virden-illinois-coal-mine-massacre.html

Acknowledgements

This novel would not have been possible without the assistance of numerous people, whom I would like to thank in roughly alphabetical order.

John Alexander, Virden historian and owner of Books on the Square in Virden, Illinois, and his wife, Jeannie Alexander, were the best sources of information about Virden, Illinois, and the Battle of Virden.

Stephanie Anderson, Gold Nugget Publishing, current publisher of the *Virden Recorder*, allowed John Alexander and me to dig through the old copies of Virden papers, which led to our uncovering *The Virden Record* copies that had not been microfilmed. *The Virden Record*, being the Democrat newspaper, provided a different point of view from *The Virden Reporter*, the Republican newspaper, which was available on microfilm.

Teri Barnett at the Abraham Lincoln Presidential Library assisted with getting copies of *The Virden Record* to the library for microfilming.

Carolynne Calloway at Grand Prairie of the West Library, Virden, Illinois, helped me in providing references and in getting a new microfilm machine so that I could better read *The Virden Reporter* papers from 1898.

Joann Condollone, with the Mother Jones Museum in Mt. Olive, Illinois, was a source of connection to others related to coal mining and the Union Miners Cemetery.

Indigo River Publishing. I am grateful to my publisher for taking this project on. Terra Friedman King, my line editor, gave me many insightful suggestions that no doubt made this book much improved. Deborah Froese, executive editor, helped me get the novel off to a more compelling start.

Helaine Silverman, Department of Anthropology, University of Illinois at Urbana-Champaign, helped me obtain a copy of General Bradley's memoir. She is also co-director of the Mythic Mississippi Project: https://mythicmississippi.illinois.edu/.

Scott Thomas, UMWA Local President, gave me my second tour of the Illinois Coal Mining Museum in Gillespie, Illinois, and he explained the use of equipment like the parting lamp.

Dave Tucker gave me my first tour of the Illinois Coal Mining Museum in Gillespie.

Rick Wade, retired editor, *The Virden Recorder*, showed me where the old Virden papers were on my first trip to uncover the past through the local newspapers.

The following early readers were especially helpful in identifying errors or passages that needed clarification: John and Jeannie Alexander, Loretta Williams (portrayer of Mother Jones), David Schrock, Alan Schrock, Linda Cumbie, and friends I met in a Glen Workshop: Elizabeth Brown, Lauryn Francisco, Hannah Koeske, and Caleb Monroe.